Thomas Adam, junior Fellow of St. Columb's, is one of countless English travellers crossing the Channel to explore the reopened Continent after the Napoleonic wars. His motives, however, are severely academic. Romance is excluded: do not the College statutes forbid dons to marry, and is not Adam a man of honour? But once settled (or perhaps more accurately unsettled) in the beautiful lakeside town of Lucero, he finds himself tempted to exchange his learned pursuits for others less learned, and by the end of the Long Vacation he is faced with problems for which all his classical scholarship has not prepared him.

by the same author

★

SNARED NIGHTINGALE

SO WILD THE HEART

BY

GEOFFREY TREASE

LONDON

MACMILLAN & CO LTD

NEW YORK · ST MARTIN'S PRESS

1959

MACMILLAN AND COMPANY LIMITED
London Bombay Calcutta Madras Melbourne

THE MACMILLAN COMPANY OF CANADA LIMITED
Toronto

ST. MARTIN'S PRESS INC
New York

PRINTED IN GREAT BRITAIN

For

PETER AND JOCELYN

Chapter One

HEARING the Warden's cautious gouty tread, so unmistakable although (on Number Five staircase, Front Quad) so unfamiliar, Adam did not wait to sand the wet ink but whipped the paper into a drawer.

In Oxford you could not be too careful. It would be dangerous to let anyone — and suicidal to let the head of his own college — lay eyes upon that paper. He remembered the scandal of his second term, five years ago. Though it had happened in another college across the street even the italianate walls of St. Columb's had shuddered with sympathetic distaste. One of the two young men expelled had been an Etonian and the heir to a baronetcy: neither fact had saved him. What mercy then would St. Columb's show to a Fellow, a very junior Fellow, who lacked both those mitigating attributes — who lacked indeed birth and breeding of any sort, and whose very election had been no more than a misconceived concession to the new and regrettable spirit of reform? After two years at high table Adam knew pretty well the conditions on which he could survive.

Challand rapped, opened the door and peered in. Looking more than ever (thought Adam) like a fat bedraggled rook, his black amplitude relieved only by a glint of shoe-buckles, a gleam of linen bands, and of course the sanguine face, pocked and venous, under the wig he still wore, ignoring change. The face not of a scholar but of a squire.

He advanced, waving back, with a flap of gown-sleeve, the chair Adam was offering.

'Thank you, Mr. Adam, but I must not stop. Or interrupt your . . . researches.'

The grey gaze washed, cold and even as sea-water, over the strewn jumble of calf bindings and foxed pages. Adam was glad he had not cleared away his books. It was remarkable how much Challand could take in, even reading upside down. In fact there was a College theory that the Warden preserved his faculties for reading what he was not meant to by never exhausting them on what he was. But even Challand, fortunately, could not read the papers in a closed drawer.

The pouched eyes roved from the table to Adam himself, resting for a moment on his waistcoat and travelling down to his feet. Adam waited, silent, controlled, apparently deferential. He felt a trace of his freshman's awkwardness return.

'You dining today, Mr. Adam?'

'I was intending to, Warden.'

'H'm. Didn't dine, myself, yesterday.'

'We missed you, Warden.'

God forgive me, thought Adam — but how else can one live here? And it's true enough, literally. We were all conscious that the old fool wasn't there.

'It has come to my ears,' said Challand with deliberation, 'that yesterday you went into Hall and dined in — in trousers. In *trousers*, Mr. Adam.'

Adam gaped. Groping back into his memory, he could recall only that he had been working furiously and that the dinner-bell had sent him hurrying across the quad, fumbling dazedly into his gown as he went.

'You are wearing trousers now, Mr. Adam.' Adam

2

glanced down at his sober grey knitted pantaloons. The fact was irrefutable. 'I say nothing to that. You've a right to do as you please in your own rooms,' said Challand magnanimously. 'Indeed, trousers may do very well for certain informal occasions. But while I remain Warden of this College, you will oblige me by removing them before you come to dinner!'

'Certainly, Warden! It was pure forgetfulness. I——'

Challand stopped the excuse with an uplifted hand. 'Can't afford forgetfulness of that sort . . . Deplorable modern world . . . No standards left unshaken by the war . . . Trousers in Hall! It's indecent, Mr. Adam.'

'I assure you, Warden——'

'Once admit that sort of thing and we're finished. Finished. We open the way to all the excesses of the Jacobins. Don't let it occur again, Mr. Adam.'

'It won't, Warden.'

Challand went. Adam closed the heavy door behind him.

God, he said between his teeth, this is what I've come to . . .

He wrenched open his drawer, stabbed the ink-pot with his quill, and desperately, as though for salvation, began to write.

At that same moment, in the drawing-room of the Warden's Lodging, Miss Challand sat talking with her sisters, Miss Sophia and Miss Julia. As befitted the daughters of the Warden they confined their discussion to a topic of deep and permanent interest.

'Of course, he's ugly, I must admit that,' said Sophia in her usual forthright tone.

'Oh, not ugly, surely?' Miss Challand was the timid one. She twittered. She had never been good at facing facts, and, as one birthday followed another, she found

3

some facts more and more alarming. There was no longer the comfort there had once been, in childhood, in being the eldest. 'Would *you* say Mr. Adam was ugly?' she asked Julia.

Julia seldom said anything. Nor did she now. Her sisters, she had early discovered, would always say everything that there was to be said, and usually a great deal more.

'Of course he's ugly, Charlotte,' Sophia insisted bluffly.

'Well — perhaps — but in a very *distinguished* way, don't you think? Not unlike the dear Duke of Wellington? Don't you think so, Julia pet? Do say *something*!'

Thus appealed to, Julia pet conceded that Mr. Adam's big nose was not unlike the big nose of the national idol.

'Distinguished fiddlesticks,' said Sophia. 'Mr. Adam isn't even a gentleman——'

'You're not fair to him! All because he doesn't like *you*, and——'

'Fiddlesticks again! He doesn't like any of us. He doesn't like women at all — he has no use for the sex.'

'*Sophia!*' Charlotte's eyes saucered with dismay and her jaw dropped in a fatuous way which her family had tired of criticising. 'But — I thought — I mean, you don't think——'

'Oh, you needn't worry. Mr. Adam will marry in the end. And one of us, most likely.'

'*One* of us?' Charlotte had brightened, but still looked anxious. 'But *you* don't like him, and Julia's still such a child, and after all——'

'I didn't say I didn't like him.'

'No, but——'

'And Julia may be quite grown up before Mr. Adam gets a living and is free to marry.'

'Julia will have plenty of other chances! I *am* the

4

eldest, after all,' Charlotte trumpeted almost tearfully. It was not a claim she often made. In any case it was all too evident.

'You know what Papa says,' observed Sophia with malice.

'What?' There were so many things Papa said, one could not remember them all. So one selected those it suited one to remember. As Sophia did now.

'Why *should* everything go by seniority?'

'Sophia! What a thing to say! As if getting married was something like getting a College living!'

'Well, isn't it? They go together. The poor men can't marry and keep their fellowships. And they can't afford to give up their fellowships until there's a vacant living.'

This simple truth was so obvious that even Charlotte could not obscure it with ejaculations. She went off at a tangent:

'But suppose Mr. Adam doesn't want one? He hasn't taken Orders yet——'

'That's soon arranged.'

'But he may not wish to be a clergyman!'

'What else is he fit for?'

'Sophia, do you *dislike* Mr. Adam?'

'Certainly not,' said Sophia with warmth. She was indeed prepared to love Mr. Adam. 'I am merely facing facts. What other prospects are open to him? He has no interest.' By this, Sophia was not suggesting that the young man did not possess a great deal of interest for herself and her sisters, but only that, having no influence, he could hope for no other career.

'It's a shame. Still, he would make a fine figure in the pulpit. He *is* rather striking, whatever you say, with those dark brown eyes and his high cheekbones. And he has a good voice.'

5

'I've never denied that.'

'One could be very happy in a country parsonage,' said Charlotte wistfully, meaning that Mr. Adam could, but also thinking that *she* could.

'One could,' agreed Sophia darkly. 'Provided it were a *good* living.'

'But would the College ever give Mr. Adam a good living? I don't think he's very popular with some of the Fellows——'

'You know very well that the Fellows will do as Papa tells them.'

'But Papa doesn't like Mr. Adam! This morning, I believe, he was quite displeased over something or other he had done.'

Sophia looked pityingly at her sister. 'You really *are* a goose, Charlotte. Do you suppose Papa would feel the same about him if he was going to marry one of us?' She laughed. 'True, Papa is sometimes displeased — irritated, anyhow — by little things he does. But he would be getting rid of all that if he induced the College to offer Mr. Adam a living.'

The unspoken thought quivered in the air between them that Papa would also be getting rid of an unmarried daughter, and that this might be an even more powerful attraction.

'Of course,' said Charlotte, 'Mr. Adam *can* be irritating. He sometimes says and does surprising things. He is unconventional.'

'No, he is ill-bred.'

'Oh, Sophia!'

'Yes. It shows in small things. When he forgets. But nothing which can't be put right. A good wife could transform him.'

'Mr. Adam is rather a mystery. I *should* like to know more about him, wouldn't you?'

6

'I should indeed.'

'Wouldn't you, Julia?'

Julia looked up from her needlework and grunted ambiguously. She already knew all she wanted to know about Mr. Adam, and, except when embroidering, she cared little for details.

Charlotte and Sophia would battle for Mr. Adam's hand, but Sophia, for all her aggressive spirit, would not win. Julia was going to marry him herself. In her own mind that was quite settled. So why talk about it?

Adam had finished writing, and, being in no mood to return to his more academic work, had gone to the window and flung up the sash. The High curved past below, glistening after the rain, tired of the wettest summer term in memory, hardly less humid than his room. A single rider, blue-coated, gilt-buttoned, exquisitely breeched and booted, went tittuping back to Christ Church for dinner, saluting with his whip a young nobleman lounging on the front steps of University, who acknowledged the gesture with a languid wave of his gold-tasselled mortar-board. More formal greetings were exchanged as Dr. Challand emerged to encounter the Provost of Queen's: after much ceremonial bowing and capping, the two heads turned with one accord and set off, sweating under their doctors' robes, to breathe the greener air of the Broad Walk. Then, for a few moments, the street was empty — until the notes of 'Brignall Banks', played on the guard's bugle, identified the coach which was then rumbling over Magdalen Bridge and came into sight, a fraction of a minute later, spanking up the last quarter of a mile to the Mitre. After two years in Front Quad, Adam knew them all — Dart and Defiance, Tantivy, Blenheim, and the rest — and he could have set his watch by their bugle-solos, 'The Troubadour',

7

'Begone Dull Care', 'The Maid of Llangollen', or whichever it happened to be.

The coach went by. Silence flooded back. Oxford lay under the window, still and pastel-tinted as an Ackermann print. Looking at the dank grey stones, he remembered with irony that the place had not always felt like a prison. Far from it. Oxford, once, had meant escape.

Parson Jennings had started it all . . .

He had caught Adam poaching rabbits in the glebe. Instead of thrashing the urchin, he had believed his hard-luck story. It had happened to be true. Adam, though imaginative, had not needed to invent it or even to decorate it with pathetic detail. Barefoot and skeletal, with paper skin and dark avid eyes, he would have convinced anyone.

Jennings let him keep the rabbit and gave him sixpence for his mother. Nor did he leave the matter there. He had noted Adam's precocious and misdirected skill, and, himself a keen sportsman, decided to divert it into a legitimate channel. Adam was delivered from the drudgery of bird-scaring. Instead, for the same small wage the farmer would have paid him, he trudged through the fields with the old parson and his retriever, carrying a game-bag which grew hourly heavier and a flask which became inversely lighter. When the flask was empty, Jennings would declare that failing light precluded further accurate shooting. Then they would turn home, two ill-matched silhouettes against the fretted winter branches and the brazen flare of sunset. At the Rectory Adam would be dismissed with his pay and one of the less noble victims of the rectorial gun — a rabbit usually, a leveret once in a while, pigeons for a pie, and on a single handsome occasion a brace of partridges. Never pheasants. Pheasants were for gentry, and Parson Jennings, though eccentric, was not mad. So pheasant, from that time forth,

8

was never tasted again in the Adam household, despite the most pointed maternal hints and the most contemptuous reflections on the boy's poaching ability. The Rector's moral influence was not generally noticeable in Ramsthorpe, but in this one parishioner he had inspired quite incidentally a sense of honour.

A day came when Adam was not dismissed on the doorstep. He was sent round to the kitchen to clean himself up, eat the plateful of dinner doled out to him by a disapproving housekeeper, and present himself in the study, his one-time papery cheeks glowing like a copper kettle.

Jennings, originally attracted by his country lore, had discovered his wider interests. This ragamuffin, who could barely read, had curiosity, penetrating observation, and a memory like a sponge. After a few fragmentary but fascinating discussions in field and spinney, Jennings had realised that the pursuit of knowledge went badly with the pursuit of game, and that if too many conversational hares were started there would be no real ones to hang in the larder. So a curb was set on Adam's tongue until the serious business of the day was over. Then, in the white panelled study, boots and wig laid aside, the candles gleaming on his polished skull, the old Rector was only too willing to talk, to pull favourite volumes from the shelf and thumb the pages through. It was as though Adam had blown upon an ember of scholarship, still not quite cold after forty years in a remote Nottinghamshire parish.

One thing led to another. Adam began to read, at first aloud to the Rector, then increasingly to himself when the old man dozed. He spent more and more time at the Rectory. The close season did not stop his visits, but lengthened them. The Rector's books were too fine to borrow and take home to the rat-ridden hovel he shared

9

with his mother — and she would never have let him sit idly reading them. As it was, she complained. Meeting Jennings in the lane she tackled him with a boldness few women of her class would have shown — and even in her, though an inborn trait, it was fortified on that occasion by the beer within her.

'I wonder, Parson, ye don't have my Tommy move his bed over to the Rectory! Might just as well, for all I see of him.'

To her amazement, and Adam's delight, Jennings took the widow at her word. Young Tommy became nominally the garden-boy. A proper wage was scrupulously paid over to Mrs. Adam, who also received regular Sunday visits from her son. Otherwise the Rectory became more and more his home. He continued to eat with the servants, sleep in an attic, and do odd jobs. But his status became by imperceptible development that of a son, or more strictly a grandson, for the gulf in age was wide and Jennings felt affection without undue responsibility.

Adam still remembered one milestone in that development . . .

Each Sunday, in church, his curiosity was teased by the strange sonorous phrases prefacing the Psalms. *De profundis*, *Jubilate Deo*, *Adhaesit pavimento* . . . He knew they were Latin, a dead language known to living gentlemen, especially parsons. He questioned Jennings, who explained that they were the Latin equivalent of the opening English words. *Jubilate Deo* meant 'O be joyful in God', *Audite haec omnes* was 'O hear ye this, all ye people'.

'What a wonderful language, sir! So few words, meaning so many!'

'The Romans were wonderful people. They didn't waste words. They were doers.' Jennings gave colourful examples.

Adam, leafing through his Prayer Book, pounced on the 42nd Psalm. 'If you want to say, "like as the hart desireth the water-brooks", you can do it in one word. *Quemadmodum!*' He was only momentarily dashed when the Rector explained that Latin was not quite such an expressive language as that, and *quemadmodum* meant no such thing.

'Why not, sir?'

'Well . . . the Romans put their words in a different order. It isn't easy to explain.' The old man laughed away the problem. 'You'll have to learn Latin, Tommy, I can see.'

This time it was Jennings who was taken at his word. Before he knew where he was, the study had become a school-room. The garden-boy did fewer and fewer menial jobs. Soon his place was laid at the Rector's table, so that their discussions on the Gallic Wars or the adventures of Aeneas should not be interrupted. On shooting days he carried not only the game-bag but a gun, and now, despite the snorts of the housekeeper, new maids found it natural to address him as 'Master Thomas'. Mrs. Adam bore her continued bereavement with fortitude, and pocketed what was still known by courtesy as 'Tommy's wages'. She complained only once, arguing that Tommy, being older, was worth a rise. The Rector paid it. He had encouraged the boy in his pursuit of learning, and the widowed mother (though 'widow' was probably another courtesy title) should not lose by it.

Ramsthorpe, drowsing under its elms in the somewhat featureless vale, was too far from either Nottingham or Loughborough for Adam to attend grammar school except as a boarder. For a son of his own, Jennings might have seen that as the proper course. Not unnaturally, he saw no reason to incur such an expense on Adam's behalf, especially as it would have robbed him of the boy's companionship. So Adam pursued his studies alone, unaided by competition or chastisement, though not entirely missing those character-building benefits supposed to come from the rough-and-tumble of school life. The village boys supplied these generously, for they instinctively resented the way in which Parson Jennings had singled out Tommy Adam and withdrawn him, in mind and manners, from his proper place. Adam learnt that self-improvement was no substitute for self-defence. He punched, kicked and hacked as need arose and opportunity offered, and could not have borne himself better if the Rector had sent him to the finest public school.

Time passed. Greek was added . . . simple Caesar gave place to tortuous Tacitus, naïve Xenophon to subtle Plato. For relaxation there was the literature of England . . . and it was soon plain that a cultivated modern reader could not get along without French. Adam even began to dip into Dante, but here he was beyond the Rector's aid.

Two or three times a year, red-letter days, they drove to Nottingham, over the long arched bridge and the causeway across the golden meadows to where the town clung to its saddle between Castle Rock and the less dramatic height crowned by St. Mary's. Adam loved those long, full days, opening sleepily in the summer dawn and ending, an age later, in the even sleepier jog home at dusk. He loved the bustle of the vast market-place, the carriages of the gentry, and the gentry themselves, elegantly passing and repassing under the colonnades of Long Row. He loved the circumstance of dinner taken at the Flying Horse — where once, unforgettably, they were even lodged overnight — and the deference shown to Parson Jennings by his tailor and his wine-merchant (who took them down into exciting cellars hewn from the rock) and the splendours of the Duke of Newcastle's mansion and park.

12

But the highlight, beyond question, was the visit to Mr. Pritchard.

Mr. Pritchard was bookseller, printer, stationer, and God knew what else. It was incredible that so many functions could be incorporated in that gnome-like, smiling little man — or carried on in that poky back-street shop.

Adam realised more fully, in late years, how much he owed to Pritchard, the only other intellectual influence to which he was exposed in his boyhood. As a supplement — or a corrective — to Jennings, he had been invaluable.

The Rector's tastes were classic and conservative. With books as with wine, his motto was the older the better. Furious arguments used to rage in Pritchard's shop, which frightened Adam on his first visit, until he realised that the old men loved each other like brothers. Their passion for books and partridge-shooting united them in a bond which Pritchard's Unitarianism and Radicalism were powerless to weaken.

There had been a glorious conflict when Pritchard had tried to sell Jennings the new edition of *Lyrical Ballads*. Who were these young men? Wordsworth? A Cambridge man! The Rector snorted. And this Coleridge — not merely Cambridge, but expelled from Cambridge into the bargain! As for this nonsense about diction, that a poet should use the common words of everyday speech——

'The Muse is a mountain-dweller! So an elevated language is only proper.'

'Nonsense, my dear sir! The Muse lives in a man's heart.'

They had gone on for some time, without any result except full self-satisfaction. Afterwards Adam had found an imperfect copy of the book which Pritchard had slyly slipped into his pocket. He did not tell the Rector, fearing he might be vexed. It was the first secret he had ever kept from him. He rather enjoyed the poems. He kept that as his second secret.

Every year, in the autumn, Pritchard came to the Rectory for a few days' shooting. They had several evenings of splendid talk. The Rector proudly showed him the elegant verse translations Adam had begun to make of certain elevated passages from the *Aeneid*, and Pritchard had declared diplomatically that Pope himself need not have felt ashamed of them. It was Adam himself who had shown him, surreptitiously, a few scraps of his original versifying, which the Rector discouraged as unhealthy and a waste of time. Pritchard raised his eyebrows and handed them back. 'You're too young to have anything much to say yet. But you can turn a phrase. Don't be put off. Show me some more sometime.'

Adam hadn't. It seemed disloyal to Jennings to multiply such secrets. And the old parson was right. He had no time to waste.

They were thinking of Oxford now.

It had begun so naturally, with Jennings reminiscing as he twiddled his wine-glass in front of the fire. This brushing-up of his dusty classics stirred memories of his own youth — of Oxford in the seventeen-sixties, its Gothic shabbiness newly beautified with the glistening modern splendours of the Radcliffe Camera and the Clarendon Building, Peck Quad and Worcester, and Hawksmoor's Italian design for Queen's. Against this architectural background, this city of light (a somewhat rosy light, induced by the port), moved a throng of scholars, wits and philosophers, whom few people would have recognized as the Rector's contemporaries.

'Mitford? Heavens, yes! Dined with him many a time.' Adam, who had already devoured the *History of Greece*, now looked upon its author with an almost

14

proprietorial pride. Gibbon? No — but if the Rector had been up a few years earlier, he would certainly have hobnobbed with him. Bentham? Queer little fish. A precocious child, pitchforked into a crowd of seniors. Most unsuitable . . . And Charles James Fox . . . Though the Rector deplored his later career in politics, he looked back affectionately on that meteoric young man, whose mind had been so brilliant and whose reading almost excessive.

Soon Oxford, from a blurred and dazzling vision, steadied and clarified itself into the outline of a target, distant but not beyond range. Inquiry confirmed that Jennings' old college, St. Columb's, had two ancient scholarships, restricted by statute to natives of the East Midland shires. With the Rector's recommendation, Adam might get one when it fell vacant two years hence. It would help too if, in the meantime, he learnt still more Latin and Greek.

So there was no time to waste.

There weren't many distractions at Ramsthorpe anyhow. A short winter's day after the partridges, an early morning swim in summer, a walk with the Rector or alone . . . Nothing else, beyond the dwindling duty visits to his mother, who glared at him through an alcoholic haze and demanded to know where it was all leading. He assured her stiffly that she need not worry, she would not end her days in the poor-house. Whatever happened she would get her money, she would not lose by his incomprehensible ambitions.

I was almost as lonely in those days (Adam reflected) as I am now.

He had grown away from the village-boys he had once played with. He had no chance to know the village-girls — and no ladies visited at the Rectory. Jennings was not merely a bachelor: he truly had no time for women. He

15

said little to Adam on the subject, but the boy had insensibly absorbed much of his own feeling. Goings-on which could be contemplated with urbane pleasure in the pages of Propertius or Theocritus were quite different morally (however similar in other respects) from the goings-on of the young villagers in the hay-barns of Ramsthorpe. Literature and life were two separate things. And literature was what the Rectory was concerned with. A boy was expected to read all the love-lyrics and idylls of the ancient pagans without a responsive quiver or the least stirring of curiosity. Adam hadn't managed to do that, but as his situation did not offer any very tangible temptations he had done no more than write a few new verses of which the Rector would have disapproved. Otherwise, he stuck to his work.

Nowadays he knew that he could have achieved Oxford without that grind. The scholarship election was little more than a formality. But it had seemed an unbelievable triumph at the time.

He could still remember, with the vividness of yesterday, that morning when the post-boy brought the letter with the College seal. There was no one in Ramsthorpe, certainly not his mother, who would have understood. So nothing would satisfy the Rector but that they should harness up and drive into Nottingham to tell Pritchard and celebrate with a bumper dinner. When they crossed Trent Bridge and went spinning up the last mile into the town, they found the whole place making hurried preparations. Flags were going up, shops and houses were getting out illuminations and transparencies ready for nightfall, the ale-houses already resounded with song, every face was smiling, and perfect strangers waved familiarly to the parson and his boy.

It was not till they reached the bookshop that they found out the real reason: the mail-coach had come in from

16

London an hour before them, laurelled for the victory at Talavera.

What did that matter? The national triumph could not dim the personal. All the better if the whole dining-room of the inn was in festive mood. Pritchard had proposed a toast, 'to the two victors, Sir Arthur Wellesley, Commander-in-Chief in the Peninsula, and Mr. Thomas Adam, Scholar-elect of St. Columb's College in the University of Oxford'. And the other diners, catching on, had raised their glasses to the blushing boy and cheered. Afterwards Pritchard had given him a new book, called *English Bards and Scotch Reviewers*, by a young author who (though he had been at Cambridge) was a peer of the realm and a local landowner. In those circumstances, and on such a special day, the Rector was prepared to excuse his being still alive, and Adam was allowed to accept the volume. The moon was high when at last they went bowling through the honeysuckle-scented lanes, bellowing at the tops of their voices *Hearts of Oak* and *Britons Strike Home*.

Oxford had not been quite what he had expected, not quite what the Rector had described. Had he perhaps been recalling not so much Oxford as his youth? Adam had found it difficult to make contact . . . Few of the undergraduates seemed interested in what they were supposed to be studying. When he tried to join in a dinner-table discussion on 'Penelope', he discovered too late, and with embarrassment, that they were arguing the merits of a racehorse. Another time, when he had to explain to his neighbour that Socrates and Isocrates had been two quite separate persons, the youth echoed the second name with a yawn and drawled:

'Damn it, no, that's something in Euclid!'

The elegance of your Latin prose was nothing: it was the cut of your coat that mattered. To be able to construe

17

a difficult text at sight impressed nobody, but if you could handle the ribbons like a professional coachman you were a College hero. The gentleman commoners had no compulsory lectures and no one inquired into the progress of their studies. They looked down on the scholars but deferred to the biggest fool whose birth entitled him to wear the gold-braided gown of a nobleman and clap a gold-tasselled mortar-board upon his empty head.

Adam had shrugged his shoulders, gone his own way. He'd grown used to it.

At least no one stopped him from working. The libraries and bookshops were no disappointment. He got up early, kept his chapels, walked in the Meadow or in summer bathed. By nine o'clock, when lively breakfast-parties were gathering in other rooms, he would be sitting down alone with a book, a cup of tea, and a George — the penny roll and butter on a pewter plate, which his scout banged down insolently before him. So the day unrolled, till three o'clock dinner in Hall, his main social contact, and then on till bed. He got a lot of reading done.

There must have been a few men with similar tastes, scattered through the University, if only he could have found them. The examinations arrived — the new-fangled 'quackery of the Schools' as the Warden contemptuously called them, with their Classes and Honours. There had been nothing like them in the Rector's day and even now only a minority took them seriously. But Adam, who had never in his life known real competition, found that the minority had existed all the time. He missed the First he had hoped for. With it he missed his chance of a fellowship at Oriel, which had just embarked on the revolutionary policy of electing Fellows on intellectual merit, even though they came from other colleges. But from the trough of despair a new wave had lifted him to what were then (he remembered wryly) the heights of exultation.

'The Warden's compliments,' said the scout in a tone he had never used before, 'and would Mr. Adam have the goodness . . .'

And there they had sat at the long mahogany table, those dons he had venerated from afar, who had never known his face but were now ready with his name.

'Mr. Adam,' Challand had said, 'it is my pleasant duty to offer you the vacant place in our society. You have just been elected to a junior fellowship. What do you say?'

He might as reasonably have put the question to Prometheus, after offering to co-opt him among the Olympians. Adam had murmured a dry-throated acceptance. His cup had been full. Only later had he sometimes wondered whether it was full of nectar or of vinegar.

He was glad that old Jennings had lived just long enough to enjoy the news . . .

After that, Adam seldom went back to Ramsthorpe. He was able now to send money himself to his mother, but they were brought no closer by the Rector's death. Rather otherwise. Mrs. Adam was disgusted that the old man had left his money to distant nieces and that 'Thomas Adam, my garden-boy' (it was a will made years before) got only 'twenty guineas, any six books from my shelves, and my guns'. And Adam was more than ever disgusted with his mother. She should never suffer financially because the Rector had snatched him from his work as a farmer's boy, but he would never willingly spend another night under her roof. With strangers at the Rectory, Adam spent part of his vacations in Oxford and part with Pritchard in Nottingham.

He owed Pritchard a letter. The new poem might amuse him. He might as well see the whole bundle. Adam took a fresh sheet of paper and began to write:

'*You ask if I keep up my own versifying. I do, and it eases my feelings, if it doesn't add anything to the world's literature. Here you are — read for yourself, show them to anyone else you like, do as you please with them, so long as nobody but you knows I wrote them. If it got known in Oxford, it might be very awkward for me——*'

The chapel clock chimed a quarter to three. He thrust the unfinished letter into the drawer with his manuscript, and walked through to his bedroom.

'So much for the fearless rebel,' he said bitterly.

He unfastened his trousers, and, with a shrug of resignation, changed into the breeches and stockings of conformity.

Chapter Two

'**M**R. ADAM, I think the port is with you?'

'I beg your pardon, Warden.'

Adam stooped over the fender, lifted the decanter from its socket, and despatched it round the semicircle once more. This was the most important duty of the junior Fellow present, indeed the only one which was anxiously supervised by his colleagues.

Not that St. Columb's was, by Oxford standards, inefficient. The College might not ape Oriel in dangerous experimental reforms, but it had never sunk, like Hertford only last year, to a single Fellow, who had, with a fine acceptance of the inevitable, elected himself Principal. St. Columb's was well administered. Rents were punctually exacted from its farm-tenants in various parts of England, and as punctually, at the annual October business meeting, the profits declared by the Bursar and the annual dividend paid to each Fellow. Several of them had also been known to lecture, and three or four coached pupils, though strictly this was no business of the College since the men paid private fees for the instruction.

The elaborate dumb-waiter in the Senior Common Room was just another illustration of that efficiency, devotion to detail, and emphasis on fundamental values which characterised the running of their society.

A miniature tramway slanted down across the wide hearth, its higher terminus being on the left beside the chair reserved for the Warden. There were two parallel tracks, each bearing, on tiny well-oiled wheels, a truck designed to take a decanter. When the Warden had taken port or, it might be, madeira, he had only to place it in the empty truck beneath his elbow, whereupon its weight sent it trundling down the inclined rails to the other side of the hearth, and a pulley and cable brought up the second truck, ready for the next decanter which the Warden desired to pass on. In theory, the device saved unnecessary movement, which became increasingly difficult as the evening wore on. In practice, as a few of the less persevering drinkers left the Common Room, it was impossible to maintain the semicircle in all its decorous formality. The survivors had to leave their chairs at times, whether to circulate the decanters or to reach the wall-cupboards in which homelier vessels were always available for their comfort.

Life in the Senior Common Room was not entirely what Adam had once pictured it to be.

Here surely, if not among the undergraduates, there would be lively speculation and debate? There were. What would the dividend be in October? Would the elderly incumbent of a certain College living survive another winter? Would peace bring a fall in the price of claret by Christmas? How many birds would be killed in the first twelve shoots in September? Nor was there anything loose or vague about these speculations. Usually they were crystallised into a definite proposition, and entered as bets, signed and witnessed, and payable in bottles of wine, in the book provided for the purpose. It was the only book ever referred to in the Common Room and the only writing in which some Fellows ever indulged.

Not that the donnish mind was closed to wider questions. The Fellows were ready to bet on anything. There was a wager, dated 1811, on Mr. Percival's chances of becoming Prime Minister, and another, a year later, 'that Napoleon Bonaparte, commonly called Emperor of the French and King of Italy, is not alive this day twelve-month'. There were bets recorded on the dimensions of the Pump Room at Bath and (some pages earlier) on those of Lady Hamilton. This last bet had never been settled. Mostly though the Common Room was concerned with parishes and partridges, with livings rather than life. The favourite toast was 'to a rot in Leicestershire' — where the College held most patronage and there was the best hope of promotion to dead men's shoes.

Adam's neighbour spoke. Seabrook, his immediate senior, was also his only real friend. Seabrook might have grown lazy and cynical but he had a mind. He amused Adam. Adam seemed to amuse him.

'What are you going to do?'

Adam started almost guiltily. 'Do? Oh — you mean now?'

'When else? Are you going off to grind at your *magnum opus*?'

Adam considered. There were moments when he faltered in his self-appointed task of rendering Antonian's interminable elegiacs into English couplets.

'Not tonight, George. I don't feel in the mood.'

'I wonder you ever do. Antonian is thoroughly third-rate.'

Adam did not argue the point. There were beauties in the poet which appealed to him. He merely grinned and retorted:

'That's why nobody's bothered to translate him before.'

'You're backing a loser all the same. Antonian won't bring you much glory. However . . .' He set down his empty glass. 'How about a turn in the Meadow? Before it rains again!'

'If you like.'

Adam glanced round the company. They were well away. 'Slimy' Symes was dropping casual innuendoes where they would most damage his enemies and advance his private schemes. Doctor Rallingson was repeating an anecdote, which only he himself believed, of how he had once scored off Samuel Johnson. Murthwaite was chuntering on about the iniquities of the American colonists, who (he was unshakably persuaded) would one day return to their rightful allegiance, having learnt that republics would not work. Other conversations were more narrowly domestic. In the past two years Adam had heard them all. Many, many times.

'We've done our duty. We shan't be missed now,' said Seabrook.

'No.'

'If I stay, I shall only drink myself into a stupor. In self-defence.'

'Come on, then.'

They bowed to Challand, excusing themselves, and went out. Only the Chaplain took note of their going. He cocked a shaggy eyebrow and remarked offensively:

'The young men aren't what they were. Can't take their wine. Uncultivated.'

They crossed the High and cut down Logic Lane. Merton Field was mellow in the early evening sunshine. Beyond the leafy colonnade of Broad Walk the grass and buttercups and cows stretched hazily down to the meeting of the unseen rivers.

Broad Walk amused Seabrook. It tickled him to recall how the Cavaliers had laid it out to celebrate the Restoration and how, before the trees were much more than saplings, the Stuarts had been kicked out again for good. The trees remained. Now, with a century and a half of accumulated majesty, they provided Oxford with its

24

most fashionable promenade and Seabrook with an inexhaustible source of sardonic pleasure. He delighted in the spectacle of the two perambulating streams — the learned doctors and the worthy tradesmen with their wives and daughters, town and gown no more mingling than water and oil; the portentous capping and bowing of the academic hierarchy; the transparent manoeuvres of the smaller fry to win the merest acknowledgment from the Vice-Chancellor or the head of a house; and the no less transparent manoeuvres of the ladies to further their social and matrimonial schemes. Sunday morning was the best time, when twenty college chapels and half a dozen city churches discharged their congregations into the Meadow. But any fine summer evening in term gave ample scope for satirical comment.

'Any plans for the vacation?' Seabrook asked as they turned down a quieter path beside the Cherwell.

'I shall stay here for the present.'

'My God! Why?'

'I must finish my translation.'

'Oh, *that*. Must you?'

'There's nothing else for me to do.'

Seabrook looked keenly at him. He sensed the double meaning. Adam was pinning a lot of hope on this English rendering of a little-known Roman poet. He was gambling on it to establish his name as a scholar. A man like Adam, without family or influence, must publish or remain for ever submerged. Seabrook wondered whether Antonian would bring anyone much kudos, but he refrained from discouraging forecasts.

'How is it going?'

'Only a few more hundred lines.'

'Have you a publisher?'

'I haven't really thought about that side of it.'

'You should — with the end in sight.'

'I expect Pritchard will do it for me — he prints and publishes once in a while——'

'H'm . . . Nottingham. Oxford would be better — or London.'

'Pritchard would advise me, anyhow.'

'Very important to go about these things in the right way. You want to get lots of subscribers. Not just in the University. Titles. Fly high — dedicate it to a duke, if you can. Work on that old humbug Challand——'

'What does *he* care about Antonian?'

'Nothing. But he won't mind some easy glory for the College.'

Adam knew that was true. The Warden was immensely jealous of the College's good name. When he drove back from a visit to London, he always took on a couple of extra horses for the last stage over Magdalen Bridge. 'Never let it be said,' he would declare, 'that the first man in the first college in the first university in the world drove up to his lodge behind a mere pair.' It would please Challand if he could buttonhole the Provost of Oriel with the news that even the junior Fellow of St. Columb's had written a book.

Challand, if properly handled, said Seabrook, could pull many useful strings. He had influential contacts. The old registers must contain a sprinkling of St. Columb's men who had by now achieved peerages and bishoprics. Challand must get them on the list of subscribers. They need not read the book, but loyalty to the College demanded that they should lend their names and give their guineas.

Adam laughed. 'It's you who ought to be publishing. You know all about it.'

'It's merely my weakness for running other people's lives. You *must* stir your stumps, Tom, with the writing so nearly done.'

'The final polishing may take longer than you think.'

'Why?'

'There are some awkward bits that don't make sense. Where he's describing his villa in the North. You know — he had a little island on one of the Italian lakes, what he called his "*amoris insula*".'

'Did he, the dog?'

'It's always been assumed it was Maggiore. But that can't be reconciled with several perfectly clear statements in the poem. What lake he *does* mean isn't so clear — his phrasing is ambiguous——'

'I don't blame him. If I'd got a little "island of love" somewhere, I'm damned if I'd give the world precise directions how to find it. Does it matter now?'

'When I translate a piece of Latin,' said Adam mildly, 'I rather like to begin with a clear idea in my own mind of what the Latin means.'

Seabrook chuckled. 'You're over-conscientious.'

'If I *knew* the location, I should know which alternative meaning to choose.'

Adam developed his theme as they followed the river-bank to Folly Bridge and turned towards the cathedral spire to complete their round of the Meadow. Seabrook was a sound scholar and his mind still had an edge to it, when he used it seriously. It was a rare pleasure for Adam to be able to discuss his work.

Seabrook summed up the evidence.

'What does it all add up to, Tom? Two inconsistent prepositions — some ambiguous adjectives — a muddling of compass-points — one apparent major contradiction——'

'Which would disappear if we abandoned Maggiore.'

'You're still left with difficulties . . .'

'I know.'

Seabrook ruminated. They were nearly back to the Broad Walk, with its gowned and broadclothed and

c   27

muslined mannikins passing and repassing under the great trees in the oblique bars of sunshine. He tried another tack.

'Is the text certain?'

'Fairly. But one of the manuscripts could have been misread, I suppose.'

'Where are the best ones?'

'There's a good manuscript in Paris. The Vatican codex most likely stems from the same origin. There's another — the oldest of the lot — in the Ambrosian Library.'

'H'm . . . Milan's a long way. But Paris . . .' Seabrook chuckled again. 'I'm going to Paris myself when term finishes.'

'You are? George, would you verify these passages for me? Would you just go along to the——'

'No, I'm damned if I would.'

'Why not?'

'Come to Paris with me, and do it yourself.'

Adam stared. 'Paris? To check half a dozen Latin words!'

'You're not compelled to come posting back the very next day.'

'No, but——'

'Paris would be good for you, Tom. You're getting desiccated. I've watched you, term by term.'

'I'm all right.'

'That's the danger signal. You really imagine you are. If celibacy once gets a grip on you . . . Have you never been abroad?'

'How could I?'

'It was the first thing I did when they caught Boney the first time. And he dam' nearly caught *me* in Paris last year! But he won't play that trick again. Not from St. Helena. If that's what you're afraid of.'

'Of course I'm not! But if you think I'm going over to Paris merely——'

'My dear Tom, where is the devotion of the true scholar? If need be, you should be prepared to go to Milan, Maggiore, Rome — and where *do* you reckon Antonian really had his villa?'

'I don't know. But I've a theory it was Lucero——'

'Where's that?'

'Much nearer Garda and Verona. One of the small lakes. In some ways it fits like a glove. There was a Roman town there. The distances and directions are consistent. I don't know about the landscape — I don't even know whether there's an island. It's not a famous lake. Only a tiny blue spot on the map.'

'You should go there!'

'Don't be absurd!'

'Don't you be slapdash! Go there. Prove your theory. Astonish the learned world. Make mincemeat of all the previous commentators. Then you will be noticed. That way lie doctorates and professorships and even maybe — God help you — wardenships——'

Adam burst out laughing. 'But suppose, when I'd gone all the way to Lucero, the first sight of the place blew my beautiful theory sky-high?'

'If it were my theory,' said Seabrook, always honest in dishonesty, 'I'd take dam' good care it didn't. A scholar must learn to select his facts. See them in the right perspective. And interpret them. If you follow those three golden rules, you can prove just about anything.'

'I think, all the same, I'll stay in Oxford and do my work undistracted.'

'Undistracted you certainly won't be.' Seabrook dropped his voice as they turned back into the Broad Walk and came face to face with the three Miss Challands approaching under full sail, an armada which even the filmiest muslin and tulle could not render less than formidable.

Escape was impossible. Only an immediate right-about turn, abrupt as that of a stamping sentry, could have prevented the encounter.

'Why, Mr. Seabrook——'

'Miss Challand!'

'— and Mr. Adam!'

There was much social clucking, much raising of caps, much artless play with shawls and parasols.

'A beautiful evening——'

'An unexpected pleasure——'

And so on and so on, like (as Seabrook observed later) one of those damned oratorios of Handel's.

They all wheeled in the same direction. There was no help for it. Talk turned to the imminent vacation and the four months' quiet which would descend after the final academic junketings were over. Miss Charlotte was thrown into a flutter by the mere thought of anyone's going to Paris.

'The Continent, Mr. Seabrook! I should love to see the Continent — just once.'

Sophia hooted. 'You talk about the Continent as if it were a notice-board! You see it, and that's that. Europe is quite large, really——'

'I know, I know, my dear. I only meant——'

Nobody was much interested in what the eldest Miss Challand meant. It was the general feeling that, whatever she had in mind, there was ample room for it.

'We have begged Papa to take us abroad,' said Sophia, 'but he will not hear of it while Bonaparte is still alive. I am not afraid of Bonaparte. Or any other Frenchman.'

'Why should you be?' Seabrook demanded, in so agreeably gallant a tone that the question was robbed of any malicious ambiguity.

'But Papa will not budge. He will stay in Oxford until the September rent-collections. And so shall we.'

'And Mr. Seabrook will come back in October and find us just where he left us,' said Julia, speaking for the first time and with accumulated force. 'At least he will be able to tell us what the fashions are!'

'Oh, Julia *pet*! As if a gentleman would notice such things! I am sure,' Charlotte whickered apologetically, and with a sincerity which embarrassed everyone but herself, 'I am sure Mr. Seabrook has other things to do in Paris than stare at the ladies . . .'

There was an awkward silence, broken only by a smothered choking noise from behind Seabrook's cravat.

Sophia said, brightly:

'And where is Mr. Adam spending the summer?'

'In Oxford, chiefly.'

Even more brightly Sophia said:

'Then we shall hope to see a little more of you than is possible during the term.'

Charlotte supported this proposition eagerly. Julia did not feel called upon to add anything. But she looked thoughtful.

They saw the young ladies to the door of the Warden's Lodging and went up to Seabrook's rooms. It was darkening inside the thick College walls. He lit candles and got out the brandy.

'Well, Tom, you've been fairly warned!'

'Warned?'

'Of what will happen if you stay up in the Long Vacation — *I'd* as soon spend it in a cage with three healthy tigresses.'

'Oh, rubbish, George!' But he was beginning to wonder if it was.

'Though you might do worse. They're not bad-looking girls.'

'Miss Charlotte is a fool——'

'And Sophia has the makings of an ogress. But Julia is a nice little thing. She's young enough to be moulded.'

'You're welcome to her.'

'Thank you. But I have given Challand to understand — discreetly, of course — that I am promised elsewhere.'

Adam was taken by surprise. 'Are you?'

'Oh, no. But the rumour saves me a lot of annoyance. You notice they waste no time on me? Also — and this *is* true — I have the family living to go to when my aged uncle dies, which can hardly be more than another year or so. The Challands know they have no hold on me. With you it's different.'

'What hold have they on me? In that sense?'

Seabrook lit a cigar at the candle and puffed an aromatic haze across the table. 'You have no interest. No one to push you into anything?'

'Only the gutter.'

'Then you will *have* to take Orders.'

'I don't think I want to.'

'You can't stay here much longer if you don't. And how can you leave without?'

'Why not?'

'You're so stuffed with Latin and Greek by now that you're fit for nothing else. Bachelor quarters in College or married bliss in a parsonage. That's the choice, but it's Holy Orders either way.'

'But, George — I sit there in chapel, and I — I just can't swallow half of it——'

'What intelligent person could?' Seabrook drew at his cigar and sipped his brandy. The candles winked back from the panelling. 'No one asks you to. All they want you to do is preach 'em two good sermons on Sunday,

32

denouncing the sins they're least tempted to commit and sticking to comfortable generalizations about their Christian duties. A funeral as required, a baptism, a wedding or two — and the rest of the week's your own. A gentleman's life. Especially if you can get one of the Leicestershire livings. First-rate sport there.'

'I know.' Adam remembered life at the Rectory. 'But — I couldn't.'

'What else *can* you do?'

'I'd sooner be a schoolmaster——'

'I don't see you as an usher. You were never at school yourself, were you?'

'No——'

'You'd not get far, then, without Challand's backing. And you'd be handicapped if you didn't take Orders, even for that — they like clergymen to thrash their boys.' Seabrook tilted back his chair and surveyed his friend sympathetically. 'I think that exhausts all the possibilities?'

'You forget — I'm pinning a certain amount of hope on my translation.'

'Of course! I apologise to dear old Antonian. But even for that you need all the help that Challand can give you.'

Adam could not keep every sign of his irritation out of his voice. It was a pity that George, so good a friend in most ways, never quite believed in the work he was trying to do. 'If I can't get Challand's approval without becoming his son-in-law, I'll have to go without it. I can look after myself.'

'You'll need to, if you stay here through the summer! Those genteel young harpies are after you.'

'Why should they be?'

'Frankly, because their choice is so limited here. And their situation is, in a way, as hopeless as your own.'

33

'Thank you!'

'If I were a betting man, I'd lay five guineas to one that by October one or other of them had manoeuvred you into position——'

'Make it bottles of madeira, and I'll take you on myself.'

'You will?' said Seabrook incredulously. 'Didn't know you were a sporty devil!' He hesitated. 'No, I don't like the light in your eye, Tom. You've a strangely determined look.'

'As you please. I'm going now. Thanks for the drink.'

'Not Antonian at this hour? I haven't driven you to burn the midnight oil?'

'No. Just a letter I want to finish.'

'Good-night, then.'

'Good-night.'

It was dark in the quadrangle, except for one corner where the moonlight splashed down like milk. From an upper window came raucous singing, which showed that one group of young gentlemen at least were engaged neither in gaming nor in any of the quieter misdemeanours. A rumbling confusion from the black archway of Number Two Staircase indicated that Doctor Rallingson's scout was carrying him up to bed. Near the passage connecting the two quadrangles Adam came upon the Dean, no less drunk than Rallingson but more determined to be independent. He had wandered off course and was trying to walk through the solid wall, at that point clothed with an ancient and luxuriant vine. Drawn to the spot by his feverish scrabbling, Adam caught his despairing mutter:

'Losht! Losht! In 'n impenetrable foresht!'

'Allow me, Mr. Dean.' Adam got a hand under his elbow and respectfully turned him. 'You'll find the forest less thick in this direction.'

'Thank ye, thank ye. Yesh, the treesh are persheptibly thinning. Thank ye, young man. Mosht shivil . . .'

The Dean tottered gratefully away. Adam went on to his own rooms, lit a candle and finished his letter to Pritchard.

'*But the main thing is,*' he wrote, '*I shall try to let you have my Antonian by October.*' He stopped and considered, then drove on his pen with spluttering emphasis: '*As soon as term ends I am going to Italy. There are some minor points to check, and it would be a good idea to revise my translation in the country where he composed the original.*'

He signed his name after the usual courtesies, made up a neat parcel and sealed it. Yes. Italy *would* be a good idea.

Chapter Three

EXCEPT once or twice, at queasy moments in the Channel packet, Adam was never sorry he had agreed to go with Seabrook.

George was right, he had been too much of a hermit. It was absurd that after five years in Oxford — which to the village boy had seemed the gateway to the great world — he had travelled so little. Two brief visits to London, where he knew nobody, and one tiresome cross-country journey to the other university, had been the limit of his explorations. Hard necessity had kept his nose in his books. It was time he raised his head and peeped over the top of the page.

Avoiding the Challand girls was only part of it. The avoidance of women had become a habit. It was easily acquired in Oxford, where only the College heads could marry and provide daughters for the entertainment of their junior colleagues. Adam had never seriously considered looking for entertainment elsewhere — though he was not blind and knew well enough how many dons, as well as undergraduates, were impelled by Nature into the arms of their bedmakers, into discreet liaisons in Cowley or Abingdon, or into impulsive encounters in Magdalen Grove. Fortified by the Rector's precepts and (in a negative, inverse way) by his mother's example, he had repressed the first stirrings of temptation and read some more Latin. It had helped always to have his eyes fixed on the next milestone: scholarship, degree, Antonian ... If Nature became noisier in her demands, he found it a relief simply to read a little less and write a good deal more. What other course was open to a man of honour? Old Jennings had been a great believer in honour ...

Driving to Paris Adam wondered whether Jennings would have approved of Seabrook. Seabrook's attitude to many things in life was, to put it charitably, flexible. And with every mile they covered along the endless tree-lined road from Calais Adam noticed a brightening in his companion's eye, a subtle mellowing of the whole personality.

They had hired a cabriolet with three scrawny horses harnessed abreast. The diligence, said Seabrook, was painfully slow.

'We want to get to Paris while we're still young enough to enjoy the place. Anyhow, the diligence will be full of the most appalling English people.'

It was true, as they had seen on board the packet, that everyone was going to the Continent. For twenty years the quality had been denied the pleasure of looking down on the foreigner and his ways — except for those few enterprising travellers who, like Seabrook, had ventured abroad during last year's brief lull. Now peace was permanent and secure, and its blessings could be all the more fully enjoyed if one had made profits from the late war. Finally, the weather at home was unspeakable. So the deck of the packet and the inns of Calais were crowded not only with milords and miladies resuming their patronage of Europe but with new faces from the City, from Birmingham and Bristol and wherever money could be made. Not forgetting the astute merchants of the West Riding who had triumphed over edicts, blockades and sentimental scruples, and had contrived somehow to equip the French army in Poland with English great-coats; or their equally enterprising brothers in Northampton who had put boots on two hundred thousand pairs of French feet to facilitate their advance against the Allies. Other invasions were forgotten as the English middle class moved in to occupy the Continent.

Seabrook was impatient for Paris. Adam, however, found everything interesting and different, except for the weather (which continued uncertain) and the fleas at Calais which were not unlike those he had met before. Otherwise he saw novelty wherever he looked — in the straight road and the hedgeless fields and the broad-beamed women who worked there, far outnumbering the men; in the capering chattering beggars who swarmed at every post-house, and the unfamiliar uniforms, and the habits of the priests.

So this was France. And these were the strange, baffling, alarming and disgusting French (so Jennings had taught him to think of them), the nation with so little loyalty that they had murdered their king and queen, and with such an excess of it that they had blindly followed their upstart emperor even to Waterloo. These were the inexplicable people who had blasphemously worshipped Reason and behaved (by the standards of the Rectory) so utterly unreasonably.

'Things still look a bit dilapidated,' said Seabrook apologetically. 'Of course, Boney drained the country-side of men . . . and then the armies of occupation. My word, last time I came! Russians, Germans, Austrians, Hungarians, all sorts . . . Like locusts. You could hardly get a cup of coffee.'

Adam saw nothing dilapidated about Paris when they came clattering into the capital at the end of the long second day.

A light shower had laid the dust, and the sun broke

38

through just in time to bemedal the rooftops with gold. The wet façades glistened. He got a confused impression of glory, of wide streets and beetling cliffs of neo-classic architecture, of long vistas fuzzed with young trees and starred with lanterns, and of squares vast as lakes, over which currents of jingling, clopping traffic wove their bewildering way.

'Well?' said Seabrook.

'Pretty lively — for the heart of a defeated empire!'

'Ah, but the French haven't been "defeated", you see, they've been "liberated". All Boney's battles must have been won in spite of his troops. They were all convinced royalists, they were all just waiting for the day to get rid of him. That was the trouble. They all just waited.'

The cabriolet was held up by the traffic. Seabrook pointed to the façade of a theatre opposite. Even in the fading light Adam could still make out, under a thinly painted row of royal *fleurs-de-lys*, an unmistakably Bonapartist inscription.

'A lick of paint works wonders,' Seabrook remarked. 'Goes about as deep with the people, I should say.'

They drove on. The hotel he had used last year was full. They were sent on to another and were met with regrets. The driver took them to a third, a fourth . . . It was quite dark overhead, but the streets blazed with more and more lights. Waiters were bringing out chairs and tables after the rain. To Adam, suddenly weary after the long day — they had driven fourteen posts, ninety miles of bumpy French road — it seemed as though they were moving slowly past endless herbaceous borders of humanity. Nodding at his window, he could take in only a blurred composite impression of mirrors and marble and crystal chandeliers, of top hats and swarthy faces budding out of high-standing collars, of rouged cheeks and whitened shoulders and high bosoms which (Seabrook candidly confessed) reminded him of eggs half buried in a nest of filmy tulle.

They found a room at last in the Rue St. Augustin, in an establishment obsequiously renamed the Hotel Nelson. It was clean, comfortable and extremely dear.

'It'll do while we look round,' said Seabrook. 'Soon find some snug little place and leave more money for other things.'

'Yes,' Adam yawned, past caring.

'Find anything you want in Paris! Just a question of keeping your eyes open.'

They woke late. Fresh rain had cooled the July air. In the Place Vendôme a huge puddle mirrored the column in the centre. Adam greeted it almost as an old friend, it was so like Trajan's Column, familiar from pictures in the Rector's books.

'It's meant to be,' Seabrook explained. 'Boney tried to build a second Rome. Columns, triumphal arches, temples of glory — the town's peppered with them. Louis can change the labels, but he can't pull 'em down.'

Seabrook had not come to Paris to look at pseudo-Roman monuments. He said so pleasantly but with vigour. They strolled on and emerged in the Rue de Rivoli. Seabrook eyed the fashionable thoroughfare with quickening interest.

'One of Boney's better ideas——'

'This street?'

'Of course. Prinny isn't the only man who can lay out a town. Poor old Boney! Not much scope where he is now.'

Adam was thoughtful as they went on their way. This constructive side of Bonaparte was new to him. He had never heard it discussed either at the Rectory or at St.

Columb's. Even Pritchard, for all his radical sympathies, had thought in terms of a Corsican ogre.

'The Tuileries,' announced Seabrook.

Sentries in the old royal uniform strutted to and fro, guarding the tubby little Bourbon within.

'Where's the Louvre?'

'Just beyond. We're coming to it.'

'That's what I want to see.'

They found the galleries in process of rearrangement. Most of the looted treasures had by now been restored to the countries from which Bonaparte had removed them, but even the shrunken residue of antique sculpture and vases would have taken weeks to examine.

Seabrook reminded Adam that this was not the main object of his own coming to Paris. When Adam lingered to admire the proportions of the Versailles Diana, he suggested that it might be more amusing to study the no less perfect proportions of extant beauties on the boulevards.

'I'm coming. Oh — half a minute, George! — I must pay my respects to Antonian!'

'Damn Antonian!'

Seabrook swayed from one foot to the other while Adam examined a portrait bust which could only have been highly imaginative, since it dated from some centuries after the poet's death. But it pleased Adam. It caught the spirit of the man as he thought he had discerned it in his verses.

'Randy-looking devil,' said Seabrook. 'Might have been a good enough fellow to go out with — once. Not now. Come on, Tommy. *We're* alive. Or haven't you noticed? I want my dinner.'

'All right. But I couldn't just walk past him. After all, he's the reason for my being here.'

Seabrook paused, laid a hand on Adam's shoulder, and

41

surveyed him. Then he shook his head resignedly. 'Damn me, Tom, I believe he is.'

His spirits rose visibly over the meal, which they took, deliciously but cheaply, at a little restaurant near the Palais Royal. Adam was thankful his friend was there to order. So far he had been unable to make much of the French he had heard, and, when he tried to utter any, the natives seemed to have a similar difficulty. The way of life was as strange as the language. His not very wide experience of the English inn and chop-house was no preparation at all for this noisy, glittering Parisian world of the café and the restaurant.

Adam's blurred impressions of the previous evening were clearing hour by hour. The crowd, even in this quite modest place where they were dining, was almost alarmingly smart. His grey coat was, by its very drabness, conspicuous among all these sky-blue ones with their rows of buttons flashing like brass cannon. His dark knitted pantaloons, so disturbingly modern to the Warden's eye, must look antiquated against the fuller cut of trouser favoured in Paris. He thrust his long legs under the table-cloth and hoped that, by hiding them, he was not merely shifting attention to the plainness of his cravat. Even Seabrook, who had always stood out as something of a beau against the sombre background of the Senior Common Room, looked faintly provincial here. But if he was aware of it, he showed no sign.

'What do you think of the women, Tom?'

'The — the women?'

'Exactly. You may have observed that here, as elsewhere, the human race can be classified under two convenient headings?'

Adam considered. 'I wish they wouldn't wear such enormous hats. Like chimneys.'

'And with birds' nests on top of the chimneys. I'm with you there. But what about the faces underneath?'

'They use a lot of paint——'

'But not unskilfully, would you say? This is hardly the place to look for dewy milkmaids.'

Adam had never realised before what pleasure there could be in a leisurely extended meal, combined with contemplation of the passing world. Where an Englishman at home liked to get his back against a high settle, with an equally high partition cutting off all view of the other diners, and there earnestly ply knife and fork as though digging a trench under hostile fire, the Parisian took his time and enjoyed the company almost as much as the cuisine. I could be lazy here, Adam told himself with surprise. He had never been lazy before, never wanted to be. Suddenly now, with the deepening languor of the summer afternoon, the wine mounting in his cheeks as it sank in the bottle, he was astonished at other changes which seemed to be stealing over him. He felt no regret when Seabrook said:

'Too late for that library, today.'

'Lord, yes. Tomorrow will do. Plenty of time.'

'Want a fresh mind to examine a manuscript.'

'That's right, George. To be honest, I still feel a bit drowsy. It was a long drive yesterday.'

'And it's hot here.' Seabrook plucked at his neck-cloth.

It was. The savoury fumes of cooking blended with potent scents to thicken the air in the restaurant until it was almost tangible. Adam felt strangely reluctant to leave, but certain that if he stayed he would slump forward and go to sleep. Imposing an unusually deliberate control upon his legs, he managed to follow Seabrook outside without stumble or collision.

It was better on the pavement, despite the vibrating

D
43

heat. The air, if not fresh, was fresher. It smelt of horses and cigars, which was at least a change from cooking and cosmetics. And down on the *quais* it smelt of the river, green and cool. They agreed solemnly that a walk would do them good.

'A short one,' Seabrook insisted.

'Once round the Meadow.'

This remark struck them both as much funnier than it would have done at any other time. Seabrook greeted it with a most gratifying hilarity, and was doubled up with uncontrollable amusement when Adam was encouraged to add: 'If we are lucky, we may run into the Miss Challands.'

Adam himself had not drunk so much as to escape a new reflection, which impinged with the force of a minor discovery: George, dear old George Seabrook, grew simpler as he moved south; his sophistication, so marked in Oxford, was only the thinnest veneer. None the worse for that, of course . . . put them more on an equal footing . . . Good old George . . . excellent fellow . . .

With which eupeptic judgment, Adam took his friend's arm for the next hundred yards or so, whether as a gesture of affection or an appeal for support he was not himself entirely clear.

They admired the new bridges which Napoleon had built across the Seine. He seemed to have built a great number. How many was another point on which Adam remained unsure.

'Excellent things, bridges,' said Seabrook.

'Excellent. You can lean on bridges.'

They continued their promenade, pausing frequently to contemplate the beauties of the Seine.

The waning of the afternoon cooled their heads and, after strong coffee under the shady awning of a pavement

44

café, they felt ready to plan their evening. Adam had heard of the Comédie Française and would have liked to see one of the classic dramas through which he had stumbled as a boy. Seabrook had also heard of the Comédie Française and was determined to avoid it. It was a long way off . . . there was more to see at the Opera, and less language difficulty . . . Surely, he demanded, Adam liked music?

'I like Handel,' said Adam, whose musical education had been centred in village church and College chapel. He had also heard a little Mozart, tinkled out by the Miss Challands on their pianoforte. His feet always responded to the rhythm of a military band and he was liable, when feeling happy and safely alone, to burst into *Hearts of Oak* or *Tom Bowling*.

'I doubt if they will be doing any of Handel's operas tonight,' said Seabrook. 'We can but see.'

The opera billed was Lesueur's *La Caverne*. It sounded promising. On his previous visit, Seabrook explained, he had seen a most spectacular piece, culminating in a realistic Alpine avalanche. With luck, *La Caverne* might include some equally striking effects.

In this hope he was disappointed. So far as they could understand the singers, the plot concerned a young woman who — travelling with an equal absence of discretion and baggage — was captured by brigands in the mountains of Italy. Her virtue was most improbably respected until the denouement, which was as well since the brigand chief had reasons for regarding her with the most confused emotions.

'I think he's her brother,' Seabrook whispered.

'Her *what*?'

'Her brother!'

'Surely she'd know her own brother?'

'No, he's her *long-lost* brother. I think.'

45

'How did she come to lose him, then?'

'There was something about his leaving the ancestral home — years before — and going to the bad. I *think*.'

Even operas presented linguistic difficulties. The final curtain descended without the hoped-for avalanche. Seabrook complained, as they struggled to the door, that the piece had been somewhat deficient in dramatic sensation.

Still, he admitted, there had been plenty to see, and any deficiencies on stage had been abundantly made good by the audience. The trouble was, they knew nobody. Of all those glorious creatures framed in their boxes round the sweeping auditorium there was not one to whom they could pay their respects during the long intervals.

'And everyone agrees, the best part of an opera is the interval! Never mind,' he added with customary resilience. 'Supper now.'

They went to the Mille Colonnes. The café seemed huge, for gilt mirrors multiplied it in every direction and turned the press of customers into a numberless horde. It was like some fantastic forest of soaring marble trees, festooned with crystal foliage and blossoming lights. Looking at some of the faces as they pushed their way through, Adam thought that the forest was not without its beasts of prey. In the centre, at a desk raised on a platform, sat a mature nymph in claret-coloured velvet, glittering with dubious diamonds as though she were herself one of the chandeliers. Every other moment she shot out a much be-ringed talon and jingled her bell, whereupon a waiter looked up, read the edict in her lifted eyebrow, and scurried off to do her bidding.

'Mistress of the ceremonies,' murmured Adam.

'And not only of the ceremonies,' said Seabrook, seizing upon a just-vacated table. 'In her day — if day is the word — she has felt the full weight of imperial responsibilities!'

'You mean — Boney——?'

'So they say.'

The bell tinkled. A waiter took shape at his elbow. Seabrook tilted his head thoughtfully. 'A light supper, I think?'

'Nothing too heavy after that dinner.'

'Some soup then . . . chicken . . . and champagne. Iced. Plenty of champagne.'

The last words stirred a doubt in Adam's mind. 'Old Jennings,' he ventured, seeking the support of authority, 'used to tell me that champagne was a woman's drink . . .'

'And who are we to contradict him?' Seabrook's smile was ambiguous. 'For a country parson, your old Jennings seems to have been almost improperly well informed. So, as I said, plenty of champagne.' He gave the order and sent away the waiter before Adam could develop the discussion.

The café was getting fuller every minute as fresh parties came streaming in from the theatres.

Adam said, conscientiously:

'We oughtn't really——'

Seabrook interrupted swiftly, a suggestive twinkle in his eye: 'In Paris one does a lot of things one oughtn't.'

'I only mean, to have taken a table for four. When the place is getting so crowded.'

'Shall we invite someone to join us?'

'Well——'

Seabrook turned his head. 'How about some of those delightful-looking young ladies?'

'Good Lord, George! Young ladies surely wouldn't ——' Then, following Seabrook's glance all the way, Adam stammered: 'But those — aren't they, well — they look to me more like——'

'*Filles?*'

47

'Er — yes——'

'What do you expect? The Miss Challands? These girls can be damned good fun. What's the harm in buying them a bite of supper? No obligation. Shall we get a couple of them over? I rather fancy the buxom one in green — sea-green, if not perhaps incorruptible——'

'George!' said Adam agitatedly. 'I shouldn't know what to talk to them about——'

'Don't be a wet blanket.'

While Adam was still hoarsely protesting things just seemed to arrange themselves. A brief billowing of draperies, a flash of teeth and eyes, an aura of flower scents (such as his classical reading had taught him to associate with the sudden materialization of a goddess) . . . and there they were, Rose and Gabrielle, seated on either side of him, uttering soft-voiced giggles, addressing him as 'milord', and exclaiming as the champagne rose bubbling in their glasses. Rose was the one in green, Gabrielle wore pink. Adam found it difficult to distinguish them otherwise. They might as well have been called Rosencrantz and Guildenstern, for all the individuality they displayed.

Seabrook was chattering happily. His grammar was simplified, by a linguistic method of his own, almost to extinction. He made up for it by his abundant self-confidence. Adam, anxious not to seem discourteous, ventured a few halting sentences. He encountered wide-eyed incomprehension, a polite request for a repetition, and then peals of bosom-heaving hilarity. He said to Seabrook, in English:

'I seem to be affording them a good deal of amusement.'

'It's the *words* you use, Tom.'

'I warned you I should be no good at this sort of——'

'But they're loving it. They won't believe you're not

48

putting it on.' Seabrook wiped the tears of laughter from his own eyes. 'They say it's as good as the theatre.'

'It's the only French I know——'

'And it couldn't be better! The French of Corneille and Racine,' Seabrook declaimed magnificently. Recognizing the names, Rose and Gabrielle exploded anew.

Adam wished that he had acquired a somewhat less literary vocabulary for these everyday conversations. He had long suspected that his pronunciation too, derived from the Rector years before, had not quite the authentic ring of the native.

'I wish they wouldn't keep calling me "my lord",' he grumbled.

'I've explained to them that you're an eccentric English aristocrat.'

'Oh, damn it, George——'

'It's half true. You are eccentric. Nowadays people are lucky to get half the truth.'

'Why am I eccentric?'

'How else can I explain your clothes? I've told them you're a man of such distinction that, if you appeared in your normal *tenue*, you'd be instantly recognised by the crowd and——'

'I don't believe a word of it.'

'I don't suppose they do. That's something you have in common.'

'There's not much else.'

'I don't know what you expect. Personally,' and at this point Seabrook's smile could only be described as a leer, 'I find the essential difference far more amusing.' He turned to Rose again and engaged her in a cajoling whisper. She responded with every appearance of good humour. For all the barriers of language she and Seabrook had quickly achieved a complete understanding.

49

Adam looked round him desperately. Gabrielle looked round her, bored. Communication, as he understood it, was impossible. That would not have troubled Seabrook, in his place. Gabrielle was pretty, in her standardised way. When she was not silent and bored, her dark eyes scintillated, her lips promised acceptable substitutes for conversation. When she leant towards him across the table, Adam weakened for a moment. His mind was in a flurry, as when two opposing waves crash together . . .

He was never quite clear, afterwards, what decided him. Was it memories of the Rector's moral training? Cowardice — the inhibitions ingrained in him by years of enforced withdrawal into his books? A fastidious reluctance to buy, for cash, an experience which he had always pictured in so different a context?

Anyhow, it was no good. No good at all. He felt as cold as the ice in the champagne bucket. He mustn't let this thing go on any longer, drifting to the end the others so obviously assumed. With some difficulty he got Seabrook's attention.

'I'm sorry, George——'

'What's up?'

'I'm no good at this sort of thing——'

'You don't have to worry——'

'I'd better excuse myself before the situation gets any more awkward.'

Seabrook flushed with annoyance. 'Damn it, Tom, you can't let me down!'

'You let me in for this. I asked you not——'

'Oh, all right! Go to the devil!'

'Will you explain? Tell them — well, tell them whatever you think best——'

'They'll think you more than eccentric,' said Seabrook crossly. 'All right then, you awkward old devil. You'd better just excuse yourself — less embarrassing if they think you're coming back. And when you don't, oh, I'll think of something.'

Adam got up, bowed to the girls, and left the table as naturally as he could.

Outside, alone, he was surprised to find himself as confused and divided as he had been at the table a quarter of an hour before.

Suppose he went back — at once? It was not too late. Only Seabrook would be surprised, and Seabrook wouldn't show it. He'd be only too pleased if Adam changed his mind.

No . . . no.

Adam strode away through the thinning crowd on the pavement. To want and not to want . . . To be offered and to reject . . . His head spun with the contradictions of his own nature.

Seabrook would laugh tomorrow. Let him. Let him think Adam desiccated, with nothing but ink in his loins . . . He wouldn't try to explain himself to Seabrook. Stalking past the bright café windows, he realised that he had never before even considered explaining himself — to anyone. It was the world around one that one tried to explain, surely, not oneself? Were there things, then, that defied the philosophic approach? All too clearly there were.

The sultry Parisian midnight teased his senses. He seemed to be the only person in all the city walking alone. The women passed, leaning each on her escort's arm, faces upturned, vivacious, enigmatic, rapt . . . Cabs went clopping by, their dark interiors full of laughter and whispers . . . Even the most silent doorway exuded a sense of unseen occupancy. The very shadows were alive and heady with perfume. Behind the thick walls

51

the stairs rumbled to mounting feet, and the lights died behind upper windows.

Late as it was, it was not too late. No man in Paris need be lonely — if he were not too particular. Even in Oxford life was not so blinkered that Adam had not seen how these things were managed. Perhaps if he turned away from the busier streets and strolled along the *quais* where they had been this afternoon? By the bridges, Seabrook had told him——

No, said Adam, almost aloud, between gritted teeth. I will not rent an amiable animal, however alluringly scented . . . Love must be worth waiting for.

He recognised a street-corner, got his bearings, and concentrated on finding his way back to the hotel.

He never heard Seabrook come in. But that gentleman, when at last he woke up towards noon, appeared much refreshed, and there were no recriminations over Adam's desertion of the night before.

However, it was clear as the day advanced that they had already reached a parting of the ways. Seabrook was anxious to leave the Nelson and find a room elsewhere. Adam sensed that he would not object to sharing such a room, but that he was not seriously considering Adam for the purpose. They arranged to dine together at the Quadron Bleu, and Adam went off to the National Library to inspect the Antonian manuscript. It did not throw any fresh light on the particular textual problems troubling him, and he came away feeling that there was nothing to detain him in Paris. When he met Seabrook at the restaurant he said:

'I've booked a seat on the Dijon coach for tomorrow.'

Seabrook did not try to dissuade him. Seabrook had a preoccupied air. They spent a pleasant, rather desultory afternoon together, visiting Notre Dame and the Madeleine, and had supper at Tortoni's. Then, pleading his early start in the morning, Adam went back to the hotel. 'I'll stay a bit longer,' said Seabrook. 'I'm not sleepy. I'll have another drink and watch the world go by.'

When Adam was called at dawn, Seabrook's bed was still unoccupied. Clearly, not quite all the world had passed him by.

Chapter Four

THE Rector would have disapproved of the Alps. He would have found them, Adam reflected more than once as the diligence crept slowly up and down Switzerland, uncouth, over-large, and probably deficient in partridges.

The Kidderminster lady in the corner opposite gave it frequently as her opinion that the Alps were awful. But she delivered this opinion in so warm a tone, frequently adding 'sublime' or 'inspiring', for she was a lady who by nature preferred three words to one, that she and the Rector would clearly have disagreed at every stage in the long journey.

Adam was surprised to find how far his own tastes coincided with those of Mrs. Simmonds from Kidderminster, tiresome though she might be in the sentimental reasons she so volubly gave for them. Even Mrs. Simmonds could not diminish these superb rock masses with her chatter.

Adam had never before seen hills bigger than the gentle green undulations enclosing the Thames Valley or the Vale of Trent. The Rector had instilled in him a gentlemanly love of order, in park and garden, meadow and plantation, as in thought and speech. The uncultivated filled the old man with distaste, in landscape no less than in manners. These Alps, with their jagged untidy outlines, their tangled almost vertical pinewoods defying planned forestry, would have revolted him. And then the monstrous *size* of everything. . . How could one quote, 'Man is the measure of all things', when the dimensions of the background reduced the most impressive human figure to a scrambling, overshadowed speck?

Adam, on the contrary, found it rather stimulating to have his old accepted standards roughly turned upside down by what he saw. Next time he went to stay with Pritchard, he must really give Wordsworth's poems a fair trial. Perhaps there was more in them than he'd realised? He'd let Jennings prejudice him too often against Pritchard's enthusiasms. It had been easy to say he was too busy with his ancient authors to read this modern stuff. Once Antonian was finished, he would have time for exploration.

Was Seabrook right? Had he been getting desiccated — intellectually and otherwise? He smiled as his thoughts went back to Seabrook still in Paris, so determined to get his wild oats sown in due season . . . so anxious at the same time to broaden his friend's mind. Adam had not regretted his abrupt departure from the city he had scarcely seen. He would go back to Paris, one day, when he was ready, but not with Seabrook. A queer, good fellow, George, so cynical in Oxford, so fundamentally earnest in Paris, plunging with conscientious abandon into his painstaking little peccadilloes . . . Still, he owed a lot to George for dragging him out of his academic rut and setting him on the road to Italy.

His thoughts were recalled to the road itself by a fresh flight of fancy from Mrs. Simmonds. Her sensibility was so extreme, she explained to the company, that she could not contemplate these romantic vistas without being almost overwhelmed by the most elevated emotions.

This caused her husband to open his eyes and remark dryly that a sense of elevation wasn't remarkable, considering that they must be now at least five thousand feet above sea-level.

'Mr. Simmonds is not romantic,' Mrs. Simmonds informed her fellow-travellers apologetically. No one contradicted her.

'Oh, look, Mr. Adam! Another splendid cataract!' Adam had given up to her, at the beginning of the journey, his own forward-facing corner-seat, so that all his view of Switzerland was retrospective. Mrs. Simmonds showed her appreciation by warning him of each natural feature before it came into his line of vision, and of the emotion which it would be proper for him to feel. Sometimes it was not a splendid cataract but a picturesque cascade. In all the considerable length of the pass there were no mere waterfalls.

This time she prodded her husband into attention. 'Do look, Mr. Simmonds! Such a majestic torrent, falling from such an eminence! Isn't it wonderful?'

'There is nothing to prevent it, my love. I should wonder a good deal more if it stayed up there or stopped half-way down.'

'And look down here!' With Mrs. Simmonds' ample bonnet and shoulders filling the window, no one else could. 'Hurling itself madly into the abyss!'

'Just falling, my love. You speak as though it were deliberately committing suicide.' There was a wistfulness in Mr. Simmonds' tone as he pronounced the last phrase.

His wife withdrew her head, sat back, and rolled her china-blue eyes at the unresponsive company. 'I declare, Mr. Simmonds is too bad. He spoils everything. Doesn't he, Mr. Adam?'

By this time Adam was pressing his face to the window to get his first glimpse of the receding waterfall, and was trying to form an independent impression.

Not even the woman's background babble could spoil

the Simplon. The fantastic, almost perpendicular heights and depths, the strained unfamiliar angles of vision, the great lacey shawls of foam racing over rock slabs, the spray billowing up again in cold white clusters like blossom — all these, with the grey-green snow-water of the rivers, were utterly different from anything he had ever known.

The diligence climbed at a plodding pace, in spite of the extra horses taken on at the foot of the pass. Bridges gave sudden alarming glimpses of the depths only a yard from the wheels. Mrs. Simmonds would close her eyes and shudder theatrically, or fan herself out of a threatening swoon. They drove through rock-hewn galleries. Mrs. Simmonds squawked when the dripping walls closed in and plunged them into gloom.

'Do you know, Mr. Adam, I cannot *bear* to be boxed in?'

If Adam had not known before, he did by now. There were times when he would gladly have consigned her permanently to that condition.

They would regain the daylight, and there would always be some fresh chasm, abyss, or gulf to excite her fearsome enthusiasm. For Mrs. Simmonds every crag beetled, every height frowned and every depth was bottomless. The same, thought Adam regretfully, as she once more leant half out of the window, monopolizing the view, could hardly be said of herself.

Mr. Simmonds remarked that the French, whatever their faults, were good engineers. Europe owed something to Bonaparte, if only the Simplon road.

Mrs. Simmonds refused to believe that any credit was due to him. If Frenchmen had really made these bridges and tunnels (which she doubted), they could only have been good Frenchmen and loyal subjects of their king.

'But, my love——'

57

'Propaganda! Mr. Simmonds will believe anything,' Mrs. Simmonds assured Adam, the Danish couple, and the Austrian captain, who made up the complement of the diligence. 'I assure you, I'm quite nervous that people will take him for a Jacobin. It's only that he's so easily imposed on.'

Adam said he could believe that. The Danes, who knew no English, smiled amiably and said nothing. The Austrian, who knew a little, said nothing and frowned with class-conscious hauteur.

Things were better (and not only for the horses) when they were over the summit. At well over six thousand feet Mrs. Simmonds found that her sensations were almost uncomfortably elevated. She particularly disliked the sight, recurring at every turn in the descent, of a frail fence nakedly outlined against empty air. The horses might stumble . . . bolt, even . . . Much as she admired the beauty of the cataract, she had no desire to emulate it. Adam's offer to change seats again was gratefully accepted. Mrs. Simmonds journeyed on, blind to the horrors of each dizzy bend, and for the first time Adam was able to look forward literally, straining his eyes for the first glimpse of the Italian plains.

They soon stopped for dinner. They were ready for it. They had been travelling since six o'clock. At Berisal, where they had changed horses, there had been time only for a cup of coffee. Adam asked the Captain how soon they would reach the Italian frontier. The Austrian stiffened. His white tunic visibly swelled.

'There is no such thing, sir.'

'I beg your pardon, Captain——'

'There is no frontier of Italy. How can there be? There is no Italy. There is Piedmont, Parma, Modena, Bologna . . . many small states.' The thin lips curled as the names were ejected. 'But when we pass from

58

Switzerland we enter Lombardy-Venetia. A territory belonging to His Imperial Majesty.'

Adam kept a straight face with difficulty as the Captain clicked his heels. 'I am sorry, Captain. A mere slip of the tongue.' It was understandable that these Austrians should be touchy about the status of what still (in his own mind) he would persist in calling Italy. Napoleon had kicked them out of Lombardy and they had only got back by courtesy of the Vienna Congress.

The Captain did not seem inclined to develop the discussion. So, when they all climbed into the diligence again, the journey proceeded in a silence which suited Adam very well. For Mrs. Simmonds, having indulged liberally in food and (for her unaccustomed) wine, slept soundly over the next few miles. Adam was able to enjoy the most spectacular part of the drive without distraction. What Mrs. Simmonds would have said about the Gorge of Gondo, the boiling maelstrom of the Fressinone, and the two-thousand-foot precipices on either side, was all too easy to imagine.

So, at early evening, they came to the frontier of Lombardy-Venetia and pulled up at the barriers painted wasp-like in garish yellow and black stripes. Tall solemn Austrians in badly-cut white uniforms peered owlishly at their passports. For the first time since coming abroad Adam felt like a suspected person. It was also, he realised, the first time he had entered the territory of a British ally.

In spite of the uniforms and the Hapsburg eagles and the guttural, expectorant speech of the border officials, Adam persisted in his private conviction that he was now in Italy. How else could he think of a countryside he had known since he first read Latin, the birthplace of Vergil, Catullus and Antonian, of the Plinies and Cornelius Nepos and——

Everything which met eye and ear and nose was Italian. There was Italian music in the very cry of 'Milano!' on the driver's lips. The soldiers might be big and blond, but the people still labouring in the fields, long-shadowed in the evening light, were small and sallow. They straightened up as the diligence sped by, and volatile faces flashed smiles from under huge straw hats or red stocking-caps. Vibrant voices sang greetings. Mrs. Simmonds bowed like a duchess. The Austrian captain sat rigid, as though the countryside were uninhabited.

'The peasants look very romantic,' said Mrs. Simmonds. 'I only hope that none of them are brigands. However, the country is much *flatter* here, isn't it? So I expect we shall be all right.'

Next morning, as they skirted Maggiore, Adam had the pleasure of overhearing her ask the Captain:

'It is all *very* Italian, isn't it?'

It indisputably was. The confident sunshine, the priests, the beggars; the silver-nosed donkeys and their panniers, the milky-hided oxen with mild eyes fringed against the flies; the tall campanile, the faded frescoes and the wayside Madonnas; the red and yellow lateen sails dotting the blue lake, the oranges glowing hotly gold against their green leaves, the shrill girls in gay petticoats filing through the groves with long wicker baskets on their backs . . . Yes, this was indisputably Italy.

'Such a confusing language,' said Mrs. Simmonds. '*Gerla* doesn't mean the girl herself, you know, but the basket she's carrying. A girl is *ragazza*. You must think of ragamuffins!'

Adam's spirits rose with every mile they covered, and not only because each mile brought him nearer to Milan and the parting from Mrs. Simmonds. Italy was so much more than he had expected. He had thought of the country as an extensive classical ruin, the sites of anti-quarian importance separated by tracts devoid of interest. He had looked at engravings, read Smollett and one or two other travel-authors. Nothing had prepared him for the living Italy, this flood of warmth and colour, this land where even a scolding mother made a kind of music as she resonantly denounced her urchin son.

True, Milan herself bore the imprint of various foreign régimes. As the capital now of the kingless Kingdom of Lombardy-Venetia, it had an archduke as viceroy, taking orders from the imperial court in Vienna. His main task was to convince his reluctant subjects that they were still living in the seventeen-eighties, that there had been no revolution in Europe, no Bonapartist union of Italy . . . It was not easy, but he was doing what he could.

Gentlemen (Adam noticed) were expected to powder their hair as a sign of political reliability. Trousers were as suspect here as in the Senior Common Room at home. Fortunately his own Englishness was obvious to the police (and to the beggars) from the far end of the street, so his consistent refusal either to powder his hair or to leave off his trousers caused him no embarrassment.

Here, as everywhere, was the inevitable triumphal arch set up to commemorate Napoleon's victories. It was too good and too solid to demolish. So it had been renamed the Arch of Peace, and fresh bas-reliefs had been added to illustrate the late war from a different point of view. A statue of St. Ambrose (which free-thinking Liberals had ingeniously changed into one of Brutus) was now being carefully restored to its original saintly character, a task less difficult than might have been imagined, since no one in Milan had the least idea of what either Brutus or St. Ambrose had looked like.

61

Adam was less interested in the statue than in the great library which bore the saint's name. It was, he knew, next to the Vatican, the finest in Italy. Its codex of Antonian was older than the manuscripts in Rome or Paris. The morning after his arrival he hurried to the library.

The word 'Oxford' opened all doors. He found himself addressed at every turn as '*dottore*'. It was no good explaining that he had not yet proceeded to his M.A. In polite conversation, he learnt, every educated man was credited with a doctorate, even if, in fact, he had been expelled from his university in the first term.

'*Il dottor Adam* . . .' It sounded well. Was it so impossible? His dreams revived at the sight of the manuscript, so venerable, so evocative with its faint aroma of scholarship . . . Suppose he *were* able, not only to produce an elegant translation, but to upset the accepted tradition of Antonian's birthplace and the whole background of his poem? That was the kind of thing to make a young scholar's name and open up a career. It was feasible, if only he could dispose of a few verbal difficulties. There would, of course, be automatic opposition. A few dons would stir in their slumbers to differ and debate. But there was no reason to fear strong reaction, for the last editor of the text had been dead for seventy years. No living scholar — even in Germany, where nowadays they were scurrying about with an antlike industry which disgusted Oxford — had a vested interest in the *status quo*.

Adam's fingers were trembling slightly as he took hold of the codex . . .

It was, indeed, very old. The sepia-coloured writing was crabbed and pale, the scribe's abbreviations at times confusing. Adam wished he had had more experience of deciphering such early texts. He was thankful that he was not concerned with the whole book, only with the few crucial passages. Even they took time to identify. Slowly, with his printed version beside him, he checked them one by one.

Ah! A small point, but worth winning . . . The writing was crowded, the letters in this line elbowing each other into uncertainty . . . The reading he wanted *was* possible . . . No, probable. He pored over the tiny strokes and squiggles . . . He would back his own, young man's, eyesight against the middle-aged, probably spectacled, editor who had made a different guess in 1738. To be on the safe side he fetched the kindly old priest who presided over the manuscripts. With exquisite courtesy and without a moment's hesitation the Italian agreed that *il dottore* was undoubtedly correct.

Exhilarated, Adam continued his researches. This wrapped-up reference to an unnamed 'older poet' and Antonian's graceful regret that he himself had been born too late for them to exchange visits. Catullus, on Sirmio? Why not? And if not, where was the point of this reference lower down to 'Benacus' — it *was*, manifestly, 'Benacus', as he had always hoped it might be, though the Parisian and Vatican manuscripts had 'Revacus', and the editors had followed each other like cows in declaring the place unidentifiable! It *was* 'Benacus'. The librarian, for all his bleary eyes, saw it at once. Benacus was the name by which the Romans had known Lake Garda. Antonian's own lake was clearly not Garda, but the implication was that it would have been near enough for easy visits to Catullus there. '*Not long the road: even a winter sun would have carried his torch to the end of the journey.*' That ruled out Maggiore, Como, all the western lakes. Antonian's must be within a short day's drive of Garda. That narrowed the field. Only Lucero fitted the other requirements. If Lucero looked right when he got there

63

— if, above all, there was an island on which Antonian's villa could have stood — Lucero must be the place.

There was no sense in staying longer in Milan. He booked a seat in the diligence leaving for Verona next morning, and ignored the eyebrows which were raised incredulously when he said that he wished to get out at Lucero.

And when he actually did so, shortly after noon on the second day of his journey, there was equal surprise on the face of the Austrian who stamped his passport at the town gate.

'You propose to stay the night here, Herr Adam?'

'Certainly.'

'But the diligence goes on — the fresh horses are ready — no doubt these rascals have misled you? You can be in Verona for supper!'

'I have been told so.'

The official stared and shrugged. 'There is nothing in Lucero.' He spoke with feeling, nostalgic for Vienna.

'Nothing? Why, this very arch is obviously Roman!'

'Most likely. This is such a backwater. Nothing is ever rebuilt. If you are interested in antiquities . . .' The Austrian chuckled cynically. 'One night, then, Herr Adam?'

'Two or three.'

The passport was handed back with another despairing shrug. If Adam wished to prolong his stay it would be his own funeral — but not a very lively one by normal funereal standards. Adam bowed. These officials were extremely punctilious and papers seemed so important that it was best not to offend them. Nor were the resources of all his modern languages combined equal to developing the discussion any further.

The main part of the gate was certainly Roman. Only

64

the upper storey, with its balconied windows, had been added. Perhaps Antonian's curricle had gone spanking under this same arched mass of masonry, when he fled homewards from the hot season in the capital . . . He must come back later and try to decipher the inscription. But first he must arbitrate between the half-dozen ragamuffins who were fighting to carry his bags. Knowing the weight of his books, he humanely engaged two.

'*Albergo.*' He stated his wants economically. '*Letto.*'

'*Si, signore!*' The dust-caked oval cracked across to create a subservient smile.

'*Pulito!*' Adam insisted with a severe expression. Looking at the boy, he wondered if he knew the meaning of cleanliness in any language.

'*Sissignore!*' The answer was shrill with indignation.

'Milord!' amended the second boy diplomatically. Under the coffee-tinted patina of dirt, this one had the cheeks, curls and benevolent serenity of a baroque angel. The serenity was destroyed a moment later when the two colleagues turned and began to shriek in each other's faces the names of the establishments they favoured.

'*Tre Corone——*'

'*No, no! Colomba d'Oro!*'

'*Tre Corone!*'

'*Colomba d'Oro!*'

These comparatively simple exchanges led on to insults of such elaborate obscenity that Adam was spared any clear understanding of them. Lapsing into English, he said: 'Look here, you little devils——' The little devils naturally did not. The strident antiphony continued until the Three Crowns triumphed over the Golden Dove. After receiving a clout on the ear and a stamp on his bare foot, the advocate of the Dove dropped the bag he was carrying and fled, turning only to shoot Parthian shafts of harmful innuendo. The victor ignored them. Bestowing

65

a discouraging grimace on a third party who tried to pick up the bag, he seized it himself in his other hand without apparent distress, and smiled up at Adam with a lightning resumption of angelic nature.

'Milord?' he said with exemplary courtesy, and started down the street with the bags bumping against his tattered breeches.

Lucero was more of a town than Adam had been led to expect. They crossed one corner of the Piazza del Duomo, a not unimpressive square, with a pink-and-white striped cathedral bulging into it and, on the other side, a florid little opera house. In the middle a bronze archduke sat a rampaging bronze charger with a smugness of expression he could not long have kept up in real life.

'*Bello, milord!*' The jerk of the angelic head took in the whole square and its components. Understandably, the burdened ragamuffin had little breath to spend on more particular comments. He went lurching forward, into the shadows of an arcaded side-street, and out again into the full dazzle of the afternoon sun.

Adam blinked as he saw for the first time, across the paved expanse of the Piazza delle Erbe, the lake itself.

It was not blue at this hour, but, in the heat haze of July, it had the opalescence which had caused Antonian, so often, to bring pearls into his similes. To the north the Alps, their foothills veiled, floated palely in the sky. '*My swans . . .*' Antonian had liked to call them. To Adam the moment was one of recognition, almost of revelation. He did not know that much the same effect could be seen from innumerable towns on the Italian lakes.

'Milord!'

The boy's resonant call brought him back to the nineteenth century. His guide had swung off to the left, picking his way between stalls and tilted hand-carts. Adam stalked after him, the heat pressing down upon his

66

shoulders. At this hour, the market drowsed. Theirs were the only footfalls. Here and there an eyelid lifted to reveal an inquiring eye, but no one troubled to cry his wares. Adam walked on, past mounds of oranges like golden cannon-balls, dangling fringes of *pasta*, dozens of straw-hats telescoped one inside another, early grapes clustered like swarming bees, shoes, shawls, and fish, the bright silver of life tarnishing with every hour they remained on the slab.

In the centre rose a slim column, and glancing up with shaded eyes Adam saw the Lion of St. Mark, emblem of the old Venetian Republic, which no one in this quiet town had thought of removing. At the base of the column was a poppling little fountain, presided over by a much weathered Madonna. It looked so old, the statue might have been there in Antonian's day. The chiselled drapery strongly suggested Diana rather than St. Mary. No doubt the town and its statue had been converted at the same time.

The piazza was oblong, one side open to the lake. Here, beyond a line of wide-spaced plane-trees, the fishing-boats were moored, their brightly-coloured sails furled, their awnings rolled away to reveal bare ribs, arched over like barrel-hoops.

'*Ecco, milord! Tre Corone — albergo molto buono!*'

Here, down a cobbled by-way, not fifty paces from the piazza and the waterfront, was the inn. It was a small, decent-looking place, with a fig-tree in its paved yard, vine trellises, and strawberry-pink stuccoed walls, against which an unsystematic profusion of outside staircases slanted and twisted crazily up to various wrought-iron balconies and blue shutters closed against the palpitating glare.

The ragamuffin deposited the bags in the shade of the fig-tree. Then, effortlessly, he raised a cry which, had he been an angel indeed, would have made the Last Trumpet quite unnecessary.

'*Signora! Si-GNOR-a!*'

'*Si, si, Checco! Un momento!*'

From the kitchen doorway emerged a Junoesque but homely figure, wiping brown hands on her apron and bringing with her an aura of savoury steam and garlic.

'*Buon giorno, signore——*'

'*Milord,*' insisted Checco.

'*Signore,*' said Adam with a smile, privately regretting that he could not say '*dottore*'.

A coin from Adam, an affectionate cuff from the land-lady, and the grimy angel withdrew well satisfied. Adam's requirements were so obvious that no strain was laid upon his small knowledge of Italian. The Signora nodded and bobbed, her wrinkles multiplying as she smiled and pattered assurances of welcome and comfort. Then, limping heavily across the yard, she set her hand on the iron rail at the foot of one staircase, raised her head, and called:

'*Brigitta!*'

The blue shutters flew back with suspicious suddenness.

'*Si, Signora?*'

Brigitta looked over the balcony, and came running down with a soft slap-slap of flat sandals. She was a colourful young creature, all ballooning white sleeves and flouncing striped skirt of green and red radiating from a tight little bodice of black velvet embroidered in gold. She listened, smiling, to the Signora's instructions and stooped, attractively, to pick up the bags.

The Signora indicated, with an apologetic gesture, that she found stairs difficult. Her legs . . . If the gentleman would go with Brigitta——

Adam nodded sympathetically, and did so, following her across the courtyard to another staircase. Front

Quad, Number Two, he thought to himself, with an incongruous recollection of St. Columb's.

There was nothing wrong with Brigitta's legs. Like the arms which sprang, golden and rounded, from the froth of sleeve, and the bare shoulders which spread their smooth crescent of flesh between her low bodice and the black hair bunched and ribboned at the nape of her neck, Brigitta's calves and ankles seemed to Adam, as they mounted the steps level with his eyes, to combine grace and muscle with unusual felicity.

This staircase ended not in a balcony but in an open door. He followed her into what was, after the glare outside, a cool darkness which momentarily blinded him. He was aware of her moving shadowily down a passage in front of him. There was a pleasant smell of recently scrubbed woodwork. Then, at a sideways push from her hip, a door creaked open at the end of the passage, and she was silhouetted against the brightness of an unscreened window.

'*Signore* . . .'

'*Grazie!*'

She passed inside with the bags. He followed. The room was soon taken in — a bed, table, chair, bowl and jug, simple but all he needed, and apparently clean. He crossed to the window. It faced due north, straight towards that ethereal skyline of the Alpine snows. That was why the shutters were folded back against the wall outside. The room would be cool even now in July. As he stepped out on to the balcony the freshness of the lake came up at him. Leaning over the balustrade, he saw that this wing of the inn-buildings rose sheer from the water. Had he yielded to so juvenile an impulse, he could have spat into the boat that was moored at the landing steps below.

He turned back into the room. Brigitta stood hand on hip, waiting to know if the room was approved. Her

69

recent exertions had brought a pleasant glow to her cheeks, and her quickened breathing emphasised the salient attractions of her figure.

Adam smiled, trying to express thereby what his Italian was inadequate to do, his complete satisfaction with the accommodation and in particular the outlook from the window. In his anxiety to do so, he inclined (as foreigners will) to an exaggeration of emphasis. The smile became a grimace. Some might have interpreted it as a leer.

'*Bella!*' he exclaimed. '*Molto bella!*' he added with feeling. He had in mind the Alpine horizon.

Brigitta dropped her eyes, and then flashed them at him through a fringe of superb lashes.

'*Grazie, signore,*' she answered in a modest murmur that was almost caressingly intimate after the resonance of her normal speech.

Good Lord, he thought confusedly, she thinks — she must think I——

'*No parlo italiano,*' he began hastily.

'*Monsieur parle français?*'

'*Un peu, mademoiselle.*'

Brigitta beamed. Clearly there need be no obstacle to communication. She chattered brokenly in French while she spread sheets, thumped pillows, and filled the ewer with fresh water. Adam asked how she had learnt the language.

'Lucero was much occupied by the French armies . . .'

Adam could believe that the French armies had been much occupied with Brigitta.

As she knelt to unlace his boots for him he became more than ever conscious that she was a young woman with conspicuous attractions.

'Monsieur has everything? Monsieur requires nothing more?'

70

Adam was not quite sure of her meaning. Nor was he quite sure of his answer. He thought it best to say: 'Thanks, no, nothing for the moment, thank you.'

'If Monsieur wants anything, he must go to the top of the steps out there and call. There is no one up here. Monsieur can be very quiet here with his books, no one will come.'

She went with a flounce of her striped skirt, a final flash of smile. How the devil, thought Adam, does she know I mean to stay longer than I said?

Chapter Five

H<small>E</small> felt curiously at home as, after washing and putting on a clean shirt, he set out his books and writing materials on the table. He could not have settled in Paris, even without Seabrook's distracting company. Even Milan would have been too big and noisy. He wanted to be quiet now, and finish his translation in sight of the same unaltered horizons which had inspired Antonian so many centuries ago. Here in this lakeside room he could enjoy the peace of an Oxford quadrangle.

But not just yet. After so many days of bumping across Europe, he wanted to stretch his legs, to breathe something else than dust and the staleness of coach-leather and fellow-travellers. And he wanted to eat.

He went downstairs and investigated the geography of the inn. The common dining-room was a low vaulted apartment, with crude but gay paintings on the white plaster. Brigitta was talking to three men, one a priest and the others decently dressed townsmen, who sat at one end of the long table. They greeted Adam with a nice blend of civility and curiosity. Brigitta broke off her talk with them and asked what he would like for dinner.

'Whatever is ready, mademoiselle.'

'At once, monsieur.'

She whipped away and was soon back with a mountainous risotto, fragrant and saffron-gold, snow-capped with Parmesan. Veal followed, flavoured with lemon and some herb which eluded him and which Brigitta could not name in French. The red wine was a little rough to his taste — it would have been thought poorly of at St. Columb's — but he had taken 'When in Rome . . .' as his motto. As he peeled himself an orange by way of epilogue, he felt more than ever disposed to settle in Lucero.

'Monsieur will see the town?'

'Yes, I am going now. . . .'

'There is much to see. Monsieur would like a guide?' Adam hesitated. 'Checco would show Monsieur the way——'

'Thank you, but this evening I think I will just take a little promenade by myself.'

'As Monsieur pleases.'

How obliging these people were! So different from the surly ruffians of the coaching-inns, both at home and abroad. This Brigitta, in particular, seemed ready to oblige.

The fierce heat had faded. The plane-trees along the waterfront were lengthening their shadows, the mountains were taking on the bolder outlines of evening. He crossed the Piazza delle Erbe, now stripped of its stalls, and followed a street of arcaded shops which slanted away in a new direction. The town was waking up now. Male laughter rumbled from the low-ceilinged wineshops, where already lanterns swung to disperse the gloom. White-coated soldiers of the garrison strolled up and down in little groups or, where the street broadened into a small piazza, lounged at café tables on the pavement. Women hung over balconies or tripped self-consciously along in pairs and trios, swinging their hips and laughing secretively. At rare intervals a cart or a donkey plodded by, and twice a genteel carriage. Lucero evidently had its polite society. This was still more certain when he found

73

himself straying into a quieter, shopless quarter with tall palladian houses — palaces, these Italians would no doubt term them — some blank and haughty of façade but others offering, through elegant wrought-iron grilles, a glimpse of a colonnaded courtyard musical with splashing water. Sometimes the music was not of fountains but of a guitar or a piano in some upper room.

Adam liked the place more and more. Even the iron-grilled *palazzi* gave him no sense of exclusion. There was something in the very air of Lucero which welcomed him.

It was a fair-sized town, spread over a gently sloping triangle of land where the hills dipped to the lake and a river came tumbling down, zigzagging now from side to side of what was its full bed when in spring-time spate. Adam made his way to the bridge which spanned it just before it entered the lake. On the far bank the road seemed to enter open country, and, as there was a gate-house with the usual complement of Austrian guards, he felt there was no point in crossing over and going through a lot of formalities. He turned back into the town.

That must be the medieval castle, up the hill there, its pink granite flushed by the last sunshine which had already left the streets below. . . . It had tooth-shaped machicolations — the long line of the ramparts stood out like a giant saw-edge against the pale apricot sheet of the sky. A romantic-looking place, but probably a barracks now for the unpopular *tedesci*. . . . He must find out if it was permitted to go in.

Not tonight, though. It would too soon be dark. He was more interested in finding, if there was still time, the ruins of the Roman theatre which Lucero was supposed to possess. There was a good passage in Antonian (though rather too reminiscent of Ovid) where the poet described a flirtation at the theatre which had been more absorbing to both parties than the crude pantomime on the stage. *'But at least,'* Antonian had written in another passage, *'our little provincial theatre has something yours in Rome cannot boast: when our eyes weary of the players' nonsense, they can stray beyond them to the lake and the perpetual snows.'*

It didn't prove anything, Adam warned himself. . . . Any Italian town under the Empire probably had a theatre of sorts. . . . But if this was the one Antonian meant, it must be high enough on the hillside to command that kind of view.

He stumbled on through malodorous by-ways. The inevitable ragamuffin appeared. Adam asked:

'Teatro?'

'Sissignore!' But the boy pointed emphatically back into the centre of the town. Adam was about to turn back when the boy added, gratuitously, *'Domani, signore!'* He was warning Adam that the theatre was closed today. He must mean the modern building.

'No, no. Teatro — teatro romano.'

'Ah! Teatro antico! Si, signore!'

Delightedly the small boy went capering ahead and beckoning. Adam's sense of location had not deceived him. Five minutes brought them to an open stretch of hillside, strewn with fallen columns and shattered tiers of stone benches, curved round a paved acting area below. He saw at a glance that three-quarters of the masonry had been carted away in later centuries to build into the houses of Lucero. Despite that, and despite the wild thyme which had invaded it and the cypresses rooted here and there among the fragmentary pillars, it was still possible to imagine the seats packed with toga-draped theatre-goers. He was helped by the rapidly failing light, which lit the sky with fire but blurred all the details below.

He gave the boy a coin and sent him off. He could find his way back alone. He wanted no distraction. He sat down on a slab of marble, half-way down the auditorium, and surrendered himself to the spirit of the place. How had he rendered Antonian's couplets?

> *'But stay, what spectacle have they to show,*
> *One half as splendid as the lake below?*
> *While the comedians, with vaunted art——'*

Shadowy figures moved suddenly across the ruined stage. There was a grey-white glimmer of draperies. Adam, sitting squarely on his marble bench, entertained no romantic illusion that his thoughts had conjured up ancient ghosts. The glimmer came not from white togas but from muslin dresses. Laughter and voices, too low for the words to carry at that range, showed that a mixed party had come into the ruins from below. He remembered that the moon should soon be rising.

It was goodbye to imaginative reconstruction. After a louder burst of laughter, one of the men in the party leapt the front barrier and came charging up the twilit theatre, stumbling and panting and dislodging loose flakes of masonry as he ran. He kept straight up the central gangway and passed Adam, sitting twenty yards or more to one side, without apparently noticing him. Adam kept still. If he moved now he might startle the other visitors.

The flying feet continued to the broken colonnade which ran along the top of the theatre. Silence showed that their owner had stopped. Then the silence was broken again from below, as one of the darker figures stepped forward and Adam heard (to his surprise) a broad Yorkshire voice declare with conviction:

'"Society in every state is a blessing, but government,

even in its best state, is but a necessary evil; in its worst
state an intolerable one. Government, like dress, is the
badge of lost innocence; the palaces of kings are built
upon the ruins of the bowers of paradise . . .'''

The voice continued for a full minute in this strain.
When it paused, a younger, more polished, but no less
English voice interjected from above with a slight sus-
picion of hastiness:

'Excellent! Every word clearly audible in the back row.'

'You are satisfied, then?'

'Completely satisfied,' admitted the second voice.

'I told you the acoustic properties were remarkable.'

'You did,' agreed the second voice with fervour. And
before the recitation could be resumed from the stage,
the footsteps were heard descending again with the
alacrity of an avalanche.

'Splendid stuff,' boomed the Yorkshireman. 'Tom
Paine, y' know.'

'Of course!' gasped the invisible scrambler.

But, thought Adam, that young man has no more read
Tom Paine than I have.

'I could go on for whole pages,' shouted the Yorkshireman regretfully.

'I'm sure you could, sir.' There was deference, but no
regret, in the younger voice. During the renewed laughter
and chatter which broke out as the man rejoined his
companions, Adam seized his chance to slip away quietly.
He would come again to study the ruins in daylight and
again, perhaps, to see them under the moon. There was
no point in staying now to share them with a noisy party
of English tourists.

Ten minutes of stumbling down by ill-paved, ill-lit
lanes brought him to the back of the cathedral. Beyond, in
the Piazza del Duomo, there were lights in plenty, and
several cafés, one with music. The opera-house was dark

and closed, but the play-bills newly posted outside announced three special gala performances. The titles and the composers meant no more to him than the names of the artists.

He sat down in the café which had musicians. There were half a dozen officers at one end, perhaps twenty townspeople and their ladies at the other. Adam took a table in the no-man's-land between them, and almost felt the crossfire of glances from both directions. Englishmen seemed a rarity in Lucero — but that was to be expected. More remarkable was the coincidence of the other tourists' passing through.

After a light supper he took a final turn round the square, examined the architectural details of the cathedral, now shown up in relief by the risen moon, and made his way back to the Tre Corone. Of Brigitta there was no sign, but, as he hesitated in the courtyard, wondering about a light for his room, the Signora waddled out of her kitchen, her face creased with welcoming smiles, and handed him a small lamp to carry upstairs.

'*Grazie, Signora.*'

To his surprise she bent her grey head forward and pressed her lips to the back of his free hand.

'*Felice sera, Signore!*'

And still smiling she watched him mount the outside staircase.

Under his balcony the lake was like black glass, shattered by the lemon-coloured fragments of the moon's reflection. A single boat was gliding across it. The boatman stood up, faced the way he was going, and pushed at his oars. He was singing. The voice came in a poignant tenor across the cool water:

'*Ne di giorno, ne di sera,*
Non passiamo la selva nera.'

78

Adam had not the faintest idea what the song was about, but the refrain was soothing.

He closed the shutters against the night air, climbed contentedly into his bed, and knew nothing more until Brigitta's voice roused him.

'You did not call me, monsieur,' she said. 'At last I think: I will go. That was right, monsieur?'

'Quite right, Brigitta.'

Adam yawned and struggled into a slightly less submerged position. The shutters creaked back and tapped the wall outside. Daylight washed over the room. Fresh air rushed in to meet the fragrance of coffee.

Brigitta turned, smiling as she pushed aside his books so that she could unload the tray.

'You were tired last night, monsieur?'

'I — I must have been. Is it very late?'

Brigitta shrugged. 'We have a saying in Lucero: "It is never *too* late." What does it matter? Monsieur is on holiday?'

'In a way.'

'There.' She inspected the breakfast-table. 'Coffee, milk, bread, butter, honey, fruit. There is nothing else you require?'

'No, thank you, Brigitta.'

She straightened the top book on the pile. Aloud she slowly spelt out the author's name. Adam asked, curiously:

'Have you ever heard of Antonian?'

She considered gravely, then shook her head.

'Was he a saint, monsieur?'

'Not exactly.' Adam chuckled. 'He was a poet.'

Brigitta took the point well. She laughed wickedly. 'Ah, they are anything but saints, that lot!'

He wondered if she had ever met a poet. He thought of

79

his manuscript book with its hundreds of patiently polished couplets. Even a translation, if in verse, was surely worth a sprig of laurel? He wagged his finger at her as she turned in the doorway.

'You must not say that, Brigitta. *I* am a poet. In a very small way.'

'Monsieur? A poet?'

Brigitta dissolved into confused laughter, but, when she recovered, she looked brighter and more interested than ever. He began to wonder if it had been wise to tell her so much. She might get quite wrong ideas about his versifying. But how explain his translation to her when she had never heard of Antonian and could barely spell out his name?

'Brigitta——'

'Monsieur?'

'There is something else I shall want——'

'Yes, monsieur?'

She came back into the room and let the door swing to behind her. She really *is* a pleasant young woman, he thought. She had never looked so cheerfully obliging.

'In half an hour, when I have had breakfast——'

'Yes, monsieur?'

'I should like some hot water. Boiling.'

She stared, echoing the last words.

'To shave,' he explained patiently, fingering his speckled jaw. 'Englishmen shave every day.'

'There is a good barber. Checco would fetch him, or——'

'I prefer to shave myself.'

'But——' Her eyes danced with amusement. 'No one to talk to? If Monsieur does not go to the barber, how does Monsieur hear the news?'

'And how much news will Monsieur understand — in Italian? I must depend on you, Brigitta, for any news I hear in Lucero.'

80

She giggled. 'I cannot stand talking to Monsieur while he shaves. In the morning, I have my work to do.' And on that line she made her exit, and Adam was able to swing his bare legs out of the bed. Pulling his trousers over his night-shirt he hurried to the table before his coffee got cold.

The view was clearer this morning, the colours brighter. He could see the length of the waterfront with its bobbing rank of gaily-painted boats, its line of spreading plane-trees with their mottled silver trunks, and a segment of the Piazza delle Erbe with its motley awnings like the banners of a halted army. Beyond stretched the reedy little delta where the river came swirling under the bridge and into the lake, dropping such bits of the Alps as it had not previously deposited along its course. Beyond the river, filling the middle distance and screening the upper reaches of the lake, a narrow promontory stretched far out into the water, which was so glassy this morning that the pink granite cliffs and dusky pines were exactly mirrored. A huddle of white walls and terra-cotta roofs, at the landward end, must be the village of La Lingua which he had seen named on the signpost by the bridge last night.

He had just finished his breakfast when there was a knock. The boy Checco entered, grinning through the steam of the shaving water.

'*Buon giorno, milord!*'

'*Buon giorno, Checco.*'

Adam had hoped it would be Brigitta. He had been thinking that she could clear up for him, at once, the question of Antonian's island. But when he named her, with raised eyebrows, Checco executed an elaborate mime to show that she had gone marketing. Could he make Checco understand what he wanted to know?

'*Checco——*'

'*Si, milord?*'

'*Insula?* I mean — what's the word? *Isola?*'

'*Isola?*' Checco looked dubious for a moment. Then his black eyes twinkled delightedly, until they narrowed to slits with the violence of the amusement which shook his bony frame. '*Isola!*' he echoed, with an effort at self-control which faintly puzzled Adam — had his own pronunciation of the word been so ridiculously different, or did it mean something else? But, no, Checco obviously knew he was talking about islands on the lake, for he pattered to the balcony on his coffee-coloured feet and pointed in the general direction of La Lingua, wagging his head and still gurgling with suppressed amusement. '*Si, si, milord. Isola. Isola.*'

That was all Adam wanted to know: that the lake *had* an island. If there was one, he had already assumed that it must be somewhere on the far side of the headland, for the southern stretch of Lucero was almost all visible from his balcony and its surface was unbroken by so much as a rock. When he had shaved and dressed, he would walk out to La Lingua. It would be no more than a pleasant country stroll and those wooded heights at the far end should give a clear view in both directions.

Checco showed a tendency to linger, fascinated by Adam's razor-case and the deliberate ritual which accompanied it. Adam preferred privacy. With a menacing gesture which delighted the urchin, he sent him scuttling from the room and settled to the task of lathering his face.

So . . . it was all right about the island. Not that he had seriously doubted its existence. Everything about Lucero seemed to fit. The place looked right, felt right. . . . Already he had thought of a dozen subtle changes he could make in his translation. Sight of the actual lake, the hills, the theatre, had suddenly illuminated the Latin. He would have sung aloud if it had been feasible while tensing throat and face against the scrape of the razor.

A lane, turning off the high road, brought him to La Lingua within half an hour. It was a ramshackle village of cobbled lanes, scampering goats, and round-eyed children. He stopped for a few moments by the church. It was not the little Madonna in her recess, with fading flowers at her feet, which had caught his eye, nor the still legible slogans, *Evviva Bonaparte!* and *Vincere o Morire*. It was the sight of small Roman bricks and one slab of stone, carved in bas-relief, which had been incorporated in the general patchwork of masonry and were now showing through the broken skin of plaster.

It was a wonder that any scrap of classical Lucero remained *in situ*, when even the country villages had treated the ruins as a quarry.

After the houses came a grove of lemon-trees. It was like walking down an avenue of lamps. Then came a silvery shimmer of olives, and the lake came into view again on his right, blue, almost violet, behind the twisted, rheumaticky trunks. The foliage cut off the more distant view.

Now the headland grew stonier, useless at this point to anyone but a persistent goat. It was pinched in, and he saw the flash of ripples to the left as well as the right. The track wound on between pines and cypresses, wide enough for a carriage and pair, but so neglected that probably none had driven over it in the past twenty years. It dipped to the waist of the headland and for a hundred yards or so ran above twin stretches of glistening sand, shaded only by a single file of ragged pines leaning away from the prevailing wind. Then the ground rose again and broadened, and the carriage-drive wound up into the woods, while faint paths branched right and left like the veins of a leaf.

Adam bore to the right, letting the pleasant view of the town vanish among the trees. His immediate concern was with the promised island. So far he had seen no sign of it, but a good area of the lake was still masked by the knobbly promontory in front of him. He quickened his pace, scrambling and slithering along the gritty path, sometimes almost vertically above the lake, at others dropping sharply to some miniature cove before rising like a rocky staircase. The water, changing from sapphire to emerald at close quarters, tempted him — his linen was clammy after his hot walk and, with the last houses left far behind, it seemed a convenient place to swim. But first he must get a glimpse of Antonian's island. . . . This afternoon — or tomorrow if it looked a long way out — he must get a boatman to take him there. Brigitta would find him a man. . . . He would take food and wine in a basket, picnic there, and, while the good fellow took his siesta, he himself would poke about for fallen statuary and overgrown mosaic floors. What if the island proved a tiny Pompeii? Excavations were all the mode now. Suppose he appeared before the learned world as the re-discoverer of Antonian's villa? Returned to England with half a dozen boxes full of classical antiquities, distributing them generously to the University and other learned bodies? These pleasant day-dreams did nothing to cool his brow or quieten his pulse as he hurried up and down the looping path.

Surely he would get a clear view soon? The cliff in front was the highest yet, and it jutted out to make a miniature promontory of its own. He should see some-thing when he got to the top of that. . . . He would have to stop anyhow, if only for a minute, to mop his face and get some breath back into his lungs.

Yes, he grunted, as he plodded upwards, *must* see something from the top of that.

It was not, however, quite what he had expected. As he collapsed on the soft pine-needles and looked down the far side, he saw another of the little coves which had already tempted him. Rosy crags, warm even in the slants of shadow, dropped into a soft green translucency. In a cooler moment some erudite tag would have sprung unbidden to his lips, some reference probably to 'a haunt meet for nymphs and oreads'. As it was, he had breath only to gasp one syllable.

'God!'

Even Parson Jennings would have forgiven such an exclamation in the circumstances.

The cove already had its nymphs. One, crowned with a nimbus of corn-coloured hair, had just pushed off from the cliff face and was swimming out into the open lake. The other — there seemed to be no more — was sunning herself on a granite slab which jutted out from the shadows. For a mere moment or two she sat there with pale arms uplifted, fingering some ribbon which held a mass of dark, almost black hair bunched up clear of her shoulders. He was near enough to see how the sun's brightness picked up the glistening wet furrow of her spine as she bowed forwards, struggling with the knot.

Then she dropped her palms to the granite slab, wriggled herself forward, and slid feet first into the water. A few seconds later she reappeared on the far side of the rock, swimming vigorously in the wake of her companion. All too soon they had both vanished round the next little headland which formed the other horn of the cove.

The water deepened rapidly, but it had a crystalline clarity. Every stone on the bottom was visible, down to ten or twelve feet. Only motion (such as the passage of a swimmer) imparted a fantastic illusion of wavin⁀s even to the straightest line — an optical effect which, Adam thought, in some cases created a beauty of its own.

Still prone on the pine-needles, he took rather longer than he had expected to recover his breath.

Who were the swimmers?

Not nymphs, certainly, in any strict mythological sense. Not nymph-like hallucinations, induced by too much celibacy and classical scholarship. Though any young Oxford don might have been subject to such hallucinations, his fevered fancy would hardly have gone to the length of providing towels.

One unmistakable towel he could now see, white against the rocks below. And, half hidden by the overhang of the cliff, a suggestion of mortal garments heaped together.

Adam took this as a strong indication not only that the swimmers were equally real but also that, before long, they would come back.

His first instinct was to stay where he was.

To contradict this came, from beyond the grave, and somewhat muted by distance, the Rector's favourite reminder of the principles governing the conduct of a gentleman. There was no doubt that, in this context, they involved an immediate and considerate withdrawal.

That was all very well for the Rector. He had gone to a place where he was no longer troubled (if he ever had been) by the flesh, and where no secrets were hid. But Adam had not yet achieved emancipation from desires and curiosities. Though he could not bring himself, even in silent thought, to 'damn the Rector', he did reflect rebelliously that the old man had restricted him enough as a boy at Ramsthorpe, steering him away from the mildest flirtations in the hayfield, and he had certainly no right to rule him now.

Why should he turn back, when so near the objective of

his walk? It was not his fault if two young females took the risk of bathing near a path.

Very well, then, urged the spirit of the Rector, wearying. In that case hurry on, before the ladies come back. On your return journey see if there is an equally convenient path on the other side of the headland — or perhaps the carriage-road would be best if it goes all the way? And you could sing to give warning of your approach. *Rule Britannia* or *Hearts of Oak* or *Britons Strike Home*.

The phrase with which Adam mentally countered this conscientious suggestion would have meant more to the village lads of Ramsthorpe than to their pastor.

He was tired and hot. He was going to sit there under the pine-trees just as long as he wanted to. If the ladies came back before it suited him to move, he could always look the other way. Not that he necessarily would. . . . What was that handy tag of Terence? '*Homo sum: humani nihil a me alienum puto . . .*' Well, why shouldn't he too consider everything human to be his business? And if he had already proved to himself that his translation of Antonian would be the richer for seeing the landscape Antonian had depicted, how much stronger was the argument for——

There was no need to go on wrestling with his conscience. Conscience was down, both shoulder-blades touching the ground.

At that moment he caught the splashing sound of a returning swimmer. He sat up, then stretched himself flat again upon the pine-needles. The only really un-gentlemanly thing would be to cause embarrassment by revealing his presence: so long as he kept quiet, there was no harm in the world. . . . That was certainly what George Seabrook (if not the Rector) would have told him.

He waited. The swimmer must be hugging the base of the cliff on this side of the cove — the rhythmic sound of the parted water was unmistakable, but there was a tantalising interval before the glistening figure came into view, clambering out of the shallows and over the rocks to the towel and clothing.

Adam gasped again. With his froth of white hair and whiskers, and the darker mat on his chest, the swimmer looked (as Adam told Seabrook some months later) like nothing so much as 'a bloody great sheepdog'.

Chapter Six

DRYING himself vigorously, the stranger began to sing — or rather to bellow to the echoing rocks:

'*Allons, enfants de la patrie,*
Le jour de gloire est arrivé!
Contre nous de la tyrannie
L'étendard sanglant est levé . . .'

Adam thought he recognized the tune. Yes, it must be the revolutionary *Marseillaise.* He had heard it sung once or twice by undergraduates more as a joke than as a seditious gesture.

The voice was unmistakable. He had heard it, last night, declaiming in the Roman theatre.

The song broke off abruptly. Lifting an irate whiskered face in Adam's direction, the stranger demanded:

'What the devil are you doing up there?'

Adam stood up sheepishly, dusting his knees. 'I beg your pardon——' he called.

The stranger instantly became more genial. 'Come down!' he roared. 'I thought you were one of those infernal foreigners spying on me.'

'But you spoke English?' said Adam, scrambling down the rocks to join him.

'Of course. No good trying to talk to these fellows in their own language. They only take advantage.'

'I haven't met anyone in Lucero who understands English.'

'Oh, they do. You'll see. You just have to keep on, over and over again, getting louder each time and more emphatic. It needs patience.'

And lungs, thought Adam.

'You must try the water. It's so much warmer this side — the river chills it nearer the town. Apart from the filth they throw into it.'

'I don't think I'll bathe at the moment, thank you, sir.' As the stranger showed no sign of dressing but had enthroned himself on a sunny rock, like a rather paunchy and bedraggled Neptune, Adam diffidently added: 'I ought to warn you — there are some young ladies not far away.'

'Ah, you saw 'em?'

'Well . . .' Adam hesitated. 'I caught a glimpse of their heads as they swam round the point,' he said diplomatically. 'That was all.'

'A pity. I'm afraid they won't come round again,' said the stranger apologetically. 'In theory they agree with me absolutely — the human form is an object of beauty, not of shame.' He scratched himself complacently. 'Newton taught me that.'

'The astronomer?'

'No, no. Don't you know the Newtons? Charming family. Friends of the Godwins in Skinner Street. Five children. Run about the house with no clothes on. Admirable. You would like them,' said the stranger, on what seemed to Adam inadequate evidence. 'One might develop Newton's idea into a whole philosophical scheme. Well, as I say, the young ladies — Harriet especially — are in full agreement. But the effects of bad early training die hard. A certain vestigial prudery still resists the appeal of reason. In short, they insist on disrobing in a little grotto which they have made their own. . . .' He jerked a thumb towards the next little headland round which Adam had seen them disappear. 'I blame Sally. A good enough girl. But she lacks Harriet's intellectual grasp.'

'They are English, then?'

'Thank God, no. American.'

'Are you American, sir?'

'I, sir, would prefer to describe myself as a citizen of the world.' The effect of this statement was slightly spoilt by the stranger's rising at this point and thrusting one leg into a pair of cotton drawers. 'However, for the convenience of these damned Austrian bureaucrats and their papers, I am compelled to call myself an Englishman. To you, sir, I would add, "an Englishman in self-imposed exile".'

Adam did not know quite what to make of this. He merely said:

'My name is Adam. I come from Oxford.'

The blue eyes, which had been childlike under the shaggy brows, narrowed suspiciously.

'Not a parson?'

'No, sir.'

'Then I can shake your hand.' Having completed the adjustment of his underwear, the stranger was doubly free to do so. 'I, sir, am Matthew Mortimer.' He smiled warmly in Adam's face. 'I have no doubt the name is not unfamiliar?' A lurking anxiety behind his smile suggested that a certain amount of doubt existed.

Luckily Adam had a good memory for book-titles and he had seen the name in Pritchard's shop.

'Not,' he exclaimed, 'the author of *The Rebellion of Reason*?'

The incredulity in his tone delighted Mr. Mortimer, who did not, fortunately, suspect its cause. The book had been a best-seller in the seventeen-eighties. It had not occurred to Adam that its author could be still alive.

'Have you read it, Mr. Adam?'

Adam felt that honesty would be the safer policy.

'No, sir. A friend — a bookseller — told me it was not necessary——' From the way Mortimer bristled, he sensed that honesty could be carried too far. He concluded diplomatically: 'My friend said that its influence in the past had been so wide that its basic thought had been incorporated into all subsequent literature on the subject.'

Mortimer swallowed this sweet mouthful without any sign of strain. His geniality flooded back, and his face emerged smiling from the shirt he now pulled on.

'My worst enemy would hardly accuse me of vanity. Still, I flatter myself the book was not without influence in its day.'

'And after, sir.' Adam was enjoying himself. It had also occurred to him that, by prolonging the conversation, he might make the acquaintance of Mortimer's young friends. 'It might be said with justice, sir, that all books fall into one of two categories. Those written before *The Rebellion of Reason* and those written afterwards.'

Even the most modest author could scarcely contradict that statement. Mortimer did not try to. He drew on a pair of yellow nankeen trousers and purred with gratification.

'Young man, you must come to dinner with us.'

'I should be honoured. Where are you staying, sir?'

'I am not staying.' Mortimer braced his trousers high under his armpits, tied his cravat with the decisive gestures of a professional garotter, and stuck his arms into the coat and waistcoat which Adam held out for him. 'I live here.'

'You have a house in Lucero?'

'I have a house *here*. On the very tip of La Lingua.' Mortimer clapped a peasant's sombrero on his damp grey curls and led the way forward up the rock. 'A villa — a ruin, rather — let to me by a titled scoundrel. However, it serves for the present. Fortunately I am quite indifferent to material comfort.'

The Villa Gandolfi, which they came upon suddenly after another five minutes' brisk walk through the wood, was a rather more attractive place than this description had led Adam to expect. The shutters could have done with a new coat of paint, certainly, the walls were blotchy with a kind of architectural dermatitis, and both paths and flowerbeds were overgrown. But the place was no ruin. It rose proudly in balustraded terraces from the water's edge and at one end it overhung the cliff, jutting out in an elaborate likeness of a ship's stern. Within the circling screen of pinewood the gardens made a sunny oasis. There were magnolias and oleanders, a walnut-tree and a cedar, cypresses and date-palms, orange-blossom and roses. Peaches and nectarines splayed their tendrils against the terrace walls, and the balconies of the house itself were enwreathed in wistaria.

Adam was pleased to hear feminine laughter and to catch sight of figures on the terrace.

'I have to feed these damned things,' said Mortimer abruptly. 'It's in the lawyer's agreement. And they just trail round the place uttering the most appalling noise.'

He indicated a peacock — not even a coloured one, but dead white, as though it had been kept in a dark cellar. The bird returned his stare with obvious dislike, and walked away, pausing only to utter a cry of such horrific discordancy that Mortimer's resentment seemed fully justified.

93

They made for the uppermost terrace, from which rose the house itself. Adam saw now, with disappointment, that the woman seated there, writing at a table, was of the homeliest appearance. Could this have been the fair head he had seen breaking the waters of the lake? As for the laughter, that was explained by the sight of two little girls in billowy frocks and pantalettes who pattered squealing along the terrace in the opposite direction, unaware of Mortimer's approach. At least, thought Adam, they *were* fully clothed. In the Mortimer ménage he must be prepared for anything.

'Are we interrupting you, my dear?'

'Not at all, Matthew,' the lady called back in a resigned tone. She laid down her pen, and looked over the parapet. Seeing Adam, she stood up.

Mortimer led the way up the steps and introduced Adam. The table was strewn with manuscript, the loose sheets held down with a variety of geological specimens.

'Mrs. Mortimer also does a little writing,' explained her husband kindly.

Mrs. Mortimer smiled wanly and said nothing. She must, Adam supposed, be about forty. Possibly, though, the lines on her face were not solely due to the lapse of time. Feeling required to say something, he inquired if she wrote on geology.

She looked surprised. 'Oh, no. Why?'

'These specimens——'

'They are only paperweights. Now that Mr. Mortimer no longer collects them.'

'But don't throw them away,' Mr. Mortimer interposed anxiously. 'I might take up the study again.'

'Very well, Matthew.'

'And it is good that the children should have the materials for a scientific education ready to hand.' Turning to Adam, he said: 'Mrs. Mortimer writes stories for

94

young readers. Not mere entertainment, naturally. There is a good deal of wholesome information in all her books.'

'And a moral,' insisted the authoress, with more spirit than Adam would have expected from so meek and comfortable-looking a figure. 'You mustn't forget the moral, Matthew. I pride myself, Mr. Adam, on incorporating a sound moral in every story. Not only does each one conclude on a moral note, but that note rings, unmistakably, through every page.'

'I am sure,' said Adam, 'your books must give a great deal of pleasure. And profit too,' he added hastily.

Mortimer's attention had momentarily wandered, since he was not himself speaking. 'We are glad of such small sums as they bring in,' he conceded loftily.

'Matthew! You *know*——' Mrs. Mortimer stopped short, biting her lower lip as if to snap the thread of her unfinished remark. A flush of confusion swept up over throat and face. Her husband noticed nothing, for he was galloping away on a new hobby-horse.

'All booksellers and publishers are scoundrels. I except poor Godwin. He's too inefficient to be a scoundrel. But I knew he would get nowhere with his Juvenile Library. Mrs. Mortimer publishes elsewhere now. As I told her, an author may get something at least out of a scoundrel. He'll get nothing from a bankrupt.'

Mortimer paused to give effect to this dictum. His wife took the chance to ask:

'Is Mr. Adam staying to dinner?'

'Of course, my dear. Where are the others?'

'I imagined *you* would know where Miss Seeley and Miss Forester were. I was writing all the morning.' She began to gather up the pages with a slightly wistful air. 'It seemed a good chance. Villiers took the boat across to the town.'

95

'We shan't wait dinner for him. My tastes are simple, Mr. Adam — my material wants are almost ridiculously few — but I never wait dinner for anyone.'

'If you will excuse me,' said Mrs. Mortimer, 'I will tell them to lay an extra place, and make sure that we have ——' She bit her lip again, and, as though a fresh and alarming thought had struck her, inquired: 'You are not a vegetarian, Mr. Adam?'

The term was unfamiliar. Adam stared. Did she mean that some people ate only vegetables?

'Why, no, Mrs. Mortimer. Are you? Is the family——'

'Not now,' said Mrs. Mortimer with feeling. 'It was a view that Mr. Mortimer held — strongly — at one time.'

'I have no use for a man who cannot change his views,' said her husband grandly. 'As I once wrote: "An Englishman changes nothing willingly except his linen." I might have added that with Continental nations the exact converse applies. But the brotherhood of Man is too precious to damage, merely to shine as a wit.'

Mrs. Mortimer had gone. Adam saw, strolling across the garden with wet towels in their hands, a fair girl and a rather smaller dark one. Mortimer bellowed to them jovially, and, as they mounted the steps to the terrace, plunged into introductions.

The fair one was Miss Seeley. Harriet Seeley. A beauty in the classical tradition, straight of nose, candid of eye. She was tall, and fashion had made her look taller by drawing a fantastic waistline just beneath her breasts, so that the dress flowed down almost endlessly, like a Greek column.

Miss Forester, whom the others addressed as Sally, was of a honey and chestnut colouring, though, being wet, the brown of her hair had darkened almost to black. Her face, small-featured in any case except for the eyes,

96

was shadowed by a big straw hat, worn gipsy-style with a bright handkerchief tied over it and under her short chin.

Miss Seeley had too much sense to extinguish her sculptural beauty under such a covering. She wore only a twist of stuff, turban-fashion, round her head. She approached with radiance unclouded. With, thought Adam, the grey gaze of Minerva. . . .

Mortimer was still talking.

'You haven't seen Mr. Adam before,' he said, 'but he has seen you——'

'In the open-air theatre last night,' Adam interrupted hastily. He felt his cheek-bones glow as the blood washed round them. 'Mr. Mortimer was demonstrating the acoustics——'

'You heard me?'

'Admirably.'

Mortimer was so charmed with this tribute that he allowed the conversation to be deflected.

'It was Mr. Villiers you heard at the back of the theatre,' explained Miss Seeley. She pronounced the verb 'heared'. Both she and her friend used certain colonialisms which to Adam were novel and, on such lips, quite charming. 'Have you met Mr. Villiers?' she inquired.

'*He* writes too,' said Miss Forester with ill-disguised enthusiasm.

'He is a young man who may well do something,' Mortimer conceded generously.

'He knows Lord Byron quite well,' Miss Forester rattled on. 'He met him at Geneva only a month or two back. I guess Mr. Villiers is rather *like* Byron. In some ways.'

'That is a doubtful tribute,' said Miss Seeley with a laugh.

'It depends on *which* ways,' suggested Mortimer.

Miss Forester made such a violent grimace that the handkerchief slipped its knot under her chin, and the straw-hat tilted back rather becomingly. 'I reckon you're both horrid about Byron.'

'It's only that you're such a child, darling.' Miss Seeley's arm went round her friend's waist — her real waist — in an affectionate, almost protective gesture. 'You do have such enthusiasms.'

'Enthusiasms? I like that! What about——'

A servant-girl appeared in the doorway and announced, with bell-like clarity, that dinner was on the table.

Although the elusive Mr. Villiers did not appear, they sat down ten to the meal. There were five children, so varied in looks and age that Adam found some difficulty in sorting them out. By the end of the meal he had decided that the small pink-faced vociferous Charles James in the high chair was, with the befrilled and pantaletted Virginie and Aspasia, the joint production of his host and hostess. An older boy, of about ten, was introduced as William Butts. He seemed to be Mrs. Mortimer's child by an earlier marriage. Finally there was a swarthy, aloof girl of thirteen or so, who was addressed as Primavera (though she did not audibly respond) and whose origin was left unspecified. Only later did it emerge that Mortimer had once made a sea-voyage, for his health, to Jamaica.

Mortimer beamed down the table, right and left, with indiscriminate benevolence.

'A happy family, Mr. Adam. I only wish my lads were here to meet you.'

'You have — more children?'

'Three. But they are grown up and out in the world.'

It was the first time Adam had ever sat down to eat in company without anyone saying grace. He was taken momentarily off balance. Not shocked, for he had often revolted inwardly against the automatic religious observances, but surprised by the omission of a formality he had come to regard as inevitable. But Mortimer obviously did not fail to appreciate the bounty of the earth, for he heaped his own plate higher, if anything, than anyone else's. There seemed no need to express that appreciation in words, Latin or English: the flash of his blue eye, the lively sword-play of his knife and fork, were eloquent. For a man so indifferent to material things, Mortimer attacked his dinner with remarkable gusto.

He had put Adam on his right, facing the golden beauty of Miss Seeley. Miss Forester slipped into the seat on Adam's other side, and he was hardly aware of her except for an occasional laugh or exclamation and a small white hand passing him a dish. As for his hostess, he was given no chance to pay her any attention, for she was separated from him by the length of the table and the clamour of the children. Mortimer held that political ideals should be worked out in the family. Adam was not quite sure whether his ideal, at the moment, was democracy or anarchy. He was still wondering at the end of the meal, when William Butts knocked over a carafe of red wine, transforming his stepfather instantaneously into a positive (and not unduly benevolent) autocrat.

Up to that point it had been possible to ignore the juvenile company and carry on an independent conversation.

Miss Seeley and her friend were making an indefinite stay in Italy. Miss Seeley's father had been one of the leading shipowners in Boston — she was bitter against the English because of the blockade, which had considerably diminished the fortune she had inherited, but she did concede that Adam was no more personally responsible than Mortimer. However, all that was over. The war and blockade had ended within a few months of her coming of age. There had been nothing but the disapproval of her aunts to prevent the fulfilment of her girlhood dream: with no chaperone but the faithful and contemporary Miss Forester, she had embarked for Leghorn and arrived, pilgrim-fashion, at the door of the author she venerated.

'And do you write, yourself, Mr. Adam?'

Adam hesitated. Then he told her about his translation.

'Always the past! You British are forever looking back. Mr. Mortimer tells me you have mounted sentries in Whitehall, still guarding a palace which was burnt down more than a hundred years ago!'

'I can believe it. I didn't know. But,' said Adam with a laugh, 'I've often thought what a lot of meaningless things we go on doing at Oxford, just because they were done centuries ago.'

'In my humble opinion,' Mortimer pontificated, 'Oxford and Cambridge should be swept away: they are beyond reform. New universities should be created on new lines. In cities like York and Norwich — indeed, why not even in Birmingham or Manchester? The poorest men should be admitted, but only those genuinely devoted to study——'

'And women,' said Miss Seeley quickly.

'Of course, women, my dear Harriet. What did Mary Wollstonecraft say? "*If woman be not prepared by education to become the companion of man——*"'

' — "*she will stop the progress of knowledge,*"' said Miss Seeley like a flash, '"*for truth must be common to all.*"'

Adam, to keep his end up, began to say that female

education was referred to by Plato. . . . But nobody wanted to hear about Plato.

'My chief objection to Lord Byron,' said Miss Seeley, 'is his unfairness to the educated woman.'

'Oh, but——' That, of course, was Miss Forester.

'Now Mr. Shelley. . . . Do you know Mr. Shelley, Mr. Adam? I believe he was at Oxford?'

Adam swallowed a mouthful hastily. 'He — he was not up more than a term or two. I didn't know him.' He remembered the uproar over Shelley's expulsion. The fellow had written something. . . . He had gone on writing since then. Adam had no idea what.

'Mr. Villiers knows Mr. Shelley,' shrilled Aspasia from the far end of the table.

'*And* he knows Mr. Walter Savage Landor,' cried Virginie, not to be outdone. 'He went to stay with him at Como!'

Adam would have guessed as much. Mr. Villiers seemed to enjoy a wide literary acquaintance. Unable to compete, he tried to draw the conversation back to higher education for women.

'How,' he asked Mortimer — thinking it too pointed to ask Miss Seeley, 'would you combine it with marriage, which surely is——'

'Marriage is a withering institution.' Mortimer looked anything but withered by his repeated experiences. 'I mean, marriage as now understood is destined to wither away as woman achieves her freedom. Marriage is a monopoly, and the worst of all monopolies.'

'Godwin,' said Miss Seeley automatically.

Mortimer glared at his disciple. 'What do you mean, Godwin?'

It was unlike Miss Seeley to look nonplussed, but she did. Clearly she had thought to show an intelligent interest by identifying a quotation, but Mortimer had not intended it as such. 'I'm sorry,' she said weakly, 'I fancied that Godwin said something like that some-where——'

'He may have done.' Mortimer's smile returned. 'I flatter myself I have not been without influence on Godwin's opinions and writings.'

That was the moment William Butts chose to knock over the wine. The children were banished from the table. The maid brought in a tea-tray. Mrs. Mortimer poured out and then, pleading her need to finish a chapter of her story, left the room.

'Miss Forester will play for us,' said Mortimer. She stood up and went over to a piano in the corner. 'But nothing too tinkly, mind. Music after a meal should be gentle and relaxing.' Miss Forester merely inclined her dark head. Her fingers began to stray tentatively over the keys.

Mortimer finished his tea with audible satisfaction and set down the cup and saucer on the table with a decisive clatter, almost at arm's length in front of him. Adam was reminded for a moment of the Rector. Mortimer was the first man he had met, since leaving Ramsthorpe, who kept up the same old-fashioned table-manners. But the Rector had never fallen asleep while still sitting upright. This Mortimer, after dabbing his whiskers with a red silk handkerchief, proceeded to do.

Adam found himself alone, to all intents, with the girl facing him.

He would have liked to go on with the conversation. To talk to an intellectual young woman was a new and stimulating experience. But with his host breathing rhythmically between them, and with Miss Forester obediently trying to entertain them at the piano, he could hardly do so.

It was Miss Seeley who leant towards him and murmured:

'Do you like Beethoven?'

He was unsure of the name. He craned over and whispered back, thinking she was still on the subject of books and authors:

'Has he written much?'

Her grey eyes opened. 'Surely? The seven symphonies, and a whole heap of——'

'Of course!' He checked her with a lifted finger. 'I misunderstood. I didn't catch the name.' The name was, in fact, vaguely familiar. Composers weren't much talked of in Oxford. Certainly not modern ones. But yes, he had heard of Beethoven. Presumably Miss Forester was playing one of his pieces. It was not like music as he had always understood it. It was almost as though she were making it up as she went along — hesitating before choosing which note to strike. There was nothing that Adam would have called a tune, nothing to march to or dance a minuet. . . . But no doubt Mortimer found it difficult to sleep through Handel or Haydn.

Suddenly Miss Forester — or Beethoven — seemed to come to a decision. There *was* a tune. Rather a grand deep tune. . . . It emerged, recognizably, from a flurry of notes that were no more than foam on the surface of a rising tide.

Glancing up, Adam saw that Miss Seeley's eyes were shut. But she was not asleep. She had retreated into a realm of bliss which he could imagine, though he lacked the musical experience to enter it himself.

Miss Forester finished the piece and came back to them. Playing had improved her colour and Adam, facing her for the first time without her gipsy headgear, saw that she was better-looking than he had realised. She had not the serene high forehead of her friend, so, declining to compete, she had dressed her hair with a fringe of little curls. He had noticed the style in Paris. *A la bacchante*, it was called, according to Seabrook.

'I adore Beethoven,' she said. 'He's so romantic. A Byron in music.'

'Yes,' said Adam.

'It must be wonderful to live in Vienna and hear great symphonies — with the full orchestra——'

'Wonderful.'

Miss Seeley had opened her eyes. 'We shall go on to Vienna when we are ready,' she said a trifle sharply. 'There are lots of things to be done here, first.'

'I know, Harriet. I didn't mean——'

Mortimer woke up. 'Magnificent!' he rumbled. 'I trust, Mr. Adam, you share our love of music?'

'I think I could develop it. I — I've never had much chance, except in church——'

'*Church!*' echoed Mortimer and Miss Seeley together.

They went out on to the terrace. Of Mrs. Mortimer and her writing-table there was no sign. A screech from the shrubbery indicated the presence of a peacock or a child. There seemed no need to investigate which.

'Isn't this view just heavenly?' asked Miss Forester.

The terrace commanded the whole northern half of the lake, including all that could not be seen from the town. The placid waters stretched to the vine-clad foothills, and beyond them Antonian's swan-like Alps floated on the violet haze.

Adam stared, looked left and right, sweeping the view like an anxious admiral. He realised that there was nothing in sight which could possibly be called an island. There was just one whalebacked rock, thirty yards from the landing steps, growing a few blades of grass and one struggling bush. It was not big enough to carry even the most modest of Roman villas. It would not have taken any building much larger than the rose-wreathed

Jericho at the bottom of the Rectory garden. No wonder Checco had laughed over the *isola*. . . .

'As you are so fond of music,' Mortimer was saying, 'you must give us the pleasure of your company tomorrow evening. Villiers has got us a box at the opera.'

'Thank you,' said Adam in a dull tone.

Chapter Seven

B ACK in his room at the Tre Corone, Adam surveyed
his manuscript with some uneasiness.

Brigitta seemed aware of his dejection. She
brought up a lamp as the light began to fail, kissed his
hand (which appeared to be the conventional but no less
charming gesture of these Italian servants), and wished
him *felice sera* in a tone that was almost a caress. Adam
saw little prospect of felicity in the evening which lay ahead.

So Lago Lucero was not Antonian's lake. It couldn't
be. Everything else fitted, but there was no island on
which the poet could have lived. Had he invented the
island? Had he, for that matter, invented everything —
love-affairs included? No. There was nothing of fantasy
in Antonian. He was writing for contemporaries in
Rome, who sometimes visited him and who knew his
villa so well that it had never occurred to him to include
its address in his poems. Antonian's island-villa was as
real as Horace's Sabine farm. But it could not have been
on Lucero.

I suppose a true scholar (Adam reflected gloomily)
would pack up tomorrow and continue the search elsewhere. He would visit every lake and lakelet in Northern
Italy until he found an eligible island in the required
surroundings.

Adam wondered, almost for the first time in his life, if
he were a true scholar.

Certainly he had no desire to take to the road again. He had had enough of bumping diligences. He had just made some new and stimulating acquaintances. For the moment he had become more interested, he had to admit, in the Villa Gandolfi than in the Villa of Antonian.

He tried to forget the tiresome problem of geography. The final pages of Latin lay before him, the elegiac couplets running on, in and out of the margin, like the regular left-right-left of soldiers' feet. There was no doubt about *them*, anyhow, except for those few phrases he could skate lightly over with the airy freedom allowed to a literary translator. There was nothing to stop his getting on with his original task. It was only the Introduction — so brilliant and bold in conjecture, so epoch-making in its conclusions — which was now a fading dream.

No, there was no reason why he should not buckle down this evening and render another two pages of elegiacs into smooth, well-mannered rhyming couplets.

He sharpened a quill and, with a groan, resumed what he had always considered a labour of love.

At least, the next evening, there was the opera.

The Piazza del Duomo became a microcosm of Milan. Adam would not have believed that Lucero and its neighbourhood maintained so many crested carriages and cockaded footmen. Among so many powdered heads and silk stockings he found it hard to distinguish servants from local celebrities. Even the flunkeys in the foyer looked like generals posing for a group portrait of the Emperor's staff.

To his relief Mortimer was trousered like himself and, save for a clean cravat and a plum-coloured velvet waistcoat with silver braid, had made no particular concession to the formality of the occasion. At his elbow was an elegant — in fact exquisite — young man, with tawny wavy hair, a high-bridged nose, and an air of permanent amusement. His tall collar, narrow waist, and complicated cravat would have marked him out even on a Parisian boulevard.

'Mr. Adam — Mr. Villiers!' Mortimer announced with a heartiness which made every head turn and would not have been out of place if he had been summoning the whole company to dinner.

Mr. Villiers transferred his stick to his left hand, which already held a top hat of curly brim and well-groomed glossiness, and greeted Adam with easy friendliness.

'The ladies have talked of nothing else since yesterday! It's been positively irritating.'

The ladies, it seemed, were already in their seats. Mortimer led the way up the carpeted stairs and flung open the door of the box.

Bare shoulders gleamed in the mellow diffusion of the chandeliers. The American girls were both in white dresses, cut low; bright shawls were looped with fashionable negligence over their forearms as they sat. Mrs. Mortimer was grand in a pale blue gown spangled with what Adam thought of as grass-green asterisks. She wore a tight little silk turban with a long slanting spray of plumage. This (as he correctly foresaw) was to prove a great nuisance to the gentlemen sitting behind her.

Miss Seeley was more splendidly like Minerva than ever.

Miss Forester, with her big brown eyes, looked like a lively but well-controlled bacchante, surprised in the depths of a wood.

Mrs. Mortimer looked, unalterably, like Mrs. Mortimer.

They all turned as the men edged their way into the box.

Miss Forester's quick glance did not fail to note the modest efforts Adam had made to smarten himself up for the occasion.

'My!' she said, with an amiable familiarity which he supposed must be normal in the Republic, 'But you *are* elegant!'

While Adam was wondering what to say, Villiers remarked smoothly:

'Who else but Adam should appear in — full fig?'

Mrs. Mortimer choked and dropped her fan. Adam dived for it. Wiping away her tears she said:

'Villiers is *so* amusing. We can never be dull when Villiers is here.'

Adam felt, after a few minutes, that he himself could be very dull — must seem very dull, that is, in the eyes of his companions, by comparison with the quick-tongued Villiers. He had never practised the pun. He was unused to flicking feather-light compliments round a mixed company. His own talk must seem the plainest homespun stuff.

He must beware, though, of dismissing Villiers as a buffoon. Artificial, yes. A poseur. But no fool.

As the theatre filled, he treated them all to a running commentary. That was the old Marchese . . . down there was the new young doctor, who, it was an open secret in Lucero, was having an affair with the notary's second wife . . . the smouldering beauty who had just come into the box opposite was the Contessa Navarina — no, the Conte was the insignificant little fellow on her far side, and the man with the cloak was her *cicisbeo*——

'Her what?' asked Adam involuntarily, with the scholar's instinct not to let pass an uncomprehended term.

'Her *cicisbeo*. You know, her *cavaliere servente*.'

'I'm afraid I don't know.'

'Mr. Adam,' said Miss Seeley kindly, 'is quite new to this country.'

Between them, they explained to Adam that Italian marriages were so invariably unromantic that a publicly acknowledged lover, constantly in attendance, was essential equipment for every self-respecting married woman.

'Disgusting,' said Mortimer.

'I thought, sir,' said Villiers, 'it was the monopoly of marriage which you most objected to?'

'This isn't the solution. Men and women should be free to love. Free as air.'

Mrs. Mortimer did not join in the general assent to this principle. She looked thoughtful. She was in fact (as she told Adam later) trying to work out a satisfactory dénouement for the children's story on which she was engaged. Four children had been shipwrecked and doomed to spend the rest of their all too natural lives upon a desert island. The varied composition of the party (industrious and resourceful Tommy, idle Sam, vain Polly, and virtuous Eliza) had furnished ample scope for moral examples, especially when Sam had discovered the cheerful properties of fermented liquids. Mrs. Mortimer's problem, as she delicately indicated to Adam under cover of some quiet music in the Second Act, was to sustain the high moral note all the way through the book until the rescue-party arrived twenty years later. Adam was tempted to reassure her by suggesting that few of her readers would be likely to get so far, but, as this might have seemed discouraging, he whispered back: 'Couldn't you let them be rescued sooner?' 'Yes — perhaps — but how much sooner?' Again, casting his memory back to his own childhood contemporaries at Ramsthorpe, he was tempted to say: 'I wouldn't risk leaving them on the island more than a fortnight!' But so short a book would not have satisfied Mrs. Mortimer's publisher.

Meanwhile, the opera had not even begun. Though it

was about to. The central box was filling with white uniforms. Medals and orders winked back at the candles. The officers of the garrison had also turned out in full fig.

There was a good deal of bowing from box to box. Fans and handkerchiefs fluttered. Many of the men, Adam saw, carried fans. Powdered heads and bald heads and even, occasionally, an old-fashioned wig inclined gravely towards the military party.

From the middle classes, mostly ranged below in the stalls, there were only black glances and a sibilant murmuring of the hated word: '*Tedesci!*'

'Major von Schaumberg,' Villiers whispered to Adam. 'The little old man in the centre with the shiny nob——'

'Odious tyrant.' This comment emerged, in a throaty growl, through the screen of Mortimer's whiskers.

'Oh, he's not so bad, sir, in himself. Talk to him about horses, and——'

'I'll not talk to him about anything. I'll not shake hands with oppression.'

Flunkeys extinguished the main house lights. The curtain rose and silence fell, at least in the Mortimers' box. They did not, like the music-loving Italians, maintain a running conversation throughout the actual performance.

The opera, as Villiers obligingly explained to them all in the first interval, was of the fashionable kind known as 'rescue opera'. The ladies need not distress themselves on account of the handsome young tenor who had just fled from his country's oppressors. True, many perils lay in front of him — though none probably graver than those he had just survived when taking, so literally and weightily, to the painted mountains at the back of the stage. By the end of the penultimate act they must steel themselves to a dungeon scene in which, having exchanged a price on his head for a ball and chain on his left ankle, he would sing one of those interminable arias suitable only for tenors facing lifelong solitary confinement. But they were not to worry. The substantial soprano would arrange his rescue in the last act, if necessary (or even if not strictly necessary) stimulating a national rising to facilitate it.

'Nothing to worry about at all,' said Villiers soothingly. 'They won't even let him sing the whole aria — they'll bring down the curtain after a bit and leave us to imagine him going on and on through the night.'

The opera followed this outline with remarkable fidelity, though Villiers swore that he had never heard it before. All rescue-operas, he insisted, were the same. No one was in a position to contradict him. No one else could follow the words. Villiers had a genuine grasp of Italian which continually aroused the admiration of Miss Forester and (Adam had to admit to himself) his own mild irritation.

The members of the party were curiously varied in their reactions to the performance.

Villiers listened with what Adam came later to call his 'Harrow-and-Trinity' expression. He had been at both places with Byron, whom he appeared to have studied with even more diligence than the subjects officially prescribed.

Miss Seeley listened with all her intellect, her fine eyes riveted upon the stage as though in quest of social significance.

Miss Forester was rapt. She appeared to surrender herself completely to the music — though afterwards she surprised Adam with a quiet comment that it was second-rate stuff compared with Beethoven: she would dearly love to see *Fidelio*, which had the same kind of plot, but must be immeasurably finer.

Mrs. Mortimer did not react at all. She was not listening. She was on a desert island with her own characters.

Mortimer himself listened in the way which would probably have most gratified the composer and the cast. His eye flashed and rolled in general sympathy with the hero, heroine, and chorus of rebels. He breathed deeply and groaned. His whiskers were electric with hatred of the villainous tyrant, who matched depth of voice with depth of dungeon and depravity.

The mass of the audience took the performance in much the same spirit. Though the story was laid in an unspecified period of the Middle Ages and in a country which (since the scenery would have to serve again, frequently) might have been anywhere, the topical parallel was too obvious for anyone to ignore. Louder and longer grew the applause for what were (according to Villiers' whispered interpretations) the liberal sentiments expressed by the hero. The tyrant was hissed and booed at every entrance. When the trapped tenor defied him, sword in hand, from a staircase, the applause was long and tumultuous. The tyrant's minions had no choice but to release him, hand him back his weapon, and regroup themselves in attitudes of suspended hostility until the whole aria had been sung — and applauded — again.

'Von Schaumberg isn't going to like this,' said Villiers with a chuckle.

And, when the curtain rolled down a few minutes later, the manager appeared in front of it, bowing timidly to an audience which booed his announcement.

'What did he say?' demanded Miss Seeley.

'That there must be no more excessive applause. "By order of the Garrison Commander."'

'Poltroon!' said Mortimer. 'Lackey!' He had often a somewhat old-fashioned vocabulary.

113

After an interval even longer than usual the curtain rose on the next act. If anything, the audience in the stalls and gallery were even more demonstrative. The curtain was rung down at one point, the manager made another appeal for order, and the performance went on with the incongruous addition of six Austrian soldiers standing stiffly to attention at the sides of the proscenium arch and facing outwards into the auditorium. This did not have the desired effect. Instead of being intimidated, the audience were the more encouraged to identify the minions of the chorus with their modern oppressors. The act struggled through, with difficulty, to its climax, but before the curtain could descend on the hero in his dungeon there was a violent commotion in the stalls. Lacking confidence in the abilities of the substantial soprano to break open the prison in the next act, the spectators had decided to carry out the rescue themselves. They surged over the footlights and came to grips with the white-coats. The curtain came down, and not surprisingly did not rise again.

Even George Seabrook would not have complained that the opera was deficient in sensations.

Mortimer himself was restrained from leaping over the front of the box and joining in the charge only by the realisation that there was a drop of twenty feet below. Red-faced and bellowing, he allowed the others to lead him bull-like from the theatre.

'Have you a carriage?' Adam asked Mrs. Mortimer anxiously, thinking that if so it would not have been ordered for another hour.

'No. We have our boat.'

The air outside was deliciously fresh. Even Mortimer cooled rapidly. The moon was up over the hills. They could see clearly across the bay to the dark pines of La Lingua. When they reached the lakeside Mortimer said:

'Come back to supper.'

Adam was tempted. 'It's rather late——'

'Nonsense! Those Austrian scoundrels have cut short our evening. We won't let them ruin it.'

'Very well, sir. Thank you. It will be a pleasant walk back in the moonlight.'

'The gates will be closed by then,' said Mrs. Mortimer.

'I'll bring him over in the boat,' Villiers offered. He handed her into the craft while Adam steadied it.

'Here you are, Sally.' Miss Seeley took her own seat and draped her shawl around her, patting the vacant cushion at her side.

'I think I'll sit here, thank you, Harriet.' Miss Forester's voice, which Adam had come to think of as a particularly *warm* voice, was as light and cool as the night breeze ruffling the lake. She stepped into the bows and reclined there picturesquely. Villiers took the next seat, and necessarily with his back to her, since he rowed English-fashion, but he minimised this disadvantage by frequently turning his head and throwing light remarks which the others missed. Mortimer bluffly refused Adam's offer to take the other oar. Adam took the empty place beside Miss Seeley, who engaged him in conversation with an almost deliberate brightness. He was flattered. It was a delightful, almost a dream-like, experience to be gliding over the moon-spangled water beside a girl who was both handsome and intellectual.

Three or four other boats were putting out, whether of fishermen or of opera-goers returning like themselves to lakeside villas. Lanterns twinkled. One party had a mandolin. Adam recognized the refrain he had heard on his first evening:

> '*Ne di giorno, ne di sera,*
> *Non passiamo la selva nera.*'

He asked Miss Seeley if she knew the meaning.

'Oh, I can manage that! "Neither by day nor by night do we pass the black wood." I don't know *why* they don't! But the words evoke a kind of atmosphere, don't they?'

As the distant singing faded across the water, Villiers was emboldened to strike up himself. He had a pleasant, light voice, and controlled his breathing well, so that despite his rowing the words came smoothly. After a few moments Miss Forester joined in, her Italian a trifle shaky, but musically confident.

> *Scendi propizia*
> *Con tuo splendore,*
> *O bella Venere,*
> *Madre d'Amore.*
> *Madre d'Amore,*
> *Che sola sei*
> *Piacer degli uomini,*
> *E degli dei . . .'*

It was the last touch needed to perfect the magic of the evening. Adam was sorry when the last notes died away, and Mortimer called over his shoulder:

'What was all that about, Villiers?'

'Metastasio's *Ode to Venus*.'

From the bows Miss Forester added:

'Villiers is teaching it to me. To help my Italian.'

Villiers obligingly translated some of the Ode. '*Descend propitious in thy splendour, O beautiful Venus, Mother of Love. Mother of Love, who alone art the pleasure of men and of gods . . .*'

'We can all make out that much,' Miss Seeley murmured restlessly to Adam. 'But I don't see how that kind of Italian will help Sally in everyday life.'

116

'Well,' he said pacifically, 'it was very appropriate.'

'Appropriate?' Her voice went up sharply. 'Why?'

'I mean to the moment. This romantic setting. The moon — the water — the mountains in the distance——'

'Oh, that. Yes, I suppose so.'

It was impossible to continue the conversation. Mortimer conceived that it was now his turn. He began to boom out *Ça Ira* in a defiant voice which echoed round the lake and was clearly meant to carry to the fortress and annoy von Schaumberg. When he paused, Mrs. Mortimer quickly called out, before he could start on the *Marseillaise:*

'What a musical evening we are having! Do *you* sing, Mr. Adam?'

Adam had no wish to contribute anything from his limited repertoire. In any case, most of the songs he knew were popular patriotic ballads inspired by the exploits of the British Navy. They might not have been acceptable to the present company.

Luckily their boat was now rounding the tip of La Lingua. There were the landing steps, the moon-washed terraces, the house with its lamp-lit windows muted by the brilliance outside.

'Ah,' said Mortimer, shipping his oar with a grunt of deep satisfaction. 'Supper!'

Over the meal Adam's host treated him to a survey of the political situation.

'You saw for yourself tonight, in the theatre! In the other boxes the simpering boot-licking aristos: down below, the People.' Mortimer could, by his very tone, put capital letters to any word he chose.

Here in Northern Italy, he explained, one could see something like France before the Revolution: not only an oppressed peasantry but a middle class who, whatever

117

their education and professional standing, had no voice in the country's affairs. It was hard for an English gentleman to grasp. And whereas at least the French, in the old days, had been ground down by their own nobility, the real tyranny here was foreign: the Italian lordlings were mere lackeys to the Austrians.

'They will be swept away, along with their masters! The Italian people will rise, as the French did. They tasted liberty under Napoleon——'

'Liberty?' queried Adam.

'Certainly! They knew nationhood — unity. When you have once tasted such things, you don't forget them. No, the day isn't far off, Mr. Adam — the day of glorious liberation. The *tedesci* will be kicked back over the Alps where they belong, Lombardy and Venice will link up with Piedmont and the Papal States, the Neapolitans will throw the Bourbons into the bay——' He paused for breath and to cut himself another slice of veal.

'It will be a glorious day,' said Miss Seeley, her eyes shining.

Villiers thought it would take rather more than a day. Storming fortresses, he suggested, was a little harder than storming footlights.

'You are a cynic.'

'Of course.'

Villiers withdrew from the discussion with a smile. Adam thought, amusedly, there are enough tensions in this household to string a harp. . . .

The meal petered out in a desultory peeling of oranges, a shifting of chairs. Mortimer continued to hold forth. His political ideas must have matured — or at least stopped developing — more than twenty years before. He talked as though the Bastille had been stormed last week, and nothing that had happened since could modify the views he had formed then. Robespierre, Bonaparte. . . .

there was no fact so awkward that he could not smooth its edges and build it into the fabric of his philosophy. Those authors who had revised their opinions of the French Revolution were turncoats.

Adam was not sufficiently well informed to argue with him. It was no good pitting the prejudices of the Rectory and the Common Room against such a flood of generous idealism. He listened courteously. And Miss Seeley, beside him, listened with shining eyes and rosebud lips ajar. Happy pilgrim (he thought) to have reached the shrine and be so satisfied with her saint. . . .

Mrs. Mortimer rose and excused herself. Adam apologized for the lateness of the hour and began to make his farewells. She waved him back to his seat, smiling, her eyes blinking with tiredness in the lamp-light.

'Please, Mr. Adam! There is no need, just because I . . . Mr. Mortimer will tell you, I am sure, there are no conventions in this house.'

'None at all! We live by Reason.'

'It's only that my eyes get tired, Mr. Adam — I do so much writing during the day. Do not disturb yourselves.'

She went away. Adam could not help wondering whether it was not the light of Reason, rather than of the lamp, which wearied her.

'All the same,' he said to Mortimer, 'I ought to be going.'

'Where is Villiers?' cried Miss Seeley. Spell-bound by Mortimer's eloquence, she had not seen him slip from the table. Miss Forester had also vanished. 'Villiers was going to row you home.'

'It doesn't matter. I can walk.'

'You're forgetting, the gates will be shut.'

'I expect I can scramble over somewhere,' said Adam lightly. More than once, having walked too far from

Oxford on a summer evening, he had come back late and entered College unofficially.

'You'll do no such thing,' said Mortimer. 'You don't want a bullet in your head. Those white-coat scoundrels aren't particular.'

'We must find them,' said Miss Seeley with determination.

'Them?'

'Villiers, I mean. He promised Mr. Adam——'

She rushed out on to the moonlit terrace. Mortimer gazed fondly after her.

'A superb creature,' he said. 'Such beauty, such brain. You know, Mr. Adam, when I first ran my fingers over her skull, I was tempted — very sorely tempted — to resume my study of phrenology. But, alas, there isn't time for everything.'

Adam agreed sympathetically.

'Miss Forester is amiable enough in many ways. But there's no comparison. Strange that Villiers seems to prefer Miss Forester.'

'Very.'

It was some minutes before Miss Seeley, after running up and down a great many garden-steps and along a number of shadowy paths with skirts upheld against the dew, returned panting but triumphant with the missing pair.

'It's all right,' said Mortimer jovially. 'I've prevailed on Mr. Adam to stay the night.'

Chapter Eight

'I THOUGHT——' said Brigitta almost tearfully when Adam returned to the Tre Corone late the following morning.

'*What* did you think, Brigitta?'

'I did not know what to think, monsieur. Your bed was not slept in — you had been going to the opera, and all the town is talking of the trouble there last night! Anything might have happened. You might have been hurt — or arrested by the police——'

'I'm sorry. I'd have sent word if I could. But you know how it is — one thing leads to another, and then it's too late——'

'Yes,' said Brigitta darkly, 'I know very well how it is. How one thing leads to another.'

'I told you, I stayed with friends.'

'Yesterday Monsieur said he knew no one in Lucero.'

'Yes, but these friends I had made live out beyond La Lingua. A famous English writer,' he added. In his ignorance of contemporary literature he still imagined naively that this made it sound more respectable.

'Not the Villa Gandolfi?'

Her eyes, like thunder-clouds, flickered lightning at him. She tossed her head.

'Monsieur is English, of course. Perhaps all the English like that sort of . . .'

'Sort of what?'

She shrugged. 'Monsieur does not want to listen to servants' talk.'

At that moment Adam would have rather liked to. What was the gossip about the household at the villa? Probably nothing of consequence. Mortimer was rather a flamboyant figure, certainly, and, as a foreigner, bound to attract attention. The children, too, running wild on the promontory in accordance with his latest educational theory. . . . And the young Americans — they could hardly fail to arouse gossip, especially if they had been seen swimming. . . . Small country communities were, as he knew too well, critical of the slightest departure from convention.

He began to gather up his books and papers.

'Brigitta——'

'Monsieur?'

'I want you to ask the Signora for my bill——'

She stared, dismayed. 'Monsieur is not going? I have not offended Monsieur? I did not mean to suggest——'

'No, no, Brigitta. But I *am* going — for the present anyway — and I want you to explain properly to the Signora for me. I have been most comfortable here, everything has been excellent——'

'Yet Monsieur is leaving us?'

What an emotional race they are, thought Adam, tears are quivering on her eyelashes . . . and what eyelashes . . .

'Yes,' he said in as matter-of-fact a voice as he could manage. 'My friends have asked me to move over to their villa. Being English, you see, they think I shall not be so lonely——'

'Monsieur need not have felt lonely here!'

'Er — no . . . well . . . will you explain to Signora Corvesi? I don't want to hurt her feelings. You do understand?'

'I understand very well,' said Brigitta, sweeping like a

tempest to the door. 'I have heard of the Villa Gandolfi! I thought Monsieur was different. But it is true as they say: the quiet ones are the worst!'

After a few days at the villa on La Lingua, Adam was still waiting for the nameless orgies to begin. Even Mortimer's philosophy of nudity was relegated to the limbo of forgotten causes. True, Harriet — as Adam by the custom of the house now called Miss Seeley — did not go back to the shapeless blue flannel bathing garb she had apparently worn on her first arrival at Lucero, but she and Sally Forester kept their distance from the men. As for Free Love, though the theory seemed to be warmly accepted at the villa, there was no sign of its practice. Harriet might write embarrassingly outspoken pamphlets on the Equality of the Sexes, and Villiers might throw off a few daring stanzas of Byronic type — it was usual to read these, and other literary productions, round the table in the evening — but Adam saw no tendency to cross the border-line between literature and life.

He himself contributed to the readings with a few pages of Antonian in his own version. Unfortunately Mortimer was going through an anti-classical phase at the time, so that Adam's choice was criticised as a sad misdirection of a modest talent. However, talent there was, he grudgingly admitted. Harriet naturally agreed with him. Sally began to say something, and checked herself. Villiers said his verses were neat, but in too old-fashioned a way: nobody wrote like that now. Adam concealed his irritation, which was all the deeper because he felt that Villiers was probably right.

Mrs. Mortimer, who every day wrote more than the rest of the household put together, read none of it to them. It was tacitly assumed that her work, being intended for children, was not worth any critical consideration. Mrs.

Mortimer herself, Adam noted with some compunction, did not seem to be very highly considered.

'Of course, I'm sorry for her,' Sally confided to him. 'But she should never have married a man like him.'

'No?'

'It can't have been a marriage of *spirits*, can it? I mean, she doesn't believe passionately in all the things he believes in, she doesn't really *share* his ideals. . . .'

'I admit, she isn't an intellectual woman.'

'I don't know how important that is, Adam.' She laughed. 'I'm not an intellectual woman myself — not like Harriet. I'm very ignorant. But . . . well, I suppose Mr. Mortimer *is* a great man?'

'I suppose so,' said Adam gravely. It was the tacit assumption at the villa. Mortimer himself had never denied it.

'Then,' said Sally earnestly, 'I reckon Mrs. Mortimer ought to devote herself more to him, not to go away into a corner and scribble her own little stories all day. You can see he feels lonely and neglected. The way he turns to Harriet for sympathy and understanding . . .'

'I have noticed it.'

'Harriet would have been the right sort of wife for him.'

Adam looked aghast. 'But — he's old enough to be her father!'

'I guess Harriet wouldn't mind that. In some ways . . .' Sally hesitated, seemed almost to shiver. 'In some ways, Harriet's odd about love. Though we were friends as quite little girls, I've never fully understood what she wants in life. . . .'

'She is a remarkable person.'

'You realise that?' said Sally gratefully.

'Oh, yes.'

'I was afraid you did not like her.'

'Good Heavens, no! *I* was afraid at first she did not like me.'

'Harriet is rather prejudiced against the British. That's natural, after all. But you and Mr. Mortimer are different.' She did not, Adam observed, include Villiers among the exceptions.

He found it difficult to adjust himself to the ways of the Villa — the tireless discussion of each other, the constant dissection, explanation, and justification of oneself. Sally, though romantic enough in her enthusiasms, was at least not as self-conscious as some of the others. Adam found it refreshing to talk to her for a change.

'I think,' she said, closing that particular topic, 'it must be wonderful to be married to a famous author, to give up one's own life to helping him in his work. Yet when one looks around at people like Lord Byron, and — well, to be candid, poor Mrs. M.——'

The Rector's shade tapped Adam on the shoulder and reminded him that a gentleman did not take part in criticising his hostess while still under her roof.

'I know nothing about Lord Byron,' he said. 'Is there a Lady Byron? Villiers said nothing——'

Sally's large brown eyes grew larger. 'Don't you *know* what they say about the Byrons?' She proceeded to tell him with gusto.

Mrs. Mortimer, Adam soon discovered, was not in the fullest social sense their hostess.

As he walked with Villiers to their bathing place (Mortimer having departed to harangue the children over some iniquity which conflicted with his current theory of education), Adam happened to remark on her assiduity at the writing-table.

'Of course. The poor woman daren't stop.'

'*Daren't?*'

'Someone must pay the bills. Those trashy stories of hers keep this place going.'

'But — Mortimer? He's famous!'

'How long is it since he published a successful book?'

Adam admitted that he knew nothing of modern literature beyond what he had learnt in the past most stimulating week.

Villiers laughed. 'It's arguable whether poor old Mortimer comes under the heading of "modern". How long is it since he made such a stir with *The Rebellion of Reason*? Nearly thirty years. If he doesn't do something big very soon, he'll be written off as a "has-been".'

'You mean . . .' Adam was appalled. 'The Mortimers are actually in financial difficulties?'

'I should say so. Old Matthew didn't come here for his health, you know — or to dodge political persecution, though he rather likes to hint as much. He left London when he found he could no longer live on his writs.'

Villiers chuckled again. Adam thought the pun rather tasteless in that context. As he peeled off his clothes he considered the implications of what he had just heard.

'I can't stay,' he burst out. 'I can't take their hospitality if things are as bad as that.'

'There's no need to go, my dear fellow.'

'But——'

'We all pay our whack, Harriet and Sally and I. Share the housekeeping. It's a help to them really.'

'Do you think I could suggest to Mortimer——?'

'I'd save your breath. The matter can be settled in two minutes' sensible conversation with his wife. She's a practical woman. If you feel the least embarrassment about it, I'll fix it up with her myself.'

'I wish you would,' said Adam, much relieved.

Villiers was a good fellow at heart, he decided, even though his witticisms jarred at times.

'*You would like Villiers*,' he wrote to Seabrook at the collecting address they had arranged in Paris. '*In many ways you are very similar*.' Having written it, he sat back and reflected what a naïve statement it was.

There was a similarity between the men. But Villiers was the successful sophisticate — too much what Seabrook yearned to be, without the necessary equipment and opportunity. Seabrook would have looked a little pale in Villiers' presence. He would not have enjoyed the juxtaposition for long.

Adam himself, though, found the same sort of interest and amusement in Villiers' company as in Seabrook's. Villiers got into the habit of dropping in for a final word and cigar before bed. He had the excuse that Adam's room had a balcony, which his own next door had not. But sometimes he had things to say which were best not spoken to the outer night and the open windows of the other bedrooms. He would perch on the end of the bed.

'That woman is a dragon.'

'What woman?'

'My dear Adam, who do you think? Harriet, of course.'

'What has she done?'

'Oh, just the usual. "I guess it's late, Sally darling — I wouldn't go wandering about in the garden at this hour — you might catch malaria." Chasing her off to bed like a little child! Though even the children in this menagerie go to bed when they like — and probably with whom they like,' Villiers added darkly. 'She as good as called me a liar — when I said I wanted Sally to hear the nightingales in the wood, she implied I'd never heard any there.'

'And had you?'

'No. But how the devil was she to know I hadn't?'

'She's a very perceptive young woman,' laughed Adam.

'She must be. She sits at the feet of the sage, drinking in every word he lets fall — but if Sally takes ten paces out of the room, it's as though she'd got eyes in the back of her head. Sally hardly gets a minute to herself. And why they have to share a bedroom in this half-empty mausoleum, well, it beats me.'

'Your very tone,' said Adam dryly, 'suggests the beaten man.'

Villiers gave him a sharp look, then grinned disarmingly. 'I like little Sally. She isn't such a damned blue-stocking as Harriet.'

'She's no fool.'

'Did I say she was? But she lets Harriet dominate her too much. Of course, it *is* awkward.'

'Awkward?'

'Oh, you haven't realised? The money's all Harriet's. Sally hasn't any. And I think she broke with her people — very straitlaced Bostonian Puritans — they didn't hold with this gallivanting off to Europe. So it puts Harriet in a strong position.'

'It's horrible to be dependent.' Adam spoke with feeling. But perhaps it was not so bad for a girl: it was the natural consequence of her sex. It could hardly be worse to be dependent on a sympathetic friend like Harriet than on disapproving relatives. 'Still,' he said, 'Harriet's very fond of her.'

'Too fond. She's possessive. She has a very hard streak in her, our Grecian beauty. She keeps a tight hold on her dollars, too. Mortimer is finding that.'

Adam looked mystified. Villiers explained that Mortimer had come out with a new scheme a month or two ago, for the launching of a literary review to provide a platform for enlightened and progressive theories. Mortimer of course would be editor: 'Give me a platform,' he had quoted modestly, 'and I will move the world.'

Villiers himself had been asked to contribute and to use his acquaintance with Byron, Shelley and other promising young writers to enlist their pens also in the enterprise.

'And Harriet has been offered an open field to write on whatever she likes. She has also,' chuckled Villiers, 'been offered the honour and privilege of financing the whole adventure.'

'Has she accepted?'

'She is considering it. As I say, our handsome Sappho has quite a hard head when it comes to her dollars.'

Yes, thought Adam, this household is all tensions, drawn in criss-cross lines from individual to individual, forming themselves into overlapping triangles such as one might doodle during a mathematics lecture.

There was Harriet, venerating the old man, despising his wife, dominating Sally, obstructing Villiers in his flirtatious designs. . . . And Sally, torn between loyalty to her friend and the Byronic attractions of Villiers. . . . And Mrs. Mortimer with her own understandable resentments against the two beautiful young Americans — for, yes, Sally was beautiful too in her unusual way. . . . And Villiers, possibly loving her (if that wasn't too strong a word?), and quite certainly detesting Harriet. . . . Even the children were not outside the emotional network. The way William Butts looked at his stepfather . . . and Primavera looked at them all. . . . In all this fantastic household there were only two who gazed out upon the world with frank self-assurance: Charles James in his high chair and Mortimer himself.

And what about me? Oh, I stand outside the whole thing, he reflected. I'm a mere bird of passage, in the villa but not of it. I am not emotionally involved. I am free to go whenever I like.

Villiers was saying:

'They blather on about the liberation of Italy — how

about a little liberation nearer home? It's Sally who needs liberating. And, damn me, I'm going to have a shot at it, if only to annoy Harriet. You're a sport, Adam — I shall rely on your co-operation.'

'How?'

'Oh, I don't know. Just put a spoke in Harriet's wheel when she interferes too much. Give me a chance to get two words alone with Sally, once in a blue moon. It makes me laugh,' said Villiers sourly. 'Harriet sits there scribbling away about Free Love, Female Emancipation, and Lord knows what nonsense — but if she realises that Sally and I are out on the terrace by ourselves, she shoots out as if there'd been a fire-alarm.'

Adam surveyed the figure sitting elegantly on his bed in frogged dressing-gown and tasselled smoking cap. He did not entirely like Villiers' cynical tone.

'I shouldn't say,' he remarked dryly, 'that you were a highly inflammable person.'

He liked even less the ring of Villiers' laugh. 'Ah, but what about our little Sally? You don't know about *her*, do you?'

'Do you?'

'Not yet. But our acquaintance will develop — given time and opportunity.'

Adam was glad when Villiers took himself off to bed. Of course, he told himself, trying to be fair, this Harrow-and-Trinity manner always rubbed him up the wrong way, always made him feel inferior and unsure of himself.

He stepped onto his balcony to escape the lingering scent of the cigar which, though pleasant enough, reminded him too much of his visitor. How placid, how unruffled, the lake stretched beneath the stars! Had it half the undercurrents of the Villa Gandolfi?

130

Chapter Nine

FOR weeks after the demonstration in the opera-house Mortimer continued to fulminate against the Austrians and all their ways.

Monarchy he detested at any time: Reason demanded republics everywhere, and he pointed to America as a country in which a logically worked-out constitution had made corruption and oppression unthinkable. A foreign monarchy was a double abomination. Though at other times he would proclaim the brotherhood of Man and the unreality of national barriers ('invented by despots to divide their dupes'), he was emphatic at the moment on the essential difference between Austrians and Italians. They were better with the Alps between them, as Nature had intended. And the day was coming when a glorious national rising would drive the invaders back to their proper side of the mountains.

Adam, though sympathetic, thought it would take some doing. Villiers, he knew, shared his doubts, though he humoured Mortimer and the girls in their ardent idealism.

'Well,' he remarked as they all sat drinking tea on the terrace, 'if von Schaumberg achieved nothing else that evening at the opera, he doubled the membership of the Coal-heavers.'

'Of the what?' inquired Mrs. Mortimer.

'The Coal-heavers. That's what "Carbonari" means.'

'And who are the Carbonari?'

'Oh, Mrs. Mortimer!' both the girls protested together. 'Surely——'

'The Carbonari, otherwise known as the Good Cousins,' said her husband patiently — or at least fairly patiently, 'are a secret society. I thought everybody knew that.'

'If everybody knew it, my dear, I don't see how it could be a secret society.'

'It's secret from the Austrians. Naturally every Italian is with it heart and soul.'

'They're supposed to have branches all over Italy,' said Harriet, growing warm with enthusiasm. 'They call them *vendite*, don't they, Mr. Mortimer?'

'But why?' Mrs. Mortimer still looked puzzled.

'*Vendite* means "sales-centres". For coal, you see.'

'You mean, they *sell* coal?'

'Of course not!'

'Then why——'

'It's a cover for their real activities,' said Villiers kindly. 'And actually, though everybody knows vaguely that the Carbonari exist, those activities are kept very dark. Membership is pretty strict. After all, it means a treason charge if they're caught. That's a capital sentence— and even if they're not executed, they're shut up in the Spielberg for years, maybe for life.'

'It makes my blood boil,' said Mortimer. 'This is the liberty we gave Europe after Waterloo!'

'It seems very wrong,' said his wife. 'How do you hear of all these things, Villiers?'

'Oh, I have my friends in the town . . .'

'Do you know some of the Carbonari?' inquired Sally, wide-eyed.

'Of course.'

'How romantic!'

'Villiers has a great advantage over the rest of us,' said Mortimer, a trifle pettishly, 'knowing Italian. I think,

132

my dear, I shall really get down to a serious study of the language——'

'We might all join his class,' said Harriet. 'After all, he is supposed to be helping Sally now. But it would be better if we organized a proper group.'

Mortimer was not the only one who looked put out by this idea. He said hastily:

'I'm not sure I have the time to begin now. I thought perhaps next autumn — when the dark evenings——'

'It *is* better,' said Villiers, 'to tackle a job like that thoroughly . . . or not at all.'

'I hope I am always thorough, whatever else my short-comings? Nothing if not thorough!'

'Exactly, sir.'

On the following day the subject of the Carbonari came up again. The three men took the boat across to Lucero in search of newspapers. As they sat over a glass of wine in the piazza before going back, Villiers leant across the table and remarked in a low voice:

'We were speaking of the . . . Coal-heavers.'

'Yes, the Carbo——'

'Sh! If you don't mind, sir — not the Italian word, here.'

Mortimer took the correction with unusual meekness. He apologised, glancing round him with a conspiratorial air which would have aroused the interest of any police-man within view.

'I've just been told,' Villiers continued, confidentially, 'there's to be a meeting at — well, not more than a few miles out of town. If it would amuse you to go, well, I think it could be arranged.'

The effect of this offer was remarkable. Mortimer could hardly control his delight. His blue eyes brimmed with fervour.

133

'It would not "amuse" me, my dear fellow — it would give me the profoundest pride and satisfaction! To range myself, if only for an hour or two, beside the heroic champions of liberty. To demonstrate to my Italian brothers, that I, though an Englishman——'

'It would be better not to demonstrate too much,' said Villiers tactfully. 'As I say, I think it could be arranged, but they are rather strict against admitting strangers.'

'I understand, I understand! Say no more. Naturally, it's dangerous?'

'Well . . .' Villiers hesitated. Watching his face, Adam felt sure he was going to continue, 'not really'. But, anxious not to diminish the old man's pleasure, he went on: 'There *is* danger . . .'

'Excellent! I thrive on danger.'

Mortimer bristled pleasurably. It was a source of perpetual regret to him that an accident of geography had prevented his assisting at the storming of the Bastille and the Battle of Valmy.

Villiers looked at Adam.

'It's tomorrow night. Will you make it a trio?'

'I should like to come, if three isn't too many?'

'I'll fix it. We can take the boat, and then it's about two miles to walk.'

'Say nothing to the ladies,' Mortimer ordered. 'Mrs. Mortimer has a horror of my getting, as she puts it, "mixed up in things". Not that there would be any cause to worry. If we were caught, what would these scoundrels dare to do to a British subject?'

So, thought Adam, we attend the meeting as citizens of the world. We only remember we are British if we are caught by the Austrians.

Villiers said, soberly:

'All the same, it would be better not to land ourselves

134

in trouble. Our passports would save us from the Spielberg, but we should probably be kicked out of the country.
And I, for one, don't want that.'

'Nor do I,' said Adam.

'I don't know,' said Mortimer, his eye kindling with
imaginative fire. 'Could they expel us without a trial?
I suppose they could? But if it meant a chance to testify
to my convictions in open court, the whole thing might
be well worth while. I should welcome the opportunity
to tell them . . .'

Failing that, he told Adam and Villiers instead.

For the next twenty-four hours Mortimer was happily
pregnant with their secret.

He would draw the young men aside with a warning
finger laid on his lips and a discretion so elaborate that
the rest of the family, children and ladies alike, were
soon consumed with curiosity.

'We should go armed, I think? You agree we should
go armed?'

'I have my stick,' said Villiers. It was a sword-stick,
which he sometimes whipped out and demonstrated.

'But you have pistols too?'

'Oh, yes.'

'What about you, Adam?'

'No.'

It had never occurred to Adam that pistols were a
necessary part of a gentleman's equipment for a foreign
holiday.

'I am sure Villiers will lend you one of his——'

'I shall be delighted,' said Villiers.

Adam did not like to damp them by refusing. He was
not at all pleased to hear that Mortimer had a pistol himself. They would all have been safer without. The Rector
had long ago drilled him in a proper respect for firearms,

which were best kept out of excitable hands. At all events, if he accepted Villiers' loan, he could make sure that one of the three pistols did not go off.

An hour later it was their dress which Mortimer was concerned with. He drew Adam mysteriously aside.

'Have you a cloak for tonight?'

'I shall be warm enough as I am, thank you.'

'Don't you think we ought to wear cloaks?' Mortimer was anxious to do the right thing. 'Something dark . . . we don't want to attract notice.'

Adam had an overcoat which he had not worn since the Channel crossing. It was not a romantic garment, and Mortimer was obviously disappointed, but he agreed that at least it would cover the white expanse of neckcloth if Adam turned up the collar. It was a pity that Adam had only a top hat. . . . What was really needed was a soft-brimmed sombrero to pull down over his brows. If necessary, Adam must tie a handkerchief across the lower half of his face . . .

'If necessary,' Adam agreed. He escaped on the pretext of working on Antonian. The translation had gone slowly and a little half-heartedly of late. The atmosphere of the Villa was unsympathetic. Feeling that he would not long be safe in his bedroom from Mortimer's next idea, he took his writing materials into the gardens and found a corner sheltered from the sun.

Antonian. . . . He read a few pages of the fluid Latin, trying to get back into the mood of a week or two ago. It was not easy. Was the fault in himself, he wondered — had he surrendered too willingly to the distractions of the life around him? Or was it Antonian's? Had Seabrook been right when he said that Antonian was third-rate? The doubt was insidious. Of course, it had not helped when there had proved to be no island on Lucero, and his ingenious theory had been demolished. All the same, the work must be finished now he was so near the end. Pritchard would be expecting the manuscript in October.

After some frowning and quill-twiddling, he achieved half a dozen lines which reproduced, more or less neatly, the meaning of the original. He was fated to get no further that afternoon. The approach of female voices made him look up.

Harriet and Sally, their arms affectionately entwined, were coming round the curve of the path. That was not remarkable. Harriet rather liked to maintain an actual physical hold over her old schoolfellow.

What made Adam blink was the fact that she was wearing a pair of men's trousers.

The two young women laughed and waved.

Harriet said: 'There's Adam. You could ask *him*.'

'Very well. I will. You go on.'

Sally disentangled herself. Harriet let her go without demur, smiled at Adam, and disappeared towards the house. She doesn't mind Sally talking to me, he thought. She isn't jealous of me, I don't count. I'm the dry fellow from Oxford. Harmless as a neutered cat.

Sally came into the spangled shadows, swinging her hat.

'May I interrupt you, Adam?'

'Please.'

'Will you loan me a pair of trousers?' His jaw dropped. 'For tonight.'

'What do you mean — tonight?'

She laughed. 'Oh, Harriet's got it out of Mr. Mortimer. And we're coming to the meeting with you.'

'The devil you are!'

'But we'll have to dress up as men. Harriet has made Mr. Mortimer loan her some clothes——'

'So I see.'

137

'I would ask Villiers. But I calculate nothing of his would fit me.'

'Would mine?'

'I could at least get into yours. It wouldn't matter how *big* they were. It'll be dark. And we're all to muffle ourselves up.'

The emancipated Miss Forester made her outrageous request with a most engaging candour. Laughing up into his face she looked quite ridiculously feminine. She was right, he thought, to come to me. Villiers' skin-tight elegance had been tailored for no form but his own. For all my height and breadth of shoulder, my clothes are at least possible. If they hang like sacks, it isn't my fault. . . .

'Very well,' he said.

'Thank you, Adam. You know,' she added, as he gathered up his papers and started back to the house with her, 'I felt you would. You're not as solemn as you look.'

'Do I look solemn?'

'Often. As if you were summing us all up.'

'Perhaps I am.'

'And do you find us amusing?'

'Very.'

'This is all very different from Oxford?'

'Somewhat,' he said dryly.

They crossed the hall and climbed the curving staircase under the indifferent gaze of plaster cherubim.

'Shall I . . . bring them? Which is your door?'

'Oh, mayn't I choose for myself?'

'You'll find my wardrobe sadly limited.'

She followed him into his bedroom as though it were a public place. Why not, he told himself? There were no conventions at the Villa Gandolfi. Reason was the only law. Mortimer had said so, frequently.

'These are your other books? All Latin?'

'I'm afraid so. I brought the bare minimum for my work. They weigh heavy. Not that I wanted to bring a lot of clothes. I don't possess them.'

'I *love* clothes! Mr. Mortimer talks about the hypocrisy of decking our bodies — but it's a mighty pleasant form of hypocrisy!'

'I'm afraid you won't derive much pleasure from anything *I* can lend you. Now. You'll want a coat?'

'I guess not. I have a redingote for cold evenings. It's quite military. If I turn up the collar — and at night my hat is very like a man's——'

'Then all you need——'

'Is trousers. As I said.'

It was refreshing not to hear them called 'unmentionables' or 'inexpressibles'. She wanted to cover her legs, not her lower limbs.

'It's a choice of these, then — or these.'

'Oh, these.' She pounced on the knitted pantaloons. 'These won't hang so loose.'

'No . . .'

'Thank you, Adam. It's going to be quite an adventure! Like something out of Shakespeare. I'll feel like Jessica or Rosalind.' She bundled up the trousers and crept out of the room with exaggerated stealthiness. In theory, the expedition was still a secret from the children and the servants.

Adam put away the rest of his clothes and straightened his books and papers, well aware that he would get nothing more done that day.

Villiers strode in a moment later without the nominal tap on the door which he usually gave from force of habit, however much Mortimer despised it as a meaningless convention. He was not, for once, smiling.

'Well, I'm damned!'

His face was darkly flushed.

'What's up?' asked Adam innocently.

'I might ask you that, Adam!'

Oh, Lord, thought Adam, not yet another line of tension drawn across this happy family!

He did his best to convince Villiers that he had nothing to be jealous about. It was not easy. On this occasion Villiers showed a surprisingly suspicious nature and deficient sense of humour.

It was dark and moonless when they all groped their way down to the landing steps. Mrs. Mortimer, of course, was not going. She had no taste for adventures beyond those she experienced, vicariously, when writing her stories.

'There had better be no talking,' said Mortimer. 'Voices carry across the water.'

The five of them arranged themselves as quietly as they could. Villiers pushed off and, giving a wide berth to the rock now mockingly known as Antonian's Island, they put out into the open lake. The water was like oil under their gunwales. Only an occasional light in the distance indicated roughly where lake and sky and shore drew close together. After some minutes Mortimer asked:

'Are you sure of the direction, Villiers?'

'Yes, sir.'

'I don't see how you can be on a dark night like this. We don't want to go wandering off our course and miss the meeting.'

'I've guarded against that possibility. You see——'

'All right, all right. I think we agreed that there must be absolute silence? Every little sound is clearly audible for miles. If we are detected, we bring danger not only on ourselves but on all these good people who have let us into their secret.'

'Yes,' said Villiers.

For the next five minutes there was no sound but the measured suck of the oars, the soft slap of ripples against the waterline. Then Sally leant forward, tapped Villiers on the knee, and whispered:

'A little more to the right.'

'What's that?' Mortimer demanded behind him.

She repeated the words in a slightly amplified whisper. 'Villiers told me,' she added, 'to look out for a waving lantern.'

'Oh?' Mortimer turned to see for himself, caught a crab, and expressed his annoyance in a loud undertone.

Adam now saw the light referred to. It went off and on, and moved a little from side to side. Villiers brought the nose of the boat round and pulled for the shore at that point. Considering that he had the embarrassment of Mortimer's help, Adam could only admire the accuracy of his navigation.

A low voice challenged them from the gloom. Villiers gave the password:

'*Italia rigenerata!*'

And the voice answered:

'*Vincere o morire!*'

They had to duck as overhanging branches scraped their heads. Adam clutched his top hat in the nick of time. The boat glided in, the dripping oars were shipped, unseen hands gripped the gunwale . . .

'Don't hand the ladies out,' Mortimer ordered in a hoarse whisper, 'or it'll give them away.'

Harriet and Sally showed themselves quite able to disembark unaided. They all bunched together in the darkness while Villiers carried on a discussion with the lantern-waver. The lantern was now masked.

'What's to do?' Mortimer demanded. 'We're wasting time.'

'He wants ten scudi. Two each.'

'Then give him the money. It's for the cause?'

'I think so. I hope so.'

There was a series of chinks as Villiers counted out the silver into the hand of friendship which had been extended to them. Then, without more ado, they filed off along a path through what appeared to be an orange-grove.

Harriet, close behind Mortimer, turned to whisper that it was like something out of Walter Scott. Sally agreed. Adam, of course, did not know.

Somewhere to the left an owl hooted, startling them.

'A signal,' murmured Sally with an appreciative shudder. Adam was inclined to think it was a genuine owl, but he realised that so prosaic an opinion would be unpopular.

Next, their ears picked up the sound of gushing water. A minute later they reached a stream, swirling along in a businesslike manner between deep-cut banks, almost like a mill-leat. They picked their way carefully along the ribbon-narrow path beside it, then crossed it by a single plank.

'Careful,' Villiers muttered in front.

Adam felt his hand caught impulsively. He steadied Sally as she walked over, drawing him after her. It was too dark for the Italian guide to see the feminine gesture. Adam hoped that Villiers had not noticed either. He could be unreasonably jealous. Until that afternoon, Adam had not guessed what passions lurked beneath the polished surface.

'How much further?' Mortimer grumbled. 'I hope we can trust this fellow? We're not being led into a trap? Villiers——'

'Yes?'

'Tell him I have a loaded pistol. At the first sign of treachery——'

142

Villiers murmured something to the guide, but Adam felt sure he was telling him nothing of the sort.

They walked on, the stream now on their left.

'Horses,' Adam whispered suddenly.

'I didn't hear anything,' Sally answered, her voice still further muted by her upturned collar.

It was Adam's nose, not his ears, which had informed him. Mingled with the night scents was the pungent reek of sweating horseflesh. Somewhere just ahead were animals which had been ridden hard within the last few minutes.

A building loomed in front, dark and solid, blotting out a great part of the star-pricked sky. A mill, Adam decided . . . Yes, the stream *was* a mill-leat. . . . But, though there were horses tethered in the yard, and chinks of yellow light faintly outlined the door, the mill had the air of a normally deserted place.

A youth's voice, tense with excitement and self-importance, demanded the password. Their guide gave it. The door opened, and they followed him into a long barn, dimly lit by a couple of lanterns. Two or three dozen men were sitting on benches or on bales of straw. Some talked in undertones. Others sat hunched in silence, as though uncertain of their neighbours. The party from the villa took their places unobtrusively at the back, where a flat-topped cart offered raised seating and a clear view of the proceedings.

It was all (as was agreed afterwards) excessively romantic.

A semicircle of square logs, in front, provided seats for the officials of the *vendita*. On a central block sat the president, a fiery-eyed haggard-featured man of about forty, perhaps (Adam speculated) a lawyer in private life who had become bored with the law. He played nervously with a hatchet, but, as it proved, this was merely the

143

symbol of his office, the equivalent of a masonic mallet. Indeed, as Villiers later explained, the Carbonari had a lot in common with the Freemasons.

On another log, draped with white linen, stood a crucifix as though on an altar. A ball of thread symbolized the linen woven by the Madonna and the link uniting the members of the movement. At least, it was supposed to symbolize those things, but, according to Villiers, many of the Good Cousins preferred to see it as the hangman's rope intended for their enemies, just as the president's hatchet was the weapon of revolution.

A few more muffled figures came in, one or two at a time, and sat down. Some looked like peasants or fishermen. Most, Adam would have guessed, were middle-class idealists like those who had invaded the stage during the opera. They were young, mainly. There might be a student or two from Padua or Bologna — perhaps even a boy still at school. There was little risk that Harriet and Sally would be conspicuous by their slightness and delicacy of feature, especially in that light.

The proceedings opened with a solemn ritual. The Rector would have called it mumbo-jumbo. Adam felt it *was* mumbo-jumbo. But it seemed to induce the desired atmosphere of enthusiasm and patriotic dedication. Stealing sideways glances at his companions he saw that they were as rapt as the Carbonari themselves, even though the flood of Italian passed mostly over their heads. Adam could understand little except a recurring phrase about 'getting the wolves out of the forest' and such cries as, 'Victory!' and 'Death to tyrants!' and 'Long live Liberty!' which exploded from the audience when their emotions demanded relief.

Adam was as sympathetic as the others to the cause of Italian unity, so far as he was informed about it. But if all the revolutionary movement was like this, he did not feel optimistic about its chances. Half a dozen mounted yeomanry would be enough to break up this assembly. Compared with a similar number of Luddites or Nottingham Lambs on a drunken spree, the combined *vendita* (hatchet and all) looked unlikely to cause any government authority much alarm. That this estimate, though unflattering, was not unfair was proved before the meeting had lasted half an hour, when the door was flung open and a nerve-shaken voice cut across the president's rhetoric.

'*Tedesci! Tedesci!*'

There was an impressive demonstration of unity as every man rushed for the door.

Chapter Ten

MORTIMER instantly revealed himself as the fearless man of action he was. He drew a formidable pistol from the folds of his cloak and began to shout exhortations in a mixture of Italian and Yorkshire. Finding himself ignored, he turned to Villiers.

'Explain to them! If we stand firm, we can hold this building against a regiment——'

Villiers begged him to be quiet and put his pistol away. If the crowd noticed him at all, they were more likely to imagine from his foreign speech that he was an Austrian police spy.

'We must get the girls out of here,' he urged.

'Come on then! Follow me, all of you! I'll clear a way.'

Mortimer flung himself massively upon the press of figures struggling to depart. At that moment the second of the two lanterns was put out, plunging the place into darkness. The most immediate danger to the girls, Adam realised, was that they would be trampled underfoot in the general panic.

'Wait!' he shouted, trying to make himself heard against the uproar. 'Not that way!'

It seemed not to have occurred to anyone else that there must be another exit. The ox-cart could never have passed through the ordinary door. Now that the lanterns were out, he could see, faintly pencilled in grey upon the blackness, the outline of a tall opening which would have admitted a laden hay-wagon.

'*This* way,' he shouted, and made for it, groping for the bolts. It took a few seconds. The barn-doors of Lucero and of Nottinghamshire did not follow the same pattern. But he got the hang of it. The rusty bolts screeched back, he caught his finger and felt the raw scrape, the welling up of the hot blood. . . . Then one side of the double doors creaked outwards, making a tall panel of night sky. The cool air rushed round him.

'Come on——'

He looked back. There was only one dark figure behind him.

'Who's that?' he asked.

'Me. Sally.'

'The others?'

'I guess they didn't hear you. I shouted too. But they must have——'

A shot rang out from the other side of the buildings. It was followed by two or three more. The pistols, barking and snapping like ill-tempered lap-dogs, sounded extraordinarily trivial in the greatness of the night. There were loud shouts in German, too, the trample of hoofs, the jingle of military ironmongery.

'We must get away from here,' she panted.

They ran forward as fast as they could over the uneven ground. On this side of the mill there was long wet grass, loose stones in patches, invisible briars that reached out to fasten on sleeve and shoulder. There was no more firing, but a good deal of contradictory shouting and rushing about. Lanterns began to twinkle as the Austrians searched the mill and its surroundings. There must be a big force of police and soldiers, Adam judged. They were sending out patrols in quest of the fugitives.

He put a restraining hand on Sally's shoulder.

'Stop a moment——'

'But — they'll catch us——'

'No. Keep absolutely still.'

She obeyed unwillingly. He drew her close to him against the trunk of a tree, so that their figures made no outline against the gloom. She was panting uncontrollably. Gently he turned her face so that it was half buried in the upstanding revers of his overcoat and the sound of her breathing was muffled. They stood like that for perhaps five minutes, not speaking, listening to the hubbub of the search-parties. One filed past within a few yards of them. His arms were round her shoulders, just as hers had instinctively closed about his waist. Speech being too dangerous, he could do no more than tighten his hold to reassure her. He felt, through the thick layers of cloth, an answering pressure from the small hands on his back.

'Now,' he said at last, gently disengaging himself. 'Slowly. Mind where you put your feet. No noise.'

He had been getting his bearings while they stood there. The lake must be somewhere to the left. . . . They had better make for it. If they could not find the boat, they could at least walk home by following the shore.

He discouraged all attempts at conversation until sight and sound of the Austrians had faded behind them.

'We should be all right now,' he murmured softly. 'I only hope the others got away.'

'I guess they did. From what the soldiers were shouting to each other. I don't think they'd caught anybody at all.' She laughed, very low. 'They sounded so cross.'

'German always sounds cross to me.'

'It was cute of you to make me stand still. I wouldn't have dared — I'd have gone on running full pelt, and they'd have heard me, and I'd have been caught.'

148

'That's what I was afraid of. When people are chasing you — in the dark, anyhow — it's usually much safer to freeze where you are. If you've a background to merge into, like that tree.'

'You talk like an Indian-fighter! Or are you a smuggler back home?'

'I did a lot of poaching when I was a small boy.'

'So that's why you move about so confidently in the middle of the night! I suppose you poached for fun?' she asked, curiously. 'From what Villiers says, the young gentry in England get up to all kinds of devilment — playing tricks on the watch and the toll-gate keepers and——'

'I poached because my mother and I were hungry. I am not . . . gentry.'

'I'm sorry——'

'You needn't be. I'm not ashamed of it. At least — to be quite honest — there are times when I am. And afterwards I am even more ashamed for having *been* ashamed of it.'

'I think I understand.' They had struck a cart-track between the orange-groves. Walking was easier, and there was no longer any need to worry about the Austrians. If, by mischance, they ran into a patrol and were challenged at this stage, no one could prove that they had been present at the meeting. To walk through the countryside at this hour might be eccentric, but it was not illegal.

'Why were you poor?' she asked. 'How did you get to college?'

He cut the long story as short as he could. When he had finished, she exclaimed:

'My! How romantic!'

'It isn't romantic in the least. And don't get any false ideas about my poor old widowed mother at home in the village. She is *not* proud of me. She is no more sentimental about our relationship than I am. I have a duty

149

to her. I do it. I send her what I can afford. If I am ever richer, I'll send her more — though I know perfectly well she will only drink it.'

'Oh, Adam! How sad!'

'The truth often is. I hate humbug.'

They walked on in silence for a little way. It was as though the fierceness of his tone had nipped a flame, as one snuffs a candle.

What an ill-assorted pair we are, he thought, to be trudging through an orange-grove in the middle of the night — or, for that matter, anywhere else at any time! It should have been Villiers. . . . No, perhaps it was as well it had not been. It would have been amusing to see Harriet's fury, but — better not. As it was, she would have no cause for concern. And Villiers would just have to accept his explanation that they had got separated by accident.

God knows, Villiers need not worry.

If Sally was not in love with him, at least she was under his spell. With his looks and clothes and tongue, he would have fascinated most girls. To Sally, a fugitive from the prim restraints of a New England upbringing, his airs and graces must be irresistible. One had only to watch her, drinking in his words as he talked of fashionable London and Brighton or referred familiarly to his literary acquaintances. How her eyes burned when, in serious mood, he put forward some Utopian scheme or recited poetry! And how readily she laughed when, with some outrageous epigram, he appeared to demolish one of the long-established principles of morality.

I am jealous of him, thought Adam, I must face that. I can be satirical on paper. But I cannot throw off these fireworks in conversation. No use to try . . .

Sometimes it seemed to him that even Villiers tried too hard. But perhaps that was jealousy again? Everyone

else found him amusing. Should satire stand analysis?
Must an epigram remain Truth, merely with its point
sharpened — or was one justified in saying anything, true
or false, to win a laugh?

I know what the Rector taught me, he said to himself.
Perhaps different views obtained at Harrow and Trinity.

'Look!' Sally plucked at his sleeve.

They were coming down to the lake. On one side of
them was an open meadow. Bright green points of light
flashed metallically in the gloom.

'Are those fireflies?' he asked wonderingly.

'Yes. Haven't you ever seen them before?'

'Never.'

She seemed generously pleased that he was seeing
them now.

They reached the water's edge and sat down on a rock.

'Do you know where we are?' she asked.

She had lost her hat when they ran out of the barn.
He could see her pale face above the high collar of her
redingote.

'The boat — if it is still there — must be further along
that way.' He indicated the shore curving away to the
right.

'Oh, yes,' she said quickly, 'we never crossed back over
the creek, did we? So we can tell by that. If we walk
along, we'll come to the creek first — it must flow into
the lake — and then a little further on we should get to
the place where we landed.'

'But will the boat be there?'

It was hard — impossible, in fact — to be sure.

If the other three had got back to the boat, how long
would they have waited? Would they have dared to wait
at all, if the Austrians were on their heels?

'I don't suppose,' said Adam, 'that we are more than
an hour's walk from La Lingua, if we turn left now. If

151

we go looking for the boat we shall be walking away from home all the time — and if it isn't there, we shall be stranded.'

'You decide.' He could tell from her voice that she was beginning to feel tired.

'Then I think it would be safer to start walking home the quickest way. Otherwise, we may waste time and double the distance we have to walk before we finish.'

'I'm in your hands, Adam.'

'Drink this, first.'

He unstoppered his brandy-flask and pressed it into her hand. She sipped at it gratefully.

'Is this another idea you picked up when you went poaching as a little boy?'

'No. Later. When I went shooting with old Jennings.'

She began to shake with silent laughter. The flask clicked against her teeth.

'Is that so funny?'

'No, no! I was thinking of Boston. What the folks back home would say — if they could see me now, in trousers, swigging brandy with an Englishman, at — what time of the night?'

'I can't see my watch. From the stars I should think it is well after midnight.'

'Oh, later, I reckon. The meeting was eleven, and it didn't begin punctually.'

They started to walk along the side of the lake. It was not so dark here. The open water reflected a dim luminosity. At times they could move at a good pace, but at others they had to push their way through dense thickets or squelch through boggy patches to an Aristophanic chorus of croaking frogs. It had sounded simple, just to follow the lake-shore round until they got to La Lingua, but it was not so easy as that.

'I calculate the others are safely home by now,' she said.

'I hope so. I wonder what they're thinking——'

'I know what they're *saying*. Mr. Mortimer anyway.'

'What?'

' "Supper!" ' she said, giving the 'u' its Yorkshire value. They both laughed. He was glad to know that she *could* laugh at Mortimer. So she was not, like her friend, overwhelmed by reverence.

'Which reminds me,' she went on, 'I don't suppose you have any food, as well as your flask? Your youthful training didn't make you fill your pockets before we started?'

'I'm sorry.'

'So am I. Oh, I *am* empty.'

He was quite upset by her pathos. Never in his life before had he found himself responsible, like this, for a companion of the opposite sex. Was she liable to swoon, unless instantly fed? He had an exaggerated idea of feminine fragility. She soon brushed aside his fussy inquiries.

'I'll be all right, Adam. I only said I was hungry.'

'If only I'd thought! But — well, this situation is rather unforeseen.'

'Don't you like the unforeseen occasionally?'

He considered. During the last few plodding years it had seldom entered into his life. Certainly, though, in recent weeks a lot had happened which he could not have foreseen when he left England. On the whole he had liked it very much.

'Yes,' he admitted.

'This is an adventure. I adore adventures. I came to Europe because I wanted adventures.'

'Will you tell me,' he asked diffidently, 'about *your* life?'

He need not have been diffident. He should have known by now that nobody at the villa could resist such an invitation.

153

As they trudged on, past glimmering water and flashing fireflies, with an accompaniment of croaking frogs and an occasional watchdog barking furiously in the distance, Adam was transported in imagination to New England. Sally had been the fourth daughter of a serious-minded apothecary . . .

'Every one thinks my name stands for Sarah,' she confessed. 'You might as well know — it doesn't. My real name is Salvation Forester.'

'Never mind,' he said sympathetically.

Her childhood had been narrowly confined. It had been enlivened by nothing more exciting than a picnic up the Charles River, a supervised stroll over the Common or up to Beacon Hill, or an extra-long sermon by a fashionable preacher at the Old South church. Music had been permitted, and the reading of approved books. She had never set foot in a theatre before landing in Italy, and, though she had (thanks to Harriet) read innumerable plays, she had still to see one acted in her own language.

It was Harriet who had freed her from the shackles of Puritanism. Harriet with her big, wealthy home, where the ships' captains came to dine and brought not only presents for the owner's schoolgirl daughter but (what was more important) a whiff of the outer air.

'I guess I was always the rebel in our family,' Sally reflected. 'But if it hadn't been for Harriet I reckon they'd have beaten me.' She laughed. 'We used to say it was my private War of Independence, the second American Revolution.'

Harriet had lent her forbidden poetry. She had discovered *The Last Minstrel* and *The Ancient Mariner*, *Childe Harold* and *Kubla Khan*. Harriet had insisted that ideas and ideals were as important as emotions — sometimes the boundary was, for her, only raggedly defined — and Sally had smuggled tracts and pamphlets to her room

154

very different from the theological or philanthropic ones favoured by her parents. Tom Paine, Mary Wollstonecraft, William Godwin . . . these became the new prophets, displacing for the two girls the great names of the Old Testament. Above all, Matthew Mortimer . . .

'In those days,' said Sally, '*The Rebellion of Reason* was our Bible.'

'In those days?'

She hesitated. 'Well, naturally, it's not the same now we're here. I mean—we have Mr. Mortimer in person.'

'True.' Adam could imagine: it made a difference.

In those days Matthew Mortimer, and the Europe he personified, had seemed as remote as a star. If the girls could escape as far as the Faneuil Hall, to attend some heated protest meeting on an unsuitable social problem, it was as much liberty as they dared hope for.

Mr. Seeley's unexpected death changed everything. 'It was an old will,' Sally explained. 'He didn't figure, when he made it, that Harriet might be his only child — or that she might turn out the way she has. I guess he'd never gotten around to revising it in time.'

Anyhow, Harriet had been left with a financial independence to match the independence of her mind. After twenty-one her trustees had no more than a loose general check on her capital. She had an income and complete freedom to do as she liked.

'So she came to Italy — and brought you?'

'Yes. She'd been writing to Mr. Mortimer for ages. He used to write such wonderful letters. As if he were in the room with us.'

'And your family? What did they say when you announced you were off to Europe?'

'You can imagine! A great many stupid, unjust things — as though I were a baby, and didn't know the world. If they'd realised some of the *books* I'd read!'

'H'm,' said Adam.

'I've finished with my family. The family's a worn-out social institution, anyway. It hasn't any function in the new age. Mr. Mortimer says that children belong to the community, not to their parents.'

'That's exactly what Plato says, in the *Laws*.'

Sally turned her face, her eyes larger than ever in the gloom. 'Plato? Does he, now?'

'No doubt,' Adam could not resist saying, 'he was deeply influenced by Mr. Mortimer.'

She laughed. 'Maybe I never read enough of the *old* books. Barring Shakespeare and Dante, Harriet and I were all for the new ones. The newer the better.'

'I wish you could have met my old Rector.'

'I wish I could, Adam.'

They had been talking so busily, they had forgotten to be tired or hungry. Nor had they noticed the stealthy creeping up of the dawn. Now, though, they suddenly realised that the night had gone. The sky was grey, the water was a vast expanse of softly gleaming mother-of-pearl, and only half a mile away were the clustered houses of La Lingua. Dark with its trees the promontory stretched out across the twinkling lake, dipped, and climbed again to its final knob. From this side they could clearly see the white walls of the villa, the rising terraces, and the twin pillars flanking the steps below.

'There's the boat,' she said. 'It looks as though they got home all right.'

The village was awakening to the new day. They gave it a wide berth and started along the last mile. Warm with their long tramp they carried their top-coats over their arms. She made a quaint, but not unattractive, figure in the borrowed trousers and a long-sleeved muslin spencer of her own. After the night's adventures and the loss

156

of her hat, the unkempt curls more than ever suggested the bacchante.

In the lemon-grove they surprised a village couple in the moment of farewell. Ramsthorpe and La Lingua, thought Adam, there is not much essential difference. Crushed grass tells the same story, the world over. Before they reached the villa they passed two other places where the story was repeated.

'It's a favourite place for lovers,' said Sally. 'All the boys and girls in La Lingua come out here to do their courting. Even from Lucero.' She laughed tolerantly. 'There must be something in the air.'

'There must,' he said gravely.

From the garden in front a white peacock greeted their arrival with a derisive scream.

Chapter Eleven

I T WAS an amiable feature of the Mortimer ménage
that, however hot-headed, they were no less warm-
hearted. The sound of returning footsteps brought
a rush of welcome. Adam and Sally had to thrust their
way indoors through a clamant pack of adults and
children in all stages of undress. Though it was four
o'clock in the morning, everyone in the villa appeared
to be wide-awake. It would indeed have been remarkable
if anyone had been otherwise.

'My dear!'

Mortimer enfolded Sally and pressed his whiskers
against her pallid cheek. He had changed his clothes,
Adam noted, and despite the early hour was arrayed with
extreme formality.

'We were going to give you another hour——' cried
Harriet.

'And then,' said Mrs. Mortimer, 'Mr. Mortimer was
going straight to the police.'

'To demand your immediate release,' he explained.
'To *demand* it. In the name of His Britannic Majesty,'
he added with, for a convinced republican, surprising
gusto.

'What the devil happened to you?' Villiers asked Adam.
'We only got away by the skin of our teeth, ourselves.
We knew you'd been behind us——'

'I was terrified the Austrians had caught you,' said Harriet. Relief was giving place to reaction. She sounded a little sharp.

Adam tried to explain briefly how they had escaped from the mill. On the whole it seemed lucky that they had used the other exit. The children pressed round, demanding details.

They had by now reached the living-room. A servant flung back the shutters, and the blinds rattled up. The day's first sunshine splashed on the wall. Sally sank wearily onto a chair, and closed her eyes.

'She's in a state of collapse,' cried Harriet. She turned on Adam accusingly. 'I don't know what you've been doing——'

'We've been walking,' he said shortly.

'All this time?'

'Of course. That's why she's tired. It's a long way, following the shore round.'

'I suppose so.' But the grey eyes gave him the sort of look which was generally reserved for Villiers.

'The girl wants breakfast. We all want breakfast,' said Mortimer. The idea seemed to raise his spirits. After his first delight at the return of the wanderers, he had seemed a trifle disappointed at no longer needing to issue an ultimatum to the authorities.

'*Caffè!*' His wife bustled the two goggling maids from the room. '*Molto caffè! Colazione. Presto!*' She turned to the others. 'What are we to tell the servants?'

'Better not mention the Carbonari,' said Villiers.

'Certainly not,' agreed Mortimer. 'Not a word about the meeting.'

'Then what?' she demanded.

'Why say anything?'

Mrs. Mortimer's customary meekness was less in evidence at this early hour of the morning. 'Don't be ridiculous, Matthew. After all this uproar and excitement, we must give them some kind of explanation.'

'Can't we just say that Adam and Sally went for a walk and got lost——'

'And were out the whole night?' interrupted Mrs. Mortimer witheringly. 'I wouldn't dare to introduce such a story into one of my books — even for children! What do you want the maids to imagine?'

'Mamma means,' said Primavera, making one of her rare interventions, 'they will assume that Miss Forester and Mr. Adam have been——'

'Hold your tongue, Primavera!'

William Butts was heard to whisper, in an interested tone: 'What were you going to say?' and his coffee-tinted stepsister to promise: 'Later. Meet me — you know where.'

'I really don't see,' Mortimer was protesting, 'it is, after all, quite easy to lose one's way in the woods at night——'

'And one's reputation, even more easily! You can sneer at me, Matthew — say I am conventional——'

'You are!' It was a quarrel Mortimer never tired of. 'Can't we have an enlightened community even within the four walls of this house? Are all our "principles" to curl up and wither at the first breath of reality?' (Probably, thought Adam, but kept out of the argument — or rather forebore to interrupt the monologue.) 'Reputation? This "bubble reputation"? *Sally* is not worried about her "reputation".' (The girl certainly did not seem to be: she was leaning forward, elbows on the table, head on hands, the slim trousered legs slanted together, like a bird's, in an attitude of blank exhaustion. She was barely conscious even of Harriet fussing round her.) 'She has long liberated herself from the shackles of an outworn ethic. She believes that Woman, like Man, was born to be free. Why should she worry about the tittle-tattle of servants,' Mortimer continued, giving the last word a contemptuous inflection not quite consistent with his theories of human equality, 'when, if she *wished* to take a lover——'

'Hush, Matthew!'

'Let's not be mealy-mouthed!'

'The children——'

'The children benefit from listening to our discussions.'

'So you say. But when we are speaking of persons — of ourselves——'

'Papa says that knowledge never did anyone any harm,' said Primavera with relish. She glanced at William Butts with a thoughtful expression.

'What was I saying?' Mortimer demanded.

Nobody prompted him. His wife said:

'Well, thank God — or Reason, if you prefer it — everyone is back safely, and that's the main thing. You know what *I* thought of the whole escapade from the moment I heard of it.'

' "Escapade?" ' Mortimer was deeply aggrieved. 'I regret nothing. It was a practical demonstration of our sympathies with the cause of Italian liberation. That is the trouble with you, my dear — the moment I attempt to *do* something, you throw cold water on it. But words are not enough. I sometimes think there is too much talk in this house——'

'Yes,' said Mrs. Mortimer. But whether in irony or sheer fatigue was not apparent, for at that moment the maids came in with laden trays of breakfast.

Flat on his bed, blinds drawn against the glare of sun and water outside, Adam found himself surprisingly disinclined for sleep. The events of the past few hours went round and round in his slightly aching head.

Seabrook would laugh himself silly if he ever heard the story of last night — not so much at the fiasco of the Carbonari meeting as at Adam's subsequent lack of initiative. To have been alone, so long, so late, with a girl who was not only pretty but who boasted emancipation . . . '*I'd* have emancipated her.' He could almost hear Seabrook saying the words, almost see his colleague winking at him across the brandy-glasses.

Adam could not say, with strict honesty, that he had never thought of Sally like that during the hours they had been thrown together. There had been times — as when they had clung to each other in the darkness outside the mill — when he had been almost excessively conscious of her as a young woman. But danger first, then exertion and tiredness, had prevented any further development of such feelings. The protective instinct had triumphed over any others. His only concern had been to get Sally back to the villa. It had no doubt been very unenterprising of him. But he would do the same again, if — God forbid — they had to repeat their expedition tonight. Seabrook might say that was another symptom of desiccation. Seabrook would never have understood the pure pleasure — yes, pure pleasure, and let Seabrook twist the phrase as mockingly as he liked — of just walking beside a lake with a girl and talking to her.

'Some fellows have all the luck!'

Adam opened his eyes, surprised to find that after all he had been asleep, and, by the feel of it, for several hours. The figure sitting at the foot of the bed, striped with thin lines of light by the Venetian blinds, was not Seabrook, of course, but Villiers.

'Ah-ow,' Adam groaned. 'What time is it?'

'Dinner in an hour. I came to tell you. I was saying, some people have all the luck. If *I* could get Sally to myself for half an hour, never mind half a night——'

Villiers laughed, rather complacently. Damn him, thought Adam with a sudden rush of exasperation, though he envies me the accident which left Sally with me instead of with himself, he isn't jealous any longer. *He* saw at a glance, even if Harriet didn't, that nothing had happened between us. He has written me off as only half a man.

'Harriet was in a frenzy,' Villiers continued with reminiscent pleasure. 'First she pictured poor Sally at the mercy of the licentious soldiery. Then, as time passed, she began to think that a dissolute young don might be an even graver peril. You know, Adam, she was prepared to credit you with the basest appetites.'

'Aren't *you*?'

Adam went over to the wash-bowl and began to splash his face and chest with cool, faintly greenish water, smelling of the lake. He turned and faced Villiers squarely as he towelled himself. It was an instinctive movement of pardonable vanity, to show Villiers a chest and shoulders he could not compete with. Physique didn't prove anything, of course, but he wasn't going to have Villiers, as well as Seabrook, talking as though he were some bloodless marionette.

'Oh, I'm sure you're a devil when you're roused,' agreed Villiers amiably. '*When* you're roused.'

Adam pulled his shirt over his head to hide both his face and his feelings. Villiers went on:

'If it had been *I* who'd got so conveniently lost with Sally, I can't imagine what poor Harriet would have done. Though admittedly with more cause.'

'You flatter yourself.'

'Meaning?'

'I know that Sally's views are . . . unorthodox——'

'Unorthodox? My mother would say that was putting it mildly.'

'But even if she believes half she says about Free Love
— and isn't just agreeing with you others for the sake of
harmony — I don't see why you should assume that she'd
seize the first time she was alone with you to — to——'
Adam left the sentence unfinished, not through any
prudery, but from a sudden distaste (so violent as to
surprise him) for visualizing this very particular situation.

'Oh, she'd have to be worked up to it,' Villiers conceded, swinging a leg elegantly. 'That's why time and
the hour must conspire to create the mood. She's much
more heart than head — just the opposite of Harriet.
Harriet would go to bed to prove a principle — and I'll
bet she'd prove an icicle!'

'*Very* funny.'

'How sour you scholars get when the talk turns to a
topic outside your own field! Now with Sally, as I was
going to say — give me a summer's evening, a sunset,
nightingales if possible, a romantic ruin or a convenient
cave, a great surge of sympathy for a young poet (myself)
unappreciated by the English public——'

'You make me sick,' observed Adam quietly, putting
on his shoes. Straightening up, he said: 'Do you want
to marry her?'

'Marry her? My dear fellow, marriage in this enlightened household is practically an obscene word.'

'You know as well as I do, Villiers, there's a wide gulf
between theory and practice in this house. And, hang it,
for all the nonsense Mortimer talks, he did marry Mrs.
Mortimer.'

'Is that a very persuasive argument for marriage?'

'Maybe not. But these girls . . . well, it's different.
They've got hold of these half-baked theories — and *you*
know they're half-baked as well as I do, you only pretend
to believe in them because they're amusing — and convenient——'

164

'I deny that. You're accusing me of insincerity.'

'Well, I don't care a brass farthing whether you are insincere or not. What I do know is that the girls — Sally, anyhow — will grow out of these notions in a year or two——'

'Hence the urgency of my problem,' said Villiers, nodding.

'You mean, then, you have no intention of marrying her? You just want to take advantage of her——'

'You make her sound like a servant-girl. Shall we say rather, "take advantage of her present opinions"? You can't blame me, my dear fellow. These girls are asking for it. The books they read, the things they come out with in discussion. . . . I don't say I wouldn't want to marry her if she had half Harriet's income. Unfortunately she hasn't.'

'Is this,' inquired Adam, using some self-control, 'what you regard as the new romantic attitude?'

'I'm sorry if I shock you.' Villiers got up off the bed and lounged gracefully against the window. He was, Adam had to face it, what women regarded as handsome. The sun turned his long brown hair to a glinting aureole, and today, imitating Byron, he wore his shirt open at the neck. That was sensible enough, in the Italian heat, but Adam resolved he would choke before he would imitate Villiers. While he fastened his own cravat, Villiers drawled on: 'If you're so great on the institution of marriage, I wonder you don't propose to her yourself.'

Adam wondered if his eyes were really bulging, or if it was mere fancy, induced by surprise and the unwonted violence with which he had tied the knot. Easing it slightly from his throat he retorted:

'If I wanted to marry Miss Forester I couldn't. I'm in no position to marry anyone.'

'Or to criticise. Till dinner, then . . .'

Villiers drifted from the room.

For some days after the Carbonari meeting the villa reverted to its normal routine.

On the terrace, Mrs. Mortimer wrote with terrifying fecundity, putting her juvenile heroes and heroines through a series of misadventures designed to test every weakness in the human character. The real children eddied round her or disappeared for long periods in pursuit of their own interests. One could only hope that their activities were equally productive of moral benefit.

Mortimer and Harriet spent many a happy hour drafting the prospectus for their new literary review which, once launched, would blow the *Edinburgh* clean out of the water, along with the *Quarterly*, *Blackwood's* and the *British Critic*. Mortimer was prepared to do battle with them all.

'I have never,' he declared, 'been one to do things by halves.'

'Except,' Villiers remarked aside, 'brothers and sisters.'

He himself, meanwhile, taught Sally more Italian. 'You should study the language too,' she urged Adam ingenuously.

'My vocabulary is adequate for my purposes,' he said more sharply than he had intended. 'I know the meaning of *dilettante*.'

She flushed and turned away. Villiers raised an eyebrow. When not giving Italian lessons he was understood to be engaged on a long narrative poem. He read the first few stanzas one evening after supper.

'Oh, it's splendid!' cried Sally. 'It's as good as Byron.'

'It's very like Byron,' Harriet agreed.

'It promises well,' said Mortimer warmly. 'We might publish the first canto in the review. What do you say, my dear?'

Mrs. Mortimer glanced up from her sewing. 'Are you asking my opinion — or Miss Seeley's?'

'In this case I meant Harriet, my dear. Since she will be associated with me — I hope — in publishing the review.'

'I like the poem,' said Harriet carefully, 'but it would not be fair of us to try to commit Villiers at this stage. He may prefer to bring the whole poem out together, in a book——'

'And become famous in a night, like Byron!' Sally exclaimed. 'That would be wonderful. They say that seven editions of *Childe Harold* were printed in a single month——'

'Of course,' Harriet reminded her, 'editions vary greatly in size — don't they, Mrs. Mortimer?'

'John Murray himself told me,' said Villiers casually, 'that ten thousand copies of *The Corsair* were sold on publication-day.'

'One *day*!' echoed Sally. 'If only that could happen to you!'

And they all, in graduated degrees of enthusiasm, played with the agreeable day-dream. Villiers, for all his nonchalant disclaimers, contributed just those first-hand, knowledgeable touches needed to make it vivid. Glancing across at Sally, Adam knew that her eyes were shining in the imagined blaze of chandeliers and carriage-lamps. She was sweeping down great staircases at Holland House, at Lady Jersey's, at Lady Melbourne's. . . . She was sitting in her box at Drury Lane with the new poet whose name was on every tongue . . . dancing at Almack's, walking in Bond Street, driving in the Park, talking books in John Murray's drawing-room at Albemarle Street . . .

He could not despise her for it. In his heart he knew he would have enjoyed a taste of that world himself. Only a taste — and then perhaps another taste after a due interval — but a taste, certainly. It was all part of the world, part of life. Like a woman, it could be ridiculous and alluring at the same time.

He had written two short poems himself since the Carbonari meeting. They stayed folded in his pocket. They were too personal to read to that assemblage.

For all her preoccupation with Mortimer and his schemes, Harriet had a sheep-dog's talent for keeping the flock together. Nor did the great man (much as he enjoyed his *tête-à-têtes* with her) care to lose his larger audience for long at a time. As his wife was unyielding in her resolution to scribble her daily stint, and as Adam insisted on retiring occasionally to work on Antonian, any attempt by Villiers to detach Sally for more than the odd half-hour was easily noticed and frustrated.

One evening Sally seemed to be taking longer than usual in choosing the Beethoven she meant to play. Villiers had already taken up his position by the piano, ready to turn over her music, but his insistent murmur appeared to be delaying the start of the recital. Harriet, who added a dog's hearing to her other canine attributes, turned from the table and interposed serenely:

'That sounds like an excursion we would all enjoy.'

'Eh, what? Who's off where?' Mortimer demanded, emerging from a digestive coma.

'Villiers was offering to show me the monastery on the other side of the lake——'

'What monastery?'

'It's only a ruin,' Villiers explained, his enthusiasm evaporating. But he had miscalculated. Both Harriet and Mortimer preferred their monasteries in decay. Not only was a ruin far more romantic, but it symbolized the overthrow of superstitious religion.

'We might all go,' said Mortimer. 'Take the children. Good for them. Instructive. Rid them of any nonsensical notions about celibacy.'

Adam privately doubted whether any educational effort was needed in this direction. Villiers said, with a slight edginess roughening his normal urbanity:

'We couldn't all get into the boat.'

'We could hire another boat then. Or a carriage, and go round by the road.'

Villiers said it was a long way by land. He would not like to suggest a big family expedition which might disappoint. There was little to see but the ruined cloisters, their capitals carved like oranges and lemons, which the monks were said to have introduced to the shores of Lucero.

'One could wish they had introduced nothing worse,' cried Mortimer good-humouredly. 'Never mind, Villiers, it will make an expedition — some day. There will be the prospect of the lake and mountains from another angle. Who could tire of that?'

Mortimer himself could, and very readily, but nobody said so. He often grew eloquent on what he termed 'the sublime in Nature', but two minutes' contemplation of it, without a listener, irritated him to distraction.

'We must fix something next week,' said Harriet. 'The work on the review is going so well, we mustn't interrupt it while Mr. Mortimer is in the mood.'

Villiers did not press his suggestion. He seemed to have lost interest. Sally began to play the piano.

After breakfast, the next morning, Adam had some small shopping to do in the town, and decided to row across. Mortimer and Harriet were deep in conference, Mrs. Mortimer (though physically present on the terrace)

169

was in essence several thousand miles away, rescuing an imprudent boy-hero from the predicament of the moment and therefore not to be disturbed, even if Adam had desired her company. Neither Sally nor Villiers was in sight, but it was all too probable that they were together. He did not much want the companionship of Villiers, and there was small hope of getting Sally's without it. So he must go alone.

Wait, though. . . . The children sat in line along the crumbling balustrade, drumming with their heels, sour with boredom. He had often felt sorry for them, wanted to make some friendly gesture, shy though he was. He addressed himself, as a matter of courtesy, to Primavera.

'I'm going into Lucero. Would you like to come?'

She brightened instantly. 'Me?'

'Yes. Any of you. All of you.' He had begun to visualize a happy little group round one of the tables in the piazza, spooning up ices and stuffing cakes.

Primavera's smile faded, as though she had been thinking of a somewhat different expedition.

'Too hot,' she said.

'I didn't mean walk. I'm taking the boat. You can help me row, William.'

'I can't,' said William Butts regretfully. 'Mr. Villiers took the boat. He wouldn't take me. I asked him.'

'You mean — he's got the boat?' Adam bit his lip, not merely because he had looked forward to sculling across the cool water. 'I suppose Miss Forester is with him?'

'You suppose right,' said Primavera with a kind of gloomy glee.

'They're only going round the point and back,' said little Aspasia reassuringly.

'That's what he said,' Virginie corrected her. Virginie

was eighteen months older than her sister. 'I think Mr. Villiers is in love with Miss Forester.'

'Oh, no,' protested Aspasia.

'Why not, silly?'

'Because he was whispering to Maria by the kitchen-door, ever so close, and Primavera says that when a man and a servant-girl carry on like that it only means one thing!'

'I expect he was asking her for some food,' said William, who had done much the same thing himself in his time. Adam, listening to this animated crosstalk which he could think of no easy way to stem, was relieved to find that the boy's sophistication was no greater.

'If you believe that,' said Primavera darkly, 'you'll believe anything.'

'Besides,' Virginie instructed Aspasia, 'Mr. Villiers may lust after them both.' (She studied the Bible a good deal, unknown to her father who would have been horrified at the thought of her pure young mind being contaminated by religious concepts.) 'After all, there is no reason why a gentleman should not lie with two ladies at the same time.'

'Not at the same time,' said Primavera. 'As Papa always says, get your facts right.'

'Would anyone like to *walk* to the town?' Adam seized the chance to inquire, before the discussion could develop further.

Primavera tossed her lank hair. The two smaller girls would have found the dusty miles rather far for their pantaletted little legs. Only the boy said:

'Please, sir, I'd like to come.'

'Go on, then!' burst out Primavera with surprising viciousness. 'Don't imagine *I* want you. Go on — little boy!'

'It's you who go on,' said her stepbrother, unmoved.

M   171

Primavera flung away to the end of the terrace, where the garden-boy was weeding with a defeatist air. Virginie and Aspasia raced after her, squealing, but their attendance seemed unwelcome and they were quickly sent about their business. Adam and William started along the rocky path to La Lingua.

'What a lovely place this is,' Adam sighed, conscious that the weeks were slipping by and the shadow of term was looming nearer. 'You're lucky to live here all the time.'

'I'd sooner be in London. Perhaps, if this magazine gets started, we'll be able to go back.'

'Why do you want to?'

'I ought to be at school,' explained William soberly.

'I thought your mother gave you lessons?'

'She's too busy writing stories. Mr. Mortimer used to, when we were all by ourselves. Now he just tells us to read books and study Nature and learn to think for ourselves. Mamma was cross about that.'

'What did she say?' Adam's curiosity was ignoble but irresistible.

'Oh, she burst out at him, as she does sometimes when there aren't any visitors there. She said, "Good God, no, Matthew, let them learn to think like other people."'

'So — you'd rather be at school. Why?'

William considered. He was a stolid little boy and the circumstances of his life had (Adam judged) developed a habit of reflection.

'I'd like to learn Latin,' he said at length, 'and all about the ancient Romans. Like you.'

Here we go again, thought Adam. For a few moments he was no longer a young man tramping between the twisted silver olive-trees, with the sunlit lake glittering through the branches and William Butts trotting at his side. He was a boy again himself, walking the frosted furrows with the Rector, while a December sunset died behind the leafless elms.

'If I were staying longer——' he began, and stopped.

No. Why put out a hand, even with the kindest intentions, to draw another boy on to the same treadmill? William Butts would find his own future when the time came.

They reached the town and Adam bought the oddments he had come for, William proving a great help as an interpreter, for he had acquired quite a flow of servants' Italian during the family's erratic travels. As they made for one of the cafés in the piazza, they encountered Brigitta, who bobbed and flashed an April smile.

'Who's that, Mr. Adam?'

'Brigitta. The maid at the Tre Corone.'

'Oh. She looks nice.'

'She is.'

'But she seemed a bit . . . cross.'

'She was sorry when I moved to the villa.'

'She would be. Is she married?'

'Good Heavens, I've never noticed! I shouldn't think so.'

'Well, she's no chicken,' said William in his old-fashioned way. 'I bet she's between twenty and thirty. I thought she seemed just a *bit* motherly — though a very young sort of motherly.'

'She tried to mother me,' Adam admitted with a chuckle. 'That's why she was cross when I left.'

They sat down. He ordered a glass of wine for himself, an ice for William. The boy said, abruptly:

'I like Miss Forester much better than Miss Seeley. Miss Seeley may be nicer-looking——'

'I see nothing wrong with Miss Forester's appearance,' said Adam quickly, 'though I agree that Miss Seeley is more of a classical beauty.'

173

'And she's cleverer, of course. Everyone says that.'

'Possibly. She is intellectual. Perhaps Miss Forester is just——' Adam paused, trying to sound impartial. 'Just intelligent.'

'I like her better, anyhow. And so does Mr. Villiers. Don't you?'

'I don't think I ought to state a preference.'

'*Are* you a cold fish?' inquired William with interest.

'Who says I am?'

'Oh . . . I forget.' Life had taught William that if he was too straightforward it only led to a head-on collision with trouble.

'Well, I don't know.' Adam considered his empty glass with good-humoured detachment. 'I don't think a lot about my own feelings. Not to be picking them to pieces all the time and laying them on the table for everyone to admire.'

The boy wagged his head with approval. 'It makes me sick.'

Perhaps after all, thought Adam, he had the stuff of classical scholarship in him? Better not encourage the tendency too far . . .

'That's not the same as saying I don't *feel* anything. As my bedmaker at College is very fond of remarking, "I 'as me feelings, same as what you 'as, sir." '

William chortled appreciatively, and accepted another ice. He was a pleasant, ordinary little boy. It was good to get away, however briefly, from the forcing-house atmosphere of the villa.

'Can we look round the market before we start home?'

'Why not?'

William finished the ice, Adam paid the waiter, and they walked through the cool sun-streaked arcades into the Piazza delle Erbe. It was getting towards noon, and the tumult of the market was rising to a crescendo. They worked their way round, enjoying the noise and the colour, until, as they reached the tree-lined waterfront, William let out an exclamation:

'Isn't that our boat, Mr. Adam?'

'Where?'

Adam's first impulse was to run his eye along the moored boats bobbing against the steps. Perhaps Villiers had seized his chance and persuaded Sally to prolong the half-hour. Perhaps they too had come into Lucero and were even now drinking coffee somewhere nearby.

But the boy was pointing out over the lake. A couple of hundred yards out, but making straight for the landing-place, was a fishing-craft. Towed astern, empty but unmistakable, was the Gandolfi boat.

Adam's heart bumped within him. 'Good God,' he said. 'That conceited fool——'

He saw everything. Villiers, showing off ridiculously, had somehow overturned the boat. Somewhere, far out in mid-lake, weighed down by wet clothing, lungs choked with green water, Sally was drifting, pale and drowned . . .

William's command of low-class Italian now proved of great practical value. Forcing their way through the crowd of excited bystanders — who were agglomerating at the landing-stage with the spontaneity of a bee-swarm — they were able to accost the fishermen the instant their craft drew alongside. Out of much chatter and finger-pointing William extracted and interpreted the gist.

'They say it was drifting — over there — it hadn't been upset or anything——'

That much was obvious. Though the cushions were missing, the Gandolfi boat was quite dry within. A volume of poems lay open and wind-ruffled just where it had been left. Nor was there any sign that the occupants had gone overboard to swim: there was no heap of clothing.

One of the fishermen was drawing attention to the painter. William said:

'It was trailing in the water. He thinks it wasn't tied up properly.' The fisherman gabbled on, with much illustrative sweeping of the arm. Adam gathered, even before William spoke again, that the lake-currents would never have taken the boat to the point where it was found if it had broken loose from its normal mooring below the villa. The fishermen had come upon it at the south-western corner of the lake, near the old monastery . . .

Everything was suddenly plain. Adam tried to sound relieved and matter-of-fact, though one cause for foreboding had replaced another. He thanked the fishermen and rewarded them with a couple of *scudi*. Then he took hold of the sodden painter as an indication that he was assuming all further responsibility. The crowd, disappointed in its hopes of tragic drama, dissolved into the market again.

'They must have gone over to look at the ruins,' said Adam.

'That place they were talking about yesterday?'

'Yes. I expect they landed just for a few minutes — they'd be horrified when they came back and found the boat gone.'

'They mayn't have found out yet.'

Adam gave him a keen look. It was just what he was afraid of, himself. 'What makes you say that?' The children growing up in the villa, seemed to develop a precocious insight.

'I don't think Mr. Villiers meant to be back for dinner,' said William. 'Primavera laughed at me when I said he was whispering to Maria about food. But he *was*. She gave him a little basket, with a white cloth over the top, and there was a bottle of wine sticking out. He smuggled it down to the boat. Nobody but me saw him.

176

Even Miss Forester didn't know. I expect he was planning a nice surprise for her.'

'I expect so.'

There was a moment's silence before William said: 'It's not a bit like Mr. Villiers——'

Adam was afraid it was all too like Mr. Villiers. He was considering rapidly what it was best to do. 'What isn't?' he asked mechanically.

'Not mooring the boat properly. He knows more about boats than any of them. He taught me how to do knots.'

'Perhaps,' said Adam grimly, 'his mind was on other things.'

'How will they get back? It's miles and *miles* round by the shore. And it's all woods over that side — no villages or——'

'I shall row across to them.'

'Oh, can I come with you?'

Adam hesitated. For some reasons he would have liked the boy's company. His presence might have helped to ease a situation which promised to be tricky. Damn it, though, these poor children were sufficiently involved already in the follies of their elders! Why drag the boy into another?

'I think you had better go back to the villa. Somebody may have seen the boat being towed — or some rumour may get round to them — they may have a fright. So, go home as fast as you can. Explain to your mother what has happened. Say I'm taking the boat over to pick them up. It may take time. Don't worry if we don't get home for dinner.'

'Then it's a good job I'm not coming,' said William, holding the boat while Adam stepped into it. 'I don't suppose Mr. Villiers took enough food for four.'

'I doubt if he bargained for three,' said Adam.

'Shall I give you a push?'

'That's just what I need, thank you, William.'

The boy shoved the boat out, Adam unshipped the oars, and swung clear of the other craft. For a few moments the boy stood waving under the plane-trees. Then he turned and trotted obediently away into the crowd.

Chapter Twelve

RECLINING on boat cushions and the wild thyme which carpeted the roofless cloisters, the truant couple could not see the lake behind them, now ruffled by Adam's gradual and slightly erratic approach.

'The monks chose a good spot,' said Sally drowsily, 'if they really wanted to get away from the world.'

Villiers too thought the spot well chosen.

Not only had it an isolation which suited him as well as its monkish builders, but Time had dressed it in romance and ivy. Owls must, almost certainly, nest in the crumbling campanile. The shattered framework of a chapel window rose starkly beautiful above the cypresses: the full moon could be relied upon to shine straight through it, provided that one stood on the right spot on a fine night when the moon was full. In life, the monastery of San Remigio had been architecturally insignificant, possessing only one minor feature of distinction, the luxuriant orange-and-lemon motif of the cloister-capitals, which long-dead craftsmen had carved lovingly to recall the monks' introduction of fruit-growing to the Lucero district — or perhaps, no less lovingly (Villiers speculated, as his eye roved over the voluptuous globes and tapering tips of the sculptured fruit) to recall the pleasures of the world they had renounced. These carvings, the best of San Remigio, remained. The rest of the place had acquired a distinction by decay.

179

It was undeniably picturesque. When the shadows lengthened it would qualify as enchanted. If necessary — if he could find no other excuse to bring Sally willingly into his arms — he might have to suggest that it was haunted. But that would be a last resort. He had every hope that the situation would mature long before twilight. Even if it did not, a suggestion of spectres and phantoms (however agreeable round the supper-table at the villa) might not be the most persuasive argument for passing the night where they were.

Meanwhile, the day was yet young. The cloister-garth was golden with steep sunshine. Lizards scurried over the warm masonry. There was no sound but their own desultory conversation, the tireless song of the cicadas, the chuckling murmur of the tiny stream still racing through the stone troughs in the monks' *lavatorium*.

'I could stay here for ever,' she said. She lay back, hands clasped behind her head. She had taken off shoes and stockings to dabble her feet in the ancient basins. Her feet and calves stretched, wet and glistening, beyond the patch of shade.

'What would dear Harriet say?'

'Harriet is my friend. She's not my keeper.'

There's firmness in that chin, thought Villiers, small as it is. It wouldn't do to assume an easy victory.

He busied himself with the picnic basket. The bottle of wine was already cooling in the runnel of icy water. He spread the cloth beside her, set out the pink-and-white flakes of ham, the long loaf, the olives, fruit, cheese, the hard-boiled eggs glowing like ivory.

Sally laughed. 'For a man who acts on sudden impulses, you show remarkable forethought! You've brought enough for several meals. Or——' she glanced at him. 'Did you make Maria think that there were to be more than the two of us?'

'Would you want me to tell lies to the servants?'

'Of course not! I would hate it. I hate hypocrisy — I hate all these stupid little conventions. We wanted to see the ruins. It was a delightful idea of yours to bring me. Why turn straight round and row back, merely to eat dinner round a table with the others?'

'Exactly.'

Villiers fetched the wine, its pale plaited jacket beaded with water-drops.

'I don't know why they call it "white",' she said. 'It's like liquid gold. A drink for Greek gods.'

'And goddesses.' He raised his glass to her. 'Though Byron, who has been to Greece, tells me their wine tastes of turpentine.'

'Then we are that much better off than the Olympians. I should have woven you a garland! We passed some laurels.'

'Your hair does not need a garland.'

'You like it *à la bacchante*? Harriet thinks I ought to go back to my dull old central parting.'

He exclaimed in horror. 'You might as well go back to New England!'

'So I tell her. Don't worry. I won't do either.' She took more bread. Her teeth, biting the brittle crust, were small and nearly perfect. 'Come on, Villiers, you're not eating. You should be ravenous after rowing all that way.'

Villiers was, in fact, eating with rather less than the appetite which might have been expected. He was wondering how best to plan the next few hours. Cold ham and hard-boiled eggs did not combine well with schemes for seduction. His desire was mounting with every minute, and each mouthful was an effort.

He was beginning to wonder whether he knew her quite as well as he had thought he did. How far would

181

she go to practise the theories so enthusiastically discussed at the villa? How far had she (as women did) allowed the talk to wash over her, neither challenging it nor inwardly accepting it? Was more talk — however eloquent and persuasive — his best approach today? Or would it be better to let the situation ripen by undefined natural stages? In this, surely, her temperament would be his ally? Not for nothing had he stood so often beside her at the piano. It might be more accurate to say that he had watched and felt her — rather than listened to her — pouring out the strangely unsettling music of these modern Germans.

'Don't you really want this half-egg?' inquired the romantic girl. 'Then I guess I'll eat it before the ants do.'

Villiers had considered suggesting a bathe as the next move. If she agreed, it would be instructive to see if she imposed any barriers. As sunshine must be their only towel, the aftermath of their swim might produce the decisive moment. But she was making so hearty a meal that it might be dangerous for her to enter those cold depths. It was one thing to be seized with uncontrollable passion, another to be seized with cramp.

'More wine,' he said, and refilled her glass. It might be better just to stay where they were, and trust to the help of wine, proximity, and the languors of a southern afternoon.

He must be patient. She hadn't yet even mentioned going back. It would be ironical — rather vexatious even — if she did not miss their boat until its absence was no longer vital. . . . Still, if the situation did mature faster than he had dared to hope, it would be worth having the night too in which to repeat the raptures of the afternoon.

Let tomorrow take care of itself. They would get home

eventually. There must be a farm or a village somewhere with a vehicle of sorts. . . . And the Mortimers would be scanning the lake. I can fly a signal from one of the trees on the shore, thought Villiers amusedly — my shirt, perhaps, like a castaway in one of Mother Mortimer's absurd stories — only it will hardly be a signal of distress. Quite other . . .

It was at this moment that Adam, red-faced and sweating, came stumbling urgently through the ruins and saw them there.

'Adam!' Sally's tone was incredulous. Whether she was pleased or displeased was anyone's guess. 'How ever did *you* get here?'

'In the boat,' Adam answered with deep feeling. He had sculled himself across at top speed in the heat of the day. He was also considerably moved within. His immediate emotion was intense relief. Seeing the girl reclining there beside the picnic debris, surprised but unembarrassed, he knew that all was not lost. Indeed nothing was lost, by the look of it, except Sally's appetite, and that at least was replaceable.

'In *our* boat? But you couldn't! It's tied up down there——'

'It is now,' Adam agreed dourly. He turned to Villiers, who had jumped to his feet, but seemed momentarily at a loss for words. 'It was found drifting and towed into Lucero. I happened to be in the town, so——'

' "Happened?" ' Villiers erupted. 'You've been spying on us, poking your damned long ugly nose into our private affairs——'

'Look here, Villiers——'

'If you weren't, what made you think we'd be here?'

'Oh, surely,' Sally interposed, 'didn't you say you'd told the maid where we were going?'

'I forget. I — I expect so——'

Adam turned slowly and looked down at her. She had jumped to her feet, but looked younger and smaller than usual without her shoes and stockings.

'Did *you* know you were coming here?'

She flushed at his tone. 'Not till we were on the lake. It was Villiers' suggestion. A very charming suggestion,' she added with emphasis. 'And perfectly harmless.'

'Except to an old woman like Adam,' said Villiers offensively.

'I certainly can't make out why he's so mad at us,' Sally complained. 'One might think you'd fixed it for the boat to break loose on purpose.'

'Didn't you?' Adam asked Villiers.

'I don't know what the devil you're suggesting, Adam!'

'You know perfectly well what I'm suggesting. You've as good as hinted at a scheme like this when you've talked to me——'

'*Adam!*' The sheer lack of sex-loyalty left Villiers for the moment speechless.

'I think it's pretty obvious,' Adam told Sally, genuinely thinking that it was. 'This place is miles from anywhere. Villiers wanted you to be stranded here over-night——'

'And *I* think it's outrageous!' Sally's eyes swam with tears of fury. 'You all misjudge Villiers, you're all against him. Harriet's bad enough. But if *you're* going to start——'

'He *is* just another Harriet.' Villiers recovered speech and self-confidence together. 'Harriet in trousers. Nothing more nor less than——'

'I think that's enough, Villiers.'

'If you were half a man, you'd have something better to do with your time than creeping round us like——'

184

'I said that was enough,' Adam shouted, and swung a clout to the side of Villiers' head which sent him reeling backwards over egg-shells and olive-stones.

'You — bounder!'

Villiers came forward with spirit, fists clenched and scientifically positioned. Adam, never having had the honour of sparring with Lord Byron at Cambridge, could think of only one thing to do, which was unoriginal but not ineffective. He hit Villiers rather hard on the chin. Villiers sat down on the tablecloth.

'I think that was *brutal*!' cried Sally, stooping to help him. 'If gentlemen can't settle their differences by an appeal to reason——'

'Oh, to Hell with reason!' said Adam rudely.

Villiers got up, somewhat shakily, and submitted to Sally's brushings and dabbings. 'The trouble is,' he said stiffly, 'that Adam is not a gentleman.'

'Say that again——' and it was unfortunately true that Adam's voice reverted momentarily to the rustic accents of his native village. 'Say that again, and I'll dob you another one on the nose!'

'I'm not going to brawl with you, my dear fellow——'

'Good!'

'I am quite prepared to give you the benefit of the doubt——'

'You'd better!'

'If you *are* a gentleman, you will realise that you've cast the most disgusting imputations on my honour. You will apologize——'

'I'm damned if I will.'

'Then you know what to do.'

Villiers' tone and attitude were both so melodramatic that there was no room for doubt as to his meaning. Sally put a hand to her mouth.

'No! Not a duel!'

185

Adam laughed aloud, though angrily, at the absurdity of it all.

'Don't worry. I'm certainly not going to fight any duel.'

'Then apologize,' said Villiers.

'I shall do nothing of the sort.'

'You mustn't fight,' Sally pleaded, round-eyed.

'I'm afraid we must,' said Villiers, beginning to enjoy the new situation. 'I never travel without my pistols. But if Adam prefers swords, no doubt we can get hold of some in Lucero. He naturally has the choice of weapons.'

Adam laughed again. 'Suppose I say fowling-pieces?'

'The choice must be reasonable.'

'I should say that was eminently reasonable. They are the only type of firearm I've ever handled. And I know nothing about fencing.'

'There is a certain convention about these matters,' said Villiers in his most superior tone.

'I thought you disdained convention?'

'You see what I mean?' Villiers turned appealingly to Sally. 'What can I do? This fellow doesn't speak the same language.'

Now that there seemed to be no serious danger of bloodshed the girl abandoned her pacific rôle. The idea of a duel (so long as it was not realised) was intensely romantic and might as well be enjoyed.

'I do think you're behaving rather uncouthly, Mr. Adam. You were very insulting to Mr. Villiers.'

'He was very insulting to me.'

'But you hit him too. Twice.'

'I shall be very glad to hit him again. Any time. If he's so set on fighting me.'

Villiers, who was no coward, said he was quite prepared to take Adam on with bare fists if the genteeler modes of combat were denied him.

'That's not fair,' Sally objected. 'He's stronger than you. Brute force proves nothing.'

Adam could not see that skill with sword or pistol proved much more. He shrugged his shoulders.

'I seem to have spoilt your excursion. To you, Miss Forester, I do apologize for upsetting you.'

'Thank you. You have upset me very much.' Sally's eyes were shining, her bosom heaving most attractively. She was looking at her best and most vital. She knew it.

'I'll go back to the villa now. As I brought the boat over, you will not mind if I use it for the return journey? I shall be very happy to take either or both of you with me. But if you really consider I've been poking my nose in, unwanted, you have only to stay where you are, and the *status quo* is restored. Your boat has drifted away, you have no means of getting home tonight, but — as Villiers will assure you — there is no cause for alarm.'

'Stop it!' cried Sally. 'Naturally, as you've been kind enough to bring the boat back, we'll go with you.'

'Of course,' Villiers agreed. 'In this respect — without prejudice to the other difference between us — Miss Forester and I are vastly obliged to you.'

He began rather sulkily to collect the cushions. Sally sat down with her back to them and put on her stockings. Adam, who had not dined and was now feeling hollow, seized a hunk of bread and cheese before the picnic basket was repacked.

The voyage home was taciturn. The men took an oar each and rowed with a harmony they were far from feeling. Adam, rowing bow, was able to contemplate Villiers' silken-shirted back and, beyond him, Sally's far more acceptable front. She avoided his eyes, however, and he got the impression that she was avoiding Villiers' too.

Once, in an effort to break the awkward silence, the demon of mischief impelled Adam to suggest a song.

'What's that thing the fishermen are always singing?' he asked. 'How does it go? "Neither by night nor by day do we pass the dark wood"?'

The suggestion was not taken up. It was a relief to all of them when they saw the terraced headland and the villa hanging over them like the stern of some huge man-o'-war.

It could not, of course, be allowed to rest there.

The situation offered so many fascinating facets for discussion. It was not every day that a tension in the household snapped so dramatically and (admit it) so enjoyably. The villa rustled with the exchange of confidences, comments, suppositions, innuendoes.

Mortimer was furious. He was in what the children called 'one of his tempers' and what he himself preferred to consider 'a generous anger'. Though normally (he insisted) the most placid and equable of men, he was angry that one of his guests had been mortally insulted by another, if not literally under his own roof, at least in almost equivalent circumstances.

No, thought Adam, you are really angry because it was *not* under your roof. You are furious because you were not even there, much less the central figure in the scene.

Mortimer had demanded a private word with him on the terrace immediately after supper. It would have been more private if Mortimer had not declaimed at the top of his voice. As he grew more and more excited, his accents became broader and broader Yorkshire. Adam found, to his slight irritation, that his own retorts took on a Nottinghamshire timbre.

As was the way, in argument, the original cause was

188

fading into oblivion. The dubious circumstances of the picnic were no longer under discussion. Adam had been offensive to Villiers, assaulted him, and refused him the satisfaction of a gentleman.

'I wish you would make up your mind, sir.' Adam's courtesy was wearing thin.

'Make up my mind? About what?'

'I thought you no longer believed in gentlemen. "All men are created equal—— " or whatever it is. I thought you disapproved of force as a means of settling disputes. Yet you want a duel.'

'I do *not* want a duel, if it can be avoided!'

'Yet you accept it as a possibility.'

'Only because of the disgusting accusations you have made against poor Villiers!'

'"*What is there disgusting between the free union of human souls and bodies, untrammelled by the outworn conventions of superstition and society?*"' For once, Mortimer looked less than gratified to hear an apt quotation from his own writings. Adam pressed the point home. 'I am not suggesting Villiers planned anything that *you* would have disapproved of. In theory. So, from your standpoint, there's no insult. I wish you'd be consistent.'

'"Consistent?"' howled Mortimer. 'Whatever else my enemies may have alleged against me, I flatter myself that no one has ever been able to charge me with inconsistency. I hesitate to remind you, sir, but I am essentially a philosopher. My life has been conducted in accordance with an intellectual scheme. I have made Reason and Logic the keystone of that system. You dare to stand there, and tell me . . .'

He said a great deal more. When Adam could get a word in again he said quietly:

'I think it would be better if I went.'

'So do I, sir! Much better.'

189

'I will pack my things, then.' He turned to go. But Mortimer was enjoying the scene too much to let the curtain come down so abruptly.

'You can't go tonight. The gates will be shut. And I can hardly ask Villiers to take you across in the boat.'

'Then I'll leave first thing in the morning. Perhaps you will be kind enough to lend me the garden-boy — he can bring the boat back.'

Mortimer waved away these prosaic arrangements which threatened to bring down the dramatic temperature.

'It has always been my fate to be imposed upon,' he said darkly. 'I consider you have abused my hospitality. We welcomed you to our harmonious little community — you used the pretext of your Antonian translation to settle in our midst—— '

'Don't worry,' Adam interrupted curtly. 'I told you all weeks ago that this *wasn't* Antonian's lake. Not that you were interested. I shall clear out of the whole district as soon as I can get a seat in the diligence.'

He marched off to tell Mrs. Mortimer. She seemed genuinely sorry that he was leaving, but did not try to change his mind. She merely pressed him to accept back the unused part of his weekly contribution to the house-keeping. They compromised amiably: it should be set aside for William, whose pocket-money was usually uncertain and never large.

The morrow should have been overcast, with louring cloud-masses and an imminent threat of weeping skies — if Nature had (as it nowadays seemed the fashion to suppose) the least sympathy with human affairs. Instead, the morning was radiant. The lake (as the garden-boy sculled Adam and his baggage across the bay) wore a million twinkling, rippling smiles.

His departure had been early and unobtrusive, to rob

Mortimer of any chance to stage pompous farewell scenes on the landing steps — all those balustraded flights, going down terrace by terrace, would have tempted him irresistibly. Adam was only sorry that he could not say goodbye to Sally. He suspected that she was vexed with him because he had made Villiers look ridiculous yesterday, but he could not believe that she was so small-spirited as to let him go without a word. However, the American ladies did not come down. He scribbled a polite note which was so innocuous that even Harriet would scarcely resent it. He gave it to Maria, finished his preparations, and as there was no sign of reaction from upstairs went down to the landing steps. It was hard not to glance up at the windows of the villa, but he managed not to do so.

He was not likely to see them again, any of them. Tomorrow if he could arrange things in time, he would leave Lucero. 'For ever . . .' he would have added automatically, if he had been more truly one of the Mortimer tribe. As it was, he refused to commit himself to so sentimental a decision. Some day, years hence when the Villa Gandolfi had acquired new tenants, he might well revisit the scene of this strangest vacation. Lucero would always have some exquisite memories . . .

But now he must move on. The vacation was burning away to its end. In another week or two he must be thinking of the long return journey. Was there time to go on to Rome as he had planned? Would it be simpler to go to Venice? Or should he use the dwindling days for one final effort to identify Antonian's native countryside elsewhere among the northern lakes?

He was undecided. Or rather he was uninterested. There was only one thing he felt he must do, after that unseemly row with Mortimer last night, and that was to get away from Lucero. But there was only one thing he wanted to do, and that, he realised with some disquiet at the violence of his feeling, was to stay.

The Signora welcomed him back to the Tre Corone with such demonstrations of delight that he had not the heart, in the first moment, to tell her that it was only for a single night. Soon a smile-wreathed Brigitta was conducting him to his old room, laughing and gossiping as she thumped the mattress and flapped the clean sheets.

'I knew Monsieur would come back to us. The Isola d'Amore was no place for Monsieur.'

He caught at the name. 'The — what? What name did you say?'

'Isola d'Amore. *Ile d'Amour*.'

'Oh, I know what it means. But what island? There isn't an island? I've been staying on La Lingua.'

Brigitta nodded. 'That is the proper name, yes. But there is an old name also, people use. And' — she looked over her shoulder to give Adam a smile of some intimacy — 'the young people use the place itself. Monsieur understands?'

'Monsieur understands. But it isn't an island, it's a peninsula . . .' As he spoke, he remembered the boy Checco's ambiguous giggles when he had first inquired for an '*isola*'. The reason for the urchin's amusement became apparent.

'They say it was an island long ago, monsieur — the end part, where the Villa Gandolfi stands. You know, the river brings down soil from the mountains, the bay silts up, the currents change——'

He should have guessed it the first time he crossed the isthmus. It must have been made, some time since Roman days, by the detritus swept into the lake through the river-mouth only a mile or two distant. Tradition had preserved the ancient name. The Isola d'Amore was Antonian's *amoris insula*.

Adam's academic interest experienced a brief flutter of revival. The lost island would make splendid material for his introductory essay. Also it gave him the excuse — nay, the inescapable responsibility — of remaining in Lucero.

'Yes, Brigitta,' he said. 'You can unpack the books too — unpack everything.'

Chapter Thirteen

NOT for the first time in his life, Adam turned to work as an escape from emotion. Doggedly, line by line, he sought a felicitous equivalent for the Latin. Between long sessions at his table he explored the town, viewing landmarks with the new certainty that this place was indeed the setting of Antonian's poems, and collecting what scraps of corroboration he could for inclusion in his essay.

Thanks to Brigitta, he could point out that the peninsula of La Lingua had the alternative name, in local tradition, of Isola d'Amore. At her suggestion, he went to call upon one of the doctors in the town, a keen amateur geologist who conveniently spoke French: he confirmed, without hesitation, that the isthmus was a comparatively recent formation, created by changes in the lake currents and water-level in historic times. Another clue was provided by an elderly canon of the cathedral, a classical scholar and antiquarian, whom Adam visited primarily to ask about the Roman remains in the town itself. He volunteered the information, in passing, that the Roman masonry built into the church fabric at La Lingua had probably come not from inside Lucero but from outlying classical ruins on the promontory.

'It is said that when the Villa Gandolfi was built — in the sixteenth century originally — it was built on the foundations of an ancient palace. That is what the country people call it,' added the Canon with a smile. 'It would be just a villa, of course, of the classical period.'

'I wonder if any traces would be still visible.'

'I think not. I have often been to the Villa Gandolfi, in the old days. I do not visit there now.' He smiled again. 'But you know, perhaps, the family who are living in the house at present? A countryman of yours —— '

'I know him,' said Adam briefly. 'But I do not visit there, either.'

The Canon looked relieved. 'One does not wish to be uncharitable — one must allow for the ignorant gossip of country people, especially about strangers and foreigners who are also heretics, if you will excuse the expression . . .'

Adam would have excused far worse expressions. The manner of his departure from the villa still rankled. It did not improve his temper to realize that, for several weeks past, he had been living on the very spot once trodden by Antonian, and that now he could not revisit it without the most unpalatable humiliation.

But be honest, he told himself: you care very little about poking in the wine-cellars of the villa for surviving traces of Roman masonry. You care less and less, comparatively, about Antonian and all his works. What really gnaws at you is that you are denied Sally Forester. Adam is cast out of Eden, but Eve remains inside.

I suppose, he thought, I am in love with this girl. . . . I know it is all hopeless — hopeless, that is, in any sense that would be recognized at home in England. There can be no question of marriage. Damn it (he muttered at this point, emotion bringing his thoughts to audible form), I'm no better than that dog, Villiers, really! I'd take anything I was offered, if I had the chance, if the girl went into it with open eyes. . . . Why shouldn't I, too, have my vacation romance, even if it is foredoomed to wither at the advent of the autumn term?

I am, he reflected, getting completely demoralized.

I do not care. I cannot make myself care. I am in love.

What does it matter? I am nothing to her. Probably I shall never see her again.

But he could not help hoping. As he passed through the streets and squares of Lucero he searched the arcades and shop doorways, lest he should miss a glimpse of her in the shadows. He would patrol the waterfront in case the Gandolfi boat was moored there: if he had seen it, he would have scoured the town for the chance of a meeting. Sometimes he took his writing to a café table from which he could watch the crowds passing and repassing. As a method of work he found it futile, for he could not string half a dozen words together without glancing up at the next voice or footstep. As a means of seeing Sally it proved equally fruitless. The Mortimers and their guests never seemed to visit the town.

In the solitude of his room he wrote with greater concentration. Letters, carefully phrased, which he sent to Sally. Poems, more freely expressed, which he did not. Both, in some degree, relieved his feelings. But he had to recognize that he had changed, almost alarmingly, during the past few months. The running of the ink was no longer a satisfactory substitute for the pulsing of the blood.

There were times when he wished that Brigitta would not linger, brightly chattering, when she brought his coffee or spread his bed-clothes over the balcony. It would have been easier if Sally had answered his letters, but she did not. Against her cold silence Brigitta provided a tantalising contrast.

'Monsieur is not married?' she would inquire, her tone light as the flick of her feather-duster.

'No.'

'But Monsieur is not a priest?'

He explained wearily that he was not in Holy Orders. Even if he were, that would not (in itself) prevent his marrying. Brigitta must understand that he was, from her viewpoint, a heretic.

'A heretic is a man, though,' she reminded him generously. 'But Monsieur, I think, cares only for his books?'

'Yes,' he agreed desperately. He snatched up a volume almost at random. 'I will go to the café for a little while. It will give you a chance to clean my room properly——'

'Oh, Monsieur, I must not drive you away!'

'You're not driving me away.'

'But, yes, when I come here, Monsieur always makes an excuse. He goes out. Is Monsieur afraid of something?'

She twinkled at him. She was, at that moment, irresistible. He found himself kissing her. Her co-operation was enthusiastic. Neither of them heard the tap on the door. It was repeated. This time Brigitta heard it and released him with a stammered warning.

'There is somebody——'

'Come in,' Adam shouted.

Harriet came in, coldly beautiful despite the stairs she had just climbed. She was dressed for the town, with a hat he had never seen, like a Greek helmet. She carried her parasol as though it were Mercury's wand.

'I trailed you here. The old woman pointed up the stairs.'

Adam was conscious that he must look as confused as he felt. 'I — I'm sorry about . . .' He indicated the unmade bed. Brigitta had just draped everything to air on the balcony.

'That doesn't worry me, Adam. You know the way *I* feel about the conventions.'

'You wouldn't sooner——'

'This will do well enough. For all I have to say,' she added severely. 'I just want a quiet word with you. It seems quiet enough up here.'

Brigitta flicked a chair and thrust it forward. Harriet sat down with a murmur of thanks and a long, reflective stare. The Italian girl went out, closing the door vigorously.

'I'm very glad to see you,' said Adam.

'I wondered if you were. Not without reason, you'll admit.'

Adam admitted nothing. He leant against the table. 'How is Miss Forester?'

Harriet pursed her lips. 'Well . . . but upset.'

'About what?'

'You must stop pestering her, Adam.'

'Pestering?'

'All these letters——'

'Three!'

'Three too many.'

'If she would answer *one*, Miss Seeley, at least I should know that——'

'She will answer none of them, you can reckon on that. She is not interested in your attentions. She'll continue to ignore them. And as her friend, Adam, who has known her for a good many years, I'd be obligated if you'd give over worrying her.'

Adam studied his shoes. At length he said slowly:

'I really don't see why my writing to Miss Forester should annoy her. If it annoys *you*, that's regrettable but irrelevant. So far as she's concerned, I've always understood that no young woman minds a sincere expression of admiration——'

'Sincere?' Harriet all but hooted. 'If I were to go back and tell Sally the kind of life you seem to be leading here!'

'The — oh,' Adam laughed awkwardly, 'don't jump to any false conclusions. I can explain——'

'There is no need.' Harriet rose, gathering up parasol and reticule. 'I've said all I had to say. Please stop this senseless letter-writing. It's quite hopeless.'

'Does she say that? Or do you?'

'I speak for both of us.'

Adam looked at her keenly. 'Did Sally ask you to come here?'

'No. It was my own idea.'

'Does she know you came?'

Harriet hesitated briefly. 'No. I slipped away — that's why I called on you so early in the morning. Rather *too* early, perhaps.' She flung up her head defiantly, her grey eyes meeting his stare. 'She prefers to ignore your conduct completely. It's just that I wanted to save your wasting your time. She'd be mad at me if she knew.'

'I suppose,' said Adam bitterly, moving to open the door, 'I should feel — what was the word? — "obligated" to you?'

'I am only trying to do the best for everybody. You must try to be reasonable.'

Adam opened the door. Brigitta stood on the threshold.

'You were listening?' he demanded indignantly, while Harriet's expression indicated that she was shocked without being surprised.

Brigitta's indignation was greater than Adam's.

'No, no, monsieur! I was raising my hand to knock! There is another young lady asking for Monsieur downstairs. A young English lady.'

'Sally!' cried Adam delightedly.

'A young *American* lady,' Harriet corrected Brigitta. Though deeply chagrined by this new development, she was not going to surrender what Washington had won.

199

'It is the same thing,' said Brigitta with an indifferent shrug.

'It is not the same thing,' Harriet insisted. Her French (Adam noted with gratification) was no better than his own. 'Tell the young lady I am coming down at once.'

'She has asked for me,' Adam reminded her. 'However, as you are about to go, I will see you downstairs.' He bowed. 'If you will allow me . . .' And, finding etiquette convenient, he led the way down, eager for the first glimpse of Sally and wondering in what mood she had come.

It was not Sally, however, who stood waiting with the deferential Signora in the paved yard below. The face which turned and lifted at his footstep, glancing up through the trellised vines, pink and white, like a kitten in a fashionable bonnet, was the face of Miss Julia Challand.

'Good God!' said Adam under his breath.

'Good morning, Mr. Adam,' said the youngest Miss Challand. But her welcome had curdled somewhat at the sight of Harriet.

'This *is* a surprise,' he said more loudly. This was, even by the urbane standards of an Oxford common room, a supreme understatement.

'We are just passing through on our way home from Venice,' said Miss Challand brightly. 'We are all here,' she added, as though that made it any better.

'How delightful! What a coincidence!' Adam was conscious of Harriet's brooding presence at his elbow. 'May I present you two ladies to each other? Harriet, this is Miss Julia Challand of Oxford — her father is Warden of St. Columb's.'

'Glad to know you, Miss Challand.'

'And this is Miss Harriet Seeley. She came over recently from Boston, in the United States.'

Miss Challand appeared more interested in the fact that Harriet had just come down from Adam's room.

'Indeed?' she said sweetly. 'Is it usual in the Colonies for young ladies to visit gentlemen in their rooms?'

'I have no idea, Miss Challand. I have never, thank God, set foot in a colony.'

'I am so sorry, Miss Seeley. Of course, America does not count.' Harriet let this ambiguous statement pass without comment. 'In England, of course, the conventions are stronger.'

'I guess our American conventions are as strong as anybody else's—— ' began Harriet with patriotic fervour, and then stopped, biting her lip with vexation.

Adam could not help interposing, maliciously: 'That is why Miss Seeley fled to Europe, in search of freedom.'

'I am sure she will feel quite at home here,' said Miss Challand, 'provided she remains on the Continent.'

There was a momentary pause.

'Well—— ' said Adam.

'I was just going,' said Harriet. 'I am happy to have made your acquaintance, Miss Challand.'

'You don't mind walking through these streets alone?' inquired Miss Challand. 'Your parents do not object?'

'No more than yours, apparently.'

'Ah, my father would be vexed if he knew. He left me lying down with a headache — he has taken my two sisters to look at antiquities. Then, suddenly, my headache departed.'

Harriet nodded with understanding, if not with sympathy. 'And so must I,' she said. 'Goodbye, Miss Challand.' Adam went with her to the gates of the inn-yard. She said, lowering her voice and with a meaning glance towards Brigitta who was pottering about some

domestic duty in the middle distance: 'I must admit I
had been wondering what was really still keeping you in
Lucero, when we all thought you were leaving the town.
This visit has been most enlightening.'

'Is it wise to jump to too many conclusions? After all,
Miss Challand looked very suspiciously at *you*.'

She laughed angrily. 'I am used to being misunderstood. It's no novelty. Goodbye, Adam.'

'Goodbye, Miss Seeley.'

He went back to Julia.

'You have found yourself a very pleasant haunt,' she
said.

'It is quiet for my work. I had no idea you were coming
to Italy.'

'We persuaded Papa. Everybody was coming to the
Continent this year. We met Mr. Seabrook in Paris.'

The traitor, thought Adam, half angry, half amused.
Only Seabrook, in all the wide world, knew Adam's where-
abouts. He had written to nobody else, not even Pritchard,
since he had arrived in Lucero.

The Challands, it appeared, had spent the night at the
Colomba d'Oro and proposed moving on tomorrow. They
would not have stopped in Lucero at all, but for a sudden
indisposition which had unaccountably seized Julia on
the previous afternoon, while their horses were being
changed.

'I heard you were staying in the town,' she said, as he
began to escort her across the piazza back to her own inn.
She did not say whether she had heard that morning or
(as he was privately certain) in Paris. It would be illumin-
ating to see whether her father and sisters showed surprise
at his presence. 'It would be better, though, if Papa
thought that *you* had heard of *our* arrival, and had called
to pay your respects.'

'Of course.'

'Papa would not like to think of my walking through the town by myself. The Italians *stare* at a young lady so much, don't they?' she said with transparent pleasure. 'It's most distasteful.'

'Your adventure,' he said gravely, 'shall be a secret between us.'

'That makes two, Mr. Adam.'

'Two secrets?'

'Surely. Tell me about your beautiful American lady.'

'There is really nothing to tell.'

'That usually means, there is nothing you *will* tell.'

Adam laughed. 'I can assure you, Miss Julia —— '

'Yes?'

'I met Miss Seeley at a villa near here, where she is spending the summer. I myself spent some weeks there —— '

'As her guest, Mr. Adam?'

'Heavens, no! Some English people I met by accident — Mr. and Mrs. Matthew Mortimer —— '

'Not the author? Is he still alive?'

'Very much so,' said Adam with feeling. 'Surely you have not read any of his books?'

'Papa forbade us to. He said they were immoral.'

'Possibly. I would rather say they were dull.'

'So I found. I would not tell Papa that you have been staying with such a man, Mr. Adam. He would not like the idea of your being friends with an irreligious republican. . . . We had better keep that secret too.'

'I am not friends with Mortimer — now.'

'Indeed?' Julia turned her head and looked up sharply at him from the shadowy depths of her bonnet. 'Does that mean yet another secret?'

'I think we have enough already, haven't we?'

'I might get to four — just by putting two and two

together,' she mused. 'You met Miss Seeley at the Mortimers' where you were both staying. You are no longer friends with the Mortimers . . . but I must not be inquisitive. Your friendship with Miss Seeley is unaffected, in fact you seem to be on terms of some intimacy——'

'This is a real comedy of misunderstandings,' said Adam lightly, and meant it. Julia could insinuate what she liked about Harriet, so long as she did not learn of Sally's existence.

'It does not matter if *I* misunderstand a little,' she answered generously. 'I am not a prude like Charlotte and Sophia. It doesn't shock me if young gentlemen are a little wild — before they settle down. Papa might take a stricter view. But you can rely upon me to say nothing about Miss Seeley.' The very assurance was overlaid with subtle menace.

'You might find it hard to do otherwise, as you have never — officially — visited the Tre Corone, and therefore don't know of her existence.'

'Ah, Mr. Adam, you'd be surprised how things can be made to crop up in conversation.'

They had reached the Colomba d'Oro, which stood in a busier part, just off the Piazza del Duomo. There were tables under an awning, from which the passing world could be watched through a lattice screen. Julia invited him to sit down there and wait for the return of the others. The thought of Harriet seemed to nag at her. Adam had never known her so talkative, but then he had never been alone with her. In the past half-hour she had said more to him than in all their previous acquaintance.

'Miss Seeley dresses . . . conspicuously. Not what I had imagined to be the colonial taste.'

'I fancy she has bought new clothes in Europe. Even so, Americans don't all live in the backwoods, you know.'

She raised her eyebrows at the phrase, which he realised he had caught from Sally. 'Miss Seeley belongs to one of the leading families in Boston.'

'Indeed?'

'She's extremely well-off, I believe. An heiress, you might say.'

Adam gave this explanation out of fairness to Harriet. Now his sense of humour was satisfied, he could not let Harriet be thought of as a disreputable adventuress.

'Your remark about her parents was unfortunate,' he added. 'Like you, she has no mother. Unlike you, she has also lost her father. It is not her fault if she has to come out without an escort.'

Julia received this information with ill-concealed dismay.

'You mean — she's not only an heiress, she's already come into her inheritance? She has control of her fortune?'

'I believe so.'

'Then I am sorry for her.' But Julia looked sorry only for herself. 'She's at the mercy of every unscrupulous fortune-hunter she meets.' There was a sting in her voice.

'You needn't waste your sympathy, Miss Seeley can look after herself,' said Adam with feeling, which too late he realised Julia might misunderstand.

At that moment they heard Dr. Challand's fractious voice, refusing the inflated demands of the man who had been his guide.

Dinner with the delighted Challands was inescapable. The rest of the day, Adam realised, was equally lost, and he was surprised to find how little he minded. It was a relief to talk English freely for the first time since leaving the villa. Inexperienced in foreign travel, he now learnt

the illogical pleasure of unexpectedly meeting an acquaintance — even one you normally disliked — provided the
distance from home was sufficiently great.

'We heard you had gone on to Italy,' said the Warden.
His pale eyes bulged amiably from their pouches.

'But Mr. Seabrook could not for the life of him think
where you were making for,' twittered his eldest
daughter.

'Mr. Seabrook is not so scatter-brained as he likes to
make out,' said Sophia darkly.

Julia, reverting to her normal rôle, said nothing.

'First time in my life I've missed the September rent-
collections,' the Warden explained, 'but this year I felt
I must think of the girls. They're growing up. Time
they saw something of the world. I am persuaded that
foreign travel, for a female, is highly beneficial.'

Adam had a good idea who had persuaded him.

'For myself, I'll be only too thankful to get back to
Oxford and eat a decent dinner. D'you know, Mr.
Adam, I've not come across a drop of port since we
entered Italy? Have you much luggage?' he demanded
abruptly.

Adam was taken aback. 'I'm not travelling round with
cases of my own port, if that's what you mean,
Warden——'

'No, no! Wouldn't stand the bumping about, anyhow.
Didn't mean that at all. No, I mean, you're travelling
light, I suppose.'

'Oh, yes, sir. Some books. Otherwise the minimum.'

'I thought,' said the Warden with elaborate casualness,
'you might care to travel back with us. There would be
room. We have two carriages. The weeks are slipping
by — I presume you will be planning your return very
soon now?' He looked almost wistful. He must,
thought Adam, be getting terribly tired of his daughters'

unrelieved company . . . but naturally the Warden of St. Columb's cannot cross Europe by public diligence.

'You are extremely kind, Warden — I deeply appreciate your thoughtfulness, indeed the honour you do me——'

'Not at all, not at all. Delighted to have you.' Challand's ripe face wrinkled almost benevolently.

'But I understand you are not staying long here?'

'Heavens, no. Nothing here. Want to get on, anyhow. Time I was back at Oxford.' He puffed out his cheeks at the thought of the College. 'No, we must be off to-morrow. Crack of dawn.'

He means it, thought Adam with relief. Not even Julia will get round him. He sniffs the decanters of home. . . . He won't rest now till he sees Magdalen Tower at the bottom of the hill.

'Then I'm extremely unlucky, Warden. Because I simply must have another week in Lucero.'

'Must?' echoed Sophia disapprovingly.

Challand glared, speechless at the rejection of his offer.

'Mr. Adam must have very important . . . affairs,' said Julia wickedly, 'to keep him in a quiet little town like this.'

'I have, Miss Julia. Important to me, and' — Adam turned to her father with the air of deference he liked — 'perhaps, I dare hope, not without importance to the College.'

He explained, without going into inconvenient details, the remarkable result of his researches into the life of Antonian. It was fortunate that the young ladies had never heard of the poet, for, in outlining the facts to them, he was able to inform their father without seeming to do so.

'So you see, Warden,' he concluded, 'how vital it is

to complete my work before I leave here? With these fresh facts — I might say, with this discovery — my translation may arouse a certain amount of notice in the world of scholarship. If it does nothing else, it will remind the Provost of Oriel that his college hasn't an intellectual monopoly.'

'It will give me personal pleasure to mention it to him,' said Challand, whose good-humour had flooded back as he grasped the meaning of Adam's discovery. 'You are quite right, my dear fellow. This book of yours will be an excellent thing for the College. We shall miss your company now, but a young man must put work first. Your self-denial does you credit. I am sure it won't go unrewarded.' He rubbed his hands. 'I shall look forward to seeing their faces.'

That's about it, thought Adam. You look forward to seeing their faces, but not to seeing my book. There have been some nasty digs, of late, about the stagnation of St. Columb's. You just want something to show your critics, so you can roll over and sleep for another ten years without disturbance . . .

He was agreeably surprised when the Warden reverted to the subject a few hours later when they were all perambulating the lakeside in the cool of the evening.

'If you go about things in the right way, Mr. Adam, this book of yours could be a great beginning.'

'I daren't have any exaggerated hopes, Warden.'

'Quite right, quite right. A book can fall flat as a pancake. Or it can become the foundation-stone of a reputation. I have known men,' said Challand wistfully, 'who have written one book before they were twenty-five and made such good use of it that they've lived another fifty years afterwards without needing to *read* another, much less write one!'

'How is it done?'

'Oh, interest, interest. I might be able to help you there.'

'You are very kind.'

'Not at all. I think I recognized your quality from the start. I am always prepared to back my fancy, Mr. Adam. But I do *not* like backing losers.' He glanced round. The three young women had dropped behind and were gazing raptly at the flamboyant sunset across the lake. 'There is another thing a young man must consider carefully when he has to make his way in the world. The choice of a wife can make all the difference to his career. Have you thought of marriage, Mr. Adam?'

'I am hardly in a position to do so. The Statutes——'

'You need not stay for ever where you are. The higher places in the world of learning are open to the married man. If he chooses the right partner. That is a vital point. I hope you, when the time comes, Mr. Adam, will choose wisely.'

Adam almost answered Amen. Instead, he murmured: 'I shall do my best to, Warden.'

'Do. I should not myself feel justified in exerting any influence on your behalf unless I were happy on that point.'

That's plain enough, anyhow, Adam reflected wryly.

'She must be a lady,' said Challand. 'She need not be of great intellect — that can be a disadvantage — but she must be at home in an academic atmosphere. A young man in your position can hardly expect her to bring much money with her — you have not the slightest hope of finding an heiress——'

'No,' Adam agreed. He wondered if Julia's mind was equally at ease on that point? It would be good for her if she lost a little sleep in unnecessary speculation about Harriet.

'You will pardon my frank speaking, Mr. Adam? I

believe you have no older relative to advise you on a
serious step like this? You must allow me to speak to
you as a father——'

'Of course, Warden.'

Crafty old humbug, he added to himself. Not as *my*
father, but as the father of three immovable girls.

Chapter Fourteen

Aᴅᴀᴍ despised himself for getting up early to wave the Challands on their way. But prudence certainly, if not courtesy, demanded it. What was Italy but an interlude, a rather fantastic interlude? As the Warden said, almost jovially as he waddled goutily to his carriage, 'We shall soon all be meeting again in Oxford'. Oxford was real life, all too soon to clamp round him again.

'Such a pity, *such* a pity, we cannot have the pleasure of your company, Mr. Adam! I know it can't be helped, but it *is* most unfortunate.'

'But unavoidable, alas, Miss Challand.'

'*I* respect a man who sticks to his decision.'

'Thank you, Miss Sophia.'

He helped to tuck them into the second carriage. Julia, who was to travel with her father in the first, appeared at his elbow. She smiled up at him, offering her hand and making no great haste to withdraw it.

'*I* forgive you, Mr. Adam, for staying behind,' she murmured, holding his eyes as firmly as his hand. 'Believe me, I understand. But . . . I shall look forward to seeing you next term.'

'Er — thank you,' said Adam apprehensively.

She let go his right hand only to transfer her clasp to his left, so that he could help her up the step.

'Good-bye,' she breathed.

'Good-bye, Mr. Adam,' cried her sisters.

The Warden gave a regal inclination of his head. The two carriages wheeled out into the street and went jingling out of sight.

'Thank God,' said Adam, resuming his hat. He walked down into the piazza, found a café just opening, and ordered breakfast. He was reluctant to go straight back to the Tre Corone. Though the Challands had gone, Brigitta remained, and for the moment he preferred to keep out of her way. He was not easy in the presence of that hospitable young woman. He could not honestly pretend that he had not enjoyed yesterday's brief, interrupted embrace, but he felt he should not have done. He was in love with Sally.

The past twenty-four hours had been so taken up by the Challands that only now could he review, at leisure, his conversation with Harriet.

There was only one thing she had said (he decided, biting moodily into a crisp warm roll) which he could safely believe: that Sally did not know about her visit. She had looked so alarmed when Brigitta had announced another lady.

Otherwise, he had learnt enough of women even from the Roman poets to know that Sally's reaction might take any one of several forms, and that Harriet's report of it might, again, bear no traceable resemblance to the truth.

Sally might never have received his letters: Harriet was quite capable of suppressing them.

Sally might have received his first letter — and answered it (in what terms?): Harriet was equally capable of destroying that reply and intercepting Adam's later communications.

Another thing: Harriet might have gone back to the villa and (at the price of revealing her visit to the Tre Corone) given Sally a warmly-tinted picture of himself wantoning with an Italian chambermaid. Conduct

Byronic enough in itself (if Villiers' sly hints were to be credited), but not likely to win Sally's favour for all that.

As for Miss Julia Challand . . . What would Harriet *not* make out of her sudden arrival in Lucero? By now, he thought gloomily, they have probably engaged me to her . . . She is my innocent English betrothed, who has followed me to Italy, little knowing of the double, nay, triple life I have been leading!

It was as well the Challands were now on the road to Milan. This morning, perhaps, Harriet would be sailing into the Colomba d'Oro, all primed with shocking revelations and warnings to pour (with a great show of reluctance) into the Warden's ear.

Adam took out a handkerchief and wiped his brow, which was moist either from the effects of the hot coffee or from the thoughts which crowded in upon him. A day in the Challands' company had reminded him unpleasantly of his insecure position in the world. A man must eat . . . Whatever else happened, he had got to go on living in Oxford. . . . If it came to trouble with the Warden (and Julia's manner promised it), at least let the trouble be real and based on something more than Harriet's disordered fancy.

Firmly he relegated all further thought of the Challands to the future. He could stay in Lucero another week, two weeks if he did not dawdle through France . . . But time was running out.

He must find out how things really stood at the villa. He must — somehow — get a glimpse of Sally. He could not go on like this another day. But he was not going to present himself cap in hand at the front door, giving Mortimer a chance to strike attitudes and Harriet to interfere. He would wait until dusk and be as unobtrusive as a poacher.

It was a long, long day. He had exhausted the antiquities of Lucero and he was avoiding, as far as possible, his room at the inn where he was vulnerable to Brigitta. And it was almost a fortnight since he had seen Sally.

In the end he sneaked back to the Tre Corone and borrowed the boat which was tied up, as usual, under his balcony. To have walked out to the villa, so late, would have meant applying for a special permit to re-enter the town. Since the Carbonari meeting the authorities had brought in new pettifogging restrictions. It was for that reason, too, that he found the boatmen of the piazza unwilling to hire out their craft after sunset. So he had no choice but to take the boat from the inn.

He had lived long enough at the villa to learn every yard of the indented shore. There was a good spot to hide the boat on the near side of the promontory, just where the isthmus swelled out and up into the rocky heights of the one-time island. The villa faced the other way and was screened by the woods. Unless any of the household happened to be strolling on this side — most unlikely at this late hour — his approach would be unobserved. To be safe, though, he kept as close in-shore as the river-current allowed him, hugging the land all round the margin of the bay until the twinkling lights of La Lingua village told him that he was nearing his objective.

Listening to the splash of his oars, he wished that his rowing was as quiet as his tread. But it was getting so dark now — there was just one faint patch of sunset, still echoed by the smooth water below it, and all else was a blotch of dark woodland and dark lake — that no one could possibly identify him. There was nothing in itself remarkable about a boat at this hour.

Ah, here was the spot . . .

214

He shipped his oars, put out a groping arm, met one of the overhanging branches he was expecting . . . The boat grated in the shallows . . . The side bumped against a jutting slab . . . Careful not to let go the painter, he scrambled ashore and made fast to a tree-trunk. Anyhow, he thought with acrid reminiscence, *this* boat isn't going to drift away!

A half moon, cool and yellow as a slice of lemon, stood over the vaguely piled-up mass of the town. It reminded him that it was only five weeks since he had first come to Lucero. It was the full moon before this which had brought Mortimer and his guests to see the Roman theatre on the very night of his arrival . . . Unbelievable that it was so short a time since that morning when he had first trudged up this stony path in the noonday glare, and caught that tantalizing glimpse of the unknown bathers. . . .

He trod quietly, glad of the strengthening moonshine to show up the pale ribbon of the path. Once he stopped, tense and rigid, certain that he was not alone in the fresh-scented night. A whisper, a liquid gurgle of laughing protest, reassured him that whoever was outdoors at this hour had no interest in his own passing. He went on his way silently, envying the unseen lovers. The Isola d'Amore seemed to have kept its distinctive tradition. Here Antonian had taken his pagan pleasures with slave-girl and senator's daughter. Here the village lads and lasses paired, on summer nights, as they had done down the ages, contentedly practising the theory which Harriet was solemnly scribbling tracts about, indoors, as though it were an idea newly discovered. And Sally and Villiers — where did they now fit into the island's long history of amours? What were they doing at this moment as he, rather ridiculously, an amphibious Romeo, came trespassing through the gloom?

That last question, at least, was reassuringly answered. As he came out of the pinewood and saw the house, its pale walls embroidered with great scrolls of wistaria, he heard the faint notes of the piano stealing out through the open windows. He tiptoed forward, taking advantage of the black shadows splashed by the cedar and the walnut-tree, and reached the steps leading up to the highest terrace. Here he sat down to consider his next move. The glass doors of the salon faced the top of the steps and a broad band of light poured through them. If he went any nearer, he would risk being seen, and, if that happened, he was not at all sure how he was going to carry it off.

Meanwhile, crouching below, with a shrubbery to offer cover if anyone suddenly came out to take the evening air, he could listen to the ripple of the music and imagine the scene within. Sally in the far corner at the piano, her dark head dipping and swaying as she played; Villiers, attendant beside her, bending forward to turn the music with a well-groomed hand; Harriet with grey eyes closed, in soulful communion with the composer; Mortimer, bolt upright in his chair, sleeping like a whiskered baby; Mrs. Mortimer stitching some mysterious small garment for one of the children and meditating some fantastic but eminently moral adventure to incorporate in her current story . . . He had taken part in so many similar evenings. He could see each detail, each pose, the play of candle-beam and shadow and polished surface, as though he were an artist recording it on canvas.

What now, he wondered?

In a romance, in an opera or a stage-play, things were more conveniently contrived. There would come a moment when the heroine, slipping from her piano-stool, would emerge upon the terrace in quest of fresh air, perhaps even leaning on the balustrade and soliloquizing informatively into the tops of the oleanders. Adam felt that there was little chance of Sally's coming out at all. If she did, Villiers would soon be after her. And (unless the whole situation had changed since his departure from the villa) Harriet would not be long behind Villiers.

Adam might wait all night to no purpose. Even Juliet, he remembered, had been allowed a bedroom to herself. But even if he could have trusted his weight to the wistaria, there seemed little point in climbing up to Sally's balcony.

He did not want to go back empty-handed, nor did he want to make a fool of himself. He felt sure — angrily sure — that Villiers in his place would have found a solution.

What *would* Villiers do if the places were reversed? It would depend on his mood. If feeling cool and sardonic, he was quite capable of appearing in the open doorway as though nothing had ever happened, putting on the others the onus of reviving a quarrel he chose to forget. Or, in more romantic vein, Villiers would rush in, unkempt as Hamlet, and throw himself at Sally's feet, ignoring not only the previous situation but the very presence of Mortimer and the rest. Or he would march up to Mortimer, offer his hand, and stage a manly reconciliation-scene, flattering the older man with so much deference that no one else would get the chance to enter the mildest *caveat*.

One thing Villiers would certainly not do. He would not for long sit on the steps of the terrace, listening to Beethoven.

Adam stood up, walked discreetly along beneath the balustrade, and mounted the flight of steps at the far end. Then, still more discreetly, he worked his way back, first past the blank windows of another room and then to those through which the light was streaming. Leaning cautiously forward he peered in.

There, just as he had pictured her, Sally sat at the piano, her fingers galloping to and fro across the keyboard. But Villiers was not in his accustomed place by her right elbow. In fact Villiers was nowhere in the room. Nobody else was there.

Adam did not know how many precious minutes he had wasted. He was too concerned to waste no more. The glass doors stood wide open to the night. He went in, crossed the glistening expanse of chequered floor, and stood beside her.

She was aware of him — at least she was aware of some-body — but she only bent forward with more intense concentration. Her face, he thought, studying her profile, had a hint of nervous strain — or *was* it just concentration, for the music sounded difficult? And she was paler than usual. . . . Or was that the candle-light? His eyes dropped to her hands. He had no idea whether she had been over-modest when she had said that she was an erratic amateur. There was decision in her touch, that much he could see, though his ear was untrained to criticise. Even when a series of insistent chords gave place to a quiet reflective melody, he found the same clean quality in her fingering of the keys.

He wanted to speak. The words dried in his throat. He wanted to put his arms round her. He dared not even lay an interrupting hand upon her wrist.

'I thought you had gone with the others,' she said, still playing.

There was something in her voice — what was it? But it could hardly mean anything. Her mind was on the music. Anyone would have sounded a little cold and mechanical. She had not paused, she had not turned her head. He was only a presence at her elbow, a blurred reflection in the polished rosewood. How long would it take her to realise that he was not Villiers? Would she say something more first, revealing the present state of her feelings towards that gentleman?

He could not read music, but by following the line of her eyes he judged when she was nearing the end of the right-hand page. He put out his arm, as he had so often watched Villiers do, finger and thumb poised to turn the music, as a schoolmaster preparing to tweak a pupil's ear. The effect on the girl was no less dramatic. She stopped playing, stared up at the unfamiliar hand, the unfashionable cuff, and then swivelled round on her seat, big-eyed with amazement.

'Oh, *no!*' She spoke with a strangled little gasp, as if this was really too much altogether. 'Not *you.*'

'Yes.' It was a relief to have uttered the first word. He felt as though the bottle was now uncorked. 'Why not?' he demanded.

'But — Mr. Mortimer would be furious! I thought he'd turned you out? Forbidden you ever to set foot in this house again?'

'That was the general effect, I believe. Though it was rather more of a mutual agreement at the time.'

'What are you doing here now? At this time of night?'

'I had to talk to you.'

'Oh, my God, no!' she burst out with a passion which took him quite aback. It was as though the feeling in the music had been transferred to her own life. 'I don't want to listen. I guess I don't *have* to listen.'

She turned to the keyboard with a gesture of dismissal and started to play again. The music slanted, slipped, and fell. She swept it impatiently to the floor and began playing something else from memory.

'Please — Sally——'

He put his hands on her bare shoulders. She shrugged

away the contact. He moved round the piano so that he could face her across the top. She glared at him, then avoided his glance.

He spoke through the music. 'I must talk to you!'

'There's a sight too much talk in this place,' she retorted, biting off the words as though they were threads between her teeth.

'You might stop playing——'

'Go away, Adam. If the others come back, there'll be an almighty row. *He'll* be mad at you, Harriet'll be mad at me. . . . I tell you, I can't stand it.'

As she spoke, he saw over her shoulder the door open at the far end of the long room. He braced himself for the scene she was prophesying, but it did not come. Only Mrs. Mortimer stood in the doorway, a sheaf of manuscript in her hand. She surveyed them across the desert of tiled floor and, without exclamation or gesture of recognition, went out silently closing the door after her. Adam was sure she had seen him. But Sally had seen nothing.

'Please go. They may be back any minute. You must.'

'On one condition.'

She stopped playing and looked up at him wearily. 'Condition?'

'I know we can't talk properly now. Come into Lucero tomorrow morning — make some excuse. I shall be in the cathedral at eleven o'clock. By the side-chapel, just to the right of the high altar.'

He was surprised at the incisive tone of his own voice. So was she, it seemed.

'Is that an order? I guess you all think I'm just a schoolgirl still.'

'Never mind. Be there. At eleven.'

'I'll do no such thing. Are you crazy, Adam? You act like it.'

'I wrote to you——'

'*And* I answered!'

'You did? I never got it! Did you ever get——'

There was no time for further explanation. Mortimer's rumbling voice could be heard outside, coming nearer and nearer like the first intimations of a thunderstorm. Sally jumped up.

'They're back! You must slip out the other way.'

'Promise you'll be there tomorrow morning!'

But she would not. 'If you won't go, I will,' she said breathlessly, and before he could get round the piano to stop her she went pattering across the salon and out through the open doors. He heard her greet the others with forced animation, keeping them on the terrace with her chatter about the moon and the perfumes of the garden.

She is working so hard to delay them, he thought, it would be churlish to let the effort go to waste. . . . Besides, she seemed fervently anxious to avoid a scene tonight. Had there been more scenes since he left? Was there any significance in his finding her here alone, playing to herself? She had once told him that music was something she withdrew into when the pressures of the world around her (a euphemism for Harriet?) became excessive.

He turned and slipped through the door at the near end of the salon. The room beyond was adequately lit with moonlight. He crossed to a window, raised it cautiously, and dropped into a shrubbery which on that side was eight or nine feet below. The corner of the villa screened him from the group still talking on the terrace. He would have liked to eavesdrop, but the risk was not worth while — to have been caught in that role, *after* paying his visit to Sally, would have been too undignified. Anyhow, if he saw her tomorrow she would bring him up to date with developments in the household.

If . . .

Will she come, he wondered, as he stepped with Red Indian unobtrusiveness across the garden?

She had at least answered his first letter. That meant little. It might have been no more than common politeness, an exchange of soothing courtesy after an acquaintance had ended with untidy abruptness and misunderstanding.

But had she had any of his later letters? Had she taken in the information — during those last excited whispers before they were interrupted — that her own letter had never got through to him? Looking back on those frenzied moments, Adam found it hard to be quite sure of what he had managed to say himself, so he dared not assume too much. However, she had certainly heard his demand for a meeting in the cathedral tomorrow. And, in case there was the slightest risk of her mistaking place and time, he would be in the building from ten o'clock onwards, patrolling the entire ambulatory until she came.

Surely she *would* come? Curiosity, if nothing else, would bring her. As for the practical problems of getting into Lucero and of throwing off, for half an hour, the companionship of the others, surely that wasn't beyond the wit of a girl like Sally? Easy-going she might be, but she had her rebellious moments. ' I guess you all think I'm just a schoolgirl still. . . . ' That had sounded like a cry from the heart. Yes, Sally was in a mood to come if she wanted to.

If she wanted to. . . . But she might not want to if, as something in her manner had implied, she was sick and tired of discussing personal relationships and emotional analysis — as well she might be, he reflected, after a summer in the Villa Gandolfi. If she felt no response whatever to his own ardour, she might save herself the embarrassment of coming to say so. But then, if she had never received his later, warmer letters——

If . . . if . . . if . . .

His brain spun with contradictory possibilities.

He had not even considered Villiers. If there was anything between her and Villiers, she would hardly keep a secret appointment with himself. But Villiers' name, he would swear, had never been mentioned tonight. She had been afraid of Mortimer's return — of Harriet's being 'mad at her' — but she had shown no special concern about the reaction of Villiers. So, as yet anyhow, he had no proprietorial claim.

I talk (he thought acidly) as if Villiers and I were rivals for her hand. Yet he has no intention of marrying her and I have no possibility. Antonian must have left a potent spell upon his island: it lingers still, and makes pagan satyrs of us all.

He was getting near the place where he had hidden the boat. He could see Lucero across the moonlit bay. Only an odd light pricked the huddled mass. The white walls glimmered palely. Above, darker, the battlemented *castello* crouched on the shoulders of the town.

Again he was aware that he was not alone on the peninsula, but this time, his mission finished, he did not even trouble to slacken his pace. Let the fortunate young *contadini* continue to enjoy their alfresco amours beneath the moon: he envied, but would not interrupt, them.

A white figure rose in the shadow of the cypresses. He walked on without the least turn of his head. He would pretend he had seen nothing, he had no wish to embarrass the girl. . . . But several other figures stepped out and barred his path, and he saw that they were not village damsels in white dresses but soldiers in uniform.

He did not understand their guttural questions any more than they seemed to grasp his Anglo-Italian protests.

Their levelled muskets and the firm way they gripped his arms left no doubt as to their general intention.

Adam was marched back ignominiously, through the sleeping village, along the road, and over the bridge into the town. After some tiresome formalities, lengthened by the absence of a common language, he was taken up to the fortress and pushed into a cell for what was left of the night. The cathedral clock was just striking two.

Chapter Fifteen

S UNRISE over the lake and town of Lucero was a spectacle of some considerable beauty, which in the next half-century (as the tourist traffic developed) was to challenge the brush of many an English water-colourist.

Adam, however, had seen it before — several times, indeed, during the past few weeks — and though the window of his cell high up in the *castello* provided him with a novel viewpoint he could well have dispensed with it, and with the original criss-cross effect of the grille through which he was compelled to peer.

Sleep had, of course, been unthinkable, and at first, by shouting, kicking, and beating on the door, he had tried to make it equally impossible for his guardians. They had unlocked the door once and, with a pained expression and without other reproach, taken away his boots. No one else came near him for the remainder of the night, and he decided that a dignified resignation would be the better course, especially as there was no movable furniture with which to supplement bruised knuckles and unprotected toes.

It was all, of course, an idiotic mistake. It would be put right, first thing in the morning, with suitable apologies, as soon as he could get past these illiterate numbskulls and explain himself to a responsible officer. He had been doing nothing illegal, not even poaching. Or if, by bad luck, he had offended against some new local regulation, he had only to establish his identity and British nationality, and he'd be released at once.

But they had better be prompt! He felt sour-mouthed and unshaven. He must get back to the inn, change his crumpled clothes, and swallow some breakfast, before going to wait for Sally in the cathedral.

Meanwhile, the hours were passing, and faster than they were supposed to pass for prisoners in solitary confinement. The cathedral clock marked their passage. His watch had been removed, along with his money and the other contents of his pockets. These had not, unfortunately, included his passport. Even the numbskulls would presumably have recognized a passport, and by now he would have been sound asleep in his bed at the Tre Corone. Instead of that, the passport lay safely in his room at the inn, while he peered moodily over the sunlit rooftops of the town.

The clock struck eight. For hours the place had been astir. Convent bells, market-cries, the vague rumour of the streets, came floating up, like smoke, to the square little windows under the serrated ramparts of the fort. Very soon now, Adam thought in an agony of frustration, the clock would gather its strength again, and pong . . . pong . . . pong . . . nine o'clock would be hammered out against the ancient bell. He began to drum on the door with his fists, but he remembered the solidity of the fabric and the interminable length of the corridor down which he had been dragged, and he had little hope of an answer.

However, as the hour finished striking, the door clanged back and the opening filled with uniforms. A corporal entered, said something unintelligible in German, and pointed along the corridor. Adam decided to interpret this as an invitation to leave and was proceeding to take it up when a firm hand yanked him back and another

226

presented him with his boots. He sat down again on the ledge which ran along the wall and put them on. He felt better at once. Stockinged feet gave one an immediate sense of inferiority amid all this stamping and heel-clicking.

'I am a British subject,' he announced firmly in his own language. 'I demand to see your superior officer.'

Whether or not this was understood, it was soon evident that this was just what he was going to do. After marching along even more corridors than he had traversed on his arrival, they reached a slightly less depressing part of the fortress. They came to a halt in an ante-room, where several lounging orderlies indicated, with whispers and head-jerkings towards the inner apartment, that the Garrison Commander was engaged on urgent affairs and could not yet be disturbed.

In one respect the ante-room was worse than the cell: Adam could watch the minutes ticking away on a large cheap clock. At a quarter past nine he jumped up from the bench on which he had been allowed to sit, only to be jerked back by the soldiers on either side of him.

'Look at the time!' he shouted furiously, freeing one arm long enough to point a quivering finger at the dial. 'I am a British subject. I have an important appointment——'

'Sh!' said the corporal, who understood only that he was making far too much noise for the commanding officer's ante-room.

At that moment the door of the inner room opened and a man backed out obsequiously. From the paraphernalia he carried — bowl, towels, and razor-case — it was obvious what urgent military business had just been completed within. Two minutes later, a young lieutenant poked his head out and barked at the orderly sergeant, who barked at Adam's corporal, who barked — but whether back, or to the privates, or to Adam himself, Adam was not sure. Somehow, after a good deal of stamping, clicking, pivoting at right-angles, and further barking, they managed to get themselves into the room with Adam still in their midst. As the vibrations and echoes of the exercise died away, he found himself facing the shiny-skulled little major (whom he remembered from the night at the opera) across a desk impressively cluttered with documents, paper-weights, and ink-stands.

The young lieutenant sat at one side, and, seeing that Adam knew no German, addressed him in Italian.

'I do not speak Italian.' Adam refused to conduct the interview at a disadvantage. 'I am a British subject. English.'

The two officers conferred in some dismay. The Major spoke for the first time.

'Perhaps you speak French?' he inquired in that language.

'A little,' Adam admitted guardedly. At any rate, the vocabulary of Racine might be slightly more in keeping here than it had been on the boulevards.

'What is your name?' Adam gave it. 'Can you prove it? You have no passport.'

'Of course I have!' he said irritably, conscious of the ticking minutes. 'It is in my room at the inn. The Tre Corone.'

'This must be verified,' said the Major solemnly. He wrote it down and murmured to the lieutenant, who went out and came back. 'It will be verified,' the Major assured Adam. 'That is the regulation.'

'And have I got to stay here? I have important business——'

'*This* is important business,' said the Major with a hurt expression.

'By what right are you holding me here? What have I done?'

'You were found wandering about the countryside in a suspicious manner at midnight,' said the Major, poring over a form in front of him and hesitantly translating its contents into French for Adam's benefit. 'When challenged, you were unable to give a satisfactory account of yourself.'

'Naturally! I don't speak German and those idiots didn't speak anything else!'

'You will not improve matters for yourself, Monsieur Adam, if you insult the uniform of His Imperial Majesty.'

'I am sorry, Major.' Adam realised the truth of this. He was prepared to swallow his indignation if it would help him to get down to the cathedral before Sally went away. 'But in England a gentleman does not become a suspicious character because he takes a country walk, even at night——'

'You say you are not a suspicious character,' the Major interrupted sharply. 'Then what is this document? What are these symbols, if not in code?' And with a triumphant gesture he slapped down the miscellaneous papers taken from Adam's pocket, fanning them out on the desk before him until he came to a few lines of Greek which Adam recognized (though few others would have done so) as a scrap of Theocritus he had jotted down to adorn a footnote.

'I apologize for my bad writing,' he said quickly. 'But if you will examine it more closely, Major, you will observe that it is merely a Greek quotation.'

'Greek?' The Major scrutinised the paper dubiously.

'That could be verified, of course.' Adam sensed that this was one of the Major's favourite verbs. 'But I am sure that you, sir, being not only an officer and a gentleman but — it goes without saying — a man of culture——'

'Of course, of course. Now I see it in a good light,

anyone can tell it is Greek. Look for yourself, Lieutenant.' And he flipped it over to his junior, who held it upside down and expressed what was obviously respectful agreement. Turning back to Adam, the Major observed blandly: 'So, monsieur, you are a man of letters?'

'In a sense, yes, Major.' Adam was gaining confidence. Release and apologies seemed to be in sight. But the Major shook him a little by suddenly rapping out his next remark:

'But so is your countryman, Mortimer. You are a friend of his?'

'I would not claim that. And he, I am quite certain, would repudiate the suggestion.'

'You do not agree with his views?'

'In many cases, no.'

'But in some cases, yes? In what cases?'

'I can hardly say. Mr. Mortimer holds views on almost everything — and he changes those views with considerable frequency. Nobody could be in permanent and total disagreement with such a man.'

'Yet you had been visiting Mortimer in his villa last night?'

'Certainly not.'

'Or — even against your personal wishes — carrying him some kind of message from, shall we say, a third party?'

'Not at all. I was doing my best to avoid Mr. Mortimer.'

'Yet you were found near his house — where you were most likely to meet him? I find your behaviour inexplicable, monsieur. Most suspicious! Can you offer any reason for the stealthy manner in which——'

'I had been visiting a young lady.' Adam felt that frankness might accelerate the interview.

'You — *what*?' The Major's faded eyes almost sprang from their sallow pouches.

'I am . . . interested . . . in one of the young ladies who are spending the summer with the Mortimers. Mr. Mortimer does not approve of that interest.'

'*Ah!*' said the Major in a significant and not unsympathetic tone.

'An affair of the heart,' said his young colleague, instinctively fingering his moustache.

Adam's confession had produced a complete reversal of the situation. Suspicion vanished. Seized with a sudden scruple of delicacy, the Major scowled at the corporal and uttered a guttural bark. The corporal barked back, saluted, and after a good deal of stamping Adam's escort achieved a retirement in due order.

'Now, monsieur, we can talk as gentlemen. Please sit down.'

'Thank you, Major.'

'I deeply regret if the zeal of my patrol has interfered with your private affairs. Fortunately' — he looked down at the document in front of him — 'it appears from this report that you had already been to the villa and were returning?'

'Your business completed?' murmured the lieutenant knowingly.

Adam said 'yes' to the Major and ignored the lieutenant.

'And you had no dealings with Mr. Mortimer? You are, in fact, on bad terms with him?'

'I am on no terms with him.'

'I ask this,' said the Major apologetically, 'because I have to make a report to Vienna. This man is suspected of being a subversive element. His writings — it seems — are notorious. It is hardly going too far to say that he is a Liberal! It is thought that he may have been in contact with the Carbonari — he may be helping them with funds.'

'I should imagine that most unlikely,' said Adam.

231

'I am glad to hear you say so, especially since you have no particular motive to defend him. Mortimer is an Englishman. We do not like to deport Englishmen, though of course Mortimer is not a man of title, and it would not involve such repercussions as — but let us not mention other names, eh? I have said enough, monsieur——'

'Yes, yes, Major!' Adam agreed readily, thinking of the time.

'—to explain why I felt it my duty to put Mortimer and his household under surveillance, and why, by mischance, you became involved in my precautions?'

'I am only sorry that my suspicious behaviour wasted your men's time.' A generous response, Adam calculated, might get him out of the Major's office faster than a show of indignation. It might be dangerous to rub him up the wrong way.

'Not at all, monsieur, not at all! I have made an arrest — that will look well in my report to Vienna.'

'But surely——'

'This interrogation will supply material for a second report, which I shall dispatch — but without undue haste — when my superiors have had time to digest the first. This will state that the case has been fully investigated and that I am satisfied of your innocence. Vienna will be satisfied, everyone will be satisfied. The main thing is,' the Major admitted with a shiny smile, 'that these people should not imagine one is doing nothing.'

Bureaucracy, thought Adam, is a wonderful thing. But he could not imagine it imported into English life. . . .

'Then I am free to go, Major?' He made an instinctive movement to consult his watch. The Major was quick to interpret the gesture.

'Ah, a thousand pardons! Of course — your personal possessions! Lieutenant, I have only the papers here. Monsieur Adam would have a watch, money no doubt——'

The lieutenant went in search of them. He was away some time. Adam apologised for fidgeting.

'The truth is, Major——' He searched for words which would most engage the Austrian's romantic sympathies. 'This morning I have an assignation.'

'Aha! The *inamorata*? The beautiful American?' The Major looked most contrite. 'We have delayed you? You have had no breakfast. And — you will forgive me for mentioning it — it would hardly do to present yourself before the lady as you are. Permit me to send for my barber again. And do me the honour to join me in a cup of coffee — I have only to ring——'

'No, please, Major — it must be almost near the time. With your permission, I will go at once——'

'But your watch! Your money!'

'Send them down to me at the inn——'

'But that is impossible, monsieur! You must sign the receipt.'

'Can't I sign it then?'

'I regret no, monsieur. The regulations demand that the personal effects must be returned, and a receipt signed, when the arrested person is released.'

Five uneasy minutes passed. The Major endeavoured to make polite conversation.

'The English — what a wonderful people! Such horses!'

'Yes.'

'Shall I tell you, monsieur, the secret ambition I have entertained since boyhood?'

'Please do,' said Adam with an inward groan.

The Major's eyes gleamed. 'To own an English thoroughbred!'

He developed the theme warmly. To von Schaumberg English culture meant, quite simply, the breeding of horses. He assumed that Adam, as an English gentleman,

233

must be an expert. He plied him with questions which even five years at Oxford had not equipped him to answer. Adam parried them desperately. He saw that, if he admitted ignorance, his whole status as an English gentleman would be suspect. Von Schaumberg was capable of ordering his re-arrest while his identity was verified.

Fortunately the lieutenant returned at that point and ceremoniously set out Adam's property on the desk in front of his superior. Adam snatched up his watch and saw that it was a quarter to eleven. He might just, by running down the hill, reach the cathedral as the hour struck.

'One watch,' said the lieutenant with a slight frown. 'The items should be checked in the correct order, monsieur.'

It was done, with infuriating thoroughness. When it came to Adam's small change, there was a deficiency of two *scudi*.

'Those bandits in the guard-room!' The Major's face took on an imperial hue.

'It's nothing——' pleaded Adam.

'The amounts must tally,' said the lieutenant.

'It must not be said,' declared the Major, saying it himself with every appearance of deep conviction, 'that we have brigands in our ranks, disgracing the Emperor's uniform.'

'I would never suggest anything of the sort, Major — there is sure to be a proper explanation — the coins may have fallen to the floor——'

'It will be investigated, monsieur. Meanwhile, permit me to adjust the deficiency out of my own pocket.' He began to struggle with that aim in view, but the extreme tightness of his breeches and the limitations of his arm-chair made it hard to extract the coins.

The lieutenant interposed: 'I am not sure, Major, that this is permitted by the regulations——'

'Damn the regulations! Honour comes before regulations.'

Two warm silver *scudi* were added to the pile. Adam seized the proffered pen, scrawled his signature, and began to shovel his possessions into the appropriate pockets. It was six minutes to eleven. . . . But Sally, if she came at all, would surely wait?

'I can go now, Major?'

'By all means, monsieur, and once more with my most sincere apologies. My own carriage is at your disposal.'

'I can perfectly well walk, Major——'

'I could not possibly permit it. You have been wrongfully arrested. I must be able to report that, once your innocence was established, you were treated with courtesy.'

'You are too kind.' Adam's fingers itched to shake the braided collar.

'We are Austrian officers, monsieur.'

There followed an excruciating delay while the carriage was ordered and made ready. When the orderly came in to announce that it was at the door, both von Schaumberg and the lieutenant attended Adam to the courtyard.

'I fear,' said the Major with an apologetic glance at the horses, 'they are very different from the sort of thoroughbred you are accustomed to drive behind in your own country.'

It was not the moment to enlighten him. 'They are not bad beasts, though,' said Adam generously. 'I can see, Major, that you have a keen eye for horseflesh.'

'That, monsieur, from an Englishman is a compliment I shall always remember!'

There was much bowing and shaking of hands, and Adam stepped thankfully into the carriage. The Major drew himself up and prepared to honour him with a farewell salute. Suddenly the lieutenant let out a cry of horror.

'Your pardon, Major!'

'What is it? What is it?'

'The Greek . . . and the other papers. Monsieur Adam has forgotten them!'

'Then get them, get them!'

The lieutenant, however, with a proper sense of his own dignity, sent for them. This took a little longer. Adam sat in the carriage palpitating with rage. The Major smiled at the window and inquired if there were royal palaces at Newmarket and Ascot.

It was half-past eleven when at last the carriage rumbled through the gate and over the drawbridge.

Chapter Sixteen

EVEN Dr. Challand, sweeping up to the main gates of his college, could scarcely have aroused more remark than Adam when he leapt wildly from the Garrison Commander's carriage and flew up the front steps of the *duomo*, almost as disreputable-looking as the beggars congregated there.

Sally was not in the side-chapel, nor anywhere in the ambulatory. He searched the rest of the dark, musty-sweet cathedral. There was, of course, no sign of her. If she had been in the building at all, she would not have muddled his directions.

He hurried to the inn, scanning each street for a chance glimpse of her. . . . Brigitta, the Signora, Checco, and other unspecified background characters, vaguely associated with the Tre Corone, emerged and surrounded him in the courtyard with tears, embraces, laughter, and ejaculations of pure emotion.

'The English milord is free, then?'

'The *tedesci* were here only half an hour ago——'

'Asking questions——'

'Searching the Dottore's bedroom——'

'They only wanted to see your passport, signore!'

'This morning, when the Dottore was not in his bed——'

'And the boat also was missing——'

'We feared that you were drowned——'

'So we were actually glad when the whitecoats came marching in just now!'

'It seems,' said Brigitta reproachfully, 'that when I imagine Monsieur has been arrested he is quite safe — and when I am certain Monsieur is at the bottom of the lake the *tedesci* have him locked up in a dungeon!'

'I am all right. Only starving,' said Adam, ignoring the rest of the chattering crowd. 'Has a young lady asked for me? An American young lady?'

'Not since the day before yesterday, monsieur.'

'Not that American young lady. Another.'

'Another? My God!' said Brigitta, rolling her eyes handsomely.

'Today. Within the last hour?'

'No American young ladies today,' she said with evident satisfaction, as though crossing them off the bill of fare.

'And no message? Nobody?'

'Only the Austrians.'

'All right,' said Adam in a deflated tone. He was aware suddenly of his own exhaustion, both nervous and physical. 'Can I have some dinner — at once, please? Whatever is ready. Then I will shave. I am sorry about the boat. I am sorry about everything.'

'It is nothing, monsieur.'

'I can tell you where I left the boat — you can send a man over for it. I will pay whatever is necessary.'

'This evening will do, monsieur.'

'In that case I shall have time to write a letter. Checco can take it for me.'

'Certainly, monsieur. There is no hurry.'

Adam composed his letter with the utmost care. It was a long letter — he wondered, re-reading it, if it were not over-long. That was the danger when one was at home with words and when, being more accustomed to

238

the leisured exchanges of scholarship, one liked to consider each hypothesis and anticipate every objection.

I don't see how I can shorten it, he said to himself with
a frown. I can't assume that she *did* keep the appointment.
Nor can I assume she didn't. Or her motives in either
case. At least, he thought, carefully folding and sealing
the papers, this covers everything.

It would have covered an elephant. It was not surprising that, under such a blanket of words, his emotions
showed through as little more than a restless twitch and
quiver.

He gave it to Checco with elaborate instructions in
broken Italian. He was to hand it only to the '*bella
americana*' — then, realising that by conventional Italian
standards this would deliver the letter straight into the
hands of the enemy, he emphasised the name, the Signorina Forester, who was '*piccola*' and whose hair (he
patted his own and ruffled Checco's) was '*neri*'. It wasn't,
quite, but he could not translate 'very dark brown'. By
crouching almost double, tiptoeing round the yard, laying
a finger on his lips, and gazing furtively to left and right,
he hoped that he had impressed upon Checco the need
for a certain amount of discretion. Checco grinned
appreciatively, enjoying every moment. Brigitta could,
of course, have interpreted and saved all this by-play,
but Adam felt a certain awkwardness about involving her
too intimately in the business.

The urchin departed with the boatman who had been
hired in the piazza to row over and tow back the missing
craft. Adam knew that he was in for a wait of some hours.
Checco would have to get Sally alone — though, provided
she was not actually out on some excursion, this shouldn't
be too difficult since Checco would be able to enlist the
help of the servants. Even so, Sally would have to read
his letter and, D.V., scribble some sort of reply. Checco

would hang on, leech-like, and do his best to extract that reply. Then he would have to scamper back to the waiting boatman and be ferried home across the bay. I may not see him (thought Adam) much before sunset.

He tried philosophically to pass the time with Antonian. But Antonian, deplorably, had only the effect of sending him to sleep. On waking, a good two hours later, he was rather ashamed of himself, though it was only fair to remember that he had passed a sleepless night and an exhausting morning, followed by an abnormally large dinner to make up for the lack of breakfast. He could not remember Shakespeare's mentioning how Romeo had spent the daylight hours. But not, presumably, in translating Latin elegiacs.

He went out on to the balcony. The lake was dotted with boats. But not one was towing another.

He washed to the waist in cold water, put on a clean shirt, and returned to the balcony. The lake was still dotted. Lateen sails, oars like insect-legs . . . but no coupled pair. A rose-and-saffron sunset was developing beyond the western shore.

He went down into the vaulted dining-room.

'Felice sera, dottore. . . .'

'Felice sera, signora. . . .'

He ordered supper. There was nothing else to do. The Signora peered at him from the doorway with solicitude. Il dottor Adam was arousing more and more interest. A political victim of the hated tedesci, a quarry for ladies of at least two nations, and yet an unhappy lover. . . . Who would have thought, when he first arrived, that the ugly young Englishman with all the books would reveal himself as so complex a character?

Adam had reached the fruit stage when Checco materialized silently at his elbow, looking like a fallen cherub on a confidential mission for Beelzebub.

'*Milord . . .*'

'Checco! Did you see her? The *bella signorina americana*?'

'*Si, si, milord!*' Triumph cut a large slice across the grimy face. '*La Signorina Forester — molto bella, bellissima!*' Checco kissed his hand airily, rolled his eyes, and made clear, with curving gestures, his precocious appreciation of her charms.

'*Lettere?*'

'*Si, si! Ecco, milord!*'

Adam snatched at the thin folded paper, broke the seal, and read hungrily.

It was brief, all too brief, but it was signed by Sally. Curiously enough, he had never set eyes on her handwriting before, though her friend's was all too familiar from the rough drafts for prospectuses and manifestos which she had been fond of circulating for approval.

'*Sir,*' wrote Sally, '*I must thank you for your letter. No apologies or explanations were called for. I am only sorry that you had so disagreeable an experience with the Austrians. I must see if I can convey to Mr. M. discreetly (without involving you) the need for prudence in his display of political sympathies———*'

'Damn Mortimer and damn the Austrians!' Adam grunted, skipping the next two or three lines and coming to the end.

'*I am not so handy as you with a pen———*'

'Is she being sarcastic? I did write too much!'

'*—but I can say sincerely that I have no wish to seem "heartless" and that I have only the friendliest sentiments for you. However, since you say yourself — several times — that your love for me is an "impossible passion"———*'

'But it's their favourite phrase!' he interjected, with a sense of injury. At the Villa Gandolfi they all doted on hopeless loves and impossible passions. He had only been trying to address her in the language she understood. He had had so little — indeed no — experience of writing to young women.

'— *I see no point in continuing this correspondence. Do try to be reasonable — you have always struck me as a most reasonable person——*' (she concluded with innocent malice) '—*and believe me, ever your friend, S.F.*'

'Damnation!' Adam crumpled up his napkin and stormed from the table. 'Reasonable? I have been too reasonable.'

He went out and tramped the streets, his thoughts as wild and cloudy as the darkening sky. Angry phrases leapt to mind, and emotion brought them back, again and again, round and round in his head, until they shaped themselves into a regular rhythm. By the time he sank wearily on to a café chair in the Piazza del Duomo, a poem was practically composed. He had only to ask the waiter for pen and ink, and dash it down while he drank his wine.

It began:

> '*So wild the heart,*
> *That will not stay for reasons——*'

and went on, mostly in monosyllables, for three brief verses. It had no elegance — the Rector would have said that it was 'proper' neither in style nor sentiment. It was as unpolished as metal straight from the furnace, and as white-hot.

In the morning, without adding any covering letter or even signing his name, he gave it to Checco and told him to deliver it to the Signorina Forester.

Three days passed. No word came from the villa, either in prose or in verse. In another day or two he must really fix the day of his departure. September had come, bringing a mellow golden glory to Lucero. Beneath his balcony, beneath a cloudless sky, the lake lay purple as the grapes now ripe for the vintage. He must leave it all. Should he make a final effort to see Sally first? What was the use? It could lead to nothing. Whatever happened now, there would always be a ragged end left in his life, teasing him as long as memory lasted.

He would make no decision. Yet. First, he would complete his translation. That was his excuse for staying on here. Once the last line was written he would face the inevitable.

The last line was, in fact, written at the unpoetic hour of seven o'clock in the morning.

He had (unusually for him) been sleeping badly. He got out of bed at the first paling sky, and, as soon as the light was strong enough for him to read the Latin, he sat down grimly at his table. It would be an hour or two before he could demand coffee. He poured himself a glass of wine — it wasn't the same thing, but he had to have something. . . . He refilled his glass, thinking how rough and sour this stuff was. . . . God, he was getting as bad as Challand — he was actually beginning to look forward to the suave full-bodied ports, the dark sweet sherries, of the Common Room. . . . With an alarming flash of foresight he saw the years in front of him. I think I shall drink, primarily, he thought, rather than take to laudanum or women. It better fitted his fastidious — or would it be honester to say his timid? — disposition. He knew he could have had Brigitta if he had wanted, he could have had her with him at this moment, if he had chosen, instead of waiting hours for her even to bring his coffee. But Brigitta was married, and though that only made matters easier by Italian standards — she did not love her husband and he conveniently spent his nights fishing at the northern end of the lake — Adam could not have brought himself (even in the extremities of frustrated desire) to play *cavaliere servente* to a married woman. He drank a third glass . . .

So, as seven o'clock struck from the cathedral clock of hapless memory, he chose his last rhyme and slipped Antonian's last not very original thought into the neat box of an English couplet. There. . . . He stretched his arms wide and yawned. Was it Antonian or was it the wine?

Breakfast cleared his head. But decision was no easier. The Milan diligence passed through after dinner. . . . He would stroll round to the posting-office and inquire if there was any chance of a seat today. If so he would — probably — take it. His packing could be done in a few minutes. But, if there was no chance of getting away from Lucero until tomorrow afternoon, then he would — possibly — consider a dignified farewell visit to the Mortimers, just to show that there was no ill-feeling. . . .

Yes, he would leave it like that. Let the issue depend on the fullness or emptiness of the diligence. . . . And there was always a chance, as he walked through the town to the posting-office, that he would run into Sally. He had never done so yet. All the more reason to hope that, some day, the coincidence would occur.

As he crossed the Piazza del Duomo, on his way to the posting-office, he did in fact encounter a familiar figure, but it was Mortimer's. The great man was sitting alone at a café table. He hailed Adam with a geniality which suggested that he had quite forgotten the circumstances of their last meeting. Or perhaps that he was prepared to do so, in his anxiety to secure a listener.

'Sit down, sit down, young fellow!'

Adam did so with alacrity. 'You're in town early, Mr. Mortimer.'

244

'Ay, a good deal to see to.' Mortimer puffed out his cheeks and caressed his side-whiskers portentously. 'A lot to arrange.'

'Are — are you alone?' Adam's eyes were roving round. Mortimer mistook the reason.

'Nay, that's my waiter, yonder. I'll get him.' He bellowed. 'You'll take wine, Adam? Or coffee?'

'Just coffee, thank you. . . . Did you say you *were* alone? Or are the others shopping?'

'Nay, quite alone,' said Mortimer, dashing his hopes. 'I walked in. Grand morning. Got to get some confounded piece of paper signed. These damned Austrians clap on fresh pettifogging regulations every day!' He glared round the piazza aggressively. If Sally had managed to convey a discreet warning that he should tone down his attitude to the authorities, it had clearly had no effect.

''They are very jumpy,' Adam agreed in a low voice. He knew, from Brigitta, that there was a fresh wave of unrest in the town. Several local worthies had had their houses searched and their bookshelves cleared of controversial volumes. It was whispered that the Carbonari were enrolling more and more recruits.

'I am sitting here,' Mortimer explained, 'because some insufferable little jack-in-office is *not* in his office when he is supposed to be. I have to go back in an hour. I am the mildest of men, Adam, but I find this kind of thing intolerable. It fills me with a generous rage. It is all part of the bureaucratic despotism under which all Europe groans. However, thank God, I shall soon have finished with it.'

Adam's heart bounded. 'You *are* going back to England, then? You and Miss Seeley are starting your review?'

'England?' echoed Mortimer scornfully. 'England is as much a tyranny as anywhere in Europe. It is tainted

245

with the sickness of the Old World. I have come to a great decision, Adam: shall I tell you what it is?'

The question was no more than a conversational courtesy. Even the Ancient Mariner, in that poem of Mr. Coleridge's, would have been easier to discourage than Mortimer when riding a new enthusiasm.

'The hope of mankind,' he declared, 'lies in the New World. But before it can reach fruition America must be civilized.'

His own mission, as he now saw it, was to guide the well-meaning but handicapped Americans along the path to enlightenment. The United States had so much — the bounty of Nature, democracy, a freedom from medieval mumbo-jumbo, from court etiquette, titles and an established church——

In short, Adam said to himself, not liking to say it aloud or indeed finding an opening to do so, the United States have every advantage except an intellectual review edited by Matthew Mortimer and financed by Miss Seeley . . .

When at last his host paused and drank loudly from his cooling coffee, Adam managed to ask:

'Are you . . . all . . . going to America?'

'I hope so! The more the merrier. Mrs. Mortimer and the children may have to wait and follow in another ship — I am off to Genoa presently, to see what can be arranged about passages. It is most fortunate that dear Harriet has such influence in that direction.'

'Most fortunate. And' — Adam licked his dry lips — 'her faithful friend will of course——'

'Sally? Oh, she'll come round in the end,' said Mortimer confidently. 'Naturally, the girl doesn't see the possibilities as clearly as I do.' She was, it seemed, reluctant to leave Europe. 'How can she see the rottenness of the Old World, after a mere five or six months?' he demanded tolerantly.

'Exactly,' said Adam. 'It's like expecting *you* to judge America before you have had the chance to see the country for yourself.'

'Exactly, my dear fellow!' If his listener's responses sounded sufficiently warm, Mortimer seldom troubled to examine them for nuances.

'And what about Villiers?'

Mortimer frowned. 'Villiers has not been entirely satisfactory, I am sorry to say. Frankly, I am disappointed in him. I am not sure that I shall agree to taking Villiers.'

Which means (thought Adam) that you are pretty sure Villiers won't want to come. So am I. I doubt if even the bright eyes of Sally Forester will lure Walter Villiers so far on such a wildcat adventure.

'Everyone in this enterprise must be an idealist,' went on Mortimer. 'Did you never feel that Villiers was a trifle . . . superficial? Of rather too gross a clay?'

'Perhaps . . .'

Mortimer seemed struck by a new thought. His eyes grew cunning over his coffee-cup. 'I always felt how different you two young men were! You, dedicated to learning and enlightenment — for I never despised the fount of knowledge, Adam, even when the stream runs down through the worn-out channels of an obsolete university system——'

Adam murmured non-committally.

'Now you, my dear fellow, would see this splendid American enterprise in a very different light. It would appeal instinctively to a generous nature such as yours. I don't know whether you have any private means——'

'Not a penny.'

Mortimer sighed. 'I feel we could have *worked* together, you and I. However . . .'

Adam hastily changed the subject. 'Will there be any

difficulty about disposing of the villa?' He knew that it had been leased for a period from the impoverished Gandolfis.

'Not the slightest.' Mortimer bristled. 'The owner has been behaving most offensively. Absurd demands, threatening letters . . . The fellow will get a shock when he realizes that I *am* going. His last communication was quite intolerable.'

'How fortunate,' said Adam smoothly, 'that you had already formed this plan of going to America!'

Mortimer looked at him sharply. 'On the contrary. I should have preferred to remain and teach him a lesson in manners. But I cannot hold up my American enterprise for some petty squabble between landlord and tenant——'

'Naturally.'

'Mind you, no one will ever persuade me there isn't a political motive back of everything. The Austrians want me out of the country, and that lickspittling lackey Gandolfi very well knows it.'

'These foreigners stick at nothing . . .'

'It will be different in America,' said Mortimer, his blue eyes shining. And he began to chant, for the benefit of two passing Austrian soldiers: ' "All men are created equal and are endowed——" ' Before he could go further, there was a dramatic interruption. Harriet appeared, distraught and over-heated, at their table. Without any greeting and without taking the seat Adam offered her, she gasped out:

'Thank God I've found you!'

'What's up?' Mortimer demanded. 'Has there been an accident?'

'No — it's Sally——'

'What?' cried Adam.

'She's run away!'

248

Mortimer exploded. 'That scoundrel Villiers! I knew it. He's been pestering the poor girl ever since she arrived. I've seen this coming——'

'She hasn't gone with Villiers,' said Harriet impatiently.

'How do you know she hasn't?'

'Because he was still at home when I found her letter. He brought me into town just now.'

'Where is he?' Mortimer clung to his suspicions.

'We thought we'd find you quicker if we divided — he went the other way——'

'You had better sit down,' Adam suggested. This time she accepted the chair. 'You look worn out.'

'I am. We had to walk in. We almost ran.'

'I left the boat,' said Mortimer irritably.

'But Sally took it. With William. She said she was taking him into the town for a treat — and they would find you, and bring you back in time for dinner.'

'Then where's the boy?'

'We haven't seen him either.'

'He'll turn up. She can't have eloped with William. But who has she gone with? You say she left a letter?'

'Yes.' Harriet fumbled with her reticule, then clasped her hands over it, leaving it unopened. 'No — I can't show it you. Not even you, Mr. Mortimer. It's horrible . . . it's so unfair, so *wounding* . . .'

'Does it give any practical information?' Adam asked quickly. 'About her immediate plans. Does she mention anyone she might be meeting?'

Harriet shook her fair head. 'Nobody. I wondered if it could be *you*, even.'

'Ridiculous,' snorted Mortimer. 'As if she'd elope with Adam! Of all people!'

'Then does she mention any place?' Adam knew that he had flushed.

'Only America.' Harriet opened her reticule now,

unfolded what appeared to be a longish letter, skimmed it tearfully and said: 'She only says that if she has got to go back to America anyway, she wouldn't dream of . . . I won't read just what she says. But she *may* mean that she's planning to go back to America by herself——'

'Then she would make for Genoa,' said Mortimer.

'Or Leghorn more likely — since she knows *we* have been talking of Genoa——'

'But *alone*?' Adam grew hotter still. 'A girl like that——'

'Why not?' Mortimer reacted instinctively. 'Though admittedly she hasn't anything like Harriet's personality.'

'I have always shielded her,' said Harriet with a quite feminine sob.

Villiers appeared then, looking surprisingly unruffled. Not that he was often ruffled, but Adam would have expected Sally's disappearance to have upset him more. He looked hot but bored. He greeted Adam affably enough, and sat down.

'What a farce this is!' he said, mopping his brow. 'I've been round the town. No news of anyone like her. Of course she may have foxed us——'

'How?' cried Mortimer.

'By not coming into Lucero at all. She might have rowed across to the other side of the lake — picked up a carriage at San Vincenzo——'

'But William! What would she do with William?' Harriet was not alone in seeing this objection. Sally had never shown so much affection for the child that she was likely to take him with her to America or any other destination.

'Well, I think she's playing a trick on us,' said Villiers. 'Whatever she wrote in this letter of hers, I think we shall find her at home when we get back.'

'But why? Why should she do such a crazy thing?'

'Possibly to teach you a lesson.' Villiers looked at Harriet with a dislike which had matured over some months. 'She's tired of . . . well, one thing and another. She wanted to give you a fright. I can understand her motives perfectly.'

'I guess you always hated me,' sobbed Harriet.

Villiers' expression was evidence that she guessed with remarkable accuracy. But the tradition of Harrow and Trinity was too powerful to let him say so.

'I have done all you told me to,' he said frigidly. 'I came into the town with you — I have searched — I have made all kinds of inquiries. If there's anything else I can do to assist, I shall be pleased to do it.'

'We had better go back to the villa for the moment,' decided Mortimer. 'I cannot believe that Sally would go without leaving a letter for *me*. She may have confided her intentions in that.'

They all walked down to the lake. There being no sign of the Gandolfi boat, they hired another, and two men to row them home. Adam was not invited to join the party.

'If there is anything *I* can do——' he said on the landing-steps.

'You have done enough, Adam,' Harriet answered in a chilly tone.

There was nothing much more he could say. He was firmly excluded from any further activities of the search-party. He leant over and addressed himself to Mortimer.

'May I at least walk over later in the day and see if there is any news?'

'Of course, my dear fellow, of course.'

The boatman pushed off. It did not seem appropriate to wave. Adam favoured Harriet with a stiff little bow, and turned away.

In the courtyard of the Tre Corone William Butts and

Checco were having a delightful game, chasing each other round the fig-tree, while the Signora laughed toothlessly from her kitchen doorway and Brigitta shouted encouragements from an upper balcony.

'William!'

Adam's thunderous shout stopped the game abruptly. William recovered his balance and ran forward to meet him with a welcoming grin.

'William! Is Miss Forester here?'

'Oh, *no*, Mr. Adam!'

William received the idea with surprise, as though it seemed utterly pointless to him. Adam took him by the shoulders.

'Then where is she?'

'I promised not to tell anybody at the villa — but *you're* not at the villa now, are you?'

'No!'

'So it'll be all right if I tell *you*——'

'Yes, yes!'

'Only on one condition——'

'Where is she, you little devil?'

'Promise *you* won't tell anybody at the villa? Otherwise, I'm not free to tell you.'

It was logical enough. And it gave Adam considerable pleasure to acquire information which he was forbidden to pass on to the others.

'I left her hiring a carriage,' said William. 'She was going to Verona, she told me, because they'd all think she was going the opposite way.'

'When was this?'

William considered. 'Two hours ago, nearly. But I bet you could catch her, Mr. Adam. If you looked lively.'

Chapter Seventeen

WHETHER or not all the world loves a lover, the saying held true in Lucero.

Adam's late mood of indecision had been blown to shreds by the high wind of events. It was assumed on all sides that *il dottore* would wish to pursue *la bella americana*. Things arranged themselves. Indeed, they had arranged themselves before ever he returned to the inn.

'I shall have to hire a carriage——'

'Signora Corvesi's brother has a *sediolo*,' said William promptly.

'What's that?'

'A sort of gig. They go like anything! Much faster than a *vettura*.' Sally had been bargaining for the hire of a *vettura* when she had taken leave of William.

'What about you?' Adam asked with a prick of conscience. 'Can you get home by yourself?'

'Oh yes, Mr. Adam.'

William had that all worked out as well. The Gandolfi boat was tied up at a private mooring, hidden from questing eyes. No, he would not risk the lake currents alone. Checco and his father would take him over to the villa.

'Tell them all not to worry about Miss Forester,' said Adam. He considered for a moment. 'Say that I have heard some fresh information . . .' William grinned. 'Say I have gone after her to make sure she is all right. But . . . I didn't tell you which way I was going.'

William nodded. 'I know what to tell them.'

'Now where's this — what is it? — *sediolo*?'

'I'll show you. It's only in the next street.'

Adam turned to Brigitta. 'Explain to the Signora — if she doesn't already know more about this than I know myself! I don't know when I'll be back. Take care of my things, though——'

'I have packed one bag,' said Brigitta, producing it. 'I did not think Monsieur would need his books?' Her eyes twinkled. She had a warm and generous nature. She only wanted everybody to be happy.

Checco seized the bag. Shouting farewells, Adam strode from the yard, the boys trotting on either side. The Signora's brother, a wiry little old man with iron-grey moustaches like ram's horns, seemed in no way surprised to see him. The *sediolo* stood ready — a somewhat rustic-looking vehicle, admittedly, by no means smart, but promising a good turn of speed with its two tall wheels and a reasonable beast between the shafts.

'Verona?' suggested Adam.

'*Si, si, dottore!*'

'His name's Giovanni. He doesn't know any French or English,' said William, 'but you don't have to explain anything.'

Not a moment was wasted. Adam jumped up and sat with his bag between his feet. Giovanni mounted nimbly beside him, cracked his whip, and they were off. The two boys waved and shouted. From the shocked laugh and playful push which William gave Checco, Adam guessed that the Italian boy's good wishes had embodied some idiomatic impropriety.

The pursuit, which had started with such a flourish, did not sustain its romantic tempo beyond the east gate of the town.

Here it was evident that the authorities cared little for

love. Romance must conform to regulations. And, in the last week or so, regulations had proliferated.

Adam's passport, which had brought him across France and Switzerland and half Lombardy-Venetia, was not sufficient to take him through the gates of Lucero. Did not his bag indicate that this was a journey, not a mere afternoon drive? The officer of the guard regretted . . . but Herr Adam must apply to the *dogana* for the necessary clearance.

Giovanni, without waiting for instructions, cracked his whip and took the *sediolo* rattling down the street again. The Customs officer spoke French and expressed his regrets in that language: Monsieur must apply first to the police, if he wished to leave the town. It was waste of time to ask for clearance at the *douane* until he could produce their permit.

'Waste of time? To hell with them,' groaned Adam, grinding his teeth. At that moment he would cheerfully have joined the Carbonari and followed Mortimer to the barricades . . .

The police expressed no regrets. They looked sour and ill-tempered. This was not surprising, for (as they finally managed to explain to Adam after various linguistic struggles) the authority to grant permits had just been taken out of their hands. They must stamp the document, yes — that shred of glory clung to them — but they could not grant it. The Signor must address his application to the military——

'*Al castello?*' Adam demanded with sinking heart.

'*Si, si, signore.*'

He rushed out and leapt into the gig. '*Al castello!*'

'*Si, si, dottore!*'

Giovanni cracked his whip. They started up the long dusty hill to the fortress . . .

By now Sally would be miles and miles away . . . With

so many hours' start she would have lost herself in the Italian landscape before he was clear of the town.

The sentry stopped them on the drawbridge, the sergeant emerged and examined them with suspicion . . . The garrison appeared to be in a high state of alertness — or at least of nerves. But the *sediolo* was of such a light and skeletal construction that it clearly could not have concealed a party of conspirators or even a medium-sized keg of gunpowder. Most fortunately one of the soldiers in the guardroom recognized Adam as the Englishman who had been dispatched, with so many apologies and compliments, in the Garrison Commander's own carriage a few days before. Things began to move more smoothly. Adam was invited to dismount, and Giovanni, instead of being made to drive off to the shade of some distant trees, was allowed to lead his horse into the fortress.

Once more Adam found himself in the ante-room with the cheap and loudly ticking clock. . . . The orderlies greeted him as a prodigal returned — so far as discipline permitted emotion to warm their manner . . . Once more, though, the Major could not be disturbed. Once more, urgent military affairs absorbed him in the inner room.

Adam took the seat offered him and glowered at the clock. This was maddening. If Giovanni drove like Jehu, he would not overtake Sally by nightfall. The scent was growing colder all the time. Once she turned off the main road or that road forked, once she went to ground in some kind of lodging or exchanged her *vettura* for a place in some public vehicle, he might never pick up her trail again.

The lieutenant came marching in from outside but even he was prevented, by a discreet whisper from the orderly sergeant, from passing through the double doors into the Major's office. He turned back with a gesture of pique, recognised Adam, bowed stiffly, and sat on the edge of a table, alternately removing and replacing his white gloves.

Suddenly the inner door opened. The Major appeared, wreathed in smiles, bowing from the waist. Adam saw a slender figure, bonneted, in a long coat of Pompeian red he recognized.

'Sally!' he gasped.

She was already halfway across the ante-room. She turned, gave him one brief glance of consternation, and fled. He tried to follow, but the orderly sergeant, having closed the outer door behind her, pivoted slowly and faced Adam, barring the way. Adam gibbered helplessly, scraping his mind for a word or two of German. Short of pushing the man aside — which would probably have meant immediate arrest for insulting the Austrian uniform — there was nothing he could do.

The sergeant was speaking in a solemn, reproving tone, as though Adam were behaving unreasonably. The gist of it was that Adam was going the wrong way, he wanted the other door, the Garrison Commander was now disengaged and would receive him . . .

Deciding to make the best of it, Adam wheeled round and hurried into the Major's office. Von Schaumberg received him with the utmost affability.

'Ah, Monsieur Adam too! Enchanted, monsieur! A chair for monsieur.' The lieutenant provided it sullenly: he had been readmitted to the sanctum. Adam sat down reluctantly. 'And to what do we owe this pleasure, monsieur?'

'I am in a great hurry to leave Lucero, Major——'

'Alas, you are all leaving Lucero! First, Beauty, and now Learning!'

Adam had no patience with these playful idiocies.

'I am told that under the new regulations a foreigner leaving the town must first apply to you.'

'That is correct.'

'So I have come,' said Adam, folding his arms with an expression calculated to discourage any time-wasting gossip.

'You have come to the right place,' said the Major agreeably. 'Will you have the goodness to complete this form? Where *are* the forms, lieutenant?' He straightened his tunic and looked smug. 'I had one a few minutes ago. Ah, thank you.'

Filling up the form took some time. There were a lot of questions. The Major had to translate them into French, which in places puzzled him. Adam, when he finally understood the questions, found some of the answers no less puzzling. However, the blanks were gradually filled in, the Major himself graciously wielding the pen.

'And when do you propose to leave?' he inquired in a leisurely tone, as though the relative merits of an autumn and spring departure might now be considered.

'At once. Today.'

'Ah! Like Mademoiselle Forester?'

'Yes, Major.'

'What a woman, monsieur! The English, I think, have the secret of breeding horses. But when it comes to young women these Americans——! What do you say, monsieur?' Adam said nothing. The white tunic heaved and wrinkled with the Major's inward chucklings. The row of medals and crosses clinked together. 'And your destination?' The Major dipped his pen into the ink and waited. For a moment Adam hesitated, fearing to make a false step. 'Like Mademoiselle Forester, also?' said the Major slyly.

'Of course, Major. The same.'

Von Schaumberg wrote *Venice via Verona*, Adam signed his name at the bottom, and the document was handed to the lieutenant for the wet ink to be sanded, the official stamp applied, and the corresponding permit to be made out.

He scrutinised the application and then, his expression blending deference with malice, murmured an apology in German. The Major snorted incredulously in the same language. The lieutenant thereupon set a manicured finger-nail against a line of insignificantly minute print. Von Schaumberg sighed, took a fresh form, and placed it under Adam's nose.

'I am so sorry, monsieur. But it says, "*in the applicant's own handwriting (unless illiterate)*".'

Adam swore in English and inquired in French:

'Cannot I be treated as illiterate?'

'It would not be true.' The Major looked shocked. 'What is worse, the form might be checked. And, since you are described here as a tutor in the University of Oxford, it would not be consistent.'

'You don't know Oxford,' Adam mumbled in English. Wearily he took the proffered pen.

'I greatly regret troubling you, monsieur. But — the regulations. One must cover oneself.'

'Of course!'

The second form was soon completed, for he had merely to copy the Major's original version. Ten minutes later he was bowing himself out of the office, clutching the precious permit. This time he took care to leave none of his papers behind.

Giovanni rose from the shade of the building as he reached the courtyard.

'Quick!' Adam shouted. 'Mademoiselle is not half an hour ahead of us!'

Too late he realised that he was still talking French, but the old man, whether or not he had seen Sally leave the fortress, was well aware of the need for haste. He was in his seat before Adam set foot on the step.

Once more, however, unkind coincidence frustrated them. As Giovanni wheeled his horse towards the gate-house there came, from beyond it, the most appalling blare and bang of martial music. The sentry barked, the guard turned out and shuffled feverishly into line. . . . Slowly, with impressive but irritating pomp, the remainder of the garrison came marching in over the drawbridge, dusty from the long morning's exercises. It was another ten minutes before the barking, screaming, and musket-slapping of the dismissal parade were over, permitting the trivial departure of two civilians.

Adam fumed in his seat. Why had he not followed his first impulse to drop the application, excuse himself from the Major's presence, and drive straight to the Porta Venezia, on the very good chance of intercepting Sally before she could comply with the rest of the bureaucratic rigmarole? Now it was too late. Having got his permit from the military, he might as well complete the formalities, so that, if need be, he could follow her to Venice itself.

Once across the drawbridge, Giovanni flicked his horse and they went down the hill with the dust smoking behind them like the trail of a torch. Sulkily the police examined the military stamp and signature and added their own. . . . 'La dogana!' cried Giovanni cheerfully. The whip cracked like a pistol. Down the street flew the sediolo. Fortunately the street was empty of traffic, for the town was just sinking into its siesta.

Less fortunately, the Customs officials had sunk into theirs. It took an hour, with much cajoling from Giovanni and several scudi from Adam, to obtain the clearance. . . .

There was something of a traffic jam at the Porta Venezia, for the siesta was over and the whole district seemed to be reawakening to life. Adam leapt down and battled through a stream of ox-carts, pannier-laden donkeys, and ample-hipped market-women to present his papers to the officer of the guard. That gentleman sorted them out and surveyed them with the thoughtful consideration of one arranging a hand at cards. Adam felt like bawling in his ear that hearts were trumps. . . .

At last, with a smile and a bow, the officer handed back the documents.

'Everything is in order, signore.'

Giovanni could not crack his whip in that crowd. But he let out a deep-throated howl, such as might have come from some remote ancestor driving a chariot in the Circus Maximus. The horse nosed forward, the slow-moving flood of donkeys' rumps and wicker baskets and heaped-up produce divided to left and right.

Adam drove out of Lucero on the trail of the beloved fugitive.

'*Eccola!*' said Giovanni, and pointed.

From the tone and gesture Adam realised that, for the first time in several hours, he himself and not the horse was being spoken to.

The old man, it seemed safe to assume, was drawing his attention not to the spreading splendours of the Lombard plain, now bathed in the apricot haze of evening, but to the carriage which was sedately bowling along about half a mile in front of them. To Adam it looked no different from several other closed, three-horse vehicles they had already seen on the road, but no doubt his companion recognized it as emanating from Lucero.

'Signorina Forester?'

'*Si, si, dottore!*'

Adam clenched his hands and, in all the languages he could think of, urged the desirability of speed. Giovanni cracked his whip impressively, but it was late in the day to expect much acceleration from the horse.

261

The *vettura* itself, however, made no great speed, despite the trio drawing it. Doggedly, yard by yard, they overhauled it. Soon they were coughing and choking in its tawny dust. Giovanni pulled out and yelled a hoarse exhortation to his beast. The two vehicles drew level and for some moments creaked and rattled abreast. Leaning over, Adam was able to peer through the window of the carriage and to recognize Sally's long redingote. As he did so, she turned her head to face him (for her bonnet prevented sidelong glances) and gave him what was clearly intended to be a look of extreme *hauteur*.

'Adam! Are you *following* me?'

'Oh, no! We just happen to be going the same way!'

'I think it's intolerable of you. How dare——'

He heard no more of her protest. Giovanni was drawing steadily ahead. A few moments later he was able to wheel across the road and force Sally's carriage to a standstill. He and the *vetturino* exchanged greetings like old friends, which, as it happened, they were.

Adam sprang down and opened the carriage door just as Sally was preparing to do so herself. Various emotions seemed to be competing for control of her voice and features.

'I reckon you think you've been pretty smart?'

'Not at all.'

Sally glanced back along the road anxiously. 'There aren't any more behind?'

'I don't think so. I hope not,' said Adam fervently. It had occurred to him frequently, in the last hour or two, that so long as he did overtake her in the end there were distinct advantages about the lengthening mileage between them and Lucero. For the first time since their nocturnal walk by the lake he would have a chance to talk to her without her friends interrupting.

Sally too seemed to derive confidence from their isolation.

'You can tell your driver to shift out of the road,' she said.

'Just a minute, first——'

'If you think you're going to make me turn back,' she exclaimed, 'I guess you——'

'I wouldn't try to make you do anything,' he said gently. 'What right have I? What right has anyone? You're not a child.'

She stared up at him. For the first time her face broke into a smile.

'My! If it isn't good to hear someone admit that!'

'I don't think I've ever questioned it?'

'No more you have,' she agreed. 'I'll say that for you. It's been Harriet and Mortimer and — oh, everybody. Managing and organizing and — and patronizing. I felt I'd just got to cut and run for it, or they'd have smothered me.' She shrugged her shoulders. 'Well, what happens now?'

'This.'

And Adam, surprising himself even more than her, seized her and kissed her with prolonged fervour. Giovanni and the *vetturino* looked down benignly from their respective perches, and, nodding their heads, looked more than ever like two wise old birds.

'My!' Sally gasped. 'The heart *is* wild.' But the blood which had rushed to her own cheeks seemed not to have done so in any spirit of outrage. 'Adam,' she said, and it was rather a purring murmur, breathed into his cravat, than any sort of reproach.

'I know I'm mad,' he said, 'but I like the sensation——'

Her brow puckered. 'Mad? Oh, you mean crazy? Perhaps I'm a little crazed myself.'

The sight of an approaching bullock-cart reminded them that they could not indefinitely block the highway.

'Do you still want to go on to Verona?' he asked.

263

'Well, I'm not going back to Lucero.'

'Verona, then. It can't be far now.' He hesitated, with an almost schoolboyish grin. 'I don't think we need to arrive as a procession . . .'

'I guess not. Send your man back and have your baggage put in the *vettura*. We might as well travel together. As you "just happen" to be going to Verona too.'

Adam began to explain in broken phrases. Never had he found his Italian so readily understood — almost, indeed, before he had found the words and framed them with his lips. Giovanni was already off his perch, lugging out the bag, and transferring it to the carriage.

'*Non fa niente, dottore, non fa niente . . .*'

Adam paid him. Sally interpreted:

'He says there's no need for lodging-money. He'll just pull in at the roadside and sleep for an hour or two when it gets dark. The nights are warm.'

Adam bade the old man an affectionate farewell and climbed into the *vettura* with Sally. The driver chirruped to his horses, and they ambled slowly forward over the last few miles. Over the city of Romeo and Juliet the eastern sky was already tinged with evening.

Chapter Eighteen

THE glimmering intimacy of the carriage made explanations extraordinarily easy, and its swaying motion helped to bring them still closer together.

'I got your first letter,' she said. 'Of course, I answered it.'

'It never reached me.'

'Harriet! And you say you wrote others?'

'Of course.'

'She must have stopped them too.'

'I began to suspect — to wonder, anyhow — when she came to see me and warn me off.'

'I never knew that till days and days afterwards. Harriet is a *bitch*,' declared Sally, deriving from the last word all the satisfaction bottled up over twenty-odd years of referring only to 'lady-dogs'.

'She believes so strongly in the Brotherhood of Man,' he suggested dryly, 'that she prefers all men to remain on a brotherly basis.'

He could feel Sally shaking with laughter. 'She got so mad at Villiers always——'

A great question-mark trembled over their relationship for a moment. He said, as evenly as he could:

'I thought you were fond of Villiers . . .'

'I was. I guess I was a bit . . . young . . . over Villiers. You see, I'd never had a beau. You *could* call Villiers a beau?'

'A most elegant one.'

'You don't think I was too silly? He made me laugh — he seemed to know everything — all the famous places and people. And then . . .'

'Yes?'

'He made me see that Harriet had gotten too strong a hold on me. I'm grateful to him for that.'

'Rightly so,' said Adam, but with modified enthusiasm.

She was quick to catch the alteration in his tone. 'But I soon saw through him——'

'Soon?'

'After you left — after all the trouble. It got worse and worse at the villa, Adam.'

'How?'

'They seemed to be at me from all sides. Villiers only wanted — well, I guess you were right about him, that day at the monastery, even though I was mad at you at the time. And Harriet — I see now why she was acting the way she was! But I didn't know then——' again Adam was pleasantly conscious of a laughing rise-and-fall in the body nestling against him — 'I didn't know she had you and all those letters to worry her, as well as staving off Villiers!'

'Poor Harriet!'

'Oh, I suppose she's all right. I reckon I shouldn't have called her what I did. She's been kind to me. But she likes to possess people. And I won't be possessed by her or Villiers or anyone else. I *had* to run away or be smothered.'

'I thought, that evening I went out to the villa, you looked — well, terribly strained——'

'I was. I'd just told Villiers I wouldn't run away with him to Paris——'

Adam exclaimed with a moral indignation which, in the circumstances, was not entirely justified.

266

'Maybe that first put the idea of running away — but not with Villiers — into my head,' she murmured. 'And when Harriet and Mortimer started this crazy new notion of publishing their review in Boston instead of London, I guess I knew I'd gotten to breaking point. And — do you know what? You were the last straw.'

'I?'

'When I told her about that very first letter, she pretended she liked you better than Villiers — she reckoned you were sincere, anyway, but she thought you were a no-account College professor who'd never do anything——'

'She *is* a bitch,' Adam interrupted indignantly, and, to disprove her, promptly did something which appeared to give Sally considerable satisfaction.

'She didn't mean *that*.'

'But I did!' And, to avoid misunderstanding, he did it again. 'Why was I the last straw?' he demanded, when the conversation was resumed.

'I didn't know whether Harriet was right or not. I was in such a state that evening at the villa — when you suddenly came up behind me at the piano I felt I just couldn't handle any more situations——'

'I'm sorry. I chose a bad moment.'

'You couldn't tell. Anyway, I felt better in the morning. I did go to the cathedral, just to find out — well——'

'And I wasn't there!'

'And I was so mad at you, Adam——'

'Darling!' said Adam, probably for the first time in his adult life, except when translating.

'I thought Harriet was right about you. That you didn't know what you wanted — that you were so ineffective you couldn't even stick to an appointment you'd fixed yourself——'

'But I did write and explain!'

'You did.' Sally gurgled. 'That letter!'

'I spent a lot of time on that letter!'

'I calculate you did. Why didn't you just come over to the villa and *tell* me? Never mind the others?'

'But — the night before — you'd begged me not to cause a scene! You seemed so upset — you practically pushed me out through the window!'

'Adam, you mustn't expect a woman to feel exactly the same the next day. And you mustn't *always* do what she tells you, really you mustn't.'

'I can see I have a lot to learn.'

'I gave up all hope for you when I read that rigmarole.'

'Your answer was not exactly encouraging.'

'Well, what was the use? You were so logical, you'd persuaded yourself everything was so impossible — who was I to contradict you? And then, instead of sending me another rigmarole, you just sent me that little poem!'

'You liked it?'

'Like it! It made me think. But then you didn't do anything more.'

Adam suddenly saw daylight. 'So *you* did? You ran away. You weren't just running away from Harriet and Villiers and America——'

'I guess not. I reckoned it out that you'd do something then — you'd just *have* to do something — if I disappeared from Lucero. If you didn't, then I'd know Harriet had been right, and I'd been wrong.'

'But,' Adam began — the daylight not yet complete, 'suppose I'd not found out which way you'd gone. . . . Oh, I *see*. Young William——'

'William's a stolid little boy, but he is reliable. And he likes you, Adam. He reckons we — well, never mind what he reckons about us. But I figured I could depend on William to do as he was told.'

'He did!'

'And here you are.'

'Here *we* are.'

The carriage drew up at the Porta Brescia. The guards
glanced at their papers in the last glow of the sunset and
waved them forward into the city.

Much had been explained: nothing had been decided.
For the moment they were happy to be swept along on the
tide of the delightful present.

The *vetturino* drove them to a respectable inn, close by
the ruined Roman amphitheatre — which even Adam (to
do him justice) did not notice until the following day.
And the innkeeper, who tempered respectability with
humanity, showed them to adjacent bedrooms overlooking
a sea of rooftops and belfries and the curious M-shaped
crenellations of the Castel Vecchio.

'You have a balcony, too,' she called across the narrow
gulf of dusk.

'Yes — but what do we want with *two* balconies?'

'Any more than two carriages!' Her laugh changed to a
cry of alarm as he flung a leg over the railings. 'Adam!
Be careful——'

'It's not much of a stretch.' He swung himself across
and joined her.

'But the drop——'

He silenced her objections in the pleasantest manner.

'We must go down,' she said gently. 'They're preparing supper for us.'

They realised that they were ravenous. Neither had
eaten since breakfast. They dealt appreciatively with all
that was set before them, working their way through from
the savoury ball-shaped *gnocchi* to the pink-and-gold
velvet peaches at the end. On the landlord's recommendation they drank a local white wine from the
Euganean Hills.

'This,' said Sally, 'is my idea of Heaven.'

In Heaven the future is no problem. Adam had still a surviving scruple, though it was fast being submerged.

'I ought to explain——' he began.

'Adam, you explain too much!'

'But——'

'Not now. Tomorrow, if you must.'

He had a feeling that tomorrow would be too late.

After supper, for form's sake, they took a short stroll in the cooling air. Verona was a crowded, lively city, in size midway between Milan and Lucero: for all the lights and faces, the cafés and carriages, they might have been alone. They saw, but without seeing, Roman relics and romanesque churches and the famous tombs of the Scaligeri, florid and fantastic in the lantern-light. Once they hung over a parapet, listening to the swirling rush of the invisible Adige — not that they had any idea of the river's name, they were conscious only of a fresh breath from the Alps, a noise and a force below them in the darkness, something that drew them even closer. . . . They followed the embankment for a little way, then turned up a side-street and, more by luck than planning, found themselves back at the inn.

It was a revelation to Adam, how much could be decided without a word said.

'You must never climb over the balcony again,' Sally whispered suddenly in the middle of the night. 'It scares me. If you slipped——'

'Darling——' Adam had taken a fancy to the word.

After an interlude Sally murmured:

'For all their cranky talk at the villa, I guess they were right on one thing.'

'What?'

' "Love is all that matters," ' she quoted, parodying

the solemn tone in which that romantic sentiment had often been voiced in the philosophical discussions after supper.

They lay laughing as they recalled those evenings. There had been so much talk about the importance of love. But then everything had been so important — Liberty and Manhood Suffrage and Magna Carta, Reason and Rousseau and *The Rights of Man* . . .

'I have taken off my blue stockings for ever,' she said.

'So I see.' It was so hot, he had got up and opened the shutters. The moon flooded in. 'You gleam — like ivory.'

She looked at him, silhouetted, big, tousled. She stretched out her arms. ' "The Noble Savage!" How they went on about it! Rousseau and everything. . . . It's better this way.'

'Much better.'

He came back to her.

What will happen to us, what will happen to us, he thought. But what *was* happening was so wonderful. . . . Tomorrow receded, in the intoxication of tonight.

When they woke it was no longer moonlight at the open window but late morning sunshine. The air was tremulous with heat. The city-noises lapped faintly below the balcony — bells, market-cries, creaking wheels, the far-off sweetness of an Austrian band.

Adam cried out: 'The *time*! The maid——'

Sally said: 'I told them not to disturb either the Signor or myself, until we rang. We might be tired after our journey. Oh . . .' She yawned, and stretched luxuriously. 'This is wonderful, Adam.' She lay back, studying the ceiling with interest: the water in the wash-bowl caught the sunbeams and reflected a wavy, flickering light upon the smooth plaster. She dropped her eyes to meet Adam's. He was standing in the middle of the room and gazing down at her.

'You look guilty,' she laughed. 'Like your namesake. But this isn't Genesis, you know.'

'You're lovely . . .'

'Darling Adam!' She sat up. She gleamed still, but not now like ivory. She was golden and warm, a creature of the sun rather than the moon. Her hair curled in dark brown twists and tendrils.

'Oh, dear,' she said, as he did not speak. 'I suppose we shall *have* to get up and dress . . .'

'You ought to wear panther skins,' he said. 'And ivy leaves. Not all that——' He looked at the clothes she had left draped across a chair.

'Not *fig* leaves?' she teased him.

'No, ivy. I wasn't thinking of Genesis. Euripides. He wrote a play called *The Bacchantes*.'

'Did he now? You must teach me, Adam. To me the word isn't much more than a hair-style.'

She spoke as if they had all the time in the world. He looked at her, sitting up with her bare shoulders and her big candid eyes. She was, in the best sense, without shame. She had, over the years, absorbed some of the notions her friends had preached and discussed so tire-lessly. Unselfconsciously, unlike them, she believed in love, in the body, in equality between man and woman. . . . Daylight brought her none of the doubts which were nagging at his own mind. She smiled at him with the serenity of a bride.

'We must talk——' he said.

'At breakfast, then.'

'All right.'

'In half an hour.' He put on a dressing-gown. 'And *not* the balcony, darling! What does it matter if you do meet someone in the passage? What does it matter if the whole world knows?'

'Yes,' he said thoughtfully, at the door. 'You *are* shameless. Quite, deliciously, shameless.'

'Only consistent. Half an hour, then.'

Shameless, but not promiscuous, he reflected, as he unpacked his razor-case in the next room. It was ironical that Villiers, after working so assiduously to deliver her from Harriet's domination and to lead her on from the realm of theory to that of practice, had ended in failure. However far Sally had travelled from the morality of her Bostonian childhood, she had refused to give herself to a man she did not love, merely as an exercise in emancipation.

She does love *me*, as I love her. . . . She must. . . .

Scraping his cheek he thought back over the night. She had a passionate nature, but that didn't explain everything. . . . God help her, he groaned, she is *in* love with me, as I with her. . . . What will become of us? Suppose——

He could hear her singing as she dressed. Not a care in the world. . . . As if this is to go on — as if we can be together always——

Before they let themselves be carried away any further, he must make her look at the facts.

After breakfast, slowly pacing the cypress avenues of the Giusti Gardens, he explained. It hadn't just been romantic rhetoric when he had spoken, in his last letter, of his 'impossible passion'. Impossible was just what it was, in spite of last night. . . .

'You see, I can't ask you to marry me.'

'Who asked you to ask me? I'm not making conditions.'

'But we can't go on like this——'

273

'Why not? So long as we love each other?'

'Sally. . . .'

'Yes, darling?'

'We're not living in a dream——'

'It feels like it.'

'But we're in the real world.'

'I don't care about the world.'

'I don't mean gossip,' he said impatiently. 'You have to eat. I have to eat. I've no more private fortune than you have.'

'I haven't a cent,' she agreed, 'once my purse is empty.'

'I've only what the College pays me. We have a Fellows' meeting on the last Thursday before term. I ought to be starting back now. I daren't stay here more than two or three days longer.'

'Then we have . . . two or three days.' There was a change in her voice. She was beginning to realise. 'If I can't travel back with you?'

'We must think about that. The point is this: I — I can't ask you to go on like this without being married.'

' I would marry you if that would help. I've no objection to marrying.'

'But — I've explained before — an Oxford Fellow can't.'

'Why not?'

'It's a condition. In the Founder's statutes.'

'How absurd!'

'There was a reason originally.' Adam found himself instinctively defending the institution to which he belonged. 'St. Columb's was founded in the Middle Ages. The Fellows had to be in Holy Orders — or to take them within so many years — so they couldn't be married.'

'But you're not a Roman Catholic!'

'Oh, no——'

'How many of them are — the other Fellows?'

274

'None,' he said promptly.

'*None?*'

'They can't be. Roman Catholics and Jews and dissenters aren't allowed in the University.'

She stopped and turned to him, laughing up in his face. 'Oh, Adam darling! Did you say Logic was one of the main subjects at Oxford?'

'It *is* absurd,' he admitted, but his answering laughter was a little bitter. 'They talk of reform. But men like Challand — my Warden — will stamp on every scheme. You see, he's a College head. *They* can marry.'

Step by step, threading the paths between the immemorial cypresses, with the rose and buff panorama of Verona laid below them across the grey-green sweep of the Adige, they went over what to Adam was all too familiar ground.

There was his mother. Keeping her out of the workhouse was first charge upon his income. What use, then, to talk dramatically of giving up Oxford and all its enforced hypocrisy, and earning an honest living with his hands? Especially now that peace was spreading unemployment and starvation through town and country alike.

What was he fit for?

'Can you see me as a school usher?' he demanded. 'Can you see yourself as a curate's wife?'

'A curate? You mean a sort of preacher?'

'The lowest sort,' he said grimly. 'Without influence one might never get higher. Besides, it would be worse hypocrisy than Oxford. I've always known I couldn't do it. Least of all, now. After . . . this. As for you, you weren't made for that sort of thing.'

'I couldn't pretend,' she agreed. After a moment, she added: 'Of course I'm not afraid of being poor. Anyway, now I've broken with Harriet, I guess I always *shall* be poor.'

'You ought to have everything! The sort of life Villiers would have given you——'

She checked him with her hand. 'No. Villiers nearly fooled me — but not quite. I won't deny it, I was tempted by . . . oh, a heap of things. All he said about Paris and London, the concerts and the operas and the brilliant people in the salons and the pretty things in the stores.'

'I know.' He spoke from the depths of his dejection. 'That's what you ought to have. What I could never give you.'

'Do you think——' Her big eyes were reproachful. 'Do you think it was because of all that — that I almost persuaded myself I was in love with him?'

'I don't know what to think.'

'It was quite different. Truly, Adam. It was a sort of dream I was in love with. I thought Villiers was a poet — a real poet — not just a poseur——'

'Oh, you saw through his stuff at last?' said Adam with gloomy satisfaction. 'I *thought* you had more taste than to go on imagining he was a second Byron.'

She flushed. 'I said yesterday — I admitted I was rather . . . young . . . about Villiers. You know how girls have romantic notions? I suppose I saw myself as companion to a genius — helping him through his early struggles and disappointments, sharing in his glory when he got recognition. Wife or mistress, I was not particular.'

'I'm afraid I can't offer you that sort of interesting future in either capacity.'

'I don't *care*——' Her voice trembled.

'At this moment you don't care. But you would come to.'

'I wouldn't, Adam! I only want you.'

'They talked a lot of high-flown nonsense at the villa,' he said harshly, 'about personality, and the individual, and the sacred duty of being oneself. But it wasn't all

276

nonsense. My god, there was a kernel of truth in it. You *can* force your nature into a boot that doesn't fit, but it leads to disaster. I know. It's what I've done. I won't let *you*.'

They walked in silence for a few moments. The midday sun grilled the path before them. The air was scented with dry conifers. Below them, Adam thought ironically, spread one of the loveliest cities in the world. The city of Shakespeare's lovers, the birthplace of Catullus . . . and they could talk only of College statutes and how to keep his mother off the parish.

Suddenly, in a pool of fragrant shadow, she paused. 'Adam! Kiss me——'

They clung to each other.

She said, fiercely: 'You don't *want* this to finish?'

'You *know* I don't. Oh — darling——'

'Yes, I do know. Well, why should it? I guess we've been fools — it's so easy really——'

'It seems hellishly impossible to me.'

'We get married——'

'But——'

'You tell nobody in Oxford. We'll find somewhere for me to live — a tiny cottage, rooms, anything would do. If Oxford itself is too dangerous, there must be other places not too far away. You'll come to me when you can — and there'll be the vacations — and if we have children——'

It all seemed so obvious now. She brushed aside the half-hearted objections he began to voice.

'Why not?' she demanded. 'You say yourself, some of the men keep women in the town — and the University turns a blind eye to it! Is it any different if *your* woman is secretly your legal wife?'

'It is to the Founder.'

'Then let the Founder turn in his grave if he wants

to! Why should he ruin our lives?' Exultantly she began to quote one of Mortimer's favourite passages from *The Rights of Man*. She imitated his Yorkshire accent as she declaimed: ' "Every age and generation must be as free to act for itself, *in all cases*, as the ages and generations which preceded it. The vanity and presumption of governing beyond the grave is the most ridiculous and insolent of all tyrannies——" '

'Hear, hear!' said Adam, laughing. 'Unfortunately, Tom Paine isn't approved reading in the University.'

'But you agree?'

'Implicitly.'

'Doesn't it satisfy your scruples?'

'I have no scruples.'

'Then——?'

'There's only the danger of being found out.'

'Will you take it?'

He hesitated. 'Yes.'

'I *knew* you'd be reasonable!' she cried delightedly.

'I thought,' he said slyly, 'you complained that I was *too* reasonable?'

'Reasonable, to a woman, means agreeing with her. And *vice versa*. Which reminds me — I wanted to ask you: who wrote that poem you sent me?'

'What, didn't you realise? I wrote it myself.'

'*You* did? Not that one? "So wild the heart, that will not stay for reasons——" I thought you'd just copied it out.'

'No. I'd just written it.'

'My!'

'You might claim — if you wished — that you inspired it,' he said with a chuckle. 'That chilly little note you sent me.'

'My!' said Sally again. 'Then I shall be marrying a poet after all!'

278

Chapter Nineteen

THEY had neither the time nor the desire to go on to Venice. Verona was enough. The clean racing Adige was more in key with their mood than a stagnant maze of malodorous canals.

They stayed three golden days before the inexorable calendar prodded them to start back. 'The Pandoro days' they nicknamed them privately, from the local cake, *pan d'oro*, golden bread, which they seemed always to be eating with their coffee or with odd glasses of red sweet Recioto or amber Euganean. And *pandoro* seemed a fitting symbol of their relationship, which (with the arrogance of lovers) they thought rare, precious, and permanent as gold, and which was, indisputably, as fresh, healthy, and good as bread. They had nicknames for many things. Adam was 'the Noble Savage', and Sally became *ragazza mia*.

So, early in September, they said goodbye to the cypress avenues of the Giusti and the slender campanile of San Zeno, the scurrying scintillant water and the fang-like battlements, and all the classical ruins — which they had inspected, rather cursorily to tell the truth, in the little time they found available.

'We shall come back, some day,' she said, as the diligence drove out through the Porta Brescia.

'When I have made my fortune,' he agreed.

She pressed his hand. She had a quite unreasoning faith in him, and the future.

They stopped briefly at Lucero to change horses and swallow a meal. Brigitta and Checco, warned by letter, were waiting with Adam's other bag. Sally had written to Harriet, but had omitted to mention that they would be passing through the town. It was too soon to think of reconciliations and reunions.

Brigitta reported that there had been much *va-et-vient*, much *brouhaha*, at the Villa Gandolfi. . . . There were all kinds of rumours in the town. Opinions varied. The English were being deported by the Government for subversive activity. They were to be evicted by the landlord for heresy, immorality, damage to fixtures and/or non-payment of rent. They were emigrating to America to found a colony for the practice of communism, atheism, vaccination, and other enormities. Alternatively, Signor Mortimer had refused to budge from the villa either for the landlord, the Emperor, or the Pope, and had promised to resist eviction at the pistol-point, if need be blowing up the whole place with gunpowder.

'Has he any gunpowder?' asked Adam.

'No. But he told the garden-boy that it was quite easy to make. He has a book . . .'

'I wouldn't worry, Brigitta.'

It was time to take their places in the coach again. Affectionate farewells were exchanged. Brigitta wished them every happiness — 'It is good,' she said wistfully, 'to marry for love.' Checco eyed Sally with frank appreciation and waved them away with a grubby paw and an even grubbier remark, too colloquial to be precisely understood. The diligence rumbled out along the road to Milan.

Adam was glad to have recovered the rest of his luggage, especially his manuscript. He read it aloud to Sally, to beguile the tedium of the Lombard plain. Antonian's regular verses went smoothly to the rhythm of the coach. Almost too smoothly. . . . More than once he glanced up from the page to see that her head was lolling and her eyelids down. But always, as though by instinct, her big eyes opened, and she smiled.

'Go on . . .'

'You're not bored, *ragazza mia*?'

'Of course not!'

But he could not help wondering. There were moments when he was bored, himself. And he, after all, had had the private intellectual stimulus of battling with the original . . .

When, at last, he had finished, her comments were brief and all too carefully phrased.

'I can't imagine how you did it. All that Latin. . . . I can't judge, really, but I guess that people who know about these things . . .'

He went cold inside. He said nothing until they were alone, that night, in the inn. He picked up the manuscript, casually, and forced himself to say:

'You didn't like Antonian, did you?'

She was getting into a dress. She looked up at him, startled, a flower half bursting from its sheath. He turned his back, making a great business of stowing the manuscript away among his books.

'I can't judge a thing like that. I reckon you'd need to know Latin——'

'No!' He spoke more roughly than he had intended to. He felt her hands on his shoulders, timid. . . . He stood up, and swung round. She dropped back a pace.

'Adam——'

'It must stand in its own right, as a poem. It's *for* people like you, who have no Latin. If it bores you——'

'I never said it bored me!'

281

'But it did. Didn't it?'

She hesitated. 'In places, maybe.'

'I knew!'

'But it's not your fault,' she said quickly. 'You can't make a silk purse out of a sow's ear.'

'I see. You mean I've wasted my time on Antonian.'

'How can I say, darling? I don't have the right cultivated taste, maybe. *I* liked those things you'd made up yourself——'

He snorted. 'You can't compare those trifles of mine with a — a solid achievement like Antonian's.'

In Verona she had made him recite to her such scraps as he could remember of his own occasional verses. She had laughed most rewardingly at the satirical stanzas in which he had described the life of the University. Delicacy had, at first, restrained him from quoting his more lyrical efforts, inspired or rather wrung from him by the sight of other, unattainable, girls before he had even known of her existence. But in the end she had drawn them out, arguing that the poem he had sent her a week ago was too good to have been the first of its kind. So, on hot afternoons in the shadowy room at the inn, at sunset among the Giusti cypresses or by moonlight in the ruined amphitheatre, he had murmured the lines — and she had not seemed to resent the fact that they had not been written for her.

'It could be,' she said now, 'that Antonian's achievement was a thought too solid.'

'What do you mean?'

'A man's poetry doesn't *have* to be good, does it — just because he was a Roman and he lived all that while ago?'

He had no ready answer. The outrageous question struck at the whole basis of classical scholarship.

'Adam, you're not mad at me?'

'No——' He turned back to his baggage. 'Why should I be?'

'You sound so — so cold.'

He felt cold. Wasn't it natural to feel cold, when you suddenly found yourself standing in the ruins of what had always seemed an indestructible fabric? The devil of it was, Sally was right. Antonian was a minor poet. His immortality was an accident: two or three parchment manuscripts had survived in odd monastery libraries while the works of better men had mouldered into dust, been nibbled by mice, or been torn into strips by ignorant monks and sold as amulets to equally ignorant pilgrims. . . . If every line of Antonian had gone down into oblivion, along with the lost books of Livy, the thirty-five vanished volumes of Cicero's letters, and a thousand alleged masterpieces mislaid by posterity, who would have worried? Antonian having survived, it was all too clear that he had little to say to the nineteenth century which some subsequent author had not said as well. And what he had to say was not improved by making him say it (as Adam had thought proper to do) in the mannered couplets of the eighteenth.

Yes, damn it, Sally was right. He had conformed once too often. He had produced the sort of thing that was expected. He had made Antonian talk like Pope or Johnson transplanted to an Italian lakeside villa under the Roman Empire. It was donnish, dignified, and — for all its occasional neat phrasings — most damnably dull.

'You realise,' he heard himself say, 'this is my one chance of climbing out of the rut — making some sort of a name——'

'I know what it means to you.' Her voice wavered. 'But — you wanted my opinion. Adam dearest, I can't pretend.'

'I don't want you to!'

'But other people may think it's wonderful. You must see what your Mr. Pritchard thinks.'

'I expect he'll say the same as you.'

The coldness remained between them all that evening. He was too proud to admit to her, at once, that she was right. But it was only a matter of time before, having admitted it to himself, he saw the absurdity of the barrier between them. By midnight he was whispering, his lips against her hair:

'You were right — of course you were right. We must never pretend to each other, *ragazza mia*. . . .'

So they crossed the Alps, and possibly more than the Alps, and at Geneva they found a broad-minded pastor who, making light of certain legal and international quibbles, sent them rejoicing on their way as husband and wife.

Meanwhile, as the September days dwindled, Oxford stirred from her unseasonable hibernation.

The grass stood tall between the cobbles of the High. Under the critical surveillance of half a dozen head porters a starveling crew of minor College servants issued from their respective lodges, and attacked roadway and pavement with a variety of garden-implements.

In the bursary of St. Columb's, over a glass of madeira, Challand inspected the annual accounts with satisfaction. Though he had not, this time, accompanied the Bursar on a rent-collecting progress through the shires, that officer seemed to have discharged his duties effectively. The rents had been extracted, despite disastrous hay-crops and ruined harvests, demands for repairs and improvements had been resisted, little *douceurs* had been gracefully accepted here and there — a cask of home-brewed cider, perhaps, or a promise of game or ham or walnuts or pippins when ripe for dispatch. . . . Yes, it looked as though it had been a fair year for the College.

'A three candle year, eh, Bursar?'

'We shall have to see, Warden, we shall have to see.'

The dividend would not be officially declared before the Fellows' meeting on the eve of term. The size of the dividend was proclaimed to the world by the number of candles lighted in the bursary window. Each candle represented a hundred pounds for every Fellow.

'So old Whittaker was gathered to his fathers while I was abroad?'

'I'm afraid so, Warden. A great loss, a great loss. . . .' The Bursar tried to conceal his smirk by taking a sip of madeira. 'He was up here in '59.'

'So long ago? Older than I thought, then. One of the richest College livings, isn't it?'

'Almost the richest. And one of the most genteel parts of Leicestershire.'

'H'm.' Challand raised his glass to the light and peered into its tawny redness, as though it were a crystal which might offer guidance in the choice of a new incumbent. 'We must look round for the right man, Bursar. Someone young, perhaps, and deserving. . . . A young man of parts.'

Yes, emphatically, a very fair year for the College.

Of course, the men would be coming up again at the end of next week. But one could not expect everything. Take it all in all, thought Challand, it was not a bad life.

On the Channel packet Sally clutched Adam's arm.

'Look — isn't that Villiers?'

Further along the deck Villiers was talking to a family group which appeared to include several personable young daughters. The sweeping but elegant gestures, the ready flow of speech and the laughter which it earned, combined with the wavy chestnut hair (no top hat could have held its place, just then, against the wind) to identify him beyond question.

285

'He has made new friends,' Adam murmured.

'Oh, yes. Quality. I noticed the old gentleman when we first came on board. They have their own carriage — he was swearing at the men as they hoisted it over the side. The one over there.'

'Crested!'

'And they had a coachman with a cockade.'

The group turned and began to move aft. But Villiers happened to looked round, and, Sally also being unmistakable in her Pompeian red, recognised them. Muttering some excuse, he left his friends and edged his way through the crowd of passengers until he reached them.

'What a delightful surprise!' he said without any marked insincerity.

'So you are not going to America?' Adam inquired.

Villiers laughed. 'No one is going to America. I think the Mortimers — and Miss Seeley, of course — are thinking of England again.'

'If that review ever gets started——' Sally began. She had her arm slipped through Adam's. She smiled and spoke easily, unembarrassed by the encounter, unruffled by anything but the Channel breeze. Adam exulted silently in the contact through their sleeves — the sense of mutual possession, of a serenity which Villiers could not disturb.

'Oh, the review's forgotten. Still-born.'

'What is it now?'

Villiers chuckled. 'When I left, it was a boarding-school to be run on enlightened and revolutionary lines. It might work, you know — Miss Seeley would presumably provide the capital and Mortimer the children. But I can't really say. I'm no longer in their counsels.'

'You have found new friends,' said Sally.

'Yes. In Paris. A charming family. I'd have introduced you, only . . .' Villiers coughed discreetly. 'I didn't want to cause anyone any embarrassment. I wasn't quite sure what the position was.'

'We are married,' said Adam, 'if that's what you mean.'

'Are you?' Villiers looked surprised and genuinely delighted. He seized Adam by the hand. 'I do congratulate you, my dear fellow. And Sally — Mrs. Adam — I wish you every happiness, I really do!' He smiled from one to the other. 'All is forgiven, eh? Friends again?'

'Of course,' they said together. No one could dislike Villiers deeply, or for long.

'I say, though——' The high-bred features clouded momentarily. 'Won't this be awkward for you at Oxford?'

'It could be . . . rather more than awkward,' Adam admitted. 'We rely on your discretion, Villiers.'

'Your secret is safe with me.' Villiers clapped a hand theatrically upon his heart. 'You know, this is a damned funny thing, Adam — I met a friend of yours in Paris, he started home two days ahead of us. Same college——'

'George Seabrook?' How lucky, thought Adam, that Seabrook hadn't left his homeward journey till today! That *would* have been an awkward encounter. He was not altogether happy that they had been forced to trust Villiers with their secret. Seabrook would have been far too dangerous a confidant.

'That was the name. He'd hardly believe me, though, when I told him about meeting you.'

'No?'

'He said it didn't sound a bit like you. But of course your name, and its being Lucero, and everything — he had to admit it must be the same person.' Villiers smiled reminiscently. 'He seemed to think you were far too dull a dog . . . but then I fell into the same mistake at first, didn't I?' Adam said nothing. Villiers chuckled again. 'And I didn't know half the story when I was talking to Seabrook——'

'I'm glad you didn't,' said Adam. 'And I rely on you not to write to him——'

'I'm relying on him to write to me,' retorted Villiers. 'I had to lend him five guineas for his journey home! Don't worry, my lips are sealed.'

In Oxford (as indeed elsewhere) September was over. The High was scoured clean of moss and weeds. In the Meadow the morning dew was whiter and seemed to linger later into the day. The trees were turning. Already the first dry leaves were drifting and rustling along the walks, much as the first gowned figures were beginning to drift and rustle through the windy streets. . . .

'It is very pleasant, really, to be home again, is it not?' sighed the eldest Miss Challand.

'One knows where one is,' said Sophia robustly. She liked to know where she was. Crossing the Continent, rattling through such a wearisome and bewildering succession of towns and villages, over rivers whose names she could seldom catch and did not recognise when she did, she had all too often been uncertain on this vital point. Meals also had been a mystery. She had not known which works of art to admire. She had not understood what people had been saying about her — and being able (up to a point) to guess had not made matters any better. 'Yes,' she went on, 'in Oxford one knows what to expect.'

Charlotte astounded her — and even Julia, who was moved to glance up from her embroidery — by disagreeing. It was only a very mild, even a timid, disagreement but it was not an echo.

'That's where I think you are wrong — mistaken, I mean — dear Charlotte. The beginning of a new term, a new academic year, is a very interesting time. One never knows quite *what* to expect.'

'Do you mean "whom"?' Sophia demanded bluntly.

'Well . . .' Charlotte fluttered, a rather dim little moth already repenting its approach to the candle-flame of controversy. 'Naturally, one wonders . . . new faces . . . one never knows . . . it is always interesting to see new faces. Though, of course, old friends are best.'

'We certainly have some *very* old friends,' said Julia with the touching innocence of girlhood. 'Doctor Rallingson — and the Dean — and the dear Chaplain——'

'I did not mean old in years, necessarily.' Charlotte never hesitated to explain the obvious — there were so few other things she was able to explain. 'I mean, just people we know. Like Mr. Seabrook——'

'And Mr. Adam?' The challenge in Sophia's voice would not have been misunderstood even in the African jungle.

'Yes, of course,' her sister faltered. 'Mr. Adam, too.'

'They should be back any day now. The Fellows' meeting is on Thursday.'

'And there will be a great deal for them to discuss. With poor Doctor Whittaker's death, and his place to fill — a most important living——'

'In Leicestershire,' said Sophia, her pensive expression not quite matching her brisk tone. 'Seven miles from Loughborough. Papa says there is a particularly fine Rectory — almost a gentleman's country seat——'

'You have taken a great interest,' Julia murmured. She had already ascertained these facts for herself. She knew also, from the Bursar, that the Squire's lady was an invalid but with a good expectation of life; for the measurable future, the Rector's wife would enjoy an almost unrivalled social eminence.

'I wonder if they will choose someone on Thursday?' Charlotte speculated.

Sophia thought they would take a little time to decide. Papa would have to make up his mind before he could assist in making up theirs. He would want to consider the matter in all its aspects.

'I wonder——'

'You are always wondering, Charlotte.'

'Oh, it's something else. I was wondering — what do you think, both of you? — when Mr. Adam and Mr. Seabrook come up, would it be proper to invite them to take tea with us?'

'I don't see why not. You mayn't get Mr. Seabrook, though — he never comes up till the very last minute, and then it's only because he's anxious about the dividend! I'm surprised Mr. Adam isn't here already. It's not like him. He always spends part of the vacation in Oxford.'

'Well, *when* he arrives — could we ask him alone?'

'Certainly!'

'After all, there are three of us.' That was the one regrettable factor in the situation, but Charlotte kept her voice bright. 'And it is quite natural, is it not?' It was all too natural, but Sophia had to be definite.

'What — exactly — is quite natural?'

'I mean — we have all just been to the Continent, we have all been to Italy — it is natural we should wish to compare our experiences——'

Contrast would be more appropriate than compare, thought Julia, threading her needle with a green silk of a peculiarly bilious shade. She considered dropping her sisters a hint about Mr. Adam's irregular life at Lucero. It would, she knew, put Charlotte out of the running: Charlotte would bolt in panic from the course. Of Sophia's reaction she was not so sure: Sophia might only be spurred on to capture Mr. Adam and reform him with a strong hand. Finally, there was Papa. Any information or inn- uendo fed to her sisters, however discreetly and under whatever oath of secrecy, would be certainly shared with Papa. It would be too bad if, after eliminating her

290

competitors and extracting a proposal from Mr. Adam, she lost everything through those two geese running off to Papa and quacking (with the most disinterested motives) to save their little sister from a misalliance with a libertine.

No, Julia decided. Better to say nothing. It nearly always was.

This term, to the mild surprise of the College servants who noticed and to the mounting annoyance of the Miss Challands (who pretended not to), it looked as though for once Mr. Adam was to rival Mr. Seabrook in the tardiness of his return.

On the Thursday of the Fellows' meeting — and less than two hours before it was due to begin — he was still miles away. Six miles, to be precise. He was standing patiently while Sally reached up to adjust a clean cravat in their bedroom at Abingdon.

They had settled on that somnolent little Berkshire market-town as being near to the city but in every other respect a world away. Adam's long legs would make nothing of the distance, yet it would be a most unlikely coincidence if any University man ever passed down St. Helen's Street at the moment of his arrival or departure. Nor was there much risk that any of Mr. 'Forester's' Abingdon neighbours would run into Mr. Adam in the lodge of St. Columb's and be struck by a certain resemblance beneath the cap and gown. Even if that happened, there would be probably no more dangerous a reaction than a sly wink, a slowly-spreading Berkshire leer. . . . The outside world had a good deal of sympathy for the reluctant celibates of the University. It was only from the University itself that danger could come.

Partly for that reason, though also to save their dwindling money, they had avoided London and the direct coach-route, with its risk of encounters with his Oxford acquaintances, and made their way to Abingdon across country. Here, using Sally's maiden name, they had taken two rooms in the house of a tradesman's widow. She was an elderly, decent body, who responded at once to Sally's charm and was sympathetic rather than suspicious when told that Mr. Forester would unhappily be absent a great deal, travelling in the way of business. It was not necessary or possible to tell her much more. Being deafer than she cared to admit, she liked to keep the ball of conversation at her own feet. Adam and his bride had little to do but mouth gratitude, surprise, admiration, and other appropriate responses.

Their bow-windowed living-room, on the first floor, looked across the street to the church and the almshouses which lined the graveyard. Thus, though there was no through traffic (this end of the town being wedged in an angle between the Thames and a small tributary), there was a constant passing and repassing along the pavement. As Adam rather irreverently remarked:

'Only the Lord would have time to watch over my comings-in and my goings-out.'

At the rear, their bedroom looked down a narrow vista of walled garden to the river. Three mossy steps reproduced, in miniature, the landing facilities of the Villa Gandolfi.

'But I guess they could be handy,' said Sally, 'in certain situations!'

'Such as?'

'Oh, I don't know. Couldn't one of the preachers you know in Oxford come out and take a service over yonder?'

'It could just happen,' he admitted.

It was a far-fetched idea, but it was reassuring to know that Adam need never feel trapped inside the house. Sally could always get hold of a boat nearby and bring it to the steps. Then a few strokes would be enough to ferry him across to the Oxfordshire tow-path, and he would be able to get back to College by another route.

He did not seriously expect any such difficulties. He would not risk, in term-time, a night at Abingdon, but his well-known habit of taking long country walks by himself should enable him to visit her two or three times a week without arousing anyone's suspicions.

'George Seabrook will be the main problem,' he said thoughtfully. 'We've been pretty good friends.'

'Can't you tell him?'

'I'd sooner not. To begin with. It's foolish to take any unnecessary risks. It might be safer if he imagined we weren't married.'

'Isn't it ridiculous? Poor darling! When we both so hate pretending. . . . It's such hypocrisy. Of course, it's much worse for you.'

'I'm used to hypocrisy,' Adam told her grimly. 'You forget, I've had years of Oxford. No, it's worse for you.'

'How?'

'I have a life — a sort of life — at the College end. Seabrook, one or two other acquaintances, my books, even my "young gentlemen" — it isn't completely unheard of for one of them to show a vestige of intellectual curiosity. But what life are you going to have? Sitting here, wondering whether I shall get over today or tomorrow. . . . Mrs. Forester, the young lady from abroad, who hasn't any friends or relations——'

She stopped him with her hand on his lips.

'I shall be all right, Adam. Truly. Mrs. Maynard says I may use her piano — nobody plays it now——'

'Oh, *ragazza mia*!' He burst out laughing in spite of himself. 'You can't play the piano all the time.'

'I might take pupils — why shouldn't I take pupils? *You* have pupils. And Mrs. Maynard is deaf. The money would help——'

'You're not to worry about money. Perhaps it will be a good dividend this year. Even if it isn't, we shall manage all right. Even allowing for my mother.'

'You ought to be starting, or you won't be there for your dividend!'

'I shall get it just the same. But I'd better go.' He put his arms round her. 'I'll come on Sunday — straight after service. I don't think I can manage it before.'

'I'll cook you a dinner!'

'I shall expect turkey and pumpkin pie. Look after yourself, *ragazza*. Think of the vacations.'

'I shall!'

'We'll go right away from here. We'll lose ourselves in London, we'll go to theatres. . . . We'll go up to Nottingham and stay with dear old Pritchard — his eyes will pop out when I write and tell him our news, but Pritchard's safe enough with any secret——'

'You must go to Oxford first. Now.'

'Too true. I've not only to go to my rooms and get my cap and gown, I must change into breeches, or Challand will be after my blood.'

They said goodbye on the landing. There had better be no doorstep kisses, no waving from windows, no turning to look back at the bend of the street. Nothing to attract unnecessary attention. That must be their life from now on.

Sombrely he walked away, skirted the tiny market-place — how different from the Piazza delle Erbe! — and left the last thatched cottages behind him. He mustn't think about the next few days and nights. He must look forward, reach out, cling to what they would have. The drab furnished rooms would brighten under Sally's hand. They would be so much more a home of his own than he had ever had before. There would be autumn evenings, tea in the firelight, music, love . . . before, damn it, the long trudge back to Oxford in the fog or the rain. . . .

He passed Bagley Wood. A bonfire threw a skein of fragrant smoke, blue as bluebells, across the gold and copper tapestry of foliage. From Hinksey Hill he looked down on the city, spiked with churches, embossed with domes and cupolas. The weather was playing its old tricks with light and shade — the colleges seemed to float on a central pool of October sunshine, an unreal island of pale gleaming stone, tufted with metallic trees.

It looked, he thought sourly, like the Land of Promise. In fact, it was more like a City of the Plain.

Chapter Twenty

ADAM thought he noticed a certain tension as soon as
he entered the Common Room.

Ordinarily, the October meeting was a relaxed —
liable to develop into a convivial — affair. Men who had
not met for months saluted each other with a tolerance, if
not a cordiality, which would wear thinner as the term went
on. They were prepared, for the moment, to listen to
each other's stories and experiences. There was gossip
to exchange. And the dividend threw a warm glow of
anticipation over the proceedings.

But ordinarily, too, he would have been there in good
time, hanging on the fringe of the group and (when
Seabrook arrived) chuckling over his colleague's whispered asides. Today he was almost late. Most of the dons
had already taken their seats at the table. That, no doubt,
explained the atmosphere.

'Good morning, Warden. Good morning, gentlemen. I
hope I have not kept you waiting?' He was still breathless
from scurrying up and down stairs. He glanced down,
furtively. The braided flap of his breeches was quite in
order, only his stockings were wrinkled. . . .

'We wondered,' said the Warden grandly, 'if you
intended to favour us with a personal appearance.'

Two of the old men sniggered. Seabrook winked across
the table. He himself had reached the meeting only a

short head in front of Adam, who had followed the whisk of his gown-tails through the colonnade.

Adam sat down opposite. Looking up the line of faces he saw that they were all there. Rallingson, just a shade less purple and puffy after some months away from the College cellars. . . . The Dean, with his milk-blue marble eyes set in their raw pink rims . . . . Blantyre, amiable, vacuous, deafer than ever, but still capable of counting the Bursar's symbolic candles. . . . Slimy little Symes, who bided his time, year after year, waiting for the right living to fall vacant, always jockeying for position, always avid for every crumb of gossip which might disqualify a rival and better his own chances. . . . The shaggy-browed Chaplain. . . . The Bursar fumbling importantly with his papers. . . . Murthwaite, Anderson, Vaughan, Gibbs, yes, they were all there. The whole crew.

'I think we might begin, gentlemen.'

They all stood, while the Chaplain invoked a blessing on the outcome of their deliberations. As this was generally assumed to refer to the fixing of the dividend, the chorus of Amens revealed an unusual depth of feeling.

'I will ask the Bursar to present the College accounts for the past year.'

That officer rose, bowed, and began to gabble. Nobody was in the least interested in the details, though Vaughan assumed an owlish expression and made one or two notes, while Symes sat with one hand cupped round his ear, as though the welfare of the College depended on his not missing a single digit. Only when the Bursar's more deliberate tempo indicated that he was approaching his climax and deserved to be listened to was there a general lifting of heads along the table.

'And so, gentlemen, although in many respects there have been adverse circumstances — our tenants have had the wettest summer in farming memory and the end of

297

hostilities has brought a steep decline in profits in many forms of enterprise — the College has contrived, by firm management and a watchful preservation of its legitimate rights, to maintain its revenues at a most gratifying level. The figures are before you, gentlemen, and you, in your wisdom, will decide. But, following our custom that the Bursar should submit his own proposal, I have pleasure in recommending that to each Fellow there be paid, this year, a dividend of three hundred pounds.'

He sat down. There was an appreciative murmur.

'Hear, hear . . .'

'*Very* gratifying . . .'

'Highly creditable . . .'

'I am happy to move that, Warden.'

'I will second it.'

There was seldom much scope for discussion of the dividend. Nobody knew enough, and everybody realised that the Bursar would make it as big as the figures would stand. If it had been disturbingly low, there might have been an outcry and a demand for simpler explanations. Thanks to Bonaparte it had never, in recent years, been low.

Today, as usual, it was adopted by acclamation.

Three hundred pounds, thought Adam. . . . It was rather more than he had dared to expect. . . . It would be invaluable in his new circumstances.

The meeting proceeded.

'You will all be sorry to learn,' said the Warden gravely, 'that one of the College's oldest *alumni*, Doctor Whittaker, passed away on the twentieth of August. This lays upon us the heavy responsibility of making a suitable appointment to the vacant living.'

There was a decent silence. Most of the Fellows looked down their noses, in the hope of disguising their feelings and suggesting a complete lack of self-interest.

Adam saw a nerve twitch in Symes's temple. . . . Was this the living that Slimy Symes had been waiting for? Seabrook winked again across the table. Yes, probably it was.

It was Symes who broke the silence.

'How true, Warden!' he said smoothly. 'The responsibility is indeed heavy. The right man to follow Doctor Whittaker will not be easy to find. I would suggest, humbly, that we do nothing precipitate. The matter calls for deep consideration and, if I may say so, prayer.'

There was a mumble of agreement. Nobody had anything against prayer, so long as there was no question of fasting.

Crafty devil, thought Adam. He hasn't had time to canvass. He's not sure who else is in the field. He may think Seabrook's in the running — or even that I am.

There was no hurry to fill the vacancy. The formalities of ordination could soon be rushed through if it were decided to offer it to a layman. Symes wanted time to work on the Warden and undermine any dangerous opposition.

Seabrook's twinkle signalled that he inclined to Adam's interpretation.

Symes was continuing, fortified by the manifest approval of his neighbours: 'In our quest for the right candidate, gentlemen, we should leave no stone unturned——'

And whom should we be more likely to find under a stone, thought Adam, than the Reverend Slimy Symes, M.A.?

'— and for that reason, gentlemen, I would suggest that further discussion of this matter be deferred to the next College meeting.'

'Agreed.'

'Agreed.'

No one seemed anxious to force a decision there and then. It would have deprived the Common Room of long evenings of enjoyable speculation and intrigue. Even those who had no thought of the living for themselves had votes which could be bartered, for real if intangible favours, to the highest bidder. Meanwhile, most people wanted to get on to the more than usually sumptuous dinner which, by tradition, followed the declaration of the dividend.

Two other matters, routine trivialities, were brought up and almost impatiently assented to.

'Is there any other business?' Half the dons were poised for flight, but several leant forward with an expectancy which seemed somehow, Adam thought, to echo the unusual emphasis Challand had laid upon his conventional inquiry. Symes was clearing his throat. The Warden looked at him along the table. 'I believe — Mr. Symes?'

'Yes, Warden. I have a certain matter to bring up — a painful matter. I do so with extreme reluctance, as you know.' Symes was speaking with controlled gusto, like a modest host introducing a vintage with which he was privately pleased. 'I have already,' he said, looking round the table with a deft avoidance of everyone's eye, 'consulted the Warden and one or two of my — er — my senior colleagues in private. They were unanimous. Whatever our personal feelings, for the sake of the good name of this college, this is something we cannot ignore.'

Seabrook arched his eyebrows. Several dons looked mystified. One or two, impatient to eat, chuntered: 'Go on, man, go on! Out with it!' The Warden and Symes's particular cronies contemplated their waistcoats.

'The fair name of St. Columb's is dear to us all. Or I should have thought it was. I do not say that the College, like all human societies, has not had its scandals in the past——'

In the *past*, mouthed Seabrook, cheerfully but silently across the mahogany. What about——?

Adam had to force an answering grin. What was Symes after? Whom, rather? All this sanctimonious preamble must be leading up to something definite, which would benefit Slimy and injure one of his colleagues. Not George Seabrook, surely? George looked as though he had returned from Paris with no worse a conscience than if he had spent the vacation in solitary angling. Anyhow, the College had no interest in its members' peccadilloes on the Continent. If Julia Challand had taken each Fellow privately aside, and described her equivocal encounter with Mr. Adam and an American lady outside an Italian inn, not one of them, even with the worst will in the world, would have held it a fit matter to bring up at a College meeting.

Anyhow, Julia Challand (whatever her defects) would not have gone to work in that way. And she would never have spoken to Symes in preference to her own father, and this was something Symes had taken to Challand.

It can't concern *me*, Adam told himself firmly. Or Seabrook. Who is it then? Surely not Anderson? Everyone had known about that woman of his at Marston for years! And Gibbs, surely Gibbs hasn't made an unwise choice of partner for his fumblings and tumblings in Magdalen Grove? Can it be some other sort of scandal? Atheism? Radical politics? A mishandling of College funds — or choristers?

The miscreant must be a Fellow. If he had been a servant or one of the young gentlemen, Symes would not have beaten about the bush like this. It must be a colleague, or he would not be speaking with such evident pleasure.

'Who's he talking about?'

Doctor Rallingson boomed out the question which was absorbing most of those present.

'Come to the point, Mr. Symes,' Gibbs demanded nervously.

'Name! Name!' intoned one or two Fellows with clear consciences.

'Very well, gentlemen.' Symes looked round, showing his teeth. 'But first, Warden, with your permission, I would like to put a question.'

'Proceed.'

'To you — Mr. Adam.'

Every head swung round to stare down the table.

No, thought Adam, in a paralysis of horror. He can't have found out. Not even Symes could nose it out in a few days. . . . Even the minister at Geneva — if he had *wanted* to ruin me — couldn't have betrayed me in this short time. And I gave Pritchard's address . . . he didn't know I was at Oxford, much less which college. Surely Villiers——

It was extraordinary how many thoughts could whip through one's mind in the ticking of two or three seconds.

He heard himself say:

'I have no idea what you are talking about, Mr. Symes, but I shall be very happy to answer any question you like — if it is a proper one.'

'My question is proper enough. I do not know about the answer. I ask you, Mr. Adam: have you recently written a book?'

Adam's jaw dropped. He almost laughed aloud with relief. And surely, even in the present low state of University culture, the writing of a book did not justify Symes's tone of concentrated disgust.

'I have.'

'You admit it?' Symes looked disappointed.

'Why not? Just because no member of the College has done so lately surely doesn't make it a scandal.'

'Opinions may differ about that, Mr. Adam.'

Is he mad, or am I, Adam wondered? There were, it was true, in Antonian as in most Roman love-poets, certain lubricious passages. But, playing for safety, he had rendered them with a verbal delicacy which would have caused no offence in a vicarage nursery. Anyhow, Symes could not have read his manuscript. Apart from Sally who had (nominally) heard it all, and the household at the Villa Gandolfi who had heard extracts, nobody in the world knew what his translation was like. And probably never would, he thought grimly.

'Well, my book is not yet published,' he said, with a puzzled expression. 'I'm inclined to think I shan't publish it after all.'

'A pity you didn't think of that before!'

'A little late in the day, Mr. Adam,' Challand broke out thunderously, unable to leave the matter in Symes's hands any longer. 'What have you to say to *this*?' With a dramatic gesture he pulled out a small volume and held it up for all to see. This was just what they could not do, most of them, for those nearest him were old and bleary of sight, and Adam himself — from the junior end of the table — could only distinguish the title *Isis Unveil'd*, which was entirely unfamiliar.

'Good God!' Seabrook ejaculated cheerfully. 'I bought one of those in London — only dipped into a page or two yet——'

'Do I understand that this volume is on sale in London, Mr. Seabrook?'

'Oh, yes, Warden. I bought one in Albemarle Street.'

'You see?' cried Symes. 'On sale in London! As I said, every college has its *private* scandals. But this is a scandal published to the world!'

The meeting was now on the verge of uproar. Several of Symes's cronies produced copies of the book which were eagerly studied by their neighbours. Seabrook himself felt in his coat-pocket and fished out the one he had bought in London. He was already exploding with laughter when Adam reached over and snatched it from him.

'For Heaven's sake, let me see!'

With trembling fingers he turned the pages. Every line was familiar. They were the poems he had sent to Pritchard at the end of last term. Only the title-page was new to him. *ISIS UNVEIL'D*, he read, *by a Gentleman of Oxford University*. Below was the imprint, Charles Herbert of Bond Street. Some friend of Pritchard's.

'It is not funny!' roared Challand. 'I tell you all it is not funny! I warn you, gentlemen, you are all *in* this book. Disgusting, libellous caricatures——'

'But too diabolically clever to be actionable at law,' put in Symes fretfully.

'But *we* can identify the references. As easily as we can identify the author.'

'There is no room for doubt, there,' said Symes. 'I have given this — this unsavoury production the same close study I would have given a classical text——'

'Closer, if I know anything,' interjected Seabrook irrepressibly.

'And there are several clues, which, to a St. Columb's man, point unmistakably to Mr. Adam!'

'I don't deny that these are my poems,' said Adam wearily. 'I did not know that they had been printed — I have been abroad all the summer. I never imagined that *you* would ever lay hands on them. But I'm rather glad you have.'

'Glad! I doubt if you will continue to feel glad, Mr. Adam.'

Challand clearly felt it was time to resume his control of the meeting.

'Authorship is admitted. Mr. Adam, indeed, seems to glory in his impudence. Gentlemen, this is the most scandalous affair in the whole history of the College. This rigmarole is circulating through the whole University. Most people, I am glad to say, share our own sense of outrage. This is a blow at all Oxford, not at St. Columb's alone. There is a minority, however, appearing to derive some amusement from it. Only this morning the Provost of Oriel had the effrontery to accost me in the High — he expressed the hope, gentlemen, that you were all reading these verses, "if you *could*". . . . Munday's were exposing several copies for sale in their window. I demanded their removal. They, of course, obeyed — but they added that they would have no difficulty in selling them none the less. So I bought the lot. Even so, I suspect that they will re-order.'

By now those who had previously known nothing of the affair had had time to glance through the several copies distributed along the table. A change had come over the meeting. Apart from Seabrook, everyone was avid for blood. Amusement at some passages had given place to fury as, one by one, each came to a satire which stung himself. They had even forgotten the dinner which was to follow the meeting.

'You may wish for an adjournment, gentlemen, so that you may study this doggerel at your leisure——'

Cries of no, no! They had read enough.

'Have you anything to say, Mr. Adam, at this stage?'

What was there to say? He shook his head.

'You have a proposition, Mr. Symes?'

'I have indeed, Warden. This falls within the category of flagrant scandals for which, if we think fit, we may take away a man's fellowship. I propose that Mr. Adam therefore be deprived of his fellowship at this College, and all emoluments pertaining thereto.'

'I second that,' cried the Chaplain. 'There is irreligion in the book as well as immorality.'

'Does it mean,' rumbled Doctor Rallingson, 'that he gets his dividend — or does it go back into the pool for redistribution?'

The Warden said, with dignity, that this point would require separate consideration. They did not want a lawsuit on their hands.

Looking up and down the rows of faces, Adam knew he would get only one vote. Better to jump like a man, than wait to be pushed. He stood up.

'I am sure you are all wanting your dinners, gentlemen. It will save further delay if I resign. Good-day, Warden.'

He bowed with exaggerated deference and left the Common Room for the last time.

Down the colonnade, across the paved quadrangle, up the age-worn oaken stairs, his own footsteps rang hollow and unreal. But no, he was not dreaming. This had happened. Not marriage, but a sheaf of verses, had finished his career. He almost laughed aloud at the irony of it all.

Well, he might as well pack up his things and clear out of here. Sally would be surprised to see him back in time for supper. She would understand. She wouldn't blame him. Nobody was to blame. Not even poor old Pritchard. He'd given Pritchard *carte blanche*. . . . Who could have foreseen that the poems would fall into Symes's hands — or those of anyone with enough inside knowledge to deduce the author's identity?

No doubt Pritchard had written. . . . It was his own fault for disappearing abroad and leaving no address. . . . Yes, his scout had propped several letters on the mantelpiece. Recognizing the top one as a tradesman's bill, he had not stopped to examine them in his scurry to change and reach the College meeting in time. Now he took them down.

His tailor . . . his bookseller . . . small bills, both. Thank God, he had never been one to get into debt. What was this? A long screed from — of all people! — Matthew Mortimer. . . . It was true, then, Mortimer *was* planning to open an academy for young ladies and gentlemen, to be educated together by revolutionary and enlightened methods. . . . It would be much appreciated if Adam, whose name as a patron would carry weight, being a Fellow of an Oxford college——

Adam tossed the letter aside with a bitter chuckle and sorted through the rest of the pile. Pritchard's handwriting . . . and again. One, two, three, no less than four letters from Pritchard. Before he could open the first, there was a knock.

'Oh, come in!'

Seabrook did so.

'I'm sorry to laugh, Tom. But——'

'That's all right, George.'

'This is the funniest thing I've *ever* seen! Old Challand — and Slimy — and all of them——'

'It *is* funny,' Adam agreed. 'And you haven't heard the whole joke yet. However——'

'It's damned serious for you, I suppose?' said his friend sympathetically, taking a seat on the corner of the table.

'Serious enough. I used to have nightmares very much on these lines. Expulsion, end of a career——'

'It may be the beginning of another,' Seabrook tried to console him. 'The book should bring you in something. My London bookseller made me buy it — said it was the wittiest, neatest bit of satire he'd read for twenty years. You *are* getting paid for it, I hope?'

'I've no idea——'

'*No idea?*'

'Keep quiet for two minutes, George, there's a good fellow. If you'll give me a chance to read what Pritchard says, I'll have a better idea what's been happening.'

Pritchard had said a good deal. Glancing from one closely-written sheet to another, Adam was too dazed to take in all the details. For the moment he could not even arrange them in chronological order.

'*I am sending your poems*' (wrote Pritchard in what proved to be the first of the letters) '*to my good friend Charles Herbert. They would stand a better chance, I fancy, under the imprint of a London bookseller, who knows the world of taste and fashion. I shall not, of course, reveal your name . . .*'

In a later letter:

'*Herbert is beside himself with delight. He writes that your poems are as amusing as Byron's and yet, in your other vein, you have so much more heart than his lordship. He cannot wait to print. You will be his perfect answer to John Murray, round the corner in Albemarle Street. But the book must have a title. He suggests——*'

Herbert had suggested more than a title and a pseudonym. He had suggested two hundred and fifty guineas for the copyright. Pritchard, on Adam's behalf, had accepted two hundred guineas for a first edition, the number of copies not to exceed——

'Fool!' Adam exclaimed. 'Throwing away fifty guineas! *My* guineas! Never mind. Two hundred guineas! Manna from heaven!'

Pritchard's most recent letter, barely a week old, indicated that he had not been such a fool after all:

'*Why do you not write? Where are you? I implore*

308

*you, when you receive this, get in touch with me at once —
or, better still, go to Herbert in London and reveal yourself.
You can trust him — only show me any new agreements first.
He writes to me by every other post, begging to know who
you are, and when you will have another book ready.
Isis Unveil'd has a sixth edition printing, all London is
talking about it — and speculating about you. John Murray
is green with envy, but declares the book is "most diverting".
Herbert is holding another five hundred pounds to your
credit, and says the golden goose is still laying hard. He
says it is time to unveil not Isis but the author himself. I
cannot get him to realise how much your academic career
means to you . . .'*

'That's rich!' sobbed Seabrook. 'That's marvellous!
It's as good as anything in your damned book!'

'I must get back and tell Sally——'

'Sally? Who the devil's Sally?'

Adam did not immediately answer. He stood by the
window with the stance of one suddenly paralysed. A
casual glance down into the High had shown him Sally on
the opposite pavement, wistfully regarding the venerable
walls which had so recently engulfed her husband.

'Come on down and meet her,' he cried thickly, and
went thundering downstairs. Seabrook followed with
an anxious expression.

As Adam emerged from the lodge, Sally turned and
started to walk hurriedly up the street without any sign
of recognition. Careless of traffic, he dived aslant the
road and caught her elbow.

'*Darling!*' she protested in an agitated whisper. 'Someone will see! We said, if we ever met in Oxford, we'd
pretend——'

'It doesn't matter. Nothing matters.' Still holding
her arm, he began to draw her back across the road to St.
Columb's.

She mistook his incoherent manner.

'Don't be angry!' she begged. 'When you'd gone, I felt I *had* to see where you'd be living. I just wanted to look. I never meant you to see me. I came in with a carrier — he's going to take me back——'

'*I* shall take you back,' he corrected her. 'We'll hire a chaise. But come up to my rooms first — I have to pack——'

In the middle of the High, dodging wheels and hoofs, he stammered the good news.

They gained the pavement uninjured, Sally by now hanging ecstatically on his arm, and both of them laughing like lunatics, while Seabrook, in the background, looked on benignly and waited for an introduction.

On the front steps of the College they came face to face with the three Miss Challands, returning from a perambulation of the Meadow. Sophia drew herself up and demanded:

'Mr. Adam! Are you intoxicated?'

'No, Miss Sophia. I am married.'

Adam made the introductions with inappropriate hilarity. Charlotte found voice for an automatic social twitter. Sophia snorted with incredulity. Julia said nothing. But her look was a little less enigmatic than usual.

The Miss Challands were nothing if not well-bred. They knew — and even in the bitterness of defeat they did not forget — that a married lady took precedence of the unmarried. Drawing back their skirts, they let Mrs. Adam walk up the steps into their father's college in front of them.

Half an hour later (another affront to tradition and almost enough to bring down the walls of St. Columb's in dusty ruin) Sally was folding and packing her husband's linen while he changed back into his trousers. From below the window came the tootle of a coach-guard's trumpet.

'What's that?' she cried, turning to look out.

'One of the London coaches. We'll be on it ourselves tomorrow, *ragazza mia*!'

And they kissed again. Faint and sweet came the guard's horn as his coach went rumbling over Magdalen Bridge, and the tune was 'Begone, Dull Care'.

THE END

PRINTED BY PURNELL AND SONS, LTD.
PAULTON (SOMERSET) AND LONDON